THE PILLARS OF DAWN

Timothy Johnson

A Vintage City Publishing book
Published by arrangement with the author

ISBN (trade paperback): 978-0-9997099-2-4
ISBN (e-book): 978-0-9997099-1-7

The Pillars of Dawn
©2017 by Timothy Johnson. All rights reserved.

Edited by Felicia A. Sullivan.
Cover design by Eloise J. Knapp,
www.ekcoverdesign.com

For Mom and Dad
who gave me the world
and the means to escape it

PART ONE
LOST

"No celestial body shall be chosen for colonization if native life is present... In the event that colonization has begun and native life is discovered, colonization shall cease immediately, and personnel shall evacuate, thus preserving the moral right of all life to develop and exist in its natural state without external influence."

—Colonization Protocols, Section 1, Article 1,
commonly referred to as the "Clause of Mortal Domain"

CHAPTER 1
THE FIRST FAMILIES

One

The colony was always there.

Through the barred window, Lincoln and Aeron Arokson gazed upon their home, Vale, the settlement between mountains. Fluorescent green lights danced in the night, spinning through the empty marketplace streets like the ghosts of patrons who had gone home hours ago. They frolicked through the commons, the great field at the center of town where only the wind now rocked the swings in the playground. They soared over the rooftops of darkened homes, and they crept over Arokson Hall and its looming bell tower. Beyond the colony center, they dashed through the farmlands, teasing the livestock. They even covered the colony's concrete perimeter wall at the edge of the wild. The lights, no doubt, blanketed all of that too.

Above it all, the aurora danced like electric flame, like Lumen, the planet goddess herself, was twirling a dress in the heavens. The aurora lit Vale in a colorful dusk that lasted all night, every night, for as long as Lincoln and Aeron could remember.

Perched on the mountain in the distance, Vale's Pillar of Dawn coughed an endless supply of atmosphere, the occasional lightning bolt crashing through the clouds, kissing the air like irradiated sparks. Even as the pillar lifted life-bringing gases into the sky, the aurora curled around the tower like ghost serpents.

In nothing, though, was the aurora's presence stronger than Lincoln and Aeron's glassy, captivated eyes.

"It's dying." Lincoln blinked, and the aurora was still there, imprinted on the backs of his eyelids. He was no stranger to penance for drinking shine, and the first ache squeezed behind his brow.

"It has to." Aeron shifted on the cot that was bolted to the wall, and the wood groaned under his solid weight. Even though he spent most of his days behind a desk, wearing collared shirts and wool pants, meeting with colonists, no one in Vale was estranged to physical labor. But Aeron's hands were soft, and he rubbed them together to remove the gritty dust that had rubbed off of the cot's wooden frame.

Lincoln took a deep breath of the cool night air. "I know," he said. "Still, it's always been there."

"I remember when it wasn't such a comfort for you."

Lincoln turned toward his big brother with a smile that, despite the years, still held hints of resentment. "Because of you. You were so mean when we were kids."

Aeron winced. "You know I'm sorry for all that, the way I treated you when we were young."

"It's all right." Lincoln waved a dismissive hand and returned his attention to the aurora in the sky. "Children do childish things."

Aeron was silent for a moment and then laughed. "I remember when I convinced you that nobody could see anything but clouds and stars in the sky and that sometimes people said they saw the aurora before the earth opened up and swallowed them."

Lincoln grunted.

"I had to stop you from running into the wild," Aeron said. "You cried about not wanting anyone else to get hurt because of you. My little brother. Selfless even then."

"Yeah? Maybe I should have gone into public service."

Lincoln's stare lingered out the window. Aeron's thin lips flattened. The air between them thickened.

"We've been through this," Aeron said. "It isn't what you think."

Jaw muscles bulging, Lincoln faced his brother. "Let me tell you what I think. If Dad hadn't—"

"Warden!" a female voice called from the hall, accompanied by running footsteps and jingling keys. "Aeron!"

Sheriff Regina Ballard skidded to a halt at the cell door, her fingers clutching the bars made from precious iron. Her narrow, hard blue eyes shined like ice, and the gold star embroidered on her shirt pulsed with the rise and fall of her wiry chest.

"You better come quick."

Aeron rose on the cot. "What is it?"

"It's Dani Hines, and the Bellman boy, James. They're missing. James' sister said they were sneaking out past the wall tonight."

Aeron grimaced and leaped to his feet. "How long have they been gone?"

"A couple hours at least."

Sheriff Ballard opened the cell door for Aeron and cast a stern gaze toward Lincoln. Her hard expression pulsed with strength and a kind of welcoming malice. She wanted Lincoln to try to leave so she could bring the full weight of her fury down on him. He'd done more than broken a few of the colony's laws. He'd invited her wrath, and it was only because of those laws that he was safe from her.

"You," she said. "Stay."

Aeron sensed her anger and knew it went beyond her charge of law and order. He eyed them both and shook his head. "Stay here, Lincoln."

"I can help."

Aeron paused, considering it. "No. It wouldn't look good to the others after what happened. Stay here and sleep it off."

The iron door banged in its frame. The rattling keys locked it again. Lincoln leaned against the bars and listened to Aeron and Ballard's heels kick down the hallway.

"Watch for Shane," Lincoln called after them, but Aeron and Ballard were gone, out into the night and a rising tide of voices.

The colony, it seemed, was not always there for everyone.

Two

By the time anyone realized Dani and James were gone, they were deep in the wild. The aurora bled through the thick tree canopy, but Dani hadn't known such darkness in all her young life. She had never been outside of Vale's walls and never been without the aurora's glow. With wide, curious eyes, she looked up at the pinpricks of light that peeked between branches and leaves, and she thought of stars, wondrous jewels in the night sky her parents had told her about.

Hacking passage with his bush knife, James led her through the thick brush. She showed the way with a flashlight, gripping his muscular shoulder.

"It isn't much farther," he said.

His breathing was labored from swinging the blade, but Dani felt in his tight torso that he was far from tired. The young man was strong and full of vitality. Dani liked the way his bicep rolled as his arm bent. She liked the sharpness of his jaw, the cut that was not quite a man's. She liked his broad chest and shoulders, his tanned skin from the long days working in the farmlands.

A breeze sighed through the trees, and Dani went along sighing with it.

"Soon, the pillar won't need so many workers," James said. "The colony's going to open its gates, and people are going to be free to leave and find their own place. I'm talking real towns, Dani. Land to call our own. Everything within those walls, we could be free of all of it."

"But it's home."

"Home is wherever we make it. Besides, it isn't what the First Families meant to be our permanent place. We came here to make a new home, and that's the spirit of the wild. We came here to grow."

James hacked through tree limbs and led Dani forward. They pushed on through severed vines and around bushes. Finally, after hours of trusting James to guide her through the darkness, Dani stepped onto a trodden path. Deadfall covered the ground. The trail cut straight ahead and curved around a hill.

"Here we go." James sheathed his bush knife on his hip.

The dead foliage felt like dried corn stalks beneath Dani's leather shoes. It hadn't rained in weeks, another sign that Lumen would soon be ready at last. It had stormed all the time when Dani was a child. She remembered storms so bad parts of the colony flooded up to her knees.

"I'm telling you," he said. "We can leave. You and me. Explore the wild. Find a piece of land to call our own. Start a family. I could provide for us by growing our own crops. And I can hunt. We could live off the land. We could do it."

James looked into Dani's eyes, and she could feel him wanting to pull her close. She sensed that the time wasn't right. Not just yet.

"Hunt?"

James smiled. "Come on."

He led her farther down the path until the forest's darkness opened, the end of a tunnel coming into view. Ahead, lights and shadows danced. The aurora showed the way.

James pulled her along faster until they were running. Dani found herself giggling. She didn't understand it other than she knew she was happy and might not ever be so happy again.

They halted at the end of the path. James beckoned. She reached for his outstretched hand, and the boy who was not quite a man pulled her, spun her around, and caught her in his powerful embrace. He turned her so that she looked out upon a rolling field that went on as far as she could see, running straight into the distant mountains. Tall grass waved, pushed and pulled by Lumen's breath.

"This is where they landed, Dani. Where the First Families touched down on Lumen. The land's changed, though. Back then there was nothing, no life at all. Now it's alive." He scanned the field and pointed. "Look."

Atop a crest of the rolling hills only a hundred meters away, five animals grazed in the field. She had never seen anything like them. They stood on four legs and craned long necks toward the ground. Their muscular shoulders pumped even as they stood still, silent, graceful in their idleness. Thick, bony antlers bucked into the air when one of them bent toward the sky and made a sound like a cough.

"What are they?" Dani asked.

"I have no idea."

"I don't understand. There shouldn't be any wildlife out here."

"But there is."

She glowed. The possibilities were gloriously endless.

"There's a whole world." James squeezed her like he'd never let her go. "Lumen's a whole world, and it's for us. It's ours."

The animals in the distance perked up. Their phosphorescent blue eyes beamed in frantic search. Dani and James were still. They held their breath, and for a moment, the animals froze, honing in on Dani and James' direction. Then the animals bolted toward the tree line.

"Must have spooked them," James said.

A strong breeze crept over the field and through the forest, urging the world into motion. A chill set into Dani's bones. Barely detectable at first, the earth beneath their feet trembled. Dani and James looked at each other, unsure what they were sensing. The tremble grew into a bouncing roll, and the wild erupted into battle, quivering trees going for each other's throats.

James pushed Dani behind him and gripped the hilt of his bush knife.

Three

The sound of screaming outside pulled Bernice Arokson out of a world of knights, orcs, and dragons. She set the book on her bed.

In her pink pajamas and bunny slippers, she raced to the window and found her Uncle Aeron in the street illuminated by the globe streetlamps. He was rubbing Mrs. Bellman's back as she sobbed into the gravel. Lights in other houses were turning on, and people were coming out of their homes and onto their porches to watch their warden console Mrs. Bellman.

Bernie's bedroom door burst open. The young girl's brother, Shane, peered at her from the threshold. "What's going on, Bern?"

Her face flushed, and she growled, "Get out of my room!"

Shane raised his hands in placation. "Take it easy. I'm technically still in the hallway." He teased her with a toothy grin.

Bernie huffed. "You could have at least knocked."

"I'm just checking to see if you're all right. I heard screaming."

"It's outside. Sera Bellman's mom. Uncle Aeron's with her."

Shane's boyish face hardened. He crossed the room, not without noticing Bernie's dramatic sigh, and joined her at the window.

Uncle Aeron was talking to Sheriff Ballard now, who was nodding dutifully. Bernie and Shane couldn't make out what their uncle was saying, but they could tell Sheriff Ballard was saying, "right" and "yes, sir," over and over. Ballard whistled into the distance and waved her hand in the air. One of her deputies raced down the street. Ballard spoke to him, and he nodded, said, "Yes, ma'am," then rushed off toward Arokson Hall.

The bell tower bellowed.

Bernie choked a gasp. "Shane, where's Dad?"

Shane hushed her, his attention glued outside. "Quiet."

She tugged on his sleeve. "I'm scared."

"Dad's not coming home tonight. He's locked up again."

"Oh." Bernie fidgeted with her golden hair.

"Stay here. I'm going out there."

Bernie's eyes shot open. "No! Don't leave me alone!"

Shane grasped her shoulder. "It's okay. Whatever it is, you're safe here. If you weren't, Uncle Aeron would be taking us somewhere else. Just stay here, and you'll be able to see me from this window."

Bernie released a quivering breath. "Okay."

"Besides," Shane said as he walked out of her room, "when have we ever needed Dad for anything?"

Shane left his young sister alone in a dark and lonely house. She glanced to the sanctuary of her book, longing to submerge herself in the world that allured her instead of the one that frightened her. However, she returned to the window, her portal to as much of the real world as she could handle on nights like this.

Four

As Shane walked toward his uncle, another deputy ushered Mrs. Bellman away. She looked as if she'd aged twenty years in twenty minutes. Her shoulders were hunched, and her face was a wet mess. When she met his gaze, she looked haunted, as if she didn't even know who he was.

The bell tower continued to ring. Neighbors stood on their front steps, peering down the street at Arokson Hall, tying knots in robes or buckling belts, each of them meeting curiosity before being fully dressed.

Shane neared his uncle and Sheriff Ballard.

"Regina, I hear you," Aeron was saying. "But we have to wait until sunup."

"But they're kids, Aeron. *Kids*. They're probably lost and scared. What if they were yours?"

Aeron sighed. "We have to wait."

"Why?"

"You, of all people, are asking that question?"

"To hell with the law, Aeron. Is that why you left your brother in my jail? Because you knew he wouldn't stand to wait?"

Aeron and Ballard saw Shane, and as adults do, they changed their demeanor and tone as if they weren't just ready to tear each other's throats out. Shane was old enough to recognize it and to wonder when they were going to stop treating him like a child.

"Hey there, Shane," Aeron said.

"Hey, Uncle Aeron. Everything all right?"

"Fine, Shane. Everything's fine. Why don't you go on back and see to your sister?"

"She's okay. See?" Shane pointed to the window in which Bernie's pale face looked out on them. She waved, and they waved back. "I figured I'd come see if there was anything I could do to help."

"That's real noble of you, Shane, but we've got everything under control. If there's anything that needs doing, you can bet I'll let you know."

Another part of being Shane's age was he was smart enough to know when someone was patronizing him.

Shane stayed even as his uncle turned back to Sheriff Ballard. He felt the lines of communication beginning to sever, and he hadn't gotten the answer to the question that was plaguing his mind.

"Is Sera Bellman all right?" Shane asked. "I saw her mom was real upset."

Aeron turned back to Shane with a grim face. "I won't tell you again, Shane. Go home."

Aeron and Sheriff Ballard walked down the street toward Arokson Hall, their voices blending in with the bell tower's singing.

For the first time in his life, Shane saw in his uncle a man that was too much like his father.

Five

Dani tripped over a tree root and fell into a bush that welcomed her with open arms. She struggled to get free, but her coat sleeves were caught in the branches of the bush. Thorns dug into her arms like clutching fingers. The earth trembled around her.

"James!"

In the darkness, the thick foliage of Lumen's wilderness left her with no sense of direction. She'd lost the path James had cut through the forest. Moments before, she'd lost her love.

"James!"

Something had found them both. She didn't know what it was. She knew only that she'd never seen anything like it before. It moved through the trees. It tunneled under the earth. The planet had come to take them.

Dani slipped her arms from her coat and pushed it up over her head. That left only her legs, and with her adrenaline pumping, she didn't even feel the thorns biting into her thighs, tearing them to shreds. She pulled with all of her strength and broke free.

On her feet again, she heard the thing that pursued her getting closer. It was no longer strictly a pounding within the ground. Now there was a chittering sound, a clicking like the train that took the workers to the Pillar of Dawn, only this was much faster, like a giant drumming its fingers on a table.

"James!"

More branches struck out at her, lashing her neck, face, and arms. More roots threatened to take her down again. The forest only got deeper and thicker. She couldn't even be sure she was running back the way they'd come. There was nothing but darkness and forest in every direction.

Then a bright red flare, like a miniature star, shot into the sky. It hovered with the aurora for a moment and then went out. In spite of the trembling behind her, she stopped. She heard the ringing of the bell tower and a human voice. She ran for it.

Another flare burst into the sky, confirming that she was headed in the right direction. The pounding weakened and stopped near where she'd changed her direction. A second later, it was chasing after her again.

She ran and ran, pushing away every branch that reached for her, jumping over the short bushes, punching through the foliage that was too tall. She never looked back because she knew to look back would mean falling again. If she fell, the trembling earth would take her. The ground would open and swallow her whole like a nightmare from her childhood.

"DANI HINES, JAMES BELLMAN, IF YOU CAN HEAR ME, FOLLOW THE SOUND OF MY VOICE," a man on a loudspeaker said.

She ran until she could finally see the clearing before Vale's wall, the exterior lighting pouring through the tree line. All she had to do was get into the open where the sentries could see her and she would be saved. They would protect her.

Dani leaped over a small bush and hooked around the trunk of a great tree. She crashed through a net of branches, and then she touched the edge of the wild.

She gave everything she had left to make the clearing, but as she tried to jump out of the forest and onto the groomed grass, something wrapped around her waist.

The thundering grew. The chittering rose like static.

"Help me!" Another flare went up. A trio of spotlights on the wall honed in on her location.

"There's the girl!" someone cried.

They could see her, but unless she made the clearing, they couldn't help her.

Struggling, she turned to face the darkness of the wild. It was going to get her. She was so close to home, but Lumen was going to take her. She would never see her mother or father again. James. Where was James?

Lumen showed Dani mercy, and the vines around her waist snapped. She stumbled into the clearing and scurried toward the wall. Finally, she saw it, the trees waving as if a gust of wind surged through them, the soil coughing into the air, the forest coming forth.

It reached nearly to the edge of the clearing, almost to where she could see it, shadows dancing through the leaves, and in the spaces between, the aurora's light hit a glossy, wet surface, like polished black bone.

Just before it came into the spotlight, it stopped.

"STAY WHERE YOU ARE, DANI. WE'RE COMING TO GET YOU."

She got to her feet and sprinted for the gate, the spotlights following her. The soil where she'd fallen opened and sucked down ever so slightly as though something beneath it had collapsed. When the spotlights returned their beams to the tree line, the trembling in the wild stilled.

Dani raced toward the gate. When she reached it, she pounded on it with clenched fists, screaming. The sentries on the wall froze and gazed into the quiet wild.

Six

Lincoln was lying on the cot in the jail cell. The pounding in his head grew, and he massaged his brow in a futile attempt to soothe the pain. At this point, he couldn't hope to sleep. He'd passed through the drowsiness and spins and into the hangover. Aeron probably had come to visit him just so Lincoln wouldn't be able to sleep. It would have been just like his brother to try to work a lesson into tonight.

"Lyle," he called, "you got any battensoft?"

"That's not going to make your pain go away," a female voice said.

It wasn't Reggie. Her voice was colder and harder, like a sheet of ice. This voice was soothing and warm.

Lincoln opened one eye and found a familiar blur. Lucy's red hair spilled over her shoulders like wine.

She wrapped her fingers wrapped around the metal bars. "You're just going to have to man up and take it," she said. "You made a mistake, and now you have to live with it."

"What mistake?"

"Drinking that shine Gill put in front of you."

"Seemed like a good idea at the time."

"That's your problem. You never think beyond the next hour. That's all shine's good for, and then it hits you. An hour of fun for a night of suffering."

Lincoln made a show of rolling over in his cot away from her. "Deputy, I'm being harassed."

Deputy Lyle Albright was asleep, his feet on his desk pushing his chair back at a precarious angle. His head lolled, and his mouth was agape

"You wake him up," Lucy said, "I don't think he'll be liable to care."

Lincoln sat up and rubbed the back of his neck. "What do you want, Luce?"

"For you to get off your ass and out of that cell."

Lincoln sighed. "In case you hadn't noticed, those bars are iron."

A jingling sound bit into Lincoln's ears. Lucy was holding the keys to the jail.

"You've always had control, Lincoln, even when you weren't in control. Just like right now. I've got the keys, but you have the power to use them."

Lincoln grunted. "Tell me what I gotta do this time."

"Why do you think I want you to do something?"

"There's a cost to everything with you. Always has been."

Lucy's brow narrowed. "I'm not the devil, Lincoln."

She pushed the key to his cell into the lock. She turned it, and the latch boomed. The hinges whined when she opened the door. "Your children need you."

"Ah, hell, Luce, I—"

"They *need* you, Lincoln."

He got off of the cot and stepped forward. Lucy tossed the keys onto Lyle's desk. The deputy stirred and fell, crashing onto the wooden floor.

He looked up and saw Lincoln. "What the hell?"

"Watch your mouth," Lucy said.

Lyle stood and picked up his chair. "He's not supposed to be out till morning. Sheriff said."

"That so?" Lucy said. "We'd better not tell her then."

"When she finds out, she'll—"

"Reprimand you for allowing someone to walk in here and take the keys off you."

Lyle gawked at Lucy and lowered his head to avert her gaze. "I'm sorry, ma'am. It's just—"

"Just what?"

"The sheriff said she don't want people thinking the warden's family gets special privileges."

"Lincoln won't be any more trouble."

"I think he means you, Luce," Lincoln said.

"Is that so?" she said.

Lyle gazed sheepishly.

"Huh." Pondering the thought, she turned and walked through the jailhouse door into the street. Lincoln followed, his headache gone.

Seven

Shane had seen the flares in the night sky, and he'd heard the sentries' shouts on the wall. His neighbors were marching down the streets in droves, dispersing across the open field of the commons and the marketplace toward the main gate. He heard their confused chatter but couldn't make out what they were saying. Hundreds of voices rumbled, none of them singularly decipherable.

He ran down the street against the direction of traffic, taking blows from elbows and hips. The Bellman house was dark, but he ascended the steps anyway and, after a moment of consideration, beat on the door.

"Sera?"

No one answered.

He skipped back down the steps into the crowd and followed everyone into the commons where the people flowed around him like a river. He searched for a friendly face who could tell him what was going on; however, absorbed in their own curiosity, none of them took notice of the boy standing in the crowd. Shane focused his attention up at the adults rushing past, and someone more his size crashed into him and took him to the ground.

"Get off!" With a grunt, he pushed the person off of him and glanced to his side to find his cousin Gabe rolling onto the grass.

Dazed, Gabe shook his matchstick head and grinned at Shane. "'Scuse me, cuz."

"What are you doing out?"

"Same thing as you, obviously." Gabe got up, brushed his pants off, and offered a hand to Shane.

Shane took it and got to his feet. "Your mom let you out?"

Gabe grinned again. "Not home. Something about helping your dad, who I assume isn't home either."

Shane shook his head. "You know what's going on?"

"I heard some kids went out past the wall and that a girl's been hurt."

"I saw Mrs. Bellman crying."

Gabe's face slackened as the realization set in. "Oh man. Sera?"

Shane grimaced. "That's what I'm trying to find out."

"Only one way to do that. Come on."

The boys followed the crowd across the commons to the main gate. When they got there, a line of towering adults stood between them and the entrance to the colony. They could barely see the top of the great wooden door as it began to descend and close. With a loud clank, the iron latch caught each tooth of the cog that allowed its mechanical control, and the door settled into place with a boom.

Shane and Gabe slithered between the people in the crowd toward the front, pushing through the crowd until they met the unyielding arm of

Alain Ducard, a monolithic sentry who looked at them with a disapproving gaze.

"No way, kid," Ducard said.

The sentries had done what they did best and created a perimeter. Instead of guarding the wall between the colony and the wild, they stood between the people and the girl Shane desperately needed to know the identity of.

"Sera!" Shane called, leaning over Ducard's arm.

The sentry tossed him back into the crowd.

Shane looked to Gabe and found that grin again.

"I'll distract him," Gabe said.

The boy pushed up toward Ducard. "I think I'm gonna be sick." He shoved his index finger into the back of his throat and vomited all over the sentry's boots.

The seething crowd of people gasped and pulled away from the sentry, who gazed down and groaned in revulsion. Someone asked if Gabe was the warden's kid. Someone else said they thought so.

"Sorry," Gabe said, spitting a long string of mucus onto the ground. He stared innocently up at the sentry and grinned.

Ducard grabbed Gabe by his shirt collar. "Let's see what your daddy thinks about you being out after curfew."

Easing through the crowd, Shane met Gabe's eyes again. Gabe shrugged as the sentry dragged him away and disappeared into the crowd. Shane hoped his cousin wouldn't get in trouble, but right now, he needed to see who was at the gate.

In front of the closed gate, Sherriff Ballard, several deputies, and some nurses were all helping someone. Shane spotted inky hair for an instant, and then it was lost again. As they dispersed, there was the girl. Sherriff Ballard was covering her with a blanket and pushing her matted and tangled hair away from her tearstained and dirty face. Her body trembled with sobs. As Ballard ushered her forward, she struggled to be free, as if she were trying to go back out the main gate, back out into the wild.

It wasn't Sera. It was Dani Hines.

The nurses laid Dani onto a pushcart with a gurney on the front, the colony's ambulance, and the crowd made way for the cart to roll toward the infirmary. Their curiosity satisfied, most of the people at the gate cleared out and turned to their homes, but Shane trailed the ambulance.

When he got to the infirmary, they'd already taken Dani inside. More sentries were holding crowds back and denying entry.

Then they were ushering Mrs. Bellman toward the infirmary. And finally, Sera.

"Sera," Shane called. "Sera!"

When she saw him, she gasped, rushed to him, and leaped into his arms.

"He's out there, Shane! He's out there, and they can't find him!"

Shane held her tightly, pressing the warmth of her tears into his chest.

"It's okay, it's okay, it's okay," he said over and over, brushing her midnight hair.

Sera's mother approached, her eyes drained of strength but glancing expectantly at the people who'd gathered. She laid a hand on Sera's back. "We should go inside."

Shane relaxed his embrace but felt no give in Sera's grip. A moment later, she turned to her mother, and Mrs. Bellman's stone gaze faltered.

"Shane, you can stay with Sera a while."

"Are you sure?"

Mrs. Bellman nodded.

He felt compelled to verify Mrs. Bellman's permission because, less than a year earlier, Sera and James had lost their father, and the last thing Shane wanted to do was cause that family any more pain.

Eight

In the infirmary waiting room, Sera had fallen asleep in Shane's arms. His shoulder ached, and his right hand was dead, but he didn't care. Sera was safe, and after fearing the worst, this was the greatest feeling he'd ever experienced.

Raised voices erupted in the hallway. Although Shane couldn't make out what they were saying, someone was sobbing.

A moment later, Mrs. Bellman came in from the hall, her face flushed, and stopped just beyond the doorway. She placed a hand on her chest and stood there for a moment, breathing. Shane was brushing Sera's tear-dampened hair behind her ears.

Shane could sense a smile in Mrs. Bellman, even if she didn't show it. Having heard the shouting, he was about to ask if everything was all right, but he knew the answer. After a moment, she approached him.

"You should go home and get some rest," she whispered in his ear.

Shane nodded and did his best to slide Sera off of him without waking her. She stirred, but with all of her emotions drained, Shane didn't think she would wake anytime soon.

The boy stood, looking toward Sera as her mother covered her with a blanket and stepped back. Shane shoved his hands into his pockets and yawned. Mrs. Bellman wrapped her arms around him and pulled him close, her chest shuddering.

Surprised, Shane returned the embrace. "They're going to find him."

She regained her composure and pulled away, wiping her eyes. Her breathing steadied, and she forced herself to nod. "I know. You're a good friend to Sera."

Though disappointed at the label Mrs. Bellman had given their relationship, Shane gave her a comforting smile and left her in peace.

Hunched over on a bench outside the waiting room, Aeron was being briefed by Sheriff Ballard and a large man Shane didn't recognize. The man wore a sentry uniform, but it was different. It had stripes on his shoulders, and he held a hat with a flat top.

"We're holding the perimeter and leaving the spotlights on all night as you said," the large man said. "Other than that, I'm not sure what else we can do until morning."

"Flares," Ballard said. "Send one up every half hour."

Aeron nodded. "Do it."

"Warden, those are intended for emergencies," the man said. "The watch doesn't have many in supply."

"Use what you have," Aeron said. "We'll make more."

Shane let the door click closed, and they noticed him.

Aeron sat up. "Hey, Shane."

"Hey."

"Rough night."

"Yeah."

Aeron noticed Shane's wary looks at the man he didn't know.

"This is Ezra Barrow. He's captain of the Sentry Service."

Captain Barrow nodded and extended his beefy hand in greeting. "Pleased to meet you, son."

Shane shook the captain's hand and was taken aback by the respect the man showed him.

"He and his men are going to find James," Aeron said.

"Me too," Ballard said. "I'm going too."

"Point is we're going to find him, Shane."

Shane saw in his uncle's eyes, heard it in his voice, that this was more a reassurance for himself.

"I know." Shane nodded and moved past them, then stopped. "Don't tell my dad I was here. He finds out I left Bernie alone tonight, I'm dead."

Aeron grinned. "Don't worry. It's our secret."

Shane left them in the infirmary's quiet gloom, expecting his uncle to come through for the Bellman family but not really sure how he would.

Aeron didn't know either.

Nine

The streets had cleared, and the Arokson household stood silent against the dark row homes. Shane rocked in a swing across the street from his house, gazing up at the second floor windows. Bernie's bedroom light was off. She was probably asleep. Their father's bedroom light was off too.

For a while, Shane listened to the creak of the chains, ticking and groaning in the silent colony. The wind whipped over the grounds, stirring the dry, cold air. The aurora hung like clouds in a snaking pattern, a glowing river in the night sky.

The spotlights still scanned the edge of the wild, casting the top of the wall in a warm glow, but all other search attempts had ceased. Apparently they were content with finding one of the children at least until morning. No one was going out there at night. The wild scared the colonists enough during the day. The truth was, while they claimed a victory, only luck had returned Dani to them, and the people of Vale didn't have the guts to go looking for James. James was on his own.

He decided the order to stop the search until morning was why Mrs. Bellman and his uncle had been arguing. Shane's Uncle Aeron had always been a caring, compassionate man. Shane had turned to him before turning to his father, sometimes because he couldn't turn to his father at all. He'd never seen this side of his uncle. He didn't understand why someone would ignore the compulsions of their heart. It frustrated him when the people in power did nothing.

Shane sighed and hopped off of the swing. It swayed in the breeze as if some part of him remained. He set off, the gravel in the street crunching underfoot. The row homes were at peace. Although everyone knew one of their own was missing, they took solace in the knowledge that they could do nothing for James. Shane didn't have that luxury. He felt like he could do something, but he was just a kid.

"Just another night for you all, isn't it?" Shane said, feeling like it was a scream, but his words died in the wind.

For Sera and her mother, their powerlessness was the source of their grief. For Shane, it was becoming a source of anger. Sera was not physically harmed, but she was hurt nonetheless, and no one seemed to care.

Dwelling on his frustration, he ascended his home's front steps, fumbling his keys. Before he could unlock the door, it burst open. Shane's eyes met his father's broad chest, and he noted the labored rise and fall. The boy didn't have to look above his father's sharp neckline to know those eyes were burning. He didn't have the courage to meet that gaze. He just stood there, dumbly holding the key out in the air.

Lincoln's strong, calloused hand grabbed a fistful of Shane's shirt and pulled him into the house. Shane spilled into the hallway and turned to his father with downcast eyes.

Lincoln restrained himself enough to close the door quietly so as not to wake his daughter, who'd come to him in tears when he'd returned home. He leaned against the door for a moment and tried to breathe, to think about what he was going to do with Shane, a problem he'd seethed over since he got home hours ago.

"Do you know what time it is?" he finally said, trying to sound concerned, but he sounded angry, his voice cutting the air. "Where have you been? Half the colony was out looking for two missing kids, and you go and become a third? Bernie didn't know where you were, and I had no idea what was going on. I almost had to go to Sheriff Ballard and report another missing child."

"Not my fault," Shane mumbled.

"What?" Lincoln pushed off from the door. "What did you say?"

Shane shook his head, recoiling. "Nothing. I'm sorry, okay?"

He moved to walk up the stairs, and Lincoln's hand clamped onto his arm. Shane struggled, and Lincoln squeezed until he was still.

"You can't just disappear like this. I need you here."

Shane's lips quivered, his mouth threatening to erupt.

Lincoln pulled his son down from the steps, taking him with both hands in a stern, powerful hold.

"I need you to be responsible, to look after your sister."

"Yeah, you need me here because you can't be." Shane was hearing himself say these things, but he was no longer at the controls. "You need me here in case you can't make it home because you're locked up for drinking and fighting again."

"Watch your mouth."

"Why are you taking this out on me? I wasn't the one in jail."

Lincoln looked at his son with something like reverence. "My failures can't be an excuse for you. You have to be better than me, Shane."

"I *am* better than you."

Shane saw the hand reel back and knew it was coming, but he never expected it to connect. The knuckles crashed against his jaw and split his lip. His head rattled, and his cheek bloomed with warmth.

The boy stumbled. Blood trickled down his chin. In defiance, he let it.

Lincoln released his hold on his son, and Shane adjusted his shirt.

His eyes no longer downcast, Shane and his father matched each other's gaze in the darkness of the hallway for what seemed like an eternity, something in both of them unwilling to let go.

Then Shane turned his back on his father and stepped calmly up the stairs. He went quietly so as not to disturb his sister.

Lincoln didn't stop him this time.

CHAPTER 2
HOUSE OF GODS

One

Morning came early for Aeron. He hadn't slept, and the dawn had just slipped on by. Sitting at his desk in his office, nursing a migraine and listening to Sheriff Ballard's droning voice, it occurred to him that the aurora was gone, and the sun beamed through his window.

Tomorrow had come. James Bellman hadn't returned. It was time to go look for him.

Aeron sighed and looked out on the commons. The morning dew sparkled in the grass. On the mountain, the Pillar of Dawn struck into the sky.

The end of the year was approaching, and with it came the winter solstice. As colony planets were always measured against Earth, Lumen tilted less dramatically on its axis. With milder seasonal change, Vale never quite experienced the depths of the freeze that once embraced the whole world, not since the Pillars of Dawn began their work. The climate had warmed, and even during the winter, Lumen's temperate zone was comfortable.

But it was still a winter season.

The Pillars of Dawn were the key to life on Lumen. They provided the planet with two things it lacked naturally. First, the pillars were belching endless supplies of atmospheric gases to raise temperatures and produce breathable air. Second, they were melting Lumen's core to kickstart it into generating a magnetic field, without which the sun would blast away the planet's new atmosphere and leave it a dead rock.

Workers were crossing the commons toward the train that would take them across the valley and up the mountain to Vale's pillar. Dressed in blue and gray coveralls, they wore orange safety vests and carried helmets. Among the colonists, even compared to the miners working in the quarries, these were the hardest workers, and it showed on their haggard faces. They didn't have any skill applicable to colony life, didn't have the capital to open a store or invest in a service for the people. They contributed in their own way, with determination for a hard day's work, and they were irreplaceable.

Over the years, as the colony had changed, the one constant had been the pillar and the people who ran it. It wasn't lucrative, but it was well respected.

"Did you hear me, Warden?" Sheriff Ballard peered at Aeron from the chair on the other side of the desk. Her pensive eyes drilled into Aeron on a level approaching scrutiny.

"Hmmm?" Aeron turned around.

Sheriff Ballard and Captain Barrow regarded Aeron from chairs set beside each other in front of the warden's desk.

Though they'd been up all night, Ballard showed no signs of fatigue. Captain Barrow looked unfazed as well, but he had the discipline of a soldier and the training of a sentry. They could stay awake and alert for days if necessary.

Aeron, on the other hand, felt sapped of his life force.

"I said the search party is assembled and ready to go. Dani Hines gave us a good idea where they were last night. We just need—"

"How is Dani?" Aeron asked.

"Fine. Sleeping. Lacerations and bruises but nothing serious. Except for the few minutes I was able to talk to her on the way to the infirmary, she hasn't woken up since they brought her in. The doctors say it's just exhaustion, but it makes me wonder what she was so afraid of."

"You ever been out in the wild at night?" Aeron asked.

Ballard narrowed her eyebrows and shook her head. Beside her, Barrow's stone face was unchanged.

"My father used to take us, teach us things we would need to know if we ever left the colony, knowing the gates would open in our lifetimes. He always brought us back by nightfall, but even in the day, it would get real dark in there. Easy to feel like something's watching or following you."

Ballard looked at Aeron with inquisitive eyes. "What if something was?"

"Nonsense. Only life that's here we put here."

"All due respect, James isn't the first, and you, more than anyone, know that. What if people aren't just getting lost or leaving of their own accord?"

Aeron looked to Captain Barrow. "What do you think?"

Barrow's broad chest swelled with a deep breath. His hands remained folded in his lap, and he was sitting with perfect posture. He eyed the sheriff and blinked lazily. He commanded patience when he spoke. Even when asked a question, he responded on his own terms.

"I think the sheriff can't rely on the testimony of eyewitnesses for a reason," the captain said. "I think there's plenty of phenomena to explain when people think they see or hear things that aren't really there. The fact of the matter is my men watch the wild twenty-seven hours a day, four hundred thirty-two days per year, and they've never reported anything but trees."

Ballard squinted and leaned forward. "Then why are you here, Captain?"

Tension descended on the room as Ballard pressed Barrow for the answer, and the sentry captain wouldn't even look at her. Aeron doubted Barrow's heart capped fifty beats per minute, but there it was: he was afraid of her.

Aeron lifted his mug and sipped. "I didn't ask if either of you'd like a cup of tea. My brother makes the best stuff."

Ballard sat back in her chair. "No thank you."

Barrow declined with a raised hand.

The sheriff crossed her arms. "I'm not so easily distracted, Aeron."

"Reggie, you bring this up every time this happens, and every time I have to convince you that—"

Ballard balled a fist and moved to slam the arm of her chair, but she settled for a tap. "That's just it, Aeron. There is an 'every time.'"

"All right, all right," Aeron said. "Look, we've known for some time that people are leaving the colony, starting on the frontier early. Freeloaders looking to ride on the coattails of our hard work. They live out there in the wild, thriving off of the ecosystem we built, and some time ago, it was decided that people like that could pose a threat. Since the mission of the colony was so critical, we started the Sentry Service."

"So you think James Bellman abandoned his mother and sister not a year after his father died so he could go live alone in the trees?"

"I don't know, but what I do know is James and Dani got past the wall somehow, and that's a security concern. Do we know how they got through?"

Barrow cleared his throat. "We don't think they snuck through any of the gates, and they certainly didn't go over the wall. The only logical conclusion is there's a breach somewhere, but we don't know where. It could take some time to find it."

"Did Dani say anything about that?"

"She claimed she couldn't remember," Ballard said. "Claimed she was just following the boy. I think she didn't want to tell me."

"Why do you say that?"

"In my position, you get used to reading people and knowing when they're holding something back. Or when they're lying."

"I see. Well, we need to know how they got out. If there's a breach, we need to know about it, and we have to secure it. We can't have anyone else getting lost out there."

"We have all the gates secured with at least two sentries at all times," Barrow said.

Aeron raised a hand. "I know. This isn't your fault, Ezra."

"No," Ballard said. "It's mine. The people in these walls are my responsibility. I'll own that."

"We're missing something." Aeron retreated into his thoughts, rubbing his stubbly chin and sipping from his tea.

"Do you want me to stay and look for it?" Ballard said.

Aeron waved his hand in dismissal and set his mug on his desk. "No, no. Take the search party out. I know you'll find James. He's a capable boy. He'll turn up."

"And the breach?" Barrow said. "It could take weeks to search the wall. I don't have the manpower to operate a search party in the wild and inspect for breaches at the same time."

"Maybe we should just table it until we find James," Ballard suggested.

Aeron shook his head. "This whole world rests upon the Pillars of Dawn, and they need the colonies to keep them running. If our colonists can't be assured that their families will be home waiting for them in the evening, they might stop going to work. If they do that, we could lose everything. Lumen isn't ready. If our pillar fails, the others could fail, and that would mean *we* fail."

Ballard fidgeted with her hands in her lap. "What do you suggest?"

"I have a pretty good idea of someone who may be able to point us in the right direction," Aeron said.

"Who?"

Aeron held his mug up. "My brother. Before you leave with the search party, go to lockup and get him. Bring him here."

Sheriff Ballard shifted in her chair.

"What's wrong?" Aeron asked.

"Well, it's going to be difficult for me to get Lincoln from lockup."

"Why?"

"Because some time during the night, he was released. Lyle said it was Lucy."

Aeron closed his eyes and sighed. "I understand. I'll take care of it. Focus on finding James."

Ballard rose from her chair but stopped when she noticed Barrow wasn't moving.

"It's all right," Aeron said. "Go on ahead."

"My men are ready for you," Barrow said.

Ballard cast uncertain glances between the men, but she was already committed to leaving. When she had closed the door behind her, Barrow gazed at Aeron for what seemed like an eternity.

"We need to tell them," Barrow said.

"We don't know that. I don't want to scare them for no reason."

Captain Barrow's eyes drilled into him. "Warden, I once knew a man, not a particularly smart man, who did things like giving me orders and sending me into warzones. One day, he ordered me to take my company out to Adagio Minor, this moon orbiting a gas giant in a binary star system. The sunsets and night skies were so amazing that it became a destination for the super rich, which turned out to be a breeding ground for the opportunity of the desperate. Adagio Minor quickly became a line in a conflict against a rebellion that your people will never need to worry about, but this man, he knowingly put my company into a meat grinder, and he kept secrets from me because he thought I wouldn't have followed his orders if I knew the truth about what he was sending us to do. I lost half my men. Our evac never even showed. We had to hide for months and then sneak onto a commercial vessel just to get off that rock. When we got back, I asked that man why he didn't tell me what he was sending us into, and you know what he said? He said he never expected me to come back. He said he didn't think he'd have to explain it."

Aeron's head was bowed. He couldn't meet those eyes anymore.

Barrow nodded acceptance, as if his investigation confirmed something he had expected. He stood and moved toward the door. "One other thing," he said. "Your son was out past curfew last night. Sergeant Ducard escorted him home personally. I'd guess your wife must have neglected to tell you."

"She must have."

"Ducard wasn't particularly pleased with him."

"Ducard isn't a particularly pleasant person."

Barrow grunted and left the warden's office.

When he was alone, Aeron looked through his window and admired the simple lives of the colonists who woke up every day, went to a job, and came home to their families at night. Those men and women didn't carry the weight of the colony on their shoulders, not like Aeron did. They didn't hold the weight of this world like the pillars did. They could leave their work at work, but Aeron felt the pressure of the colony and its pillar, its vital mission, bearing down on him all of the time. Before he took the job, he'd known it came with certain responsibilities that would isolate him from the rest of his people, but sometimes he wondered if it was too much. He wondered if he could handle it.

His pillar couldn't falter. Neither could he.

Alice, Aeron's assistant, knocked on the doorframe. "Excuse me, Warden." She pushed her glasses back on her nose. "Your morning appointments are here."

"Postpone them, Alice. I have to step out for a while." Aeron stood.

"Um, okay, yes, sir, but—"

"And do me a favor," he said on his way out the door. "Find my wife."

The warden left his assistant and a reception area full of colonists wondering what they were supposed to do now.

Two

Sheriff Ballard approached the main gate. The massive concrete perimeter wall converged on a wooden door reinforced with wrought-iron braces and a drop bar, which three men stood by ready to remove.

Twenty sentries were in various stages of preparation. The more veteran men, Alain Ducard and Kennedy Gray, had their packed bags at their feet and rifles slung. They were chuckling and kidding with the others, who were checking binding clips and zippers, bag contents for water, rations, and essential survival gear.

With untied bootlaces and his sidearm flapping in a loose holster on his belt, Deputy Lyle Albright hurried to Ballard's side.

"What are you doing here, Lyle?" she asked.

"I want to help."

"You were on third shift last night. Go home and get some rest. Anyway, the search is for the sentries, not us."

"So why are you going?"

"It's complicated."

"It's just that I feel real bad, you know? I feel like I let you down."

"You have nothing to feel bad about," Ballard said to the young man. "Lucy Arokson does as she pleases no matter who says otherwise. A sense of obligation is the worst reason to risk your life."

"The wild isn't dangerous, is it?"

"Strictly speaking, probably not, but it's untamed land. You're better off staying here."

Lyle nodded. "I know him, ma'am. I remember seeing him in school. My last year, he'd just come over from the elementary wing."

Ballard sighed. "All right, you can come, but you listen to me out there. Whatever I say, you do it, understand? Now head on over to Ducard up there, and see if he'll check your pack. You did bring water and something to eat, right?"

Lyle shook his head.

"It's fine," Ballard said. "We should have enough to go around for the day. I don't plan to be out past sundown, even if we come back without James." Ballard made eye contact with Elena Bellman who approached from the street and most certainly had heard her. "Go on." She slapped Lyle on the back, and the deputy ran up ahead. "And tie your damned boots!"

Elena's face had been a stone to emotion since Dani had returned. Ballard suspected that, somewhere inside, Elena understood her son was probably never going to be found, but getting Dani back had strengthened her resolve.

"Good morning, Sheriff." She pulled a shawl tightly around her shoulders.

"Elena, how are you?" She reached out for her arm, and Elena shrugged it off.

"These are the men who are going to find my son?" She looked them over with a disapproving expression. "Are they even all technically men?"

"They've all been trained."

"I didn't come here to be sold, Regina. I came here to address a concern."

"Which is?"

"Everyone's treating me like he's already gone. I'm concerned some of these men consider this search a formality, that their hearts aren't in it."

"I assure you that's not true."

"Isn't it?" Elena's voice echoed over the search party. Her eyes glassed over, blinking rapidly. "My James is better at this than all of you. He knows the land. He can survive out there. He's alive. Maybe he's hurt and needs help, but he's alive."

She gazed at them, letting her words do their work, letting them see her passion, then she stormed away toward the infirmary where Dani still slept.

When Ballard turned back toward the sentries, she found the sneering face of Clayton Ford, pack slung over one shoulder and sun hat pushed back on his head. His unkempt hair already shone with a sheen of grease. Perpetually appearing as if he'd just stepped out of the wild, Ford was a despicable human being whose only motivation was profit. He knew much about the wild, as his illegal expeditions often sent him beyond the walls, but he only brought back useful resources for others if there was payment involved. Clay was more of a plunderer than a gatherer. When he looked at the wild, all he saw was bounty.

"That was inspiring," Clay said flatly.

"Hello, Clay. Are you ready?"

"Yes, yes. But I wanted to talk to you before this thing gets out of the gates, as it were. I couldn't help but notice that, of all the people who are going on this search and rescue mission, I'm the only one who has any idea what's on the other side of the tree line."

"You're our guide," Ballard said. "It's your job."

Clay clapped. "Exactly! So you get it."

"Get what?"

"You understand that someone with my experience and qualifications is more valuable in this endeavor. After all, what's the point in finding the boy if the search party itself can't find its way back?"

Ballard spat into the dirt. "You want more money. You should feel ashamed to be taking payment at all."

Clay shrugged. "Maybe I should, but I don't."

Ballard stared Clay down. "Tell me something, Clay. How's the jaw this morning?"

He grinned. "How are them hips?"

"Keep it up. We've got your regular cell on reserve. It would be no trouble to put you there."

"Then who'd lead your search party? I'm all you got. There are only two people in the whole colony can bring you back from anywhere within this valley, and I don't think the other one is going anywhere. I want double."

After a moment of Ballard's silence, Clay started to walk away.

"Wait," she said.

Clay stopped.

"Fine, but the next time you run your mouth and Lincoln shuts it for you, I'm not going to stop him from taking that wherever it goes. Clear?"

Clay smiled a crooked smile. "Then maybe I guess you can get *him* to lead your search parties. Oh, but wait, where *is* the warden's screw-up brother?"

Three

Lincoln woke at his kitchen table, a half-empty jar of shine just beyond his knuckles. His headache had returned at full strength, and his tongue felt like a bag of sand. The sink across the room beckoned. If he had to retch, it would be there for him.

The floor felt shaky, but Lincoln knew it was his legs. He made it to the cabinet and retrieved a glass, wrapping his fingers carefully, deliberately around it so he wouldn't drop it onto the stone countertop. He moved to the sink and opened the tap. The minerals in the well water sparkled in the morning sunlight. He downed it and paused while it gushed down his throat and doused the fire in his stomach.

He gazed at his backyard garden. His lone oak tree swayed in the breeze, its shadow dancing on the white glass of his greenhouse.

Then his stomach contents rushed up and into the sink.

Stubborn yellow bile clung to his lips. Lincoln turned the tap on again and rinsed the vomit down the drain. The water felt cool on his fingertips, so he splashed it into his face and swept his long black hair back. Drops landed on his shoulders as he slid to the wood floor, wiping the mucus from his mouth with a dishtowel.

It always came down to this.

He crawled to the refrigerator where he kept a container of peeled ginger for these occasions. Resting against the counter, he chewed and stared through the window until he felt he could hold down some water and food. After a few minutes of just focusing on his breathing, the warmth of the sun on his face, Lincoln filled the glass again, but this time, he sipped it.

The stairs thundered. Most mornings, Lincoln loved his kids. This morning, he really didn't want to deal with Shane, but that's what parents did. In the face of their own mistakes, they dealt with their children.

Even so, he felt a measure of relief when Bernie charged into the kitchen. Already dressed for school, she pulled the stepladder from the crevice between the refrigerator and counter, planted it in front of the stove, and climbed to the cabinet above.

Lincoln cleared his throat. "What are you doing, sweetheart?"

"Making you breakfast."

She stepped down to the floor, grasped Lincoln's index finger, and led him to the table. She smiled and went back to the stovetop. The feeling of her grip lingered, and he remembered how it felt when she first took hold of that finger. Soon she would begin to take his whole hand, and then, she wouldn't need it ever again.

The childish tune she hummed in front of the stove reminded Lincoln that they still had time.

In minutes, she set a plate of steaming pancakes in front of him. The thought of eating made his stomach heave again, but he would hold it down. For her. He would do it for her.

Bernie smiled as she brought her own plate to the table, sat across from him, and began cutting her pancakes into meticulously carved, bite-sized pieces.

"I love you, Daddy," she said before she began eating.

"I love you too, sweetheart."

"I love you because you're strong."

Lincoln blew through puckered lips. "I don't feel strong this morning."

Chomping, Bernie shrugged. "Even strong men can't be strong all the time."

Lincoln blinked with bewilderment as Bernie continued like she'd said nothing of much consequence.

Knuckles rapped on the front door.

"I'll get it," Bernie announced.

"It's all right." Lincoln stood, finding his legs a bit more certain now, and walked down the hallway to the front door. He glanced through the window and grimaced. He had to open the door, but he dreaded it.

Turning the doorknob, he let the outside world in. The sunlight made him recoil. A halo of fire enveloped his visitor.

"What do you want?" Lincoln said.

Aeron shifted his weight. "Can I come in? We need to talk."

"About what?"

"Dani Hines and James Bellman."

"Now you want my help."

Aeron pleaded with his eyes, and after a moment, Lincoln stepped aside. Aeron walked into the hallway and down to the kitchen with Lincoln in tow.

"Morning, Bern."

"Morning, Uncle Aeron."

"Your daddy and I have something to discuss, Bern. Do you think we can have some privacy?"

"Let her finish her breakfast," Lincoln said.

"It's okay, Daddy. I'm done. I'll go get ready for school." Bernie took her dishes to the sink and trotted down the hall and up the stairs, her golden hair fluttering behind her like tulle.

Aeron's loving gaze followed her.

Lincoln peered at him with unyielding contempt. "What do you want?"

Aeron sighed and pulled out a chair from the table. "Can I sit?"

Lincoln consented with silence and then took a seat for himself. "Are you sending a search party out for the boy?"

"Yes."

Lincoln leaned back and rubbed his eyes. "I can be ready in twenty minutes."

"You're not leading it."

Lincoln sat forward. "Who is then?"

"Clayton Ford."

"Clay?"

"Yes."

Lincoln's expression darkened.

"Does that trouble you?" Aeron asked.

"The man *is* trouble."

"That may be, but if he finds James, what does it matter?"

"He won't."

Aeron's brow wrinkled. "Clay is knowledgeable about the wild. He's more than capable."

"He couldn't find his left testicle if he accidentally found his right."

Aeron shook his head and put his hand up in a placating gesture. "This isn't why I came."

"Then why did you come?"

"I want to know how Dani and James got out of the colony so we can secure the breach."

"What makes you think I'd know?"

Aeron's face twisted. "Please, little brother. I know you don't grow all of your herbs in the backyard. We tolerate what you and Clay do because the infirmary needs medicines, and you generally help people. You alone comforted almost an entire generation of people who died from liquid lung, and you make damn fine teas. But none of that is a priority right now. Right now, I have mothers and fathers scared that their own kids are going to sneak out at night and get lost, and I have to assure them of their safety."

"If I tell you and you close it, people aren't going to like it. It's not just me and Clay who use it, and it's not just Dani and James."

"All the more reason."

"You don't understand—"

"No, *you* don't understand. It's the law. I have to maintain order here, and part of that is assuring people that their kids aren't just going to wander off and disappear into the wild. It's part of the reason we built the wall in the first place. We can't have people leaving here. It isn't safe."

Lincoln scoffed. "Aeron, this isn't a prison."

"Brother," the warden said, "that's exactly what this place is."

While Lincoln and Aeron stared across the table at each other, Shane and Bernie lumbered down the stairs.

"Bye, Dad!" Bernie called.

"Hold it," Lincoln called. "I'll walk you."

"It's all right, Dad. We don't need you to."

Lincoln locked eyes with his son who was silently sucking his swollen lip. "Yes, you do."

"What about what we talked about?" Aeron said.

"Some of us have to work for a living, Warden. Right now, I have to make sure my kids get to school."

Shane turned away from his father and was the first out the door.

Four

Wired and electric, Lucy burst into the school's kitchen. She appeared like she had herself together with her red hair pulled into a neat bun, a steam-pressed blazer and skirt, and heeled shoes that clopped on the concrete floor, but her shoulders were wound up to her ears.

While stirring a pan of scrambled eggs, one of the cooks watched her between the metal shelves.

Lucy went to the hot water pitcher and poured a serving into a ceramic mug. She opened a canister of tealeaves and placed a heaping scoop into a metal infuser. Lowering it into her mug, the water clouded with amber and then a rich copper brown.

Breathing the steam, she noticed the cook was watching her. "Morning."

"Morning, Lucy."

"I wish we had something stronger. I do love Lincoln's tea, but after a night like last night, it just isn't enough."

"I heard other worlds get this stuff that's four to five times stronger. They say it's a bean."

"A bean?"

"Well, technically, it's a seed. But it looks like a bean, and everyone calls it a bean."

Lucy raised an eyebrow. "Strange. Thanks." She removed the infuser and stirred her tea with a spoon, escaping the kitchen with her steaming mug.

She left the cook as he was cracking more eggs into a frying pan. The cafeteria was still quiet but rising with the voices of children who were already arriving.

On the other side of the cafeteria, she climbed the stairs into the main hallway, where artwork from the eight-year-olds adorned the hallway, and Lucy smiled when she spotted Mel's piece, a hulking troll with one spiked shoulder pad and a tree trunk in his hands. She'd recognize it anywhere. It was the only piece done with paint, not dyed wax, and she was the only child who understood perspective.

Mel had always excelled at disciplines of art, and she had been born at the right time. In Vale, there hadn't been much room for artists before Lucy's generation. If Mel had been born even twenty years sooner, her abilities might have been smothered, and she might have been forced to do something else. Aeron's father had changed all of that when he had become warden. He had said the difference between a civilization and a culture was art and that, if they were to flourish on Lumen, they had to embrace and celebrate their own humanity. He had said art was the way to do that.

If Mel continued on her path, she would be one of the first to define who they were as a people, and the idea thrilled Lucy.

She exited the double doors in time to see a stream of children approaching. They were teasing and joking with each other. None of them were paying any attention.

She spotted Lincoln with Bernie and Shane, and she walked to meet them.

Lincoln kneeled and hugged Bernie.

"There's something I don't understand," Bernie said.

"What's that?" Lincoln said.

Some children walking by burst into laughter and carried on with their chatter.

Bernie squinted at them. "Someone's missing, but everyone's going on like nothing happened."

"It's how people are. Sometimes people need to be strong to move on, but sometimes, they have to be weak to live. If everyone concerned themselves with all the tragedies of the world, nothing would get done."

"There's too much sadness for them."

"Something like that."

Lucy kneeled beside Lincoln. Her smile faded as she recognized Bernie's somber mood.

Bernie was crumpling a lock of her hair. "If James and Dani knew they could get lost and no one would care, why'd they go and leave in the first place?"

Lincoln frowned and looked to Lucy.

"People care," she said. "The right people are looking for James, and you'll see. He'll turn up."

"So why'd they leave?"

"Sometimes," Lincoln said, "people just need to get away."

"From what? Was something chasing them? Like a monster?"

Lincoln laughed. "No. I mean sometimes people need to be alone."

"But they weren't alone. They were with each other."

"Exactly."

Bernie scowled. The strain of concentration appeared on her brow as she tried to make sense of it.

Lincoln ruffled her hair. "Don't worry, sweetheart. It makes sense. I promise."

Lucy stood. "Come on, kiddos. Let's get smart." She motioned for them to take her hands, and Bernie eagerly did so. Shane sulked and walked around her toward the school. She noticed the bruise and split on his lip, and she shot Lincoln a sharp look of accusation.

He looked away, unable to bear her contempt. With so many eyes and ears that would surely recount everything, it wasn't the time to handle it. She would see to it later when she could control the circumstances.

She and the kids joined the torrent of students, charging straight up the walkway toward the building. Lucy ushered them all in, and when the last of them entered, Lucy looked back toward the end of the walkway. Lincoln was still standing there.

She closed the doors on him.

Five

Daenuel Market was bustling. Lincoln stood at the edge of the commons where the two long, barn-like buildings stretched on either side of a stone plaza lined with trees and benches. At the other end was Daenuel Hall, which once was the center of the colony's government. While the first floor still held shops, the civic activity that used to take place on the second floor had moved to the newer Arokson Hall on the commons.

A man was offloading a shipment of trout from the flatbed of a pushcart. His wife stood on their shop's concrete steps, keeping inventory. When Lincoln passed, she glanced at him and missed a fish that her husband carried through the doorway.

Next door, the butcher was hauling fresh meats off of her shoulder and into her shop window. She set down a piece of beef the size of a human torso and patted it into place. Wiping her bloody hands on her apron, she too watched Lincoln walk by.

On the plaza, a fruit vendor was setting up apples and pears on display in his produce stand. The man wiped his brow with the back of his hand, smearing dirt on his forehead. He watched Lincoln pass until a customer pulled him away.

Lincoln knew them all, and they knew him.

As he approached the bakery, the sweet smell of breads and pastries warmed his insides. When he saw Gill's distillery, his guts went cold again.

Everyone who wished to be a part of the colony's budding economy had a stake in Daenuel Market. It was the nucleus of growth, the root of hope that one day their civilization could thrive and prosper. It was clear Lincoln didn't belong.

He came to Milly's flower shop, a modest stand under a tent, which housed potted plants, herbs, and flowers. The old woman was helping a mother with a newborn child, and while he waited, Lincoln browsed the herbs. He turned one over and balked at the price.

A moment later, Milly approached. "Morning, Lincoln."

"Morning, Milly. How are you?"

"Fine, dear, just fine. And you?"

"A little heartbroken to see the markup on these song blossoms. If memory serves, you got them at a fraction of the cost."

A worried expression crossed her face. "Sign of the times, I'm afraid. I hope you aren't upset. We do appreciate the discount, but with Richard's illness, we have to take advantage of every opportunity we can."

"I understand. Just as long as you're willing to help out anyone who really needs it. You know my policy."

"I do."

"Then all is well."

Milly took a deep breath. "So. Special occasion?"

"Sympathy."

She frowned. "Do you know what kind of flowers they like?"

Lincoln shook his head and pointed. "What about the white orchid?"

"Cymbidium orchid. Common on most developed worlds, but not on ours. They're durable, so they're a good gift choice." She smiled. "But I think you know all that."

Lincoln smiled back and dug into his pocket.

"We could work out something of a trade if you like," Milly offered. "I'll be needing cerebral bulbs and honeyroot soon. Nobody is as capable as you in finding them."

Lincoln pulled out his wallet. "I see any, I'll bring them to you. For now, let's settle this. I don't like debts."

"Of course," Milly said with a warm smile that highlighted the deep lines in her cheeks. "It's three."

Lincoln removed five colony notes from his wallet and gave them to her. "I'm not someone who needs the discount," he said.

"But I thought—"

"I know what it costs, and I'm happy to pay it."

Milly nodded, slipped the notes into her apron, and retrieved the orchid.

Lincoln held the plant in the crook of his arm. Milly's husband Richard was sitting in the back and hacking into a hanky.

"How is he?" Lincoln asked.

"Comfortable. The treatments help. He has trouble with stairs, but at least he can still climb them. Of course, he has his good days, like today, and he wants to be outside as much as he still can. But you know Richard. It depresses him that he can't work. The man never learned how to just enjoy the time we have."

"That I understand, but he still has time. Not everyone with liquid lung was so fortunate."

Milly frowned. She patted his arm and was silent for a moment, and then her face brightened. "Oh, I almost forgot."

She scurried behind the counter at the back of the shop and returned with a box wrapped in old, yellowed editions of the colony newspaper. She handed it to him. "Go ahead. Open it."

Lincoln set the orchid down on a table and gazed at the box, trying to guess what it was. He tore the paper off. The smooth rosewood glistened and felt warm in his palms. He flipped the bronze locking clasp, and inside was a compass on a silver chain.

"It was your father's," Milly said. "He traded it to me a long time ago for a gift for your mother. It's never worked. As I understand it, it's an heirloom, but you know your father wasn't much for sentimentality. I almost didn't take it, but he insisted. Anyway, I found it the other day."

"Why would Dad have had a compass? They don't work on Lumen." Lincoln scowled and examined the compass' face. Its needle meandered. "He'd have probably wanted my brother to have it."

"Nonsense. What would Aeron need it for? He'll never leave these walls. You're the curious one."

She smiled in reverence.

Lincoln clutched the compass. "Thank you."

"You're welcome, dear."

Lincoln left, moving down the crowded marketplace street. His whole life, his father had never given him anything with any meaning. For birthdays, Lincoln received toys and new clothes, gifts any other boy would have been happy to have. However, Lincoln had seen his father take Aeron to private places and present him with the family heirlooms. Lincoln hid in the closet as his father took his brother to the wardrobe and gave him their grandfather's wristwatch. He watched from the window as his father stood in the backyard of their home with Aeron and presented a jar of dirt from Earth. Of course, their father gave Aeron the Warden's Seal. For Lincoln, it meant that their father trusted Aeron to preserve the family legacy. It meant they shared a connection that Lincoln could never be part of.

Lincoln took the compass out of the box again and felt the cool metal in his palm. The chain dangled and rattled. He turned it over and discovered it was engraved.

In time, we find our way.

He gazed at the words and then turned the compass back over. The hand spun erratically. This compass was showing no one how to get home.

While in the marketplace, Lincoln wanted to make one more stop. Shane needed new boots. The boy had asked his father for a pair like he wore, the kind made for terrain. Lincoln had argued that Shane had no need for such footwear, and besides, he was growing so quickly it would be money gone to waste as he grew out of them. But he'd promised the boy he would have a pair of boots someday, and now would be a good time to deliver on that promise. His feet were about done growing, and maybe he would get a job soon that would necessitate such footwear. Something outdoors, perhaps working in the peace of the farmlands.

Lincoln chose a pair and inspected them closely. They were made of leather sewn together by hand and laced with thick thread. The insides were lined with a fabric padded with cotton, and the soles had built-in nubs for traction. The craftsmanship was fine, exactly as Lincoln had specified weeks ago when he'd ordered them.

After purchasing the boots, Lincoln arrived at the infirmary and stood at the entrance for a time just gazing at the swinging wooden doors. Colonists were coming and going, but otherwise it was quiet after last night's drama.

Inside, colonists waited in the lobby. A mother with a crying infant sat in the corner. A pale-faced man sat near the receptionist's window, his knees squeezing a trashcan. No one looked at Lincoln as he entered. They all had their own problems.

Lincoln gazed down at the receptionist, but she did not look up.

"I'm here to visit the Bellmans."

"They're not accepting visitors. I'm afraid you'll have to—"

"I'm a friend, and I won't be long."

She looked up at Lincoln, and her eyes sparked with recognition. "Mr. Arokson, I'm sure they appreciate your concern, but the infirmary can provide for their needs."

"I know. But wouldn't *you* want to see friendly faces?"

Casting a doubtful look, the receptionist nevertheless reached across her desk and pressed a button. The door to the back rooms buzzed.

"Thanks."

Lincoln entered the emergency department. It was a long, open room with beds on either side wall. Patients rested at some of them. Curtains were drawn on others. Nurses hustled between stations.

At the far end of the room, he went through another set of swinging doors into the part of the building where the private rooms were. Some nurses shuffled papers and whispered to each other at a desk.

Dr. Osman, one of the infirmary's few trained medical doctors, exited a room in front of Lincoln, his eyes scanning a medical chart. The old man still moved with a quickness that made his white coat flap.

"Dr. Osman," Lincoln said.

The doctor looked up and his furrowed brow relaxed. "Lincoln Arokson." Osman smiled and reached to shake Lincoln's hand. "It's been a long time."

Lincoln accepted the greeting. "It has. How have you been?"

"These last hours have been chaotic, mostly with gossip and curiosity, as I'm sure you're aware. Otherwise, I'm doing quite well. I haven't seen you, so I know you have your health."

Lincoln nodded.

"What brings you here?" Dr. Osman said.

"I came to see the Bellmans."

"Oh, well," Dr. Osman pointed with a long, bony index finger, "they are in the room at the end of the hall."

Sera waited there, back against a wall, gazing at them.

Lincoln moved to walk around him. "Thanks, Doctor."

Dr. Osman touched his shoulder. "Lincoln, we are getting precariously low on our stores of floreyfoil. I wondered if you might be able to assist us with that."

"What about deliveries from Earth?"

"You probably haven't heard. A few months ago, they reduced supplies to the colonies. A measure to lower colonial dependence on the central planets. We aren't due for proper antibiotics until quarter season."

"What about supplies from fabrication?"

"I've taken the matter to your brother, but fabrication tells him they are taxed."

"What's so important that we can't make antibiotics?"

Dr. Osman shrugged. "Aeron wouldn't say."

Lincoln nodded. "I'll see what I can do."

Sera watched Lincoln the whole way down the hall, and even when he was near, she stayed silent.

"Hey, Sera," Lincoln said. "Where's your mom?"

She gazed up to him through her red, puffy eyes. Then the door next to her opened. Elena Bellman looked out warily and ushered Sera into the room. For a moment, Lincoln glimpsed Dani Hines asleep in a bed.

"Elena." Lincoln winced. "This is for you." He handed her the orchid.

She took the flower, admiring the curved shape. "That's kind."

"I just came to ask if there's anything I can do."

"Yes. It should be you out there finding my boy, not that slime Clayton Ford." She gazed at him with hurt eyes. "But I will accept your sympathy."

Lincoln nodded. "They'll find him."

"That's why it should be you. The other men, I could tell they didn't think so. It was in their eyes. They were afraid. Not of going into the wild, but of coming back without James."

"Let me know if you need anything."

"We have your brother for *our* needs. You didn't come to check on us on your own accord, did you? Did Shane ask you to come?"

"No. I guess I wanted to come show his concern in his stead, since he couldn't be here."

"He's a good boy."

"Yes, he is."

"A bit like his father, I think."

"I hope not."

"Our children are everything, aren't they?" Elena said. "They'll be the ones to inherit Lumen. It's such a precious thing, raising children. It's not unlike making a world. Nobody can tell you how to do it. You just have to figure it out. And if they make it, we'll act like it all went according to plan, but really, it's a miracle."

"We'll find James, Elena."

She acted as if she hadn't heard a word Lincoln said and retreated into the room, quietly closing the door behind her.

Six

In the wild, millions of fluttering green hands waved at Sheriff Ballard, and she couldn't imagine what it was like at night. Her whole life, she'd watched every day as dusk yielded to twilight, and just before the first stars emerged, the aurora would materialize like a cloud-cover dome and light the world in a fluorescent haze.

Out here, without the colony's open skies and beyond its walls, not even the aurora would penetrate the dense treetop canopy. Without sight in such an untamed world, Sheriff Ballard couldn't begin to fathom how someone would navigate, let alone find their way home. Seeing it now, she understood that Dani Hines returning to the colony had been a miracle.

"James Bellman!" she yelled.

The people in the search party took turns shouting the boy's name, but every syllable died in the thick foliage.

Alain Ducard led a wing of sentries to one side of Ballard. Kennedy Gray led another wing on the other side. Lyle and Clay stayed close to Ballard as they made their way through the limbs and vines. Lyle's young, cracking calls stood out. Clay hadn't once raised his voice.

Clay stopped and crouched, peering at the ground. He picked a flower from a weed.

"Do you still have it?" the sheriff asked.

Clay ignored her.

"The trail," she said. "Do you still have their trail from last night?"

Clay held the flower up and examined it. "This is battensoft. Processed, it's an anti-inflammatory and pain reliever, especially effective against arthritis. Raw, it just sort of gets you high." He plucked a petal, placed it on his tongue, and chewed.

"That's great, Clay. Don't you think the infirmary could use something like that?"

Grinding the plant between his molars, Clay tilted his head. "Sure, but the infirmary doesn't pay very well."

Ballard sighed. "Do you still have the trail or not?"

"Of course. Can't you see? The boy was hacking limbs left and right. It's like an elephant crashed through here."

"A what?" Lyle said.

"It's an animal."

Lyle's confused expression persisted.

"Nevermind."

They pressed on, their feet kicking up the earthy scent of peat in the deadfall. The search party continued to call for James, but as they rustled through the forest, their voices disappeared in the roar of a nearby river. The tree cover thinned, illuminating this alien world in showers of champagne sunlight. For a moment, Ballard's fear of the unknown dissipated, and she lost her imagination in the wild's beauty. For a moment, she felt privileged to be there.

Clay parted some brush. "Well look at this."

He stepped through and let the opening close behind him. The branches slapped Lyle in the face, and the deputy looked back at Ballard questioningly. The sheriff shrugged and pushed through.

They found a narrow, clear-cut path. The branches of the forest reached up and over, creating an archway, nature reacting to the presence of humans.

The sheriff looked from one end to the other as each of the sentries in the search party emerged from the thick and set foot on the trail, glancing at each other in confusion.

"This what I think it is?" Ballard asked.

"If you think it's a path cut through the forest by people, then yes."

"Wait," Lyle said. "People make paths out here?"

Clay rolled his eyes. "Boy, people *live* out here. They don't tell you that in school because they don't want people thinking they can leave the colony. People have been coming and going for years though. Some families have lived out here for generations."

Lyle's face wrinkled in confusion. "Why would anyone want to leave the colony?"

"Because you put up walls, and not everyone always wants to be on the same side."

"You come out here to be alone?" Lyle asked.

Clay grinned. "I come out here because there's money to be made in things the colony needs."

"That's illegal," Lyle said. "Isn't it, Sheriff?"

Ballard looked away.

Clay laughed. "Kid, people look the other way if you can offer them something of value, especially if you supply them with something they need. Isn't that right, Sheriff?"

Ballard glared at Clay. "That's enough. Which way did they go?"

The man sneered. "Lyle, the wild has its finer points. There's truth out here. Outside the walls, people show you who they really are."

Ballard cursed and lunged at Clay, ready to tear him apart, but Alain Ducard's powerful arms wrapped around her waist.

"Whoa, Sheriff."

She struggled, but Ducard's strength locked her in place.

Clay laughed. "Easy, Reg. Don't take it personal. I'm just having some fun. James strikes me as a kid who blazes his own trails. A bit like myself in that regard." Clay pointed toward one end of the path. "They went this way."

The party fell in line behind Clay. Ballard shrugged Ducard off and cast a hot, angry stare at him. It only lasted a moment before Ballard took a deep breath and nodded her appreciation.

The path curved around a hill, dipped into running streams, and rose onto the backs of craggy boulders. In some areas it grew so thick they had to hack passage. Finally, they came upon the clearing.

Emerging from the forest into unfiltered sunlight, they gazed over the rolling hills of the field where the First Families had touched down. Tall, golden grass swayed in the breeze like the faithful in praise and worship. In the distance, metal glinted in the sunlight. Overgrown and abandoned, the hulking ship that had brought humanity to Lumen stood like a lonely, fallen column, the only remaining structure of a house of gods.

"What is this?" Ballard asked.

"This is where humans first came to Lumen," Clay said. "The earth here was a good landing spot, but it wouldn't provide for agriculture. So we left the ship there and hoofed it until we found fertile land. That's Vale."

No one spoke as the search party gazed upon their history, a story they'd all heard but never seen for themselves.

Ballard pointed. "That's the ship that brought us here?"

"Yes."

"Ever been out there?"

"Yes."

With her stern expression, Ballard pressed Clay for more, but he was unwilling.

"Maybe we should check it out," she said.

"It's secured with a chain link fence. Supposedly, the reactor is still active, so it's unsafe. I wouldn't get too close."

Ballard looked around and waded into the tall grass. "Were they here?"

"Yes, but I think they went back into the forest. I noticed impressions going the other way. They must have come here and then turned around. Probably headed back to the colony."

"Hey, I found something," Lyle called from farther down the tree line. He was holding up an object that glinted in the sunlight. He trotted back to the search party and handed it to Clay.

Clay frowned as he tumbled it in his hands. "The boy's bush knife."

It was broken mid-shaft, but the hilt was intact.

Lyle was wiping his hands on his pants. "What's that black stuff all over it? Mud?"

A viscous goo oozed down the edge of the blade and onto the handle.

Clay's face darkened. "Nothing good."

Seven

A breeze blew over the concrete train platform and chilled Lincoln's bones. He gazed at Arokson Hall bell tower looming over Daenuel Market and the commons. Aeron was no doubt there, dealing with his day-to-day duties. He would be there when Lincoln finished with his own. Confronting him was inevitable. Facing off with Clay was easy, especially with the lowered inhibitions of alcohol. However, coming to terms with family, which piled issues on top of issues for decades and couldn't be simply cast away, was something entirely different. Everything seemed intertwined, and by breaking the seam on one problem, it might all unravel.

Much of the colony had moved on even though James was still lost. Part of Lincoln had hoped the search party would have returned already, having found James not far beyond the perimeter wall. Another part of him knew this wasn't going to end so happily.

How long would Aeron look for the boy? Would he give James as long as he'd given their father? Would a week be long enough to show the public he'd given it all he could?

The train thundered into the station on clacking rails. The gust knocked him from his trance. It squealed to a stop, and he opened a door and stepped aboard.

The outside world blurred as the train picked up speed and cut through the outer residences where the dirt and gravel roads were potted and some of the less-fortunate colonists still resided in the colony's original modular homes. They called this area "the mods."

Centuries ago, when humans landed on Lumen, they had brought residences designed with airlocks and the equipment to sustain habitable environments. After the pillars finished their work on this world, none of that was necessary anymore, but people still needed walls and roofs. They still needed heat and running water. With Lumen's budding new economy, classes were already forming. Building materials like wood, stone, and metal were precious. Under the watchful eyes of the Sentry Service, expeditions had gone just outside the wall and felled trees. Almost the entire northwest quadrant of Vale was a hole in the ground, a quarry that yielded limestone and iron.

With the limitations of colonial life, using these old housing units was practical. However, the people out here weren't happy about missing out on the resources that most of them were pulling from the ground. Though, that was all Aeron's problem.

The train slowed for its first stop in the industrial district where the fabrication plants, material processing facilities, and warehouses created Vale's tools, devices, building materials, medicines, and anything else they needed. The docks were also here, platforms where the colony received shipments of resources via drones from other colonies on Lumen.

With a circumference of almost 49,000 kilometers, the planet was a bit larger than Earth. The colonies were spaced so far apart that nobody in Vale had ever been to any of the other colonies or even seen anyone from another colony. They knew they existed only from stories, radio contact, and the occasional flying robot that landed here.

The train settled into the station. A breeze whipped into the car carrying with it an odor of burning metal from the brakes, and Lincoln was glad when the train accelerated and broke free of the industrial district, leaving the smell behind.

The view opened to the rolling green hills of the farmlands. Cattle, sheep, goats, and pigs grazed in their pens. A broken down barn leaned as if the wind would push it over any day now. Lines of chicken houses stretched into the distance. Beyond, the lake shimmered in the sunlight. In those waters swam hundreds of species of fish the colonists had seeded it with many years ago. It must have been a day for harvest because the boat circled in the water with its great net cast in its wake.

The train passed through fields of corn and wheat, through the snowy-white fields of cotton, and then slowed again to serve the farmlands station. The smell of fertilizers made Lincoln feel like he was in a different world. A small drone about the size of his palm flitted in the air around the doorway, inspected him, and then flew over the train to the fields on the other side, swooping down and buzzing around the apple trees, pollinating the colony-grown plants since there were no bees on Lumen to serve that function.

The train took off again, and the perimeter wall drew nearer. The wall curved, and the trees on the other side loomed taller and greener. Finally, they entered the enclosed channel built for the train to climb the mountain. The view was no longer the green fields of the farmlands but gray stone that towered out of sight.

Lincoln sighed. There were no more stops before they reached the pillar. He shifted in his seat and closed his eyes. In his dreams, his wife's golden hair blazed in brilliant sunlight as they lay together in the fields. She laughed the way that told him she was truly happy. Her delicate hand rested on his chest. He held her close, protecting her from anything in the world that would do her harm. In his dreams, Haley lived. His children had their mother.

But in his dreams, she was always taken, clawing the earth and screaming as something pulled her into the darkness of the wild. He ran after her, but the harder his legs pumped, the faster she was pulled away until she disappeared into the thick, untamed wild.

The train's hissing brakes and flashing lights woke him. They'd arrived at the pillar station.

Lincoln blinked. He'd only slept for minutes, but it felt like hours had passed. It was darker than it had been even in the forest beyond the colony's perimeter. Here, there was no sky or sunlight, only thick cloud cover as if dusk were only minutes away.

He worked his way along the platform and down the stairs. Exiting the station, he rubbed his eyes to dig from his brain the images of Haley being taken from him.

Then there it was, like a great sword striking from the earth, Vale's Pillar of Dawn. The facade of gray metal gleamed even in the cloudy gloom, and at the top, billows of gas escaped into the sky like a volcano threatening eruption.

It still humbled him to see such a majesty that mankind had built. Lincoln had never seen Earth or any other colonies, but if humans had built such a technological wonder hundreds of years ago, a device that was the linchpin in creating new worlds, he wondered every day what else they were capable of. His own kind must have been so advanced that they'd be alien to him.

Every day, he resented them for leaving his people to build this world on their own. But it was their job, and they were doing it.

"Lincoln."

Ellis Freeman had spotted him already, and Lincoln cringed at the sound of his voice.

"Where have you been?"

Ellis hobbled across the yard, leaning on a wooden cane. He winced as a shock of pain erupted from his knee, and almost simultaneously, an electrical arc crackled in the air and curled around the pillar like a snake.

"I'm sorry I'm late," Lincoln said. "I had to make sure my kids got to school, and then I had to run a personal errand."

"A personal errand?"

Lincoln's gaze confirmed Ellis had, in fact, heard him correctly.

"What kind of errand was such an emergency that you couldn't schedule leave ahead of time or at least send word with someone that you would be late?"

"A personal one."

"You better watch it. I can't have guys who think they can come and go as they please on my time."

"So fire me."

"Fire you?"

"That's right."

Ellis' face twisted into a frown, ruffling his cotton beard. "I'm just asking you to help me out, Lincoln. That's all. Be here on time. If you can't be here on time, send word so I can get someone to cover for you."

Ellis grabbed Lincoln's shoulder, and Lincoln's gaze told him to take his hand away immediately.

"This place can't run without us, and you'd do well to remember that. Now let's go. We have a world to make."

Ellis limped toward the pillar, expecting Lincoln to follow, but spotting something valuable, he walked to the perimeter of the compound. At the foot of the wall was a weed anyone else would have passed without a thought.

"What are you doing?" Ellis called.

Lincoln plucked the floreyfoil from the earth and put it into the cargo pocket of his pants. "I know someone who can use this."

Ellis looked confused. "A weed?"

"Yes. A weed."

"Got a bad rap, do they?"

"Something like that."

Ellis shrugged. "If you say so."

"What do you think is in the tea I give you that helps with your knee?"

"That's a pain reliever?"

"No, this is an antibiotic, but the battensoft flower grows from a weed. Speaking of..." Lincoln reached into his pocket, removed a small sack, and flipped it to Ellis.

"That's why I can't fire you," Ellis said.

They laughed and crossed the yard. On the other side, a bridge spanned the electrical chasm, and beyond waited the big, gaping gate of the Pillar of Dawn.

Eight

By the time the lunch bell rang, Shane had nodded off twice. After falling asleep in English class, he had decided it was good his seat in math class was at the back of the room. If he fell asleep, maybe his teacher wouldn't notice. She was an old woman, after all.

With the rapid-fire hammer strike of the iron bell on the concrete wall, Shane's head shot forward, and his jaw snapped shut. He winced at the pain in his neck.

Dazed, he looked around the room, his focus landing on the empty desk to his left, which bore the inscription of the initials S.B. within the head of a sunflower. The thought of Sera brought everything rushing back to him.

His classmates were stuffing pencils and notebooks into their bags. Some of them had already packed in preparation to be released, stealthily working their belongings into their bags so they could be the first out the door. Wooden chair legs scuffed the tile floor. A tide of voices was rising.

The teacher stood at the front of the classroom in front of a blackboard filled with equations written in chalk, under a banner that read, "Mathematics Is The Only Universal Language." She was saying something about the homework that Shane wouldn't know how to do.

Her voice was a drone, and he understood only some of what she was saying. He'd have to ask someone. If Sera were there, he'd have asked her.

Half of the class was already out the door when Shane was coherent enough to stuff his belongings into his backpack. He rose, threw the bag over his shoulder, and fell in line behind some other shuffling stragglers who'd taken their time getting their things together.

He left the classroom and joined the river of students in the hallway, the din of voices buzzing in his head. Lockers slammed, laughter erupted, a girl screamed in playful delight.

A hand slapped his shoulder, and Shane knew it was Gabe before he turned, saw no one there, spun over the other shoulder, and found his cousin grinning.

"Every time," Gabe said. "Every. Time."

Shane sighed. "Hey, Gabe."

"I'd ask what's wrong with you, but everyone already knows. I'm surprised you're even here today."

"Dad made me come."

Gabe grinned again. "Mine too. I bet half the school tried to use last night as a reason to stay home today." He looked closer at Shane's lip. "What'd you do to your face?"

"I don't want to talk about it."

Gabe's brow furrowed. "Okay."

Shane continued silently walking down the hall, head bowed, following the heels of the kids in front of him.

"Hey, you see there's going to be a new expansion for Lore? By quarter year. I hear they're already printing decks at the fabrication plant. The Under King stands no chance against the triple threat."

Gabe had dubbed the trio of himself, Shane, and Sera in the game of Lore as "the triple threat." They mixed the three essential classes of tank, damage dealer, and healer, and together, they had raided every dungeon, cave, citadel, and villainous lair.

"Yeah, I saw."

They kept walking, and Gabe was looking at his cousin with concern.

"I heard the Under King has this mechanic where, if you do too much damage—"

"Gabe." Shane stopped and stared at his cousin. "I'm not in the mood, okay?"

Gabe put his hands up. "Okay, okay. Don't shoot. Sheesh. Just trying to cheer you up, cuz. You sure you don't want to talk?"

"Not really."

They continued into the cafeteria. Shane was silent even as he knocked the mashed potatoes spoon on his tray. They sat on the benches across from Bernie and Mel. Bernie had a smear of cheese on her cheek that she didn't know about. Mel was more concerned with molding her mashed potatoes than eating them.

"It's a mashterpiece!" Bernie declared with her mouth full. "Hi, guys."

Mel nodded a greeting.

"He doesn't want to talk about it," Gabe said.

Shane glared at him.

"Talk about what?" Mel asked, cringing when she looked up from her plate. "What'd you do to your face?"

"That," Gabe said. "He doesn't want to talk about that. Or the other thing."

"I don't blame you," Mel said. "I heard Mrs. Bellman is a wreck. I hope Sera is okay. Did you talk to her?"

Gabe crashed his sister's tray with his own. "He doesn't want to talk, tater-for-brains."

Shane looked up from his lunch. "It's all right. Sera's mom has actually been pretty strong. I'm not sure about Sera, though. It's her I'm worried about."

"I thought you said you didn't want to talk about it," Gabe said.

"I don't. It's just that, if people are going to say stuff, they should at least tell the truth."

Raucous laughter erupted from the table behind them. Shane and Gabe looked over their shoulders and found Adam Hathaway shooting glances their way and giggling.

"Just ignore them," Bernie said.

"Sure, yeah," Gabe said. "There's no way he won't make that the hardest thing ever."

As if on cue, Adam stood and crossed the aisle between the two tables.

"And here it is," Gabe said.

Shane focused on his food even when Adam was close enough to whisper in his ear.

"I heard about your girlfriend's brother," Adam said. "Idiot got himself lost in the wild and couldn't find his way back when even a girl could."

Shane sighed. The fork scraping his teeth sounded like unsheathing a sword.

"People are saying he tried to screw her and she wouldn't have it. So she ran away, and now he's too ashamed to come back."

"Who's saying that?" Bernie said.

"Nobody's saying that," Gabe said.

Adam fixed his gaze on Gabe. "Everyone's saying that. You don't know. You're not right enough to know." Adam turned his attention back to Shane. "You know what that means? It means he's chicken. People everywhere are saying it runs in families. After what happened to Mr. Bellman, we're better off cutting that bloodline. Of course, there's still Sera, but no one will love her now, not with her baggage. But, you know, I was curious to hear what you think, Shane. That's why I came over here. See, being who you are, I figured you'd have an interesting take on it."

Shane rolled his eyes. "Look, just because me and Sera are close doesn't mean you're going to get me all riled up."

"Oh, I'm not talking about you and her. I'm talking about your pa. From what I hear, your dad got taught a lesson last night. Sheriff Ballard put him in lockup for his own protection because, if he hadn't—"

With incredible speed, Shane launched and tackled Adam to the floor.

"Whoa!" Gabe cried.

The entire cafeteria population collectively gasped, shrieked, laughed, and yelled.

Adam had thirty pounds on Shane, but mounted on top of the bully, Shane pounded Adam until blood flowed from his nose and his lips.

Shane stood, stone-faced, looking down on Adam, who was moaning and clutching his face.

The cafeteria lapsed into silence. Adam's sobs echoed in the rafters. Shane crouched and bent close enough to Adam to whisper in his ear.

"Here's how this is going to work," Shane said coolly. "You don't talk about my family. Ever. Got it?"

Shouting voices drew near, and then arms wrapped around Shane's body and tore him away.

On some level, he expected the students in the cafeteria to cheer, but none did. They just gaped in silence as strong, adult hands pulled him into the cold, silent hallway, which echoed with his struggles for freedom.

Nine

Aeron slouched in his chair behind his desk. After hours of meetings with colonists, he couldn't resist the exhaustion anymore. His body was rebelling. His arms and legs felt like ropes attached to anchors. His eyelids felt as if tiny beings hung from them with increasing numbers, calling

their friends to join in the fun of making his attempt to stay awake harder. He wiped his face as if to brush them away, but they weren't going anywhere.

Benjamin Harrison, an old farmer from the far side of the colony who raised livestock and had come to the warden for help, droned on as if he couldn't tell whether Aeron was listening to him but didn't care all the same. The wrinkled, excess skin under his chin trembled as he spoke. His cloudy eyes indicated cataracts, but Mr. Harrison could see just fine. He had a way of looking directly at whomever he was speaking to as if to challenge that person to look away. Today, Aeron just couldn't hold that gaze.

When the old farmer stopped talking, silence filled the warden's office while Mr. Harrison waited for a response.

Aeron sat up and leaned across the desktop. "I believe you when you say some of your cattle have gone missing, Mr. Harrison. I really do. But I have to ask the obvious. Why would anyone take a cow from you when they can get the end product at the marketplace? And if they had some kind of interest in stealing from you, where would they put it? Chickens would be one thing, but a cow?"

Mr. Harrison pounded his cane on the floor. "The why of it don't concern me. All that matters is I got less head than I did yesterday."

Aeron rubbed his chin, thinking. "Maybe one of your employees processed some of the livestock by mistake?"

"I checked. Nothin' on the logs. 'sides, they know better."

"Maybe they forgot to log it."

"All the animals are tagged, so we can track them remotely."

"Can you find their location that way?"

Mr. Harrison cocked his head. "Might could, I s'pose. If you had the right equipment."

"All right, I'll tell you what. Get the tag information from the livestock that are missing, and give it to my assistant, Alice. I'll see what I can do about tracking them down."

Mr. Harrison stared at the warden, his thin lips set taut in his aged face. "I ain't leavin' 'til you give me your word that you take me seriously. It ain't easy to get all the way into the commons at my age, especially when my wife thinks I'm just a crazy old man too."

"Mr. Harrison, there's nothing I take more seriously. Our people have to eat, and they can't eat if our livestock go missing. I assure you we will investigate this as a priority."

The farmer nodded and took his time standing on his uncertain legs. Out of respect, Aeron walked him to the door and opened it. They left

Aeron's office together and stopped at Alice's desk. She peered at them through her glasses.

"Alice, I'd like you to get some information from Mr. Harrison here regarding some of his livestock," Aeron said. "Please notify fabrications that I'll be coming by first thing in the morning." Aeron shook the farmer's hand. "Thank you for coming in, Mr. Harrison. We'll be in touch soon."

The old man cleared his throat to speak with Alice. Aeron turned to find his lobby still full with colonists pining for a meeting with him.

He sighed. "Next on the list is Mary Barnes. Mary?"

A young woman who was twisting her dark, curly hair between pinched fingers looked up. "Yes?"

"Come on in."

She stood and walked warily to Aeron, who reached out for a handshake. Unsure, Mary gazed at his hand for a moment and accepted it.

He gave her a big, toothy grin. "How are you today?"

"Just fine, Warden. Thank you for taking the time to meet with me."

"Of course." Aeron ushered the young woman into his office and closed the door. He motioned to the chair in front of his desk. "Please have a seat. What can I do for you?"

"It's a sensitive matter, sir." She spoke in a small voice as she sat down. "I almost didn't come, but I knew I'd have to before long."

Aeron pulled his chair in behind his desk. "Please, go on. Whatever you say here is in strict confidence."

"I know. It's just that...it's just that I'm afraid what you're going to say."

This young woman didn't seem like a troublemaker to Aeron, but she clearly was in some kind of a bind. It was in her downcast eyes, as if she were turning herself in for something.

"Tell me what it is, and I will do what I can to help," he said.

"It's just that...well, I'm pregnant, sir."

Aeron smiled, relieved. "Mary, this is wonderful news. Sure, parenthood can be scary, but it's the best thing in the world. I have two myself, and there's nothing I'd rather—"

"Warden, you don't understand." Her voice was quivering now. "I already have two children, a boy and a girl."

The air fled Aeron's lungs and he grimaced. "Oh, I see."

"I know a third is against the law, but I was hoping there might be a way we could make an exception."

"Mary, you know that law serves a purpose. We have to control our population." Aeron took a deep breath and exhaled. "Didn't you get the preventative surgery after your second born?"

Mary winced. "I was going to, but I guess I just kept putting it off."

"I'm sorry, Mary, but the law is the law. I don't know if—"

"Please, Warden Arokson. Please. My husband and I, we believe in sin. We believe that, if we abort this child, we will pay with our souls."

Aeron leaned back in his chair and pursed his lips. He gazed at this young woman, and she held her breath, waiting for his judgment. He thought about his father and the wardens before him. How many times did they have to make this call? He knew he was lucky because it wasn't so long ago that they were sending women to be irreversibly sterilized and abortions were a risky procedure for the mother. Now, Dr. Osman described it as routine.

"It's not just a concern with the precedent it would set," Aeron said. "You have to understand that, if we let you keep your third child, the other parents who weren't so fortunate won't only resent me. They will resent you, your husband, your whole family. Your children will be the objects of their resentment, especially this new child."

Mary's eyes filled with tears, and she gasped. "We would rather face that than the judgment of God. I beg you, Warden. Please."

Aeron looked away, considering the woman's passion. He hated this part of the job. He liked helping people, but he hated being the arbiter of conflict because, no matter what he did, someone ended up getting hurt.

"Does your husband know?" he asked.

She shook her head.

"All right, here's what we're going to do. I'm going to bring Dr. Osman in on this. He won't like it, but he'll do it. In a few weeks, my office will announce your pregnancy, and we will tell the people your first preventative surgery failed. It's plausible. Theoretically, they're only ninety-eight percent effective. Then, when you have the child, Dr. Osman will do the surgery."

Mary's face brightened. Her tears stopped flowing, and she looked up from her lap, filling with a swell of air as she took her first breath in what seemed like minutes. "You mean we get to keep our child?"

Aeron smiled. "Yes."

Mary burst from the chair and ran around Aeron's desk, throwing herself onto him in embrace. "Thank you, thank you, thank you!"

He fought her off and set her at arm's length. "Really, it's no problem. Soon, people are going to start leaving the colony for the wild.

When that happens, the law will be unnecessary. It seems a shame to lose someone now."

Mary was sobbing with joy.

"It all depends on you, though," he said. "You can't tell anyone about this. Even your husband has to believe the failed surgery is to blame. Do you understand?"

She wiped her eyes and retreated into her thoughts. "I have to lie to him."

"Yes. Can you do that?"

Mary blinked and nodded. "But what will we say about the surgery? He knows I never got it."

"Act as if he remembers wrong. Tell him you got the surgery right after your second-born while you were still in the infirmary. He will probably be so overjoyed at being able to have a third child that he won't think on it much."

Mary laughed uneasily and shook her head. "I'm not so sure he will be overjoyed. We just get by as it is without another mouth to feed."

Aeron turned her chin so she faced him and handed her a cloth to wipe her tears. "Everything will be okay," he said. "You will get through. Let me know how I can help."

She laughed in earnest this time. "You're doing enough, Warden. I'm grateful for that."

When she was calm, Aeron walked her to the door and saw her off. Mr. Harrison was gone, but his lobby was still full of colonists, and they stared as he sent a young woman in tears away. Their expressions scrutinized him with varying degrees of curiosity and judgment.

"Alice," he said, "schedule a meeting with Dr. Osman tomorrow. Any time will do."

"Yes, Warden."

"Who's next?"

"Warden Donnelly just raised us on the radio." Alice looked over the waiting room full of colonists. "Do you want me to tell him you'll call him back?"

"No, I better see what he needs." Aeron turned his attention to the colonists. "Just a minute."

One of the men crossed his arms. An elderly woman huffed and narrowed her shrewd look.

Aeron returned to his desk, slid open a cabinet, and flipped the switch on his ancient radio.

Jack Donnelly was the warden of Horizon, a colony on the same continent as Lumen, but it might as well been on another world. For starters, by Jack's description, the land was flat in all directions, which was how the colony had gotten its name. Jack had sounded fascinated the first time Aeron had described their mountains and the valley. Horizon also was far enough away that the only way they could speak was by using the radio, which bounced signals off of a satellite they'd had in Lumen's orbit since the First Families arrived. Aeron had to take Jack's call now because, with only one satellite, the colonies only had a window of minutes before they would have to wait almost two hours for the satellite to complete an orbit so they could speak again.

Aeron checked the radio's interface. The digital readout that told him the satellite was in range, and he was still connected. He raised the microphone and spoke into it. "Warden Donnelly, this is Aeron Arokson of Vale. What can I do for you?"

The radio popped and sizzled.

"Aeron, good to hear your voice." The man's accent was foreign to Aeron, and it jarred him every time he heard it. From what Jack had told Aeron, life at Horizon was a bit simpler in some ways. They were fortunate to have extremely fertile soil for agriculture. The earth was also less rocky, which meant it was easier to work, but they lacked the building materials Vale had. Horizon also lacked trees, though it had an abundance of water from a nearby freshwater lake. All of this was reflected in their speech patterns and accents, which was much softer and lazier with the pronunciation compared to Vale's people, who tended to speak sharply and definitively.

"I know you're busy, so I'll get right to it," Warden Donnelly said. "We got a food shortage over here, and I'm hoping you can spare some while we fix up our supplies."

Aeron's brow wrinkled. He couldn't remember when Horizon ever experienced a food shortage. Food and water were two things they'd always had plentiful supplies of. In fact, Horizon often supplied the other colonies with their excess stores even when the other colonies didn't ask. Rations from Horizon would arrive unannounced at the docks with a note simply stating: *With my compliments. —J.D.*

"What happened?" Aeron asked.

"We lost a substantial number of our livestock."

"Lost? As in went missing?"

"Some of them, yes. Something spooked them and they ran off. Some of them died in the fight to get free of their pens, and we didn't get to them until it was too late to salvage. Others were hurt and had to be put down, which should do for a time. Still others broke free, and we're still trying to track them down. But we haven't been able to find them."

"I see. Well, we have a shortage of our own over here."

The channel crackled with static in the empty space, and an old man with a high forehead and wrinkles like he'd baked in the sun for years opened the warden's door. Alice followed him with a raised finger of protest. Aeron held up his hand and then motioned for her to close the door. The man sat in the chair before Aeron, crossed his leg, and leered.

"That's a shame," Warden Donnelly said.

"I'll see what we can spare and send some provisions your way, but I'm going to be honest, Jack. You might want to check with some of the others."

"I wouldn't want to take from your people if there's a shortage, Aeron. I can contact another colony."

"It's no problem. I'm happy to do what I can, but you should reach out to the others anyway."

"Thanks, Aeron. You're a good man."

Aeron forced a laugh into the microphone. "I don't know about that, Jack. It's for selfish reasons. We're in this together, right? You guys go, and we're not far behind you."

"No room for selfishness when you can't live without each other."

"No, there isn't. I'll send the shipment your way as soon as I can."

"Thanks."

"Not a problem. Take care of your people."

"You do the same."

"Vale out." Aeron flipped off the radio, set the microphone in the cabinet, and glared at the old man in front of him. Gideon Ford was a self-appointed representative of the people. The way he'd risen to power disturbed Aeron. Gideon was so politically inclined that he had fooled the people into believing they had thrust him onto their shoulders because they wanted him there, not the other way around. Gideon had masked ambition as duty, service, and sacrifice, but the man didn't know the meaning of those words.

"What the hell do you think you're doing barging in here, Gideon?"

Gideon's leer persisted. "Pleasure to see you too, Aeron, but did I hear you correctly? You're just going to give away our food?"

"Some of it. Yes."

"Unless I'm mistaken, I heard you say we have a shortage of our own to deal with, so we need that food."

"We'll spare what we can because it does us no good for the people of other colonies to starve."

"I wonder how the people of *our* colony would feel if they knew the prices at the market are going to go up because there's a shortage in supplies."

Aeron waved a dismissive hand. "What do you want, Gideon? I don't have time for this. If you hadn't noticed, I have a waiting room full of colonists, and they were here before you."

"I noticed." Gideon held his arms out in an exaggerated shrug. "I just don't particularly care."

Aeron grunted. "A real man of the people."

"Some of them."

"So what is it?"

"I'm concerned about the resources the colony is spending to look for this Bellman boy. People leave the colony all the time, you and I both know that. So what if this boy doesn't even want to be found?"

"Mr. Ford, I appreciate your attempt at insight, but James isn't the type to do something like that."

"Everyone likes drama."

"No, lots of people like peace and quiet."

"Well, anyway, if he wants to be found, he'll turn up on his own. I'm just here to inform you that some of the colonists think we ought to call off the search and put our sentries back to work here on the task of keeping us safe."

"They think that?"

Gideon cocked his head and shrugged. "I do too."

"Thanks, Mr. Ford. I'll take it under advisement. Now if you'll excuse me, those people you speak for are waiting to see me."

Aeron stood to walk Gideon out, but the old man remained in the chair. Aeron stopped when he realized Gideon wasn't getting up.

"There's one more thing," Gideon said.

Aeron sighed through his nose, stuffing down frustration. "What is it?"

"Have you given any thought to my proposition?"

"A free election?"

Gideon nodded.

"No," Aeron said. "And I don't intend to, Mr. Ford. The constitution is clear. The Warden's Seal may be passed down from a parent to a child if that child is of age and if people have a chance to protest at a public hearing. There was no protest. I was confirmed. You and I are both stuck with me, and there's no way to change that unless I break a law for which the penalty is impeachment or there's a vote of no confidence at the end of this term."

Gideon got out of the chair and stepped so close to Aeron that he smelled the old man's sour breath.

"So I guess you have work to do," Aeron said.

"I suppose we both do." Gideon forced a pleasant smile and saw himself out of Aeron's office, waving at the colonists in the waiting area as he went.

Aeron followed him out to Alice's desk and stood until Gideon reached the swinging door at the end of the hall.

"Any luck finding Lucy?"

Alice blinked from a trance and nodded. "She was tied up at the school. Something about your nephew."

The warden's eyebrows narrowed. "What about Shane?"

"He's gotten into some trouble."

Aeron flushed with frustration.

"Everything is all right," Alice said. "He just got into a fight with another boy is all." She forced an uneasy laugh. "Boys will be boys, right?"

Aeron grunted. "Like father, like son." He sighed and looked to his colonists who were waiting on him. "All right. I suppose Lucy can wait," and then under his breath, "assuming I'm able to go home sometime today."

Ten

Lucy couldn't help but stare at the deep wrinkle dug across Principal Feron's forehead every time his eyebrows jumped. Be it a habit or a nervous tick, Feron's brow creased as a kind of accent to his speech, and his long, pointy nose bobbed as if he were a squawking bird. It mesmerized Lucy, but she needed to concentrate. Her nephew needed her.

"Mrs. Arokson, you understand that Shane's actions can't go unpunished." The man spoke with a maddeningly respectful and professional tone. "I understand your point that he's under stress right now, but if we make an exception for him, other parents will find out, and then they will ask for the same exception for their children. It's a sensitive balance that could lead to the breakdown of the entire system. Consistency in discipline is key. It almost happened when your husband pardoned his brother for—"

"Lincoln did nothing wrong."

Principal Feron sighed. "Discipline must be regimented. And this isn't even considering the fallout I will have to deal with when Adam's parents get here."

"If they're your concern, leave them to me."

Principal Feron smoothed the sleeves of his suit coat. "Mrs. Arokson, I'm familiar with the way your family handles conflicts. Unfortunately, it's not the message we like to send to our children."

"The men in my family are prideful. But they're also honorable. All I'm asking is for a chance for us to show that. If you suspend Shane, you remove the power from him to address it and put the matter to rest. How are these boys supposed to learn to resolve their own conflicts if you do it for them every time?"

Feron took a deep breath. "Mrs. Arokson, we're not here to teach them how to resolve conflicts. We're here to teach them math, science, and how to read and write."

"Principal Feron, do you think we should only influence them so little?"

Lucy caught a twitch at the corner of his mouth, a slight nod.

"It isn't my job to make such a decision," Feron said.

The responsibility hand-off. It made administrating anything easier. You didn't have to defend the rules if you didn't make them. You just had to abide by them, and so did everyone else.

She smiled politely. Backed into a corner, it was time for a desperate maneuver. "Shane is a good boy. I know you know that. He's just a little like his father in that he can sometimes lose his temper. There has to be an alternative to suspension. What if he met with a counselor, and what if that counselor could assure you it wouldn't happen again?"

Feron raised an eyebrow. "And I suppose that would be you?"

"It *is* my job. I can assure you there would be no conflicts. We can even work him into the mentorship program, teach him applicable skills for a future trade, give him a place to channel his feelings. Shane likes to build things. Maybe he is a candidate for the construction focus. I'm sure—"

Feron raised a hand to cut her off. "I'm sorry, Mrs. Arokson. There's no alternative in this case. Shane has to leave school for five days. Look at it this way. It gives the kids a chance to settle down and let the whole thing blow over."

Lucy smiled. To win wars, she knew some battles had to be conceded. "Thank you for your time, Principal Feron."

"Of course, Mrs. Arokson. I'm sorry I can't help Shane more. Rules are rules. We have to be consistent in enforcing them. You understand."

"I do."

Lucy shook Principal Feron's hand and left his office. Just outside, Shane was sitting on a wooden bench. He looked at her expectantly, and she shook her head. They walked out of the school together and headed for the commons and beyond.

"I could hear some of what you said in there," Shane said after a while. "I'm not the one who needs counseling. No matter what, when I get back there, Adam won't stop."

They passed Daenuel Market and the landscape opened onto the commons. Lucy eyed the setting sunlight as it cut Arokson Hall's bell tower in half.

"I knew the school wouldn't do anything about that. We had to be realistic in our expectations. What I said to Principal Feron was just to get you off the hook."

Shane made eye contact with her for the first time since she'd come to get him. "Thanks, Aunt Lucy. Dad would have asked Feron to give me worse than five days' suspension. He would have added after-school detention, piled on community service or something."

Lucy stopped him in the gravel road. She brushed his hair aside and gazed into his eyes. "Shane, I want you to remember something. Adults don't often stop to think that punishment is pointless if you learn nothing from it. They think of it as a principle, not a learning opportunity. If you kids don't learn why you're being punished, you're only learning to resent us. So don't hold it against them, and never forget to learn from your mistakes."

She poked his nose and smiled, and they continued on.

"What do I learn from this?" he asked. "That the school is stupid and only wants to sweep their problems aside?"

Lucy snickered. "There's that. But you also learned that maybe you shouldn't try to solve your problems with a fist in the lunch room with the whole school watching."

"So what should I do?"

"Be indirect. Play with your enemies' expectations. Make him think you're going to lie down and take it, and then, when he doesn't expect it and no one's watching, not even him, you hit him sideways."

Lucy walked Shane the rest of the way home. He stomped up the stairs and crashed onto his bed. Lucy made him a cup of tea and took it to him. When he wouldn't turn over to receive it, she set it on his bedside table, sat on the edge of his bed, and brushed his silky black hair with her fingertips while Shane lay with his face mashed into his pillow.

"What else is bothering you?" she asked.

"Dad's going to kill me." His eyes became glassy. "I'm going to be stuck here in this house until they find James or longer. He's such an asshole."

She shushed him and continued to brush his hair back, mothering him the way she always had since his mother died.

"No, Shane. Your father is a good man. He may have a temper, and he may be a little bitter, but when it comes down to it, when it really matters, he will do right by you and Bernie."

"What do you know?"

"Enough." She stood and walked to his bedroom doorway. "I'll talk to him, make sure he understands."

"If he were as good as you say, he wouldn't need talking to."

"Shane, even good men need talking to from time to time. How do you think they become good men?"

She peered at him with those blue eyes that could cut right through anyone. "Remember what I said."

Lucy left Shane alone in his bedroom's slanting light.

Eleven

When the sun was once again low on the horizon and all the world was coming to a close, when the lights in Daenuel Market darkened and Arokson Hall's bell sang for the close of another day, the search party re-entered the main gate, blackened faces smeared with dirt and mud, scratches across their skin from the thick brush, weary eyes and weakened hearts from finding nothing of James Bellman that boded well.

Elena Bellman was waiting for them.

She counted each person who walked through the gate. Even as she knew from their averted and ashamed gazes that her boy was not with them, her hope persisted. She hung onto every person's image, praying one of them would be her beloved son. Even as Sheriff Ballard approached her with a stone expression, she believed James was still alive. Though, it broke her heart to know that they didn't believe it. She could see it on their faces and in the way they wouldn't look at her.

"What did you find?" she asked Ballard.

The sheriff hesitated. "Nothing. We pushed hard all day, but we only covered a small portion of the grid. We'll pick it up again in the morning." She touched Elena's shoulder. "There's no reason to lose hope."

"No," Elena said. "There isn't." She walked away, leaving the sheriff reflecting on her own failing confidence.

"Poor woman," Clay said indifferently. "I can almost hear her heart breaking apart piece by piece."

"No parent should have to go through what she's going through."

Clay shrugged. "She's doing it to herself. She's holding out hope when there isn't any."

"What if it were your child?"

Clay scoffed. "I was never stupid enough to have kids. Anyway, if I had one, my boy'd never get lost out there. I'd teach him better. He'd know his way. He'd be no fool."

Ballard squinted. "Neither is James."

"What's that?"

"James knows the wild too. Been going out there for some time."

Clay shrugged again. "It's been nice talking to you, boss, but I'm looking to get on with my night. Have you got my money?"

Ballard glared at her guide, a warning that she was thinking about drawing her revolver. Instead, she dug into her pocket and gave Clay a wad of colony notes.

Clay counted his money and sighed. "I got that other thing for you, but it's a little extra."

Ballard watched the last of the sentries leave the main gate. They didn't look at her and Clay twice, but the sheriff couldn't be sure. The quiet and stillness grew. Ballard dug into a shirt pocket, removed another wad of notes, and handed it to Clay.

Clay tossed a paper pouch at Ballard's chest, and she caught it in her fist.

"Pleasure," he said. "See you bright and early tomorrow."

After Clay left, Ballard shook the paper packet and listened to the herbs rattle inside. She placed it in her shirt pocket to be sure she wouldn't lose its precious contents.

The last of the search party vacated the main gate and returned to their lives as if nothing were wrong. Nightfall gave them the excuse to rest, enjoy their lives, and embrace their own loved ones. As always, tragedy provided the shock that made them thankful for what they had. Yet Ballard knew the day of her loss was coming soon. In a way, she envied Elena Bellman for her ability to persevere in the face of doubt. Reggie felt the paper packet through her shirt. For her, there was no hope, only inevitability.

Her home was dark and quiet. Turning on lights, she found an empty bowl with soup remnants on the kitchen counter, a pot resting in the sink. Her father had eaten. That was good.

She tried to be quiet in the hallway, but the wooden floors betrayed her with their groaning. She shirked off her clothes and showered, washing the day's grime from her body. It was only after she brightened at the smell of the lavender soap that she realized how much she must have stunk, and she was glad she chose to wash up.

After drying herself and dressing in a t-shirt and cotton pants, she entered the bedroom. The breathing machine hummed in the corner, and the sour odor of sweat hung in the air.

Her father lay in the darkness. He was still and quiet, not coughing or wheezing. Reggie eased to his side and gently placed her hand on his chest. It rose and fell.

She sighed in relief. They both knew the disease was going to kill him, but they wanted every last moment. Considering her father's suffering, Reggie might have been selfish to want to hold on, but they had agreed.

Frank Ballard's chest hitched, and then it stuttered. She grasped his shoulder as he erupted into a coughing fit. This had gone on long enough that Reggie no longer wondered if this was it, the end. It no longer frightened her. It was just another fit. Routine. And some part of her was glad he was awake.

Reggie picked up the inhaler from the bedside table. She flipped its lid and unwrapped the paper packet Clay had given to her. The minty, citrusy smell broke through the stale sweat odor like sunbeams through clouds, and she tapped a pinch into the chamber. Her father took it greedily and sucked. His coughing settled immediately, and he lay back.

"Hey, darlin'."

"Hey, Dad." She rubbed his arm with her thumb. "How are you feeling?"

He blinked lazily and shook his head. "Did you find the boy?" He wheezed deep in his chest and took another pull from the inhaler.

"No."

"You will," he said.

Sitting on the side of his bed, feeling the unsteady rise and fall of his chest and his weak grip of her hand, for some reason she couldn't explain, she believed him.

Reggie leaned over, careful not to disturb the plane of the bed, and kissed him on the cheek. "Good night, Dad."

"Night, darlin'. Sleep good."

"You too."

She left, satisfied that, even if she couldn't find James Bellman today, she could provide comfort for her father to rest in peace.

Twelve

The meatloaf was dry. Lucy had overcooked it. She pushed her dinner away, leaned back, crossed her legs, and swirled her wine beneath her nose.

With the cold outside, she loved the sweet aroma. It made her feel like she was drinking the sunshine of spring. Most people in Vale didn't know the colony's barman, Gill, could make such good stuff.

Some years ago, he had unveiled it as a secret project he'd been working on. He told people about this exotic elixir that people drank on far-off worlds, planets with culture and high societies, but the colonists went on ordering shine. Disheartened, Gill was going to pour it all out, but Lucy encouraged him to keep going with it. She told him she would buy a few bottles a month. She didn't like it initially, but over time, she acquired a taste for it.

Although it hadn't taken off yet, she got cheap wine, and she could feel good about supporting the development of her people's culture.

Her daughter screeched her cutlery against her ceramic plate, and Lucy stirred from her stupor.

The kids didn't seem to notice or care that the meatloaf had the consistency of crumbly, dry bread. Gabe chased a fleeing pea with the tines of his fork, stabbing at it and missing, stabbing at it and missing.

TINK

TINK

TINK

"That's enough," Aeron said.

The boy scooped the pea up and popped it into his mouth with a smirk.

Lucy gazed at her husband across the dinner table. He stared back at her with a stony expression she couldn't read. When she curled the corner of her mouth, he looked down to his food, which he wasn't eating so much as dissecting.

"So Feron suspended Shane?" Gabe said. "How long did birdman give him?"

Lucy showed her son that stern gaze all mothers have.

"You said you would tell me after I cleared my plate," he pleaded.

She glanced at the food in front of him. To his credit, Gabe had chased down all of his peas.

"Five days," she said.

Gabe dropped his fork onto the ceramic plate with a clang. "That's so unfair!"

"Adam was bullying him," Mel said.

Lucy held up her hands. "Children, that's enough."

Gabe and Mel scowled.

"It doesn't matter what Adam said or did to your cousin. The way he responded was unacceptable." Lucy looked to Aeron for approval, but he was more interested in mixing his peas and mashed potatoes. "You don't settle your problems with violence."

Gabe rolled his eyes and kicked the leg of his chair. "But it's *unfair*. Shane doesn't deserve to be punished. Adam should be punished. *You* should have told Feron that."

Aeron slammed the table, rattling the dishes. "Gabriel, that is enough. It isn't up to you to say who should be punished, and it certainly isn't your place to judge others for what is Shane's mistake. Now go to your room."

Mel made a sucking sound with her teeth. "Aw, Dad, he didn't mean—"

"Both of you. Right now."

The children looked to their mother in appeal, and she just kept swirling her wine. When she didn't respond, their chair legs scuffed the wood floor as they pushed away from the table and stomped upstairs.

Lucy stood to clear their dinner dishes. "That was a little quick. Where did that come from?"

Aeron wiped his mouth with his napkin and tossed it onto the table. He sat back in his chair and gazed at her. "Where were you today?"

Lucy continued to pile dishes on her forearm. "Hmm?"

"I said where were you today? I sent for you."

"I had students, Aeron. I wasn't told it was urgent. Did you need something?"

"Yes. I needed you to explain why you took Lincoln out of his holding cell before morning."

She continued her work. "He didn't deserve to be there."

"Lucy, that isn't for you to decide. That isn't your place. Every time you go against one of my decisions, you undermine me. Even worse, you make it look like we have special privileges. It hurts my ability to appear objective and unbiased."

"Oh, screw politics. He's family."

"I didn't ask for this," Aeron said. "Times have changed. Being warden used to be just a job. As long as you took care of things, people kept on working. Now it's all muddy and complicated. There are all these agendas. Everybody's got an opinion."

"Maybe you're making it difficult. Lincoln is family. If you're not going to fight for them, or if you can't, someone has to. But you don't have to hide behind the rulebook and say you're just doing your job."

"Is that what you really think of me? You have no idea what I deal with every day, what I go through."

She finally met his gaze. Her surprised eyes betrayed her. This wasn't Aeron. He didn't do things like this. She prided herself on her ability to recognize people for who they were and predict their actions. Right now, her husband was unpredictable.

"I spared a child today," he said.

Lucy froze. She winced at the dishes' growing weight and then moved for the kitchen. Aeron followed.

"I didn't have to. I should have told this young mother that she was going to have to kill her third child. But seeing how hopeful she was and knowing things are changing, waking up to the world we live in with James Bellman missing and nobody really giving a damn but me, I couldn't let it happen. Tomorrow isn't guaranteed, Luce. We forget we live on a fragile world. We forget how unstable it is. We forget anything could be out there beyond those walls."

Lucy set the dishes on the stone countertop. "What do you mean?"

He took a deep breath and blew it out, and then he threw a dismissive hand up. "Just forget it." He stepped toward the door.

"Wait," Lucy said. "If you made an exception for this girl, then you understand—"

"Lincoln wasn't there just because the law said he should be there. He was there because he screwed up and needed to know that. He needs to learn from his mistakes."

"Did he understand that? Do you know what Clay said to him? Did you even ask what set your brother off?"

"He was drunk."

Lucy sneered, a hard look that appeared out of place on her soft face. "Yes, he was, but give him some credit. You said it yourself. I don't have any idea what you deal with every day. You're right. But you're not the only one with unique experiences."

Aeron shook his head and faced her. "So what did Clay say?"

"You should hear it from Lincoln. Seems like you two need to start talking to each other anyway."

Aeron was still for a moment. Lucy began washing the dishes but watched him out of the corner of her eye.

Aeron walked to the front door.

"Where are you going?" she asked over the hissing faucet.

"You're right," Aeron said. "I should hear it from him."

The closing front door sounded so maddeningly calm and impartial that Lucy dropped the dishes into the sink and watched the water pour over the broken pieces.

Thirteen

At Gill's Still, the patrons were as raucous as ever, relieving themselves after another day of hard work. When the sun was up, Daenuel Market bustled with colonists conducting business, turning the cog in the machine that provided the people of Vale with goods and supplies. At night, those places emptied and the storefronts that had been quiet, like Gill's, illuminated with nightlife.

Vale had a budding economy. An identifiable culture was gaining a foothold. And despite best efforts at maintaining equality, classes were emerging. However, one aspect of colonial life had been constant since the First Families landed all those generations ago. When the aurora came out, people needed to let go.

At a corner booth, Alain Ducard slammed down an empty shine glass next to three others. He wiped his chin and growled away the burning in his throat.

Across from him, Kennedy Gray tapped his half-full shine glass and gazed at his fellow sentry with narrowed eyes. "What's with you tonight?"

Ducard stared at his empty glasses and lined them up. "Not enough." He raised a hand at a waitress who was meandering through the crowd, and she nodded.

Making a gun with his forefinger and thumb, Ducard shot each glass, saying, "pow," each time, and knocking each glass over with his other hand.

"It's going to be a real early morning for you," Gray said. "We got another long day ahead of us tomorrow."

"You're just jealous of my aim." Ducard set the glasses upright and lined them up again. "I'm not hurrying in the morning. They'll wait for us."

"Sure," Gray said. "But maybe this Bellman kid is waiting for us somewhere too."

"Maybe he is, maybe he ain't." Ducard pointed at the glasses. "Your turn."

Gray squinted at the sergeant. "You don't think he's alive."

"Do you?"

The waitress arrived with another glass of shine, and she had their dinners. A burger and fried potatoes for Ducard, a grilled chicken salad for Gray.

The waitress picked up Ducard's empty glasses. "Can I get you boys anything else?"

The big sentry looked at her with a displeased expression.

"Is something wrong?" she asked.

"Don't mind him," Gray said. "We're good."

She smiled and waded back into the din of Gill's. Ducard pressed his burger to his face and chewed. For a moment, Gray stared pensively into his greens before he began stabbing with his fork.

"No," he said. "I don't think he's alive."

Ducard finished chewing and gulped. "Then what are we doing out there?"

"Following orders."

Ducard laughed.

Gray chewed on a bundle of roughage. "Seriously, what's going on with you?"

"Nothing. Forget it."

"Fine," Gray said. "We're looking for a missing boy because the colony needs us to look for a missing boy."

"Our job is to secure the wall."

"No, our job is to secure the colony. For that, the people need to feel safe. So we go look for one of them because they need to know we'll do that."

Ducard watched the people in Gill's. A drunk man and woman neared fornication in another booth. Men crowded around a table of hostile gambling, which had already started an argument that sent one man to the street penniless. At the bar, a dozen colonists surrounded Gideon Ford as he twisted their minds with volatile political speech. They stomped the floor, clanged glasses, and raised their voices in assent.

"Seems they feel safe enough," Ducard said.

Gideon commanded their silence with outstretched arms. "I met with our warden today. I could tell he was keeping a secret. So I pulled it out of him. He told me he was going to send some of our food to another colony, and he told me we're already facing a shortage here."

The people sounded off their anger.

"We know what that's going to do to us here, right? It's going to raise prices at the market. Feeding your families is going to be more difficult because of the mistakes of another colony."

The people around Gideon roared.

"I say we show him where his loyalties should lie. I say we demand he keep our food here for our people and let the people of other colonies solve their own problems. Vale can't support the whole world. We have enough problems as it is here with those of you living on the outskirts in those ancient modular homes and his corrupt, crooked administration, which shows bias and preferential treatment. Vale first!"

"Maybe they don't." Gray stood and snaked through the crowd toward the bar. He pushed through the people and stood before Gideon. The old man looked at the sentry with something like distaste.

"Maybe it's time to break this up, Mr. Ford," Gray said.

Gideon raised an eyebrow. "What concern is it of the sentry service?"

Gray felt the eyes of everyone on him, turning him into the object of their deep-seated resentment born from decades of feeling overlooked and left behind.

"Our concern is always for your safety." Gray scanned the suddenly quiet room, addressing them all. "As long as you're inside the wall, you're all my responsibility."

"We have a right to peaceful assembly," Gideon said.

"You do, but that right is limited to public spaces. This is a private establishment."

"I see. If I'm not mistaken, it's up to the establishment's ownership to register a complaint." Gideon turned to Gill. "Are we a bother, Gill?"

Gill had a towel stuffed into a glass, drying it, and he scanned the crowd of paying patrons who might leave with Gideon if he sided with Gray. With the volatile economy, times were tough for storeowners in the marketplace. Not long ago, Aeron had implemented taxes on businesses to help subsidize the farmlands and mines, a measure intended to have a cyclical effect to bolster the source of goods so those in the marketplace could better provide, but those taxes were high, and small business owners hadn't seen many benefits.

"Nope," Gill said, but Gray saw the fear in the still owner's eyes.

Gideon's people erupted with insults, though they didn't dare lay their hands on a sentry. Gray turned his back on them to return to his table. Ducard was on his feet, and Gray had to pull him back down to their booth

Ducard glared at him. "Ungrateful bastards."

Gray looked down at his glass, which Ducard had emptied, and he waved to the waitress for another.

Fourteen

The train squealed into the station, the wind whipping Aeron's coat. When it stopped, the doors opened and released a torrent of orange that moved along the platform and down the stairs to ground level. The men and women of the pillar exited the tunnel and parted, some going home, others going into the marketplace for dinner and shine.

Lincoln emerged. He turned his hard hat in his hands while the other pillar workers flowed around him. He took a deep breath that Aeron interpreted as indignation, and Lincoln approached his older brother.

"Long day?" Aeron asked.

"Probably not as long as yours."

With the train empty, the last pillar workers passed Lincoln and Aeron and headed down the stairs off of the platform.

"What are you doing here?" Lincoln asked.

"We need to talk."

Lincoln sighed. "If this is about the damn breach in the wall, I'd really rather get home."

Aeron held up a hand. "Lucy had to take Shane home from school today. He got in trouble for fighting. He's suspended for five days."

Lincoln was still for a moment, then started pacing. "Dammit."

"Take it easy, little brother. Consider that he's in a rough place right now because of Sera's brother."

Lincoln spun, eyes wide. "How is that any of his concern?"

"Don't be dense. He has feelings for her and wants to be there for her, and he sees you as the thing that stands in the way."

Lincoln stopped his pacing and closed his eyes. "I know. Did he talk to Lucy? He did, didn't he? What did he say?"

"He's afraid of you. He thinks you're going to come down hard on him."

Lincoln rubbed his forehead.

"Why would he think that, little brother?"

"Because I hit him last night."

The brothers were silent. Lincoln looked into Aeron's questioning gaze.

"Sometimes he just makes me so angry," Lincoln said. "He gets out of line, and I can't make him understand. He won't learn."

Aeron took a deep breath. "I think he's learned more than you know. He's becoming a principled man, but maybe you don't see it because you're his father. Take a step back. Shane's going to be all right if you ease up."

"You think so?"

"I do. But it's important you guys work it out. Otherwise, he'll grow up resentful."

Lincoln nodded. "I'm not sure we've even had a real conversation since Haley passed. The kid was sad for only a little while. Then it was like he just got angry and never came down."

"I told you then that you alone couldn't be two parents."

"Yeah."

"Maybe that's where you should start. With her."

"Maybe."

"Lucy said some other things," Aeron said. "She can be so maddeningly right sometimes."

Lincoln laughed. "What'd she say?"

"She told me to put myself in your place. She said I'd been self-absorbed."

"She said that?"

"Basically." Aeron nodded, working up some courage. "So what happened last night between you and Clay?"

"Forget it."

"No, tell me. What did he say to you?"

Lincoln gazed at him. "What he needed to get under my skin."

"I'm sorry, Lincoln. I know it hasn't been easy being my brother, and I'm sorry for everything you've been through."

Lincoln stood back, gawking at Aeron. Never in a million years would he have guessed he would get an apology from his brother.

"I'm sorry too. You really went out for me then, and I know it hasn't been easy. I know I haven't made it easy."

The brothers stood apart from each other in silence, Aeron with his hands stuffed in his pockets, Lincoln gazing at the ground.

Aeron moved in and took Lincoln's shoulder with a stern grip. Lincoln looked up. "Now can we talk about that breach?"

Lincoln shrugged Aeron's hand off. "You're incredible. Find it yourself." He stormed off toward the residential district, and Aeron watched his brother go into the failing light.

Fifteen

Sera Bellman waited for dark to ask her mother if she could leave the hospital for a little while. She knew her mother would tell her it was okay, that she would even encourage it. Elena Bellman had always told her children never to dwell on things they couldn't change, and sitting at the hospital wasn't bringing James home. The only reason Elena was there was to support Dani, and the girl slept more than she was awake.

She had waited until dark to leave the hospital because she didn't like the thought of people staring at her as she made her way through the marketplace, across the commons, and to the residential district where she would knock on the Arokson home's front door and hope Shane answered.

When she got there, standing in the gravel street in front of their house, she saw that she was in luck. The only lights on in the entire house were Shane's and Bernie's bedrooms. That meant their father was either passed out or not home.

She climbed the steps and knocked. Someone thundered down the stairs and opened the door. It was Shane, and the first thing she saw was his busted lip.

"I heard about today." She touched his face. "Did Adam do that?"

Shane shook his head.

"Then who?"

Shane frowned. "Come in."

She followed him upstairs into his bedroom where she sat on his bed. He closed and locked the door, which was strange because his father had a rule against them being in there together with the door closed.

He sat down beside her. "It was him."

She took a deep breath but found no words. The only thing she could think to do was lay her head on his shoulder.

"He's going to kill me when he finds out I got suspended."

"No he's not."

"He always assumes I'm in the wrong. Everything's always my fault."

"My dad was the same. I think it's just the way dads are. They're trying to teach you, but they don't really know how. All they know is they don't want you to end up like them."

Shane pulled away and looked at Sera with an accusatory expression.

"What?" she said.

"That's what he said last night."

Then they heard the sounds Shane had been dreading all day. His father walked through the front doorway, boots pounding the wood floor. The coat closet opened and closed, and Lincoln ascended the stairs with heavy footfalls that came from anger, exhaustion, or both.

Shane glanced at Sera, and she looked back, worried.

"What are you going to say to him?" she asked.

Shane's face darkened. "Nothing."

They heard Lincoln walk down the hall and knock on Bernie's bedroom door.

"Hi, Dad!"

"Hey, sweetheart. I'm home. Gonna start on dinner. You finish your homework?"

"Yup! I can help you cook."

"I'd like that. Head on down, and I'll be there in a minute, okay?"

Bernie tramped down the hallway and down the stairs. Then Lincoln knocked on Shane's door. The knob jiggled.

"Shane," Lincoln said. "I'm home. Open the door."

Sera motioned toward the door with her head, but Shane was still gazing at the knob with apprehension. For fear of what he would do or what his father would do to him, Sera couldn't know.

Lincoln knocked again, this time with more weight. "Shane. Open the door."

"Come on," Sera whispered. "You're only making it worse."

Shane wouldn't budge, feeling the burn in his jaw and his split lip. He stared at the closed door.

Sera sighed in frustration. She leaped to her feet, crossed the room, and opened the door. Lincoln wasn't there. She leaned out and looked down the hallway and saw nothing but emptiness, though she heard him descending the stairs, his footfalls softer now, more resigned. An intense sadness struck her as she floated somewhere in that chasm between father and son, and she willed the edges to come back together even if it formed a scar.

On the floor, she found a pair of new boots. She grabbed them and held them up to Shane. His expression did not change.

CHAPTER 3
MORTAL DOMAIN

One

After dusk rolled over the mountains and gave way to the aurora, Ellis Freeman sat alone in the Pillar of Dawn's control room, gazing at the flat panel displays on the wall. He reviewed data from thermometers, barometers, and anemometers. He went over satellite and radar data. He monitored Lumen's vital signs.

The computers assembled it all into images of the world, showing the land that had been mapped by satellite and lidar and pinpointing the locations of the planet's six Pillars of Dawn. Vale's pillar stood several hundred kilometers from the eastern coast of a large, unnamed continent.

As far as the colonists were concerned, there was Vale, and beyond that, everything was the wild.

During these times of solitude, Ellis could hear his pillar. It was barely audible, but behind the clicking and buzzing of computers, the whir of fans, and the hum of electricity, the tower breathed.

The throat of a god exhaled life into the planet.

Ellis sighed and pressed a button on his keyboard, absently cycling among the different data views. The radar showed the funnel of atmospheric clouds expanding for kilometers around the pillar and thinning out across the land in a cyclone of continuous birth. The winds, which were establishing patterns and jet streams, swirled the atmospheric cloud cover over all six pillars and carried the gases around Lumen. Across the continent, a storm was gathering. Ellis would keep an eye on it, and he would decide later whether to include it in his weather forecast for the colony's newspaper, *The First Watch*.

As he pecked his keyboard to take notes on the storm, the pillar rumbled. There was a quick but intense buildup of pressure in the air and

then a release as the earth jumped. A radio toppled off of its receiver, and Ellis' tea sloshed over the rim of his mug.

He flipped the displays to check the seismic activity, and the readout confirmed with a jagged line that he hadn't imagined his whole world bumping beneath him.

Lumen had tectonic plates, and as the pillars accomplished their task of jump starting movement in the planet's core, earthquakes would happen. However, Vale wasn't on a fault line.

Ellis' first concern was always the pillar. He stood from his workstation with his hands on his hips, his eyes locked on the screens before him. Everything looked normal.

The pillar rumbled again, and it set Ellis on his heels.

When he regained his balance, he grabbed his cane and fled the control room. The long, dark corridor was cold and wet, but it illuminated as it detected his presence. He walked beneath dripping metal pipes, hanging bundles of wires, and exposed machinery and equipment, the pillar's ancient guts.

When he was outside, he stood on the walkway, which spanned the chasm that surrounded the base of the pillar. Below, flickers of electric arcs shot into the concrete walls, but that was normal.

Leaning on the railing, he searched the area for anything that would explain the quake. It could have been a meteor. Maybe the train had derailed. It could have been some kind of attack.

Men and women from the third shift were coming out of the facility in other parts of the compound. Something rumbled down the road that descended the mountain to the underground access tunnel. It sounded like voices, the murmur of a crowd. He hoped no one had been hurt. His knee throbbed at the thought, and he reflexively massaged it.

Ellis gazed toward the perimeter wall and the wild beyond. The wind was blowing through the trees, and he realized out here he could no longer hear the pillar breathing. Instead, it sounded like the whole world was inhaling, sucking all of the life force from that tower, and he had the feeling that the wild was grasping for them with a reach that strengthened and grew ever longer and deeper into the compound.

The breeze brushed his face like an oncoming storm, and he looked up to the mouth of the Pillar of Dawn, the rolling clouds of dark atmosphere visible in the aurora's fluorescent glow and streaks of lightning.

Then, for just a moment, the pillar held its breath. A final billow of gases ascended into the clouds, and there was nothing more.

The earth around Ellis seethed. The walkway rattled. His ears popped. A vibration rose in his chest.

The Pillar of Dawn coughed and resumed its life-birthing exhalation, a thunderous clap that echoed down the mountain and made the entire world tremble.

Two

At the center of Vale's industrial district, Aeron walked the dirt road that was blackened by soot and grime. He passed the dull, smoky concrete buildings, the windows of which were stained gray. Engineers and technicians scurried by carrying mechanical components that could have been a machine's heart or simply another piece of scrap metal for all Aeron knew.

He came to the dock, a large platform that was elevated and had a ramp on one side for accessibility and loading. A drone sat on top, and several engineers were affixing crates of food and supplies in the drone's cargo hold. Aeron got the sense from the engineers' rigid postures that they thought he was supervising. He was merely curious.

The engineers closed a compartment on the side, making the drone's body a solid black bubble.

"Wait," Aeron called. He hurried up the ramp to the dock, and the engineer that had closed the hatch looked at him with confusion.

"Open her back up, please," Aeron said.

The engineer opened the compartment, and Aeron fished a note from his pocket and slipped it under an anchor strap that was holding down one of the crates. The note read: *You go, we go. We're in this together.* —*A.A.*

He stepped back, and the engineer closed the compartment, turning a lever to seal it shut. Content with doing a good deed, Aeron strolled down the ramp with the engineers, and the drone's four propellers kicked on. The sound started as a gentle whir but soon was a buzzing scream as the blades quickened and chopped the air with intensifying ferocity. The displaced air struck Aeron, and debris around the dock circulated in the whirlwind. The drone lifted off from the dock, hovered while the engineers checked its systems, and then lurched away. It picked up speed until it zipped toward the perimeter wall. In seconds, it was a black dot and then gone on its journey to Horizon.

The drone would fly through the day and into the night. It would travel roughly 8,000 kilometers over alien terrain, splitting the gaps between snow-capped mountains, spanning a great freshwater lake, soaring over the rocky badlands where relentless glaciers had gouged deep trenches into Lumen's surface, battling high winds through open plains where spontaneous storms had been known to manifest, and finally settling at Horizon's dock the next morning.

If it got lost along the way, Aeron and the people of Vale would never know what happened to it. They would only know that it never arrived and that they would have given precious resources to the great, unknown wild.

He could do nothing now. The drone was beyond anything he could ever hope to know in his lifetime. He had to trust that his engineers had programmed and built it well enough to make the trip.

Aeron left the dock and continued down the street where he entered the fabrication plant, a vast, open, industrial warehouse where Vale's fabricators made machine parts and equipment. The screech of a drill echoed in the rafters. Sparks rained in some far off corner. Machinery whirred. Aeron coughed on the odor of burning metal.

With the stone and ores from the quarry and mine, they had used some devices that the First Families had brought with them to essentially build Vale from the ground up. Their only limitations were materials and ingenuity, and thanks to one man, Vale had no lack of the latter.

When the drilling paused, Aeron heard someone humming a happy tune. The cadence suggested the song was classical, but it had a kind of upbeat bounce that a marching band might give to it. In all of the coldness of turning gears and spinning motors, Ernest Freeman was a beacon of warmth.

Aeron found him bent over a workbench. Ernest's sparkly white hair was long and ragged down his shoulders under a bald crown. With grease-stained hands, he was toying with a small electronic component, cradling it lovingly as if it were a small, ill creature. He might have been blowing on it, but he might have also been whispering to it. Aeron couldn't tell.

The warden cleared his throat. "Ernest."

The engineer spun around, wide eyes of surprise behind magnifying goggles, one hand stroking his bushy white beard, a moment of bewilderment as his mind struggled to let go of his work and recognize the person in front of him.

"Warden Arokson!" Endearing in his eccentricity, Ernest flipped his goggles up on his head, and his blue eyes shined in the sunlight that beamed through the warehouse's horizontal flip windows. "What a surprise! What brings you out here?"

"I'd love to say I was in the neighborhood, but my job doesn't leave me with much time for social calls."

"Of course." Ernest nodded. He set the component on the bench, gently like it was a baby, and wiped his hands with a greasy red rag. It was more of a habit. Save for the dirt that would never come out, his hands were clean.

"That doesn't mean I have to be all business though, Ernest. How are you?"

"All things considered, not bad."

"Really?"

"Well, I miss Claire. But I have my work."

"Ernest, I'm sorry. I didn't mean to—"

Ernest held up his hand and tossed the rag on his workbench. "It's okay, Aeron. The worst part is people tiptoeing around me. No sense in leaving her in subtext. She was more than that."

Aeron sighed. "I know. People are still overly sensitive about my father and my mother. That never ends."

"Claire and I had a lifetime together. I'm grateful for that. You boys had to grow up too fast. And Lincoln. God, I can't imagine if I'd lost Claire so young. Terrible."

A silence grew, both men gazing into the dirt.

"So," Ernest said. "What can I do for you?"

"Ben Harrison. Know him?"

Ernest nodded. "Sure. Runs some of the livestock. Older than dirt."

Aeron grinned. "That's him. Some of his cattle have gone missing."

"Really? How do you lose a cow?"

"Mr. Harrison thinks his animals were taken."

"Who would take animals from the farm? They can get the end product at the market. Besides, where would they hide animals like that?"

"Precisely the questions I asked him. I suggested they just missed the count, and he claims that isn't possible."

"The animals are tagged, identified, tracked, and counted over wireless."

"A system you built if I'm not mistaken."

"You're not."

"Any ideas?" Aeron said.

"Maybe. The tags emit a radio-frequency electromagnetic field with a power source, so it's readable at hundreds of meters. We did that so Mr. Harrison wouldn't have to go out and scan all of his livestock individually every day. They were essentially always connected to the system wherever they went on the farm. If I can build a portable detector for the radio frequency, we could detect them within a pretty good range, but then the problem is transportation of the detector. Wandering around with a scanner on foot won't be very efficient."

Ernest retreated into thought. Mouthing what might have been gibberish, he hunched over and pressed his palm to the crown of his head. It looked like a sudden migraine had hit him, but that was just Ernest's brain working.

"What should I tell Mr. Harrison?" Aeron asked.

Ernest held up a finger and turned his back on the warden. He went to his workbench and moved various devices and tools around.

"Ernest?"

The engineer was gone, absorbed in a new project.

He patted Ernest's shoulder. "I'll get you the tag information, and you let me know what you find or if you need anything."

Ernest waved Aeron off. "Okay, good to see you."

"Likewise."

As Aeron left the fabrication plant, he took note of the quiet. None of the power tools were running, and save for some knocks and bangs from other areas in the plant, it was quiet.

And Ernest was no longer humming.

Three

Ballard held absolutely still. Clay crouched ahead, peering into a clearing, holding one clenched fist in the air, signaling everyone behind him to freeze. He brushed the edge of the wilderness aside and took a deep breath.

He didn't like what he saw.

The sheriff searched for her men. Lyle was right behind her, looking at her with wide, questioning eyes. Ballard shook her head. She didn't know.

Alain Ducard's red bandana was visible through the brush to their right. Ducard had his sentries down and quiet. Kennedy Gray was on the left with his men. They'd all responded to Clay's command with precision.

From the clearing came the undeniably animal sound that had frozen them. It was a low, drawn-out mewl that reminded Ballard of a cow. Across the clearing came another animal sound in answer, but it was more of a cough.

Watching her step on the forest floor, Ballard eased beside Clay, who placed his index finger to his lips and pointed toward the field. Ballard leaned forward and pulled a branch aside.

In the sunlit, golden field, four figures each towered on four powerful legs. Three of them bent their long necks, grazing. One of them, the biggest and most regal, looked across the field with blue eyes as brilliant as the sky. Its leg muscles rippled under a smooth brown hide, and its chest jutted forward, thick bone on the exterior like armor. On its head, two ivory antlers curved into the air and glimmered in the sunlight.

Ballard gaped with wonder. "What are they?"

"Herebors," Clay whispered. "Not dangerous, but the alphas can be if they feel threatened. That one there, he's sharpened his antlers recently. He's on edge about something. Might be lookin' to tussle."

"How do you know?"

Clay patted the tree trunk beside him, showing Ballard that, about three meters from the ground, the bark had been rubbed clean off, baring the tree's white flesh.

"I don't understand," Ballard said. "There shouldn't be any wildlife. There shouldn't be anything out here but plants."

Clay rolled his eyes. "Life is life, Sheriff. Pushing evolution with the pillars is unpredictable. What makes you think that's limited to plants? There's a whole world out here. You people really have no idea."

The alpha herebor grunted and stomped. He craned his neck into the air and mewled again. The same cough response came back, and across the field strode three other herebors. In front, another alpha male towered over the first one, its antlers reaching into the sky at a height rivaling the tree peaks surrounding the clearing.

The first herebor snorted and shook his antlers. The other herebor stared at the display with indifference.

"What are they doing?" Ballard asked.

"It's lookin' like a tussle. This could get ugly."

The herebors in the first group looked up to their leader, mashing the grass with their molars, and then went back to grazing as if the dispute meant little to them. Maybe they would follow the strongest male and it didn't matter much to them who that was. Their alpha male stomped the ground and reared up, kicking its front hooves near the other alpha male's snout, and he took a few steps back, snorted, and lowered his head.

Lyle approached from behind, shuffling leaves and cracking fallen branches. "What are you guys whispering about?"

Clay turned around with murder in his eyes. Ballard hushed the deputy.

Panicked, Clay turned back to the herebors, and for the moment, nothing moved. Both of the alpha males had heard Lyle and directed their attention to the search party's direction. The herebors' ears twitched, their iridescent blue eyes scanning the tree line. It seemed they were reactionary creatures, waiting for a threat to present itself.

A moment later, the animals bolted away in unison, soaring over the long grass in great leaping strides, their hooves thundering into the distance.

Clay sighed in relief.

"What if they'd decided attacking us was worth it?" Ballard asked.

"Our bullets wouldn't have even dented those chest plates. If they'd wanted to, they could have run us all down. The wild's no place for foolishness." Clay sneered at Lyle and pushed forward into the clearing.

Ballard offered a consoling smile to the young man and followed, squinting into the morning sunlight. The rest of the search party joined them as the herebors' galloping quieted in the distance.

"Those things," Ducard said. "I ain't never seen anything like them in my life. They were incredible."

"Sentries talk," Gray said. "Say they sometimes see things edging out of the forest. Nothing like that, though. Never."

"Lots of incredible things this side of the wall." Clay picked up the march forward. "Lots of things that can kill you too. You all best listen to me, or maybe you won't be getting back over to the safe side. It comes to it, I'll leave you behind." He walked alone ahead into the field.

Head lowered, brim of his hat casting shadows down his face, Lyle walked up beside Ballard. "I'm sorry, Sheriff."

"Pay no mind to him. He's just scared. But maybe it's best you leave him alone the rest of the day. He seems to be in an even more foul mood than usual." Ballard patted the boy on the shoulder.

The search party pressed on across the field, stopping at a stream to fill their canteens. Every once in a while someone called out for James, but the calls were becoming less frequent. If Ballard were being honest, she would have admitted she occasionally almost forgot what they were doing out there until someone called for the boy.

The sky on the horizon darkened as they worked their way toward the pillar on the mountain and its cone of atmospheric gases. None of them had ever seen it so close. Lightning struck the tower and thundered across the valley. Creation never looked so terrible.

The field ended, and they once again entered thick forest, only sparse beams of sunlight peeking through the tree cover.

Ballard pulled her map from her pack and whistled between her fingers. "Hold up a minute. Let's take a break. I'm going to check the grid. Alain, head count."

The sentry pointed at each man and woman, counting under his breath. While Ballard shaded in the sector on the map they'd just covered, she heard Ducard begin the count again. Then he counted a third time.

"Twenty-two," Ducard said.

Ballard looked up from the map. "We left with twenty-three. Who's missing?" Ballard scanned her party and knew immediately who wasn't present. "Lyle?"

Clay snorted. "One missing boy wasn't enough. We had to lose another."

Members of the search party called for the deputy in a wash of noise.

"Damn that kid." Ballard put the map away and walked several meters into the forest. "Lyle!"

"Over here!" Lyle called from other side of a thicket. "I found something!"

The search party raced over to him. When Ballard broke through the brush, the deputy was gaping at a house erected in another clearing.

Clay stepped out from the brush and caught Ballard's accusatory look.

"What?" he said. "Did you think you had jurisdiction over everyone, Sheriff?"

"That siding. It's wood from our lumberyard. Where did they get the concrete for the foundation? The glass for the windows?"

"Not everyone's willing to work for the colony to get their share. Some people just want to work for themselves. Come on. Let's find out if they've seen James. If we're lucky, he's in there. Might want to put your badge away though. These people might listen to what you have to say, but you're not their sheriff."

Passing feet had carved a trail through the tall grass leading to the front door. Along the side of the house, Ballard noticed a stack of wood, presumably firewood, and an empty clothesline strung between two posts. Beyond, the grass was stomped out, and various logs and boulders resembled a playground. It bothered Ballard because it suggested children were growing up in the wild. Despite knowing people had lived that way on Lumen for decades, Ballard didn't like it. People needed a childhood. They needed friends. They needed safety and security. They needed to experience life without responsibility, and she didn't think a family raising children in the wild could offer that. It just wasn't right.

More than that, it bothered Ballard that it was mid-day and sunny, and the children were quiet and nowhere to be seen. The house didn't only look and sound empty; it felt abandoned.

"Hello?" she called outside the front door.

Ducard swept right and peered through a window, his sentries fanning out around him and establishing a perimeter. Kennedy swept left and watched the side of the house. His sentries did the same, their rifles leveled in a display that wasn't going to help establish trust with the people who lived here.

She motioned to lower their weapons, and they reluctantly did.

Clay shrugged, trotted up the front porch, and knocked on the door as if he were an old friend. "Just because we're in the wild doesn't mean you can forget your manners, Sheriff," he said.

They waited, but no one answered the door. Clay knocked again, but the response was the same uneasy quiet.

"Is it unlocked?" Ballard asked.

Clay gave the sheriff a look of warning. "Remember why these people are out here. They like their privacy."

Ballard stepped forward and stared down Clay until he moved aside. "Since when did you care about other people's privacy?"

The sheriff pushed on the front door, and it swung wide open on rusty, squealing hinges, revealing a living room much like any they'd seen in the colony. Sofas complete with upholstery lined two of the walls. Opposite the longest couch, a fireplace was set in a brick hearth. Stairs ascended to a second level, and an archway opened to a kitchen.

Ballard stepped inside, her boots crunching dried mud and booming on the wooden floor. "Hello? Is anyone home? This is the sheriff."

She meandered around the living room, inspecting knick-knacks on a mantle over the fireplace. She ran her fingers along the smooth grain of a wooden chair, and she stepped carefully over handmade wooden toy horses and dolls.

"How did these people get all of this stuff without the support of the colony?"

Clay shrugged and crouched at the fireplace. "Some of it they made. Some of it was traded. Some of it they just walked right in and took from under your noses." He reached into the hearth and touched scorched logs and ashes. "Cold."

"They have to provide for themselves, right?" Lyle said. "There's no marketplace for them. Maybe they're out hunting."

"You think they would take their children into the forest?" Clay said, brushing ashes on his pants. "Of course not. Only we do that."

"What makes you think they have kids?" Lyle said.

Clay sighed.

"What?"

Ballard stepped between them. "The toys, Lyle. There are toys out."

Dumbfounded, Lyle frowned at the wooden figures on the floor.

Ducard knocked on the front door's frame. "Area's secure."

"We're going to search the house," Ballard said. "Keep an eye out."

Ducard nodded and ran back out into the tall grass.

"If James were here, we would have found him already," Clay said. "We should move on and search the other sectors before it gets too dark."

Ballard held up a hand. "Something's not right here. You say these people won't see me as their sheriff, but that doesn't mean we should just leave them. They might need help."

"What goes on here doesn't affect the colony. This place isn't your concern."

"Just because I'm not responsible for them doesn't mean they aren't my concern."

Clay sighed. "Fine. I'll be outside." He moved toward the door.

"Or yours," Ballard said.

Clay kept walking.

"Hey!"

Clay stopped.

"You've been hired to help us find James. That means searching for him is your responsibility and your concern."

"Exactly. It's not to bother people who live out here because they want to be left alone."

"Can you say for certain James isn't here?"

Clay crossed his arms and cast an icy stare at Ballard. The fact that he wasn't leaving was answer enough.

"All right. Let's take a look around."

They entered the kitchen. A large window over a sink bathed the room in sunlight. The wooden cabinets were faded and cracked. The countertops had split and warped at their ends. There was a table for dining, and it still had food on it, four wooden bowls with wooden spoons set in a black goo.

"What is it?" Lyle asked.

Ballard stirred the contents of one of the bowls. "I'm not sure, but it's probably not meat."

"Why not?"

"Because if it were meat, we would have known it when we walked in the door. My guess is vegetables from the garden out back. The question is how long it would take for vegetables to decompose to this state."

"A while," Clay said.

"What does that mean?" Lyle asked.

Ballard gave him a grim look.

Clay gazed into the bowl from across the room. "It means they left without finishing their meal, and it happened a while ago."

Ballard gazed into the backyard through the window over the sink. The wild seethed in the wind. She tried the faucet, but the pipes only groaned. Beyond a garden that had grown over stood a wooden shed Ballard assumed held farming equipment and tools.

They moved on, climbing the stairs to the second floor where they discovered three bedrooms and a bathroom. Lyle flipped the lid on the toilet and pulled back the cotton shower curtain.

"How'd they get running water?"

"All you really need is a water source, a well pump, and a knowledge of plumbing," Clay said. "My guess is someone in this family built some of the homes in the colony."

"Agreed," Ballard said. "The similarities to my house are uncanny."

One of the bedrooms had a large bed for adults, and the other bedrooms had smaller beds for the children. The adults' room was sparse on decorations but had all the requisite furniture made of wood for clothes storage. Ballard opened the drawers in a dresser. They were full. Wherever these people had gone, they hadn't taken anything with them.

The children's rooms were littered with more toys, and a painted mural of various farm animals adorned one of the walls.

"There's no one up here," Clay said from the top of the stairs.

They went back to the first floor and opened the door to the basement. Stairs descended into darkness. Ballard pulled a small flashlight from her belt and clicked it on. The narrow, blue beam revealed a dirt floor at the foot of the steps. Ballard hesitated briefly, thinking she should call out to announce their presence, but if anyone were there, they knew they had visitors. In the basement, they would be cornered, and Ballard had no way of knowing whether they were armed. Despite diplomacy, she pulled her revolver from the holster on her hip and held it at her side.

She eased forward, the dusty wooden stairs creaking under her weight.

Clay clicked on his flashlight behind Ballard and followed.

"Keep an eye on things up there," she called to Lyle, who waited at the door.

Lyle nodded.

Clay snickered.

The air was musty, and Ballard felt, if they were going to find bodies, this was where they would be.

At the base of the stairs, Ballard swept her flashlight around the room. Lined against the far wall, they found cordwood, old clothes folded and bound by twine, and an infant's crib. Shelves under the stairs held various canned foods and glass bottles of basic cooking and cleaning supplies. A workbench was anchored to another wall with hanging hand tools and projects at various stages of development laid out on the tabletop. Clay picked up and examined a wooden herebor and eating utensils. On the workbench were two blocks of wood glued and clamped together and set to dry. A rag lay over a metal elbow pipe, which looked to be old and dirty and in need of replacement.

Distracted by the wonder of it all, Ballard and Clay almost missed the depression in the dirt floor. They shot glances at each other, and Clay crouched by the disturbed soil, picked up some of the earth, and let it run through his fingers.

"You think this is where they're buried?" he asked.

Ballard stood back and looked on, confused. "I don't think so. When you bury something, it creates a mound, not a depression."

"So, what then? They dug up some dirt here and took it somewhere? They just dug a hole for fun and filled it back in?"

"I don't think so."

Clay rubbed the back of his neck. "So what does this mean?"

Ballard kneeled beside the crater and ran a palm over the surface. A tremble rose in her chest, and she felt like she might fall in and be swallowed by the earth. "I'm thinking maybe some of those stories they told us when we were kids, about Lumen swallowing people whole, are true."

Their laughter echoed off of the concrete walls.

"What's going on down there?" Lyle asked from the top of the steps.

The laughter ended, and Ballard and Clay held each other's gaze. Ballard was trying to read Clay, and he was trying to read her right back. In the way that he persisted to evaluate her, she saw that her guide had no answers of his own. He wasn't hiding anything.

Ballard drew a deep breath. "Nothing, Lyle. We're coming up. We should keep moving."

Clay and the sheriff ascended the stairs and met Lyle's expectant eyes in the living room.

"So?" he said. "What did you find?"

Clay released an exasperated sigh, and removed his hat to run his hand through his hair. "Nothing, kid. Nothing that concerns us. No James Bellman here."

Lyle turned his dumb expression to Ballard.

"Yeah," she said. "We should go."

She led them crashing through the front door and off of the porch. The sentries collapsed their perimeter behind them, moving in two unified lines, once again peeling back the wild and stepping through the seam.

Four

Lincoln's coring drill had jammed, and he had resorted to cursing and slamming it with a wrench.

He'd erected the drill in the pillar's yard, several hundred meters from the chasm. One of his responsibilities was to periodically drill into the earth and take a soil sample. He'd then take that sample to a small lab on site to be analyzed for contamination. If the lab detected any, it would mean the pillar's core containment was leaking.

The job was more of a formality than anything, because by the time they detected contamination in the soil, they wouldn't be able to do much about it. The pillar's core generated energy through nuclear fusion. However, whereas conventional nuclear fusion created an artificial star and was inherently safe, the Pillar of Dawn required so much energy that they needed the real thing.

The pillar's core was literally a star in a box.

Shutting it down would mean deactivating the electromagnetic field that reinforced containment, which would lead to a world-ending explosion.

Unacceptable by safety standards.

If the lab found any contamination in the soil sample, the only thing they would be able do was let the core fuse itself out until it became an immense ball of iron, which would take thousands of years, and by that time, any life on Lumen would be long gone.

Lincoln's shouts and the clanging metal echoed over the entire mountain. Other workers gawked with concerned curiosity. He thrashed against the drill bit, knocking chunks of compacted earth from the twisting grooves.

Ellis limped across the yard and waited for Lincoln's fit of rage to pass.

Finally, Lincoln let up his barrage and slammed the wrench into the dirt.

"It's been a while since I collected earth samples, but I don't think that's how you operate a coring drill," Ellis said.

Lincoln doubled over, gasping. "These things hate me."

"Machines hate anyone who beats on them." Ellis had a smug smile on his face. "It's just not how they work."

"What am I supposed to do if they never work like they should?"

"You gotta love them a little. Ask them what's wrong. They'll tell you if you listen."

Lincoln shook his head. "What do you want?"

"I have a job for you. It requires someone with a delicate touch."

Lincoln raised an eyebrow.

Ellis laughed. "Maybe you need a change of scenery. Come on."

Lincoln and Ellis crossed the bridge over the chasm between the earth and the pillar. Below, powerful blasts of arc energy leapt from the shaft to the outer wall. Lincoln could never tell if it was the crackling or the rising static discharge that made him shiver.

They entered the massive gate into the facility, and Ellis led Lincoln to the control room. Across from a wall of monitors sat a lonely desk with buttons, dials, and sliders, the purposes for which Lincoln didn't have much of a clue. Ellis limped behind this desk and waited while Lincoln finished marveling at the room and joined him.

"I need you to get under here and get something for me," Ellis said.

Lincoln sneered. "What'd you drop?"

Ellis' expression was severe. "This is the central nervous system of the pillar. From here, I control everything the pillar does. Last night, it did something I didn't tell it to, and that concerns me."

Lincoln held up his palms. "Okay, okay." He kneeled and crawled under the control panel. "What am I looking for?"

Ellis handed Lincoln a screwdriver and a flashlight. "Take off the casing, and then you need to look for a flat piece of metal about the size of a sandwich."

Lincoln removed the screws and set the panel aside. "Be honest. This is the real reason you keep me around, isn't it?"

Ellis leaned on his cane and sighed. "Do you see it yet?"

Lincoln pointed his flashlight back at the old man. "It might help if I'd ever seen one before."

"It should have a handle on it with two clips on the frame that you snap off. Then you can just pull the board out."

Lincoln was quiet for a moment while his arms worked on the undercarriage of the console, and then he put his flashlight between his teeth.

"See it?"

"Yeah." Lincoln grunted, and the clips popped and disengaged. He slid the motherboard out and tumbled it in the beam of his flashlight. "This little guy is the pillar's brain?"

"Sort of. That's this console's brain, and it controls most of the equipment in this room, which is, more or less, the pillar's brain. Unlike us humans, though, the pillar has an array of failsafes and redundancies."

"Reassuring."

Ellis extended his hand, and Lincoln took it. When he was on his feet, Lincoln handed the board to Ellis, who pulled up the glasses that hung on a chain around his neck and set them on his nose. He held the board close to his face, scanning and flipping it over.

Lincoln collapsed into the workstation's chair. "What makes you think it's a hardware issue?"

"The pillar's been stable for hundreds of years, and now it's glitching. Something is breaking down, and code in a sterile environment doesn't do that. Besides, I already ran diagnostics, and they came back fine."

"You did that for the hardware too, right?"

"It can verify the integrity of most of the components, yes."

"That came back okay, I assume. So since it hasn't happened again, why not just write it off as a hiccup? Maybe what happened is what's supposed to happen. It's supposed to quit manufacturing Dawn, right? Maybe it's just doing its job."

Ellis lowered the board and peered at Lincoln with beady eyes. "Do you know what happens if our pillar goes down?"

"I'm sure it's bad, but enlighten me."

Ellis took a breath. "The other pillars won't be able to maintain Lumen's atmosphere. We don't even know how quickly the atmosphere would collapse. With a weakened electromagnetic field to protect the planet from the sun's radiation and a slower output of gases, we could last decades, or we could last weeks."

"I get it. It's important. It just seems like you're shooting in the dark. If it happens again, we can monitor it and get a better idea of what's going on."

"If it happens again, what if it doesn't come back on at all?"

The door to the control room burst open. A supervisor from the underground compound stood in the doorway, hardhat under his arm, safety gloves clenched in his fist. Dirt clumped in his long, dark hair and beard, and sweat had drawn lines in the dust on his face. His eyes, which were ringed from safety goggles, narrowed. The tendons in his neck bulged as he gasped from running.

"Ellis," he said, his voice low and rough, "you're going to want to see this."

Ellis set the board down on the workstation and limped toward the door.

Lincoln picked it up and waved it in the air. "You want me to slap this thing back in?"

"It'll be fine for a little while. Just leave it. Come with us."

Lincoln set the board down and followed. They left the control room and walked across the compound, trailing the supervisor, who walked ahead at a pace Ellis couldn't match.

"What is it?" Ellis called after him.

"You have to see it to believe it."

Ellis and Lincoln shared uneasy glances, and the supervisor led them along the road that sloped down the mountain and curled into the underground pillar entrance. The outside of the dark tunnel was lined with yellow and black striped paint, and signs informed them of what they already knew: the tunnel provided access to the pillar's core. The signs told them proper personal protective equipment must be worn at all times. The signs told them serious injury or death could result if they didn't comply.

They didn't stop to put on the gear because they weren't going that deep. The supervisor nodded at an attendant in a booth and took them through the gates at the mouth of the tunnel, and they turned down a narrow passageway lined with old, grimy lights and wet, dripping concrete.

The supervisor stopped at a door marked MAINTENANCE and fumbled with a keychain that might have held a hundred keys. When he opened the door, Ellis and Lincoln immediately saw the hole in the concrete wall and the earth that spilled out from it and scattered throughout the room.

Ellis hobbled inside and put his hands on his hips, gazing at the wall with an open mouth. "What happened in here?"

"This wall collapsed by the looks of things," the supervisor said. "But that's not the worst part. Look over here."

He took them across the room, around some junction boxes that were locked in cages, to a far wall lined with fat, armored conduit. When the wall had collapsed, it had cracked the conduit and severed some of the cables within.

"There's your hardware issue," Lincoln said.

Ellis gawked, utterly mystified. "I ask again. What happened in here?"

"We really have no idea," the supervisor said. "Earthquake maybe?"

"Is it safe?" Lincoln asked.

"These are just low-voltage data lines. The power lines are elsewhere."

Lincoln leaned his head into one of the holes and saw some of the glass fibers splayed out like clutching fingers.

Ellis nodded in contemplation. "How long will it take to fix?"

"Not long. We can patch this. The wall is another story. I have to get a structural engineer in here to make sure it's safe before we can work on these cables, but the question of what did this is bothering me."

"Could be unrelated," Ellis said. "When the pillar trembled, it shook the ground pretty violently. We've found damage elsewhere from the tremors. Maybe this wall just collapsed."

"Maybe," the supervisor said.

"What do you think, Lincoln?"

Lincoln faced the collapsed wall, gazing into the spilled earth and scattered brick. "I think we shouldn't go shooting in the dark."

"So what do we do?" Ellis said.

"Turn on a light."

Lincoln left the men in the maintenance room and hurried up the hill. As he crossed the yard toward the train station, he eyed the drill bitterly. Ellis was wrong. Sometimes when a machine wouldn't do what you needed it to do, your only choice was to hit it.

Five

Lucy just needed a minute to herself. All day, students had come to her for help. At times, a line formed in the hall. While the colony's adults had already moved on from the missing boy, the children were having a tougher time with it. Most of them were distressed and confused. Some of them simply wanted a legitimate reason to be excused from class.

She'd always been good with people, especially children. She'd always been able to read them and make them feel comfortable. People had always liked Lucy. Loved her, in fact. She'd been the popular, beautiful girl when she was in school, and no one had resented her for it. She'd been one of those rare confluences of beauty, intelligence, and genuine goodness, and she deserved the adoration she received.

All of that had led her to become a guidance counselor. She taught as well. Very few people in Vale wore a singular hat of responsibility. Some days it was too much. It was too hard to help people with their problems when she had her own.

A minute was all she needed. She needed to sip her tea while it was still hot, cradle it under her nose, and breathe in its soothing vapors. She needed quiet. She just needed time to not deal with someone else's gaping wound.

Knuckles knocked on her door.

"Dammit," she muttered, then called, "Come in."

The door cracked open, and Principal Feron leaned his head in. "Mrs. Arokson, do you have a moment?"

Lucy set her tea down and glanced at it resentfully. It would be cold by the time this was over. "Sure. Please come in."

Feron opened the door all the way and stood aside for a boy to enter. Adam Hathaway gazed at her sheepishly with one black eye. His lip was swollen, and he had red blotches on his cheeks and forehead from Shane's strikes the day before.

"It seems Adam is having trouble after yesterday," Principal Feron said. "He could not pay attention during his math class this morning. And then during lunch, some of the other children were antagonizing him. One of those children was, reportedly, Gabriel."

Lucy narrowed her eyes. "My son, Gabriel?"

"Yes," Feron said, his eyebrows bouncing to accentuate the syllable. "I trust you can be impartial and objective here. I really do think Adam could use his counselor today."

Lucy gazed at him a moment, her exhausted mind trying to process everything. Shane, Gabriel, a bully being bullied, her responsibility to him.

"Of course. Have a seat, Adam." Lucy gestured to the chair in front of her desk and stood, circling around and ushering the principal out. "Thank you, Principal Feron. I will take care of him."

He raised a finger of protest. "Maybe I should stay."

"I don't think that would be appropriate. Counselor-student meetings must be private for the student's own good. I'm sure you understand."

"But—"

Lucy closed the door on him. She took a deep breath as she stared at the back of the boy's head. Then she circled around her desk and sat.

He wouldn't look at her. On some level, she sensed he was afraid, and she couldn't be sure if she incited that fear or if something else was the source.

"What's going on, Adam?"

He shrugged.

"I know it's hard, but you should try to talk to me. I can help."

Adam shook his head.

"No? Why not?"

"You're his aunt," he said in a small voice.

"That's true. I'm Shane's aunt, but it doesn't mean I don't want to help you. Talk to me."

The boy sat still, gazing down at the floor. Lucy sensed not many people were open with Adam. Not only did he battle with the inability to communicate because he was young, but also his expression was hindered because nobody had ever asked him to talk about himself before. Of course an adult, especially Lucy, asking him such questions would make him suspicious.

"You must feel like you lost something," she said. "Respect, maybe. You might feel embarrassed. It's okay. Whatever you're feeling, it's okay. These feelings are natural, and there's nothing wrong with it."

Adam scoffed and shook his head. "What do you know?"

"You're right. I've never been where you are. So why don't you talk about it? Tell me. Make me understand."

"What difference would it make?"

"Maybe none," Lucy said. "Maybe it will make it all go away. You don't know until you try. You've got nothing to lose. I'm not on anyone's side here. I'm not going to tell anyone what we talk about. It's just you and me."

Adam looked up and made eye contact. "You promise?"

"Of course."

He sighed heavily. "Sometimes, I feel like other people just have it easier, you know?"

Lucy nodded. "Yes I do."

"No you don't."

"Excuse me?"

Adam lost his sad, reluctant expression. It transformed into a confidence that surprised and frightened her.

"You don't understand," he said as if it were obvious. "You live near the commons. Your family runs Vale. You can do anything you want without getting in trouble. My family lives in the mods. People look at us differently, like we're dirty, and they don't want to be around us."

Lucy took a deep breath. The soft approach wasn't going to work on him.

"You're right. Some people do have it easier than others. That's life, and you have two choices. You can either ignore it and try your hardest, or you can complain and act out. If you do try, though, I promise it will get you somewhere." Lucy placed her hands on her desk. "Adam, you're on a path that leads into darker territory. Right now, you can choose to leave here and try to be good and do the right things, or you can choose to do the wrong things. But no matter where you come from, you can't expect to be bad and have people respect you for it. That just isn't how the world works. You aren't entitled to respect. You have to earn it. Understand?"

Adam nodded.

"Now here's what we're going to do," she said. "You're going to go back to class, and when school ends, you're going to go straight home. Ignore everything and everyone, and when you get home, you're going to keep to yourself as much as you can. At some point, you're going to feel like acting out or doing something you know is wrong. Instead of doing that, I want you to write it all down. Write about what you're feeling and why. Bring it to me, and we'll talk about it. Okay?"

Adam nodded, but Lucy knew he wouldn't do it.

"Okay," she said. "You can go."

The boy stood and shuffled to the door. Sitting there watching Adam leave, she wondered why she'd been so direct with him. It was against everything she'd ever learned. In a way, Adam was like Shane in that she couldn't be subtle. She had to treat them like adults because the stakes were too high.

Adam closed the door behind him, and Lucy resentfully sipped her cold tea.

Six

At the Bellman home, Shane peered through the curtains in the living room window at his classmates running down the street with their backpacks jostling. Across the commons and over the colony, the sun was setting on another day, slipping behind the Pillar of Dawn. With the failing light behind it and the first hints of a green aurora, he thought the pillar looked like a giant tree, shooting into the heavens and spreading its limbs.

Elena, Sera, and Dani sat quietly in the living room. Sera bit her fingernails and bounced her crossed leg. Dani rocked in a chair. The shock still manifested on her face, but she'd been physically well enough for Dr. Osman to discharge her from the infirmary. She'd preferred to stay with Elena instead of with her own parents because she knew the Bellmans would be the first to know if the search party had found James.

Over the last few hours, a dread had descended on the household, like the shadow of an eclipse, as each of them lost hope that this would be the day James would come home. Facing another night without knowing his fate, their hope dwindled, but they wouldn't speak of it. Initially, they talked about other things to preoccupy each other, but they had become quieter as their despair grew until another night of not knowing was all they could think about and any attempt to speak of other things felt wrong and disingenuous.

Someone knocked at the door. Everyone perked up, and Sera reached for Dani's arm. Excitement bounced even in Shane's chest as he shot up and hurried across the living room, thinking for a fleeting moment that they were free from their prison of woe.

He opened the door, and fresh air rushed into the house. Sheriff Ballard stood outside, twisting her hat in her hands. For a moment, she simply squinted into the gloom, then she took a deep, sighing breath.

"Hey, Shane. Is Mrs. Bellman home?"

Shane gazed at Ballard, his fingertips sliding off of the doorknob.

Ballard met eyes with Mrs. Bellman. She turned away, and Sera leaned onto her mother's shoulder. Shane frowned, an expression that looked out of place on his boyish face, and stepped outside and closed the door behind him.

"What are you doing to find him, Sheriff?"

Ballard blinked at the boy. "Shane, I promise we're doing everything we can."

"Apparently, it's not good enough. It's been days. I bet tomorrow you plan to just go back out there and do the same thing in another spot, don't you?"

Ballard narrowed her focus and sized Shane up. His intensity and confidence reminded her of his father, but there was something else in him, something darker and reckless. She thought about deferring to Lincoln, but something in her felt a responsibility to him, and it went beyond being the sheriff.

"You have to believe we're doing everything we can. I admire your enthusiasm, Shane. I really do. But the wild is a big place, and you don't know what it's like out there. Don't be so quick to judge."

Ballard slapped her hat into her hand and walked away.

"I know more than you think I do," Shane said.

Ballard stopped but didn't turn around.

Shane went back inside and found Elena standing at the bottom of the stairs. She looked at him with eyes of stone, and Shane felt then that she could see straight through him, into his core. She looked at him with such a heartbreakingly deep expression that Shane wondered if she could read his soul, and she was speaking to him with more than just words.

"He's still alive," she said.

"I know."

Mrs. Bellman nodded as if a job were finished, and when she got upstairs and closed her bedroom door, the children pretended they couldn't hear her sobs.

Seven

Lincoln left the train station and went straight to Arokson Hall. He walked through the front door and past the information desk. When the old woman attending to it called after him that the building was closed, Lincoln didn't stop. He marched up the staircase to the mezzanine and followed the walkway back around to the hallway, which led to the warden's office.

He walked through the door and met eyes with Aeron's assistant, Alice, who stared back in surprise. When Lincoln moved for Aeron's office door, she chased after him.

"You can't go in there," she said and chased Lincoln with a raised hand in protest.

He opened the door and saw the desk and the arched window overlooking the commons, and for a moment, he thought the man sitting behind the desk looked like his father, pale and tired in the days before he disappeared. The memory ambushed Lincoln, and for a moment, he forgot why he'd come.

"Excuse me, Warden. I told him he couldn't come in," Alice said.

Aeron raised a hand for their silence, and with his other hand, he held the radio microphone to his lips.

"Jack, I'm going to have to call back later."

A receiver on the desktop hissed with static. "All right, Aeron. I'll be here waiting. Horizon out."

Aeron set down the microphone. "It's all right, Alice. If my brother can't see me when he needs me, who can? Please give us a few minutes."

Alice pulled the door closed behind Lincoln, and the brothers gazed at each other across the office until Aeron motioned toward the chair in front of the desk.

"Have a seat."

Lincoln sat and regarded his brother with coldness.

Aeron leaned back in his chair. "Okay. I don't suppose you're here to show me the breach in the wall, so what is it that you want, Lincoln? "

"I want you to be straight with me."

Aeron's eyes narrowed. "Okay."

"You heard about what happened at the pillar and what we found today?"

"Yes. Ellis radioed down. Said everything was under control."

"We fixed what needed fixing, but I wouldn't say it's under control."

"What do you mean?"

"Something broke into that room and destroyed those cables."

Aeron nodded as if it were all routine. "I'm meeting with Ballard soon, and we'll find whoever did that."

"I didn't say some*one*. I said some*thing*."

Aeron paused, his jaw falling a little slack.

"You didn't see it, Aeron. Something dug its way in there and busted through the concrete wall like it was nothing, and the conduit...it looked like it had been chewed through."

Aeron rocked in his chair and looked down into his folded hands.

"There's something in the wild, Aeron, isn't there?"

The warden swiveled in his chair and gazed out the arch window onto the darkening commons.

"It's all right," Lincoln said. "I know about the wildlife. I know the First Families brought animals and released them into the wild to see if they could survive. I know the pillar forced them to evolve. I haven't said anything to anyone about that, but it's been really eating at me since Haley went missing."

"What do you mean?"

"I mean, I never told you everything."

Aeron settled into his chair. Lincoln now had his full attention.

"That night, when we were out in the wild, something took her. I thought maybe it was something I'd never seen before. She was there one moment and just gone the next. But all of this with James now, thinking back to her and Dad, the others who have gone missing over the years, is there something you're not telling us?"

"It will sort itself out," Aeron said.

"But the pillar is in danger. If the pillar created something that poses a threat, we have to deal with it."

"You don't understand." Aeron leaned on his desk. "The pillar was supposed to kill it."

Lincoln blinked. "You're right. I don't understand."

"It's native, Lincoln."

Lincoln reeled. He closed his eyes, leaned forward, and pressed his face into his hands. "You mean it was here when the First Families came?"

"Forget it. I've told you too much."

"No," Lincoln said. "That's what the perimeter wall and the sentries were about. All this time, you knew something was out there, and you made us think it was all just in case, but you knew. Now you're going to shut me out again, just like Mom and Dad did with everything. Kept me out of the loop. Made me an outcast. I'm not backing off this time, so tell me what you know."

Aeron slammed his fist on the desk. "I have this under control!"

The brothers' violent gazes would not break for an eternal moment, and then Lincoln stood and turned for the door.

"Lincoln," Aeron called, hurrying around his desk. "Wait. I didn't mean it like that."

Lincoln left the warden's office. With the door closed behind him, he noticed Alice trying to pretend she hadn't heard raised voices. Lincoln didn't care. All he ever wanted to do was help, but nobody ever seemed willing to let him. Lumen could plunge back into lifeless ice for all he cared. He'd tried.

His feet led him not home but toward the Daenuel Market, and before he realized where he was going, he was standing outside Gill's Still. Music poured from the door as people came and went, and he started to wonder what that first taste would be like. He wondered if he could stop at just one.

Lincoln stepped into Gill's, and it felt like coming home. As he made his way to the bar, he overheard people talking about James Bellman and the pillar's hiccup. Some cattle had gone missing. A few sentries were gathered around one of their own as he told them about something he'd seen the night Dani Hines came back, something in the trees. They listened with rapt attention.

At the bar, Lincoln found Reggie and Clay sitting next to each other, and the rage burned away any desire he'd had to drink. Clay had three empty shine glasses in front of him, and he was cradling a fourth. Ballard was nursing hers.

"Whoa!" Clay cried. "Look who it is!"

"Clay," Ballard warned, grasping the man's arm, but he shook her off.

"I been meaning to tell you, Lincoln," Clay said, "no hard feelings about my getting this gig. I know you probably could have used the money."

"I hear that's going really well," Lincoln said. "Surely you have a clue where the boy is by now."

"I ain't so much worried about James Bellman. We'll find him, but you know, I heard about your boy. Real chip off the old block."

"Way I see it, things worked themselves out."

Clay leaned in close enough to whisper, and Lincoln knew what was coming and that the foresight wouldn't take any of the sting out of it.

"Maybe what the boy needs is a female figure in his life."

"Clay," Ballard warned.

"Someone like, oh, that's right. His mother's dead, isn't she? What happened to her, Lincoln? What happened? I'll tell you what. Everyone knows it. You killed her."

Clay laughed, but no one was laughing with him. Gill's had gone quiet, and everyone was staring.

Lincoln caught him on the side of his jaw, and Clay went down, his shine tumbling through the air.

Gill's Still erupted. Some of Clay's friends rushed toward Lincoln. The last time this happened, Reggie had settled it by arresting Lincoln to protect him.

Call it a bad couple of days, but she didn't feel like doing that this time.

She caught the lead man with her boot in his groin. The next man was running at Lincoln with a raised chair, and Reggie swept his legs out from under him and sent him flying and crashing into a high-top table. The third man swung at her, but she dodged it, arm-barred his throat, and put him on his back.

When she was able to collect herself and everyone else in the bar was backing away, she focused her attention on Lincoln and Clay.

Lincoln had a fist full of Clay's shirt and was hitting him again and again.

Ballard had to step in, or Lincoln was going to kill him. She wrapped her arms around Lincoln's chest and pulled him up. Lincoln's eyes were aflame, his knuckles throbbing with pure pleasure.

The sheriff sighed. "I told him I wasn't going to stop you this time, but that's enough." She reached down and pulled Clay up. "Up you go. Let's take you somewhere for you to sleep it off."

Lincoln cast a hard look at Ballard, and she returned a look of indignation. "What?" she said. "It was just a drink."

"It's fine," Lincoln said. "You're free to do as you please."

She looked at the people who remained in Gill's. "You better go home, Lincoln. I mean it."

She pushed Clay out of Gill's, and with the show over, the patrons returned to their usual cheerful bickering.

Still catching his breath and feeling left behind, Lincoln turned back to the bar and raised his hand to Gill for a glass of shine.

Eight

Dawn crested the tree line in the eastern sky, bruised purple and fiery red emerging from the horizon. Soon, another day would be upon them, and the sentries of the watch would once again pour into the wild in their search for a boy they thought they probably would never find.

The muffled pop of an amped-down and suppressed rifle sounded from the southern wall. With roughly two kilometers of wheat fields between the watchtower here and the residential district, the discharge of this particular weapon went unnoticed.

Peering through rangefinder binoculars, Sentry Dyson huddled over Sentry Hall, who was aiming through the night vision scope of a marksman rifle mounted on a bipod. Hall took another shot. The rifle's high-powered amplifier snapped, and the recoil jolted his shoulder. The firearm launched a caseless round at 800 meters per second into a hay bale 100 meters away on top of the wall. They were shooting at a target with rings. The bulls-eye and each ring outside of it had a prescribed number of points.

Dyson lowered the binoculars. "Twenty-five."

Hall made a clicking sound with his mouth. "Dammit."

He'd hit inside the second ring. Inside the first ring was worth fifty points, and the bulls-eye was worth one hundred.

The sentries swapped the rifle for Dyson to take a turn.

Sergeant Alain Ducard ascended the staircase to the watchtower and approached Lieutenant Kennedy Gray, who was leaning against the inner ledge and watching his sentries with a smile of amusement or pride or both. Ducard couldn't decide.

Gray didn't take his eyes off of his men. "It's almost time to go again, isn't it?"

"Yeah," Ducard replied.

The lieutenant shifted his weight and looked his sergeant in the eye. "You all right?"

The big man took a spot next to Gray leaning against the wall. "Fine."

"Sleep?"

"Like a baby. You?"

Gray shook his head and nodded toward the two young sentries. "These kids."

"They do something wrong?" Ducard sprung from the wall. "I'll take care of it."

Gray caught his arm. "They didn't do anything."

Another rifle shot cracked.

"Fifty," Hall said.

"So close," Dyson said.

"My turn."

The sentries switched places again.

Gray motioned with his head for Ducard to rejoin him on the edge of the wall, and the sergeant did as the lieutenant bade.

"I'm concerned," Gray said.

"If this is about me not being hard enough on—"

"It's not about that." Gray sighed. "Look, there was a time when you and I didn't know what we were going to do in Vale. You remember?"

Ducard grunted.

"We knew what we didn't want to do, and that was pretty much everything. Working the mines or the farms, giving our lives to the pillar and being on that mountain all the time, none of it seemed like what we were made to do. So one day, the warden tells us this guy from another planet is coming here, and he needs people. He tells us he's starting the Sentry Service. He tells us it will be our job to protect Vale. Barrow shows up, and he's larger than life, talks, acts, and looks different, like some alien with super powers. And we're like, shit, sign us up. Let's be heroes. You remember?"

"I remember feeling lucky. We were gonna get to blow stuff up and shoot things for a living. Wasn't nothing cooler than that."

"Exactly. So Barrow trains us, then we wait, and wait. Nothing comes. Our whole lives, we've been waiting, and we never questioned it. Why go through the trouble of bringing in a guy like Barrow and training an army if there was nothing to fight? I thought maybe this was it. We were just meant to reassure people they were safe, but now I wonder. I don't know. What if there's something we don't know?"

"Like what?"

Another shot.

Dyson blurted laughter. "Ten."

"Dammit," Hall said.

"I don't know," Gray said. "All I know is I got a bad feeling. You saw those things with the horns and that empty house yesterday. They aren't telling us everything, and I'm worried one of these kids is going to get hurt."

Ducard snorted in mockery. "Nothing's gonna happen. Bad feeling or not, there's nothing out there that we can't take down, and we trained the boys well. You say we've just been waiting all this time, but this is exactly what Barrow trained us for. We can handle it." Ducard pointed at Hall and Dyson with his thumb. "They can handle it."

"Yeah, well, all I know is, if one of them gets hurt because we're out looking for some kid who got himself lost, I might lose it."

"Me too. Don't worry about that. It happens, I got your back."

"I know you do."

Ducard and Gray leaned over the wall toward the interior. The Pillar of Dawn to the north was beginning to gleam in sunlight. The sky was brightening over the mountains and Vale, the silhouettes of rooftops rising from the ground.

Ducard eased his fingers between Gray's, and the two sentries smiled at each other. For a moment, with the occasional pop of the rifle, they allowed themselves to enjoy the dawn together. It was the kind of moment that, for many reasons, they could rarely share, and while they were trained to fear nothing, it was the kind of moment that terrified them. The fear they felt made it all the more thrilling when they faced it together as brothers in arms, best friends, and lovers.

"We should go," Gray said finally.

"Aw, hell. All right." Ducard barked at Hall and Dyson, "Wrap it up, sentries."

"Why?" Hall said. "It isn't like we're going to find anything out there."

Ducard stabbed a finger at them. "I said wrap it up!"

Gray walked over to the sentries. He took the rifle from Dyson, leveled it at the target, and fired.

Hall peered through the binoculars and gaped. "Bulls-eye." He lowered them and gazed at Dyson. "One hundred points."

"Game over. I win." Gray shoved the rifle into Dyson's chest. "Secure that weapon, and let's go."

Dyson wrapped the rifle in a khaki blanket, tied a rope around it, then lowered it over the outside of the wall to the tall grass below. He looped the rope around an iron hook, and he and Hall hurried down the stairs without a word.

Ducard grinned. "Why are you always so hard to live with?"

"Because I always win," Gray said.

In the growing light, the sentries left the south wall and crossed the field toward the center of town, the main gate, and the wild beyond.

Nine

Like a wave breaking over the colony's perimeter wall, the morning shade drew a blanket of chill over Aeron and Ballard. Boots crunching in the frosty grass, they walked the line that marked the colony's end and the wild's beginning.

Ballard blew into her clasped hands and watched her breath escape between her fingers and rise into the ether. "Sometimes I wonder if Lumen isn't turning back into a ball of ice," she said.

Aeron squinted toward the mountains. "It's going to be winter soon. The pillars are establishing seasons."

As they walked along the wall, a sentry cradling a rifle peeked down from above. His expressionless eyes followed them as they continued their inspection.

Ballard motioned toward the sentry with a glance. "We have an audience."

Aeron looked up to the top of the wall. "Maybe he likes you."

She shrugged. "I wouldn't kick him out of bed, but even so, his eyes should be on the wild."

Aeron stopped and held the sentry's gaze long enough to show that he had the warden's attention. "Mind your post, sentry," Aeron called.

Breath streamed from the sentry's nostrils like dragon's smoke, and he lazily turned and faced the wild.

"What is that about?" Ballard said.

"They take what they do very seriously."

"So?"

"So imagine if they came into your jailhouse and started inspecting the locks."

Ballard nodded. "Fair point."

She knew the wall was everything to the sentries, and she was aware she would never comprehend that level of dedication to an ideal, not even the law.

Aeron ran his fingertips along the wall, marveling at how smooth it had become over the years of weathering. He wondered if it had weakened, but no, it would stand long after he was gone. He would never have to worry about its strength while he was warden.

Ballard twisted her hat in her hands. "I've been wondering. When do we stop looking?"

"When we find the breach," Aeron replied. "The people need to know they're safe."

"That's not what I mean. Have you given any thought to how many resources you're prepared to dedicate to finding James Bellman?"

Aeron blinked at the sheriff. She returned his gaze, and the two of them stood silently for a moment, breathing in the icy morning air.

"To be perfectly honest, Reggie, it's a decision I had hoped I wouldn't have to make."

"I know, but time's catching up with us from two angles. There's only so long he can reasonably survive, and there's only so much tension people can take in here. I think it's time we ask Lincoln to help."

Aeron smirked.

"What?"

"Nothing."

"All due respect, if he gets results, it doesn't matter what people think of him."

"Lost your faith in Clay already?"

"He was never my choice. He was yours."

Aeron's face hardened. "What makes you think my brother will help find the boy?"

"He wants to."

"He said that?"

"No, but I know him well enough."

Aeron bit his lip as he mulled a thought. "A week."

"A week?"

"That's how long they gave my father. That's how long James Bellman gets. You get Lincoln on board, you can have him, but understand something. People aren't going to like it. It's a big risk. If he's able to bring James home, that'll go away. If he can't, there will be repercussions."

"Repercussions?"

"Your badge, Reggie. I'll have to take your badge."

Ballard's face twisted with insult. "Why? It isn't on me that the kids got out. I don't even have to be out there looking for James, but I am."

"You let your guide get beat up, and then you put him in lockup. I'm sorry, Reg. I really am, but that's the reality of the situation. Bring James home before the week is out, or I'll have to make some changes."

Aeron started walking back toward the center of town, and Ballard stayed in the freezing shade, seething. She drew a conclusion.

"I threaten you," she stated.

Aeron turned. "Excuse me?"

"I was elected. You never were. You have the people breathing down your neck to secure the wall and Gideon Ford crawling up your ass for the Warden's Seal. So you're deflecting. It's you who needs results, and if you can't get them, you need a scapegoat."

Nodding because the accusation wasn't so unreasonable, Aeron looked to the pillar on the mountain. It was black with the sunrise behind it, and the atmospheric clouds were ablaze in the morning light.

"We're so close, Reg. But it's fragile. One crack, and it could all come crashing down. We lose sight of that, and people here might tear it all down. And then Lumen is just over. It's about the greater good. We can't stumble. Not now."

"Is it?" she said. "Is it about the greater good?"

Considering that accusation ridiculous, he scoffed at her and walked away with a maddeningly normal pace all the way into town. By the time he disappeared from her sight, Ballard was shivering in the cold and felt an uncontrollable urge to seek warmth.

So that was what she did.

Ten

When Aeron returned to Arokson Hall, the front steps were crowded with people waiting for him. At the front of their gathering was Gideon Ford, the voice of the people.

"Good morning, folks. What can I do for you?" Aeron asked.

Gideon cleared his throat. "If I may." He looked to the people around him for permission. He looked as if he cared about their permission. "Warden, your people are concerned. The prevailing thought is you're dedicating too much manpower to finding one boy when any of their children could follow suit and leave the colony."

The crowd rumbled with comments.

"We thought we were safe!"

"What are you doing to secure the wall?"

Aeron held up his hands. "I admit the search is taking longer than I had hoped, but I assure you everything that can be done to find and bring James Bellman home is being done."

"That's supposed to make us feel better?"

"What about *our* children?"

"Forget that stupid kid! He got himself lost!"

Aeron held up his hands again. "I know it may not seem like it, but by looking for James, I'm doing right by you all. James Bellman may not be your son. But he could be. Ask yourself what you would do if your kids were out there. Would you want us to abandon them? Or would you want us to do everything within our power to get them back?"

"That's the issue," Gideon said. "It's not their kids, and by your own admission, it could be. If we don't do something, it *might* be."

Aeron stared at his people, not liking what he saw. They didn't care about James Bellman. To them, he was just a name, a representation of the worst thing that could happen to their own children. As far as they were concerned, Aeron was doing nothing for them.

A burning sensation bloomed in his stomach. His chest trembled, and his breath hitched. Aeron prided himself on seeing through emotions, but for the first time as warden, he couldn't deny them. It felt like loading ammunition.

"Very well," he said. "If that's your concern, effective immediately, curfew at sundown. Anyone out past dark will be jailed."

A stunned silence settled over the crowd. The people gaped at him.

"Furthermore, anyone leaving the town center will need to show just cause for doing so. If you aren't working at the pillar or aren't farmland staff, you won't be allowed to leave. Sentries will be in place to enforce these new rules. You must comply with their orders, or you will be jailed."

"You can't do that!" Gideon sputtered.

"I can. You want me to abandon James Bellman, and I won't. So if your concern really is your own children, this is how we keep them safe."

Aeron moved toward the front door of Arokson Hall. Dejected, the crowd was frozen in silence, parted for him, and then dispersed, their blank faces processing the price of ensuring their children's safety. Aeron felt sorry, but he also felt vindicated. He would show them what Gideon's leadership would get them.

Before he walked away, Gideon came within inches of Aeron's face, his breath smelling sour, and Aeron could have sworn he smiled.

Eleven

Lincoln woke at the kitchen table again, his neck muscles so taut the back of his skull burned. He heard something that sounded like repeated explosions underwater. His head throbbed with each blood-surging heartbeat, but the concussive pounding came from something else. He swam in an aqueous haze, and when he surfaced, he realized someone was knocking at the door.

Deciding to ignore it, Lincoln slumped back onto the table. The knocking persisted, and ignoring it became more trouble than it was worth.

He rose on uncertain legs, using the wall for support as he stumbled toward the front door. By the time his hand rested on the knob, his chest heaved, and his heartbeat clicked in his ears. Feeling the familiar lurch in his stomach, he looked longingly toward the sink. It was much too far away.

He opened the front door and squinted into morning. A familiar, blurry shape stood there, and when it emerged from the gloom, Regina Ballard's black ponytail looked like a spout of fine ash in the sunlight. Even in her heavy sheriff's coat, she clutched herself and trembled in the cold. She stood on Lincoln's stoop looking as pathetic as he felt.

"Mornin', Sheriff," Lincoln said with as much playful sarcasm as he could muster.

"Can I come in?"

"I got work soon."

Ballard looked him up and down. "You do have some cleaning up to do."

Lincoln blinked lazily and rubbed his sandbag tongue across the roof of his mouth. He stepped aside, and the sheriff slid in. Lincoln closed the door behind her.

"Where are the kids?" Ballard asked as she pulled off her gloves and stuffed them into her coat pockets.

"Shane's staying at the Bellmans'. Lucy's taking care of Bernie. If this is about the breach in the wall, you can tell my brother he can plug up another hole."

She took off her coat, hung it over the banister, and rubbed her arms. "I'm not here about that."

He touched her arm, and it felt like ice. "Why are you so cold?"

"Because I spent the pre-dawn hours with your brother, searching the wall."

Lincoln pulled away and rolled his eyes. "So this *is* about that."

"No, it isn't."

He gazed at her, trying to read her, and she looked back at him with something in her eyes. Expectation maybe.

"I'll make you some tea," he said.

"That would be good."

Lincoln went into the kitchen, filled a kettle from the faucet, and set it on the stovetop. Then he pulled down two mugs and two infusers from the cabinet. He went to his pantry and retrieved a small metal tin.

"This about last night?" he asked as he scooped tea into each infuser.

Sitting at the table, Ballard shook her head. "Clay was asking for it."

Lincoln grunted. "Clay asks for it a lot of times, but you don't always see it that way."

"It's not always so simple."

"Yeah, usually it is."

She nodded. "Maybe sometimes the rules need interpretation."

Lincoln put the lid on the can and sat at the table, rubbing the back of his neck. "That mean we're going to get a proper judicial system?"

Ballard shrugged. "No, just discretion."

"So if you aren't here about that and you aren't here about the wall, what *are* you here about?"

He wasn't always so naive. On some level, Lincoln knew exactly why she was there, but he didn't want to admit it. Or maybe he couldn't. After years of living with the knowledge that most people in Vale hated him, he could never bring himself to believe someone yearned for him.

That suited Reggie just fine.

She stood. Her hands went to the back of her head, and her chest swelled beneath her button-up shirt. She released her coal black hair from its ponytail and it fell over her shoulders like tendrils of shadow. Her blue eyes beamed like shards of ice. Even though she was still tense from the cold, her flesh tight with goose bumps, she unfastened the first few buttons of her shirt, exposing the top of her hard yet delicate chest, the defined notch at the base of her throat. She rounded the table with purpose and determination, all the while her eyes fixed on Lincoln's, commanding him, ordering him to sit still.

Drops on the outside of the kettle sizzled.

When she reached him, still gazing deeply into his eyes, she finished unbuttoning her dress shirt. After unclasping the final button, she let her shirt fall open, exposing her white, cotton bra and her pale breasts. She brushed Lincoln's hair behind his ears, and he prayed she couldn't hear his unsteady breathing.

Reggie held that moment, hip jutting, hypnotic stare, fingertips dancing over his skin, until she grasped the hair at the back of his head and pulled his face to her chest.

Her eyes squeezed shut, and she turned to the heavens. His warmth bloomed inside her, filled her up, sent every chill in every bone racing from her body. Lincoln embraced her, and his sickness vanished. He surged with strength.

The kettle rumbled with the first hints of a boil.

Lincoln took her up, and she wrapped her legs around his torso. He set her gently on the table, and he took her then and there. He took her just the way she'd wanted him to, the way she'd told him to with those haunting eyes.

In moments, the kettle on the stove screamed. They fell into each other, collapsing to the floor, and let the water vapor fill the air.

They lay gasping on the cold wood, and then Lincoln rose and moved the kettle off of the burner.

When he turned, Reggie was standing, pulling up her pants and buttoning her shirt.

She caught him gaping at her and smirked. "Want to cuddle, do you?"

"Maybe. There's a perfectly good bed upstairs."

"I thought you had to get to work."

"I've been telling Ellis to fire me for months."

She snickered. "Believe it or not, I didn't really come for that either."

"Could have fooled me."

She shrugged, smiled, and raised her eyebrows in that innocent way that made him melt because she so rarely let it out. She never let anyone see that side of her. She saved it especially for him.

"I'm here because I need your help looking for James."

Lincoln scoffed as he pulled his pants on. "You could have just asked."

Her expression filled with mischief. "I know."

"What about Clay?"

"I question his integrity."

Lincoln sauntered to her and wrapped his arms around her waist. "You don't question mine?"

She took his hands off of her body. She caressed his broad chest, playing with the curly hairs, and looked him square in the eye. "No, never again."

When Lincoln had come out of the wild all those years ago without his wife, she'd suspected him more than anyone. That suspicion had also led her to investigate him closely, which led her to conclude Lincoln couldn't possibly have done the unimaginable because it was, in fact, unimaginable. Over time, despite her better judgment, she'd slipped into whatever it was they were doing.

"Good," he said.

She kissed the back of his hand and held it to her cheek. "So you'll do it?"

He pulled away and leaned on the counter. "Why didn't you come to me first?"

"You're hurt?"

Lincoln grunted a laugh. "No."

"I wanted to. Aeron didn't."

Lincoln felt the resentment coming back and clenched his eyes. "He needs to find James now because people are putting pressure on him."

"*We* need to find James. Or we need to find evidence of his fate."

"You need to find a body." Lincoln went back to the stove and poured the hot water into the infusers. "I understand. The colony needs to move on. That's what Aeron cares about. You care about Elena needing closure. And you think I can give it to her."

"She trusts you."

Lincoln was quiet a while as he let the tea brew. When it was ready, he brought the mugs to the table.

"Black tea with cinnamon, chocolate, and a little spicy pepper," he said. "It will warm you up." He nudged her mug in front of her. "What about you? You don't doubt me anymore, but do you trust me?"

She eyed the steam rising from the mug, the rich, reddish copper tea. "I do." She sipped and growled with the heat. "That's good."

Lincoln breathed the vapors deeply. They drank in silence, neither of them sure where to go from here because it felt like more of a confession than a bonding moment.

"Because we may yet find ourselves alone out there," he said. "In fact, if I have any say in the matter, we will."

He smiled, pleased with his attempt at lightening the mood, something he was never good at. Reggie took a healthy swallow of her tea, and then she stood, fixing her shirt and tying her hair back up.

"We leave in an hour," she said. "Meet us at the main gate."

She stared at him, and he understood she'd put the wall back up again. He was never sure how it happened or why she did it, whether it was shame or a kind of protection for herself. After all, the sheriff fooling around with the colony's only murderer at large would be a scandal that would ruin her career.

Or maybe, it was simply that she'd gotten what she needed from him and that was that.

She walked to the door. Her coat rustled as she put it on. Lincoln was sure she was gazing back at him, but he just watched his tea settle as she closed the door and left his home.

Lincoln finished his tea in silence, then went upstairs. In his bedroom closet, which was on the other side of a perfectly unused bed, he found his backpack. He emptied his pants pockets, pulling out the compass. The needle still spun erratically. He considered leaving it on his nightstand, but for a reason he couldn't understand, he slid it into his pack. Maybe it would bring him luck.

He finished getting dressed, and then he slung the pack onto his back, the metal clips and clasps jostling and jingling. The straps pulled his shoulders with a familiar weight because most of his gear never left it.

Lincoln set the bag down in the kitchen. He wrapped some bread in butcher paper, put some nuts and dried fruit into a metal jar, and slid some beef jerky into a paper bag, slipping a strip between his teeth for breakfast. He put his rations into his backpack, filled his canteen with well water from the faucet, and clipped it to the strap on the side of his pack.

Lifting it onto his shoulders, Lincoln patted his pockets a final time and looked around the house. It wasn't until that moment that he realized the depth of the silence in that home. He wondered if Shane and Bernie heard it all along.

Outside, the sun was lifting the morning mist. Taking a deep breath of the fresh air, Lincoln made his way down the street, passing neighbors who were coming out in pajamas to get their copy of the *First Watch* newspaper. They leered at him, some of them suspicious still.

He didn't cut across the commons toward the main gate. Instead, he continued down the road until he reached the Bellman home. Lincoln stood on the sidewalk, looking up the steps to the front door, paralyzed in a way. As he gazed up at the stone facade, the front door cracked open, and a face emerged from the gloom.

Elena Bellman leaned against the doorframe.

"Hi," he said.

"Hello, Lincoln." Her eyes traced the straps of Lincoln's pack, and confusion wrinkled her brow.

"I came to see Shane."

"He's asleep."

Lincoln started to ascend the steps. "It's better that way."

At the top of the steps, Lincoln heard Elena's unsteady breathing and saw the tears welling in her eyes, her bottom eyelid a dam that she wouldn't allow to break.

"Are you going?"

Lincoln nodded. "I'll find him."

Breathing unsteady and nervous, she gazed at him. Then the dam broke, and tears streamed down her cheeks. She fell into him.

"Thank you!" she said.

He rubbed her back and held her until she took a deep, trembling breath and her shoulders sank.

She pulled back, wiping her eyes and forcing an exhausted smile. "Come in."

He stepped through the doorway into heavy, oppressive air. Elena closed the door behind him.

Shane lay on the couch, a blanket so perfectly placed that someone else had to have covered him. Sera maybe. Or Elena mothering him like a surrogate for her missing son.

"He is a very strong boy," she said. "Reminds me of you in so many ways."

She smiled at Lincoln in the gloom. He crossed the room and crouched beside his son. He put his hand on Shane's shoulder and felt his steady breathing, and Lincoln stayed there for a moment, watching him. Until he had children of his own, the boy would never understand that, even now, Lincoln thought of Shane in the infirmary crib just after he was born. Yes, Shane was growing into a man, but to Lincoln, he was also still a child and always would be, even as Lincoln fought against it. A father's nature.

Lincoln brushed Shane's hair back, and the boy stirred but did not wake. Then he stood and turned back to Elena. "Is Dani still here?"

She nodded.

"Can I speak to her?"

"I think I heard her a bit ago. Come with me."

She led Lincoln upstairs to a plain bedroom. It was a place for sleeping, not living. No decorations adorned the walls. A pile of dirty jeans lay at the foot of an unmade bed, and a pair of boots stood in a corner. Dried and hardened mud littered the floor in clumps and fine dust. A disassembled piece of machinery lay out on a desk. This was James' room, and Dani sat with her back to them, gazing through the window.

"Dani? It's Lincoln." He eased into the room. "I want to ask you some questions."

She faced him with inflamed, glassy eyes, and wiped her face. "What do you want to know?"

"Tell me about when you and James were separated. Where were you? What happened? What do you remember?"

"He took me to the Field of the First Families. I'd never seen it. He told me we could make it out there, just the two of us. There were these big animals, like tall, skinny cows with horns. Something scared them and they ran away. The ground around us started shaking."

"Like an earthquake?"

She nodded. "James pushed me back into the forest, told me to get back. He pulled out his knife. I didn't know what to do. The ground was shaking harder. Even James was scared. He told me to run, so I did, and I didn't look back."

"Did you hear anything? Did James call out for you?"

Like triggering a mechanism, Dani gasped. Fresh tears streamed from her eyes, and she nodded.

"I think he was running behind me on the path, but then something stopped him."

"Did you look back? What was it?"

She shook her head and squeezed her eyes shut. "I did. I did look back."

"What did you see?"

"It was dark. Dust and dirt in the air? Rocks coming down from the sky? It was like the ground exploded."

"That's all?"

She looked at Elena with sorrowful eyes. "I was so scared. I just ran and kept running. I'm so sorry, Mrs. Bellman. I'm so sorry."

Elena swept in from the doorway and cradled Dani's head. She rocked her back and forth and hushed her like her own child.

"I'm so sorry. I'm so sorry."

"It's okay, baby. It's okay."

Lincoln squeezed the girl's hand. "Thank you, Dani. That helps a lot." He turned to leave.

Elena grasped his arm. "Is there something you want me to tell Shane when he wakes?"

Lincoln frowned. "No. Actually, unless he asks, don't even tell him I was here."

"Thank you for letting him stay with us," she said. "It's been good for Sera. It's been good for all of us."

Lincoln offered a reassuring smile and left, feeling Elena's eyes on his back as he walked down the stairs. He left the Bellman home and stopped at the top of the steps, taking a deep breath as if he'd been holding it the entire time.

When he got to the main gate, Ballard and the rest of the search party were waiting.

Sentry Ducard let his rifle hang and rubbed his stubbled chin. "Where's Clay? Don't tell me we're burning daylight for *him*."

Lieutenant Gray laughed and kicked the dirt. The rest of the sentries murmured their dissent.

Ballard ignored all of this and faced Lincoln, no indication on her face of their encounter an hour ago. "You good to go?"

Lincoln smirked. Had he imagined the encounter in the haze of his hangover? He sized up the search party. Except for Ducard and Gray, he knew none of them.

"Are they?"

"They've been out several days now. More than most."

"So they're good at doing what they're told. Will they listen to me?"

Ballard shrugged. "Maybe not, but they'll listen to me."

Lincoln looked gravely over the young men and women who thought they knew what waited for them in the wild. The last few days had built a visible confidence in them. He hadn't seen them before their first day out, but he knew, despite the typical sentry bravado, they had to have been scared. Now they seemed as comfortable as if they were going to visit their mothers, and Lincoln knew that, if there were any rules about going into the wild, the first was that you should never be comfortable.

"All right then," he said. "Let's go."

Lincoln walked forward, and Ballard signaled the sentries in the tower to raise the main gate. It opened before them, revealing the dirt road that ended in the tall grass beyond the colony's perimeter, the tree line beyond a veil to the unknown.

With the gate closing behind them, Lincoln stopped at the grass and gazed into the wild, listening to the familiar sigh of the wind through the limbs and leaves. He didn't leave the colony because he felt outcast. The truth was he loved the peaceful, natural harmony of the wild and finding a place in it. The wild's balance endured despite human presence, and the feeling was humbling, as he knew more than most that it could take that feeling of human dominance in a single, dark instant.

"Is something wrong?" Ballard asked from beside him.

Blank as stone, he looked at Reggie, and then he disappeared into the trees. The search party followed, and the sun rose over their heads like a relentless, searching eye.

Twelve

Alice rapped on the warden's office door, disturbing the stillness and quiet of the darkened room. She opened the door, peeked in, and found Aeron slumped on his desk, rubbing his eyes.

"Aeron?" she said gently. "You said to tell you if Mr. Freeman came in."

He looked up at her, trying to disguise the weight that he knew was beginning to show on his face. "Of course. Send him in."

Alice opened the door the rest of the way, and Ernest's beady eyes peered at Aeron through his glasses. His white hair splayed into the air like wings. He looked simultaneously wired and exhausted from working non-stop.

Aeron stood and greeted Ernest, motioning for the man to sit.

"Thanks, Alice," he said.

"My pleasure. Let me know if you need anything." She closed the door.

Aeron resumed his seat behind his desk. "Tell me you figured out a solution."

"Better." Ernest's giddy smile lit his face. "I found Mr. Harrison's livestock."

"What?"

The engineer leaped up and laid out pictures and detailed diagrams across the desk, flipping through them far too quickly for Aeron to follow.

"I identified the problem as the missing cattle and assumed they didn't just vanish, because that's physically impossible, and that they were still in Vale. That left me with the potential solution via search protocol, but I lacked an efficient vector to carry out said search. I knew it would take too long on foot, so—"

Aeron held up a hand. "I've had a hell of a few days, Ernest. The short version, please."

Ernest gulped and nodded. "I created a portable radio scanner set to look for the frequencies Mr. Harrison's livestock were emitting. To transport it, I used a drone." He flipped to a picture of one of the drones with extra wires running to an antenna mounted on the side and pointing forward like a lance.

Aeron gazed at the picture. "One of our trade drones?"

"The very same. They have sophisticated navigation and computation equipment. As you know, flying from here to another colony thousands of miles away, anything can happen. When we built the drones, we needed them to be able to fly themselves and make decisions based on information we couldn't possibly have before sending them on their way. We designed them to be somewhat autonomous, go from point A to point B. How you do that is up to you. Follow?"

"So far."

"Good. I stripped the autonomy from one of our drones and programmed it to cover the colony in a grid, much the same way you'd conduct any kind of methodical search. I told it to look for those frequencies and note the locations of any that matched. Then I sent it on its way, and it returned a few hours later."

"What did you find?"

"Nothing. The drone found Mr. Harrison's livestock that are on his farm, but none of them match the IDs he gave you. There was no sign of the livestock Mr. Harrison reported missing."

Aeron closed his eyes and rubbed his face. "How can that be?"

"It's simple, Aeron. Don't overthink it."

Aeron really didn't want to play this game, but he decided to humor the engineer. It was unlikely that Ernest had made a mistake in programming the drone, and assuming Mr. Harrison had given them the right frequencies, a scan of the entire colony that produced no results could mean only one thing.

"They're not in Vale."

Ernest snapped his fingers. "Exactly. Methodology was sound. One of my original assumptions was wrong. Now. I almost came to you with that, but I don't like boring results."

The engineer dug through his documents and produced a map showing Vale and the surrounding land. Five red dots were scattered beyond the colony perimeter.

Aeron gaped at it. "How is this possible?"

"I programmed the drone to start from the center of the colony and fly in a spiral-out pattern and essentially told it not to stop until it found something."

"They got out past the wall? First kids, and now animals?"

"That's not the strange part, Aeron."

"It's not?"

"This map only shows lateral distance."

"So?"

Ernest dug through his documents again and slapped a piece of paper on top. Aeron was now looking at a three-dimensional version of the map.

"These animals," Ernest said. "They're underground."

Aeron analyzed the image. It wasn't very detailed, but it showed the colony center where the commons, marketplace, and residential district were. It showed the tall industrial buildings and the farmland as a wide-open plain. It showed the towering wall and a blanket of trees surrounding the colony. Under this blanket, and beneath the grid lines that denoted the ground, the dots existed in negative space.

"Are you sure?" Aeron said.

"The signals are weak, but they're very low frequencies that can penetrate the ground. Based on a variety of factors, I'm confident."

Aeron stared at the map a moment and wiped his mouth. "What the hell am I going to tell Mr. Harrison?"

The excitement on Ernest's face vanished and was replaced by confusion. He hadn't even considered that. He hadn't thought beyond his findings or even what they meant.

"Aeron?" Ernest said. "Why are cows outside of the colony and underground?"

Aeron started gathering the documents. "You mind if I hold on to these awhile?"

"I guess."

"Good." Aeron stood and ushered the engineer to the door. "Good work, Ernest. Thanks for this. I need some time to figure out what to do. I'll let you know if I have any questions."

Aeron opened the door to the lobby, and Ernest looked at him with suspicion.

"I'm sure you have a lot of work," Aeron said. "I'll let you get back to it."

Ernest narrowed his eyes. "Yeah, okay. I guess I do."

The engineer left the warden's office, and Aeron watched him leave. When Ernest was gone, he gave the documents to Alice.

"Shred these," he said.

"Are you sure?"

"And don't ask questions."

Aeron gazed at his empty waiting room. Not a person in the colony was coming to him for help today, which suited him just fine. He returned to his office and closed the door.

Thirteen

Despite its name, the wild didn't change much. With the unfettered growth and chaotic sprawl, each tree looked like the next, each pebble, stone, rock, and boulder, all formless but conveying a sense of order in its whole. The sound of crunching deadfall never changed. The living forest breathed. The towering trees loomed like watchful guardians, permitting passage, but only just. Traversing the wild felt like crossing an alien land at the whim of the unknown. In the thick, the search party was blind, and anything could have come from any direction and taken them. That it didn't meant they were still in Lumen's good graces.

Lincoln didn't so much recognize specific landmarks as he remembered architectures. The shades of green changed. The foliage density changed; however, the shapes and figures of landmarks were constant. This was the basis for navigating in the wild.

To his right, Alain Ducard's men fanned out like a great wing. The forest was getting thicker, and Lincoln could no longer see them. He could only hear their clumsy footsteps.

"Ducard," Lincoln said, "keep it tight. Tell your men to stay within sight of each other."

Alain rested a hand on the butt of his rifle. "The more we spread out, the more ground we cover."

Lincoln pressed with an unyielding stare. "Everyone stays within sight."

The sentry looked at Ballard.

"You heard him, Alain."

Ducard said to his men, "Keep it to a ten meter spread."

Lincoln sloshed the water in his canteen. "Better tell the same to Gray."

The pillar came into view. Ballard checked their position on the map relative to it. "Lincoln, we're way east of where we're supposed to be. We've already covered this section of the grid."

"I know."

"If we're in a sector we've already covered, we're wasting daylight."

Lincoln unscrewed the top of his canteen and took a pull. He exhaled and wiped his mouth with his sleeve. "I'm taking us to the Field of the First Families. I want to see the last place Dani saw James alive."

Ballard sighed and folded the map. "When were you going to tell me?"

One corner of Lincoln's mouth curled. "When we got there."

The sheriff's face flushed. "I took a chance on you, and you pull this?"

"Come on, Reg. Trust me."

She cast a dark gaze at him. She whistled and made a circle in the air with her index finger. "Round 'em up." She focused her hard gaze at Lincoln. "If we're retreading ground, we're wasting time."

"You're the one who thought you weren't getting anywhere with Clay."

"At least he did what he was told."

Ducard trotted in, his meaty form stomping the forest floor like an herebor. Gray and his sentries emerged from the thick behind them, the rest of their men crashing through the forest.

"What is it?" Ducard asked.

Ballard held up the map. "We're way off course."

Ducard grunted in satisfaction and smirked at Lincoln. "Lose your way, did you?"

Ballard stared hard at their guide. "No, he meant to lead us astray."

Ducard's eyes widened. "What?" He broke toward Lincoln with impressive acceleration and momentum, like a train fired from a rifle, but Lieutenant Gray caught him by the shoulders.

"Easy, big guy," Gray said.

Lincoln stood his ground. "I need to see where it took him."

"What are you going on about?" Ducard threw off Kennedy's grip and raised a hand to him to signal that he was okay. "Sheriff, we don't have to follow him. I say we leave him and head back to the grid. We all know what we're doing by now."

Lincoln cocked his head and peered at the sentry. "Is that so? You spent a few days in the wild, did you? You know where you're going now? There are things out here you can't even dream about. Things that can kill you, and I'm not talking about the herebors. That's the bottom of the food chain. Have you seen the carnivorous plants? The poisonous dart launching bushes? The ivy that will make your skin bleed if you just stand downwind from it? I've been sneaking past guys like you and coming out here since I was a kid. So did my father, and so did his father, and they taught me everything they knew."

"That sure worked out for your dad, didn't it?" Ducard said.

Ballard pre-emptively grasped Lincoln's shoulder, but Lincoln was smarter than that. With Ducard's brute strength, he knew it was a fight he couldn't win, so he shook the sheriff off and walked toward the east.

Ballard cut a reprimanding glance at Ducard and chased after Lincoln. "Where are you going?"

"Come or go back to your grid. I don't care. I'm going to where I'm most likely to find something." Lincoln set off again.

"Wait," Ballard called. She looked deep into his eyes, gazing at him for a long moment, simultaneously measuring his resolve and pleading with him to not make her choose. He felt the weight of it, the strength behind those icy blue irises.

"Lincoln sees the field," she said to the sentries. "Maybe he finds something we missed. If not, we return to the grid."

Although the sentries expressed their dissatisfaction with rumbling voices, they complied.

The search party spread out and pressed on. The rays of sunlight pouring through the tree canopy strengthened until mid-day, washing the wild in more vivid, intense shades of green. Although the forest air was cool, sweat beaded on their brows and dampened their clothing. Lincoln felt the wet stain under his backpack growing, but he didn't mind. He liked feeling his muscles work. He liked breathing the earthy scent of the wild. As it came alive, he too felt more alive, a heightened sense of being.

Perhaps humans belonged out here after all.

They came to a shallow, meandering stream, and Lincoln stopped at its bank, a small drop-off with exposed roots reaching from the earthen wall. Years ago, when the rains came more often and flowed down from the mountains, this stream had been a formidable river. It reminded him that the wild was changing after all. The whole world was changing.

"This is a good place to rest," he said.

They sat along the embankment, some of the sentries removing their boots, laying out their socks in a spring of sunlight that dashed through a break in the tree canopy, and dipping their feet into the running stream. They hooted at the cold water like children.

Lincoln filled his canteen and picked from his containers of nuts and dried fruit. Reinvigorated by the break, most of the sentries ate their provisions, talked, and laughed about inconsequential things happening in the colony. Down the embankment, silent and alone, Lyle Albright gazed into the ripples on the surface of the stream. Curious, Lincoln went to him and sat down.

"Don't you have anything to eat?" Lincoln asked.

Lyle shook his head. "Forgot."

Lincoln offered a friendly smile and his container of dried fruit.

Lyle reached for the food. "Thanks."

"No problem."

The deputy chewed in silence.

"What's on your mind, Lyle?"

"Nothing."

Lincoln peered at the boy, who was still lost in the stream. He breathed in the fresh air and swallowed the nuts he'd chewed to a salty paste.

The deputy sighed. "Do you ever feel like no one takes you seriously?"

"No. I have the opposite problem. Everyone takes me too seriously."

"Ballard was a deputy before she was sheriff. So was the sheriff before her."

"And you want to be sheriff one day."

"I don't know if I'm ever going to make it."

Lincoln put the lid on his container of nuts and set it aside. "Reggie wasn't always as hard as she is. She toughened up over the years as she needed to. If there's anything I know well, it's that you can't change how people see you. You can only take care of you and hope that changes. Now, you might be sheriff, you might not, but you'll be something. You'll fall into place somewhere. That I can assure you."

Lyle looked at Lincoln shyly. "No offense, but I don't want to work the pillar."

Lincoln grunted a laugh. "Neither did I, but you know what? Maybe I wasn't cut out to be sheriff either."

"You wanted to be sheriff?"

"No. But I found my place."

"Where was it?"

Lincoln smirked. "It wasn't the pillar."

Lyle's face wrinkled in confusion.

"It's out here," Lincoln said.

Ballard approached from behind them. "We have to get moving again. It won't be long before we have to start heading back. We won't have much time at the field."

The sheriff left to deliver her message elsewhere, and when Lincoln looked back to Lyle, the deputy was already gathering his things. The boy was awkward and unsure of himself. Lincoln could see it in his demeanor and the way he moved. Not only would he never be sheriff, but he would struggle to command respect his whole life.

"You have to be what you want to be before you can be it," Lincoln said.

"What?"

"No one becomes something and changes. You change and become the thing you want to be. If you want to be sheriff, you have to start acting like you already are. Stop allowing people to push you around. If you find yourself in a situation like that, pretend you already have the badge."

They continued east, first wading through the stream and then hacking through tangles of vines and foliage on the other side. If they had left the colony from an eastern wall, Lincoln could have had them on the path to the Field of the First Families in short order. However, since they'd left from the north gate, it took hours because no one ever went that way. The going was hard, and the terrain was unforgiving, but eventually, Lincoln led them to the path James and Dani had been on the night James had gone missing.

The search party fell in line behind Lincoln. Reading the architectural signs of the wild, he knew the field lay ahead. It surprised him to find the path cut by a large depression in the soil.

They surrounded it and examined it in awe.

"What the hell happened here?" Kennedy Gray asked.

Lincoln crouched. He dug his fingers into the loose dirt and examined the surrounding brush. Twigs had snapped. Otherwise healthy, thick branches were broken from their trunks. It looked like a hurricane had crushed this part of the forest.

While the search party gathered around the crater, Ballard pulled Lincoln aside.

"I've seen this before," she said.

Lincoln rubbed the dirt into his hands. "You mean this depression?"

Ballard shook her head. "We found a home in a clearing northwest of here. We went inside to question the family, but no one was there. It looked like they'd left in a hurry. In the basement was a depression, I guess you'd call it, a lot like this one. What do you think it means?"

Lincoln frowned and looked up the path. "Show me where the broken knife was."

"Lyle actually found it." Ballard motioned to the deputy, and the boy ran ahead. "It was in the field."

Lyle led them to the Field of the First Families. The vine-covered, rusted, and weathered ship stood in the distance like an ancient monolith, gleaming in the sunlight. The grass field swayed in the breeze as if in worship.

Lyle pointed down the tree line. "It was over there."

Lincoln examined the ground. The tall grass would make it difficult to find boot impressions, but if James had disturbed the grass enough as he tore through, Lincoln would find the trail.

He waded through the field, hugging the tree line, imagining the night James had gone missing. It had been dark, and the boy was scared. His familiar path had been cut off, so he ran away and was looking for...what? A way to loop back around to get back on the pathway?

The tall grass waved and rustled against Lincoln's legs. His heart pounded from the exhilaration of feeling the chase, and his eyes searched the ground for any sign of disturbance. Looking over the top of the grass, Lincoln stopped and cocked his head. Multiple paths were carved through

the field. They originated from different points, but ahead, they converged.

"What is it?" Ballard asked from behind Lincoln, and the sound of her voice startled him from his trance. He looked back at her stoic yet beautiful face. She was simultaneously inquisitive and concerned.

"Something heavy and powerful was here, chasing him. There were three of them."

"Herebors?"

Lincoln shook his head. Then he ran to a tree at the edge of the field and climbed to the first branch.

Ducard watched Lincoln with a twisted, mystified expression. "What the hell is this guy doing?"

"I have no idea," Gray said.

"You think maybe he's not all there?"

Gray laughed.

Ballard eyed them with a gaze that froze them into sobriety.

"Sorry, Sheriff," Gray said.

From the tree, Lincoln confirmed that three paths of destruction converged. He traced them toward the direction in which they'd come and found they began out in the field, as if whatever had chased James had materialized from nothing.

"No," Lincoln whispered to himself. "Not herebors."

"It was here." The deputy waved his hand from farther down one of the paths.

Lincoln leaped from the tree and hit the ground on a trot. Ballard and the rest of the search party followed.

The deputy stood in a small arena carved out of the field. The grass was depressed and torn as if a chaotic whirlwind had descended on this specific location for only a moment and then was gone. Sharp divots dipped into the ground as if powerful fists had pounded the earth in a circular dance. Lincoln discovered deep boot impressions. James had planted his feet under him and then something had pushed him backward. The boy had made a stand here.

"Did Clay see this?" Lincoln asked.

"No," Lyle said. "I brought the knife handle to him. Why?"

Ballard and the search party caught up and stopped at the edge of the tall grass, gazing at the area in mute shock.

"Because if he'd seen this," Lincoln said, pointing ahead, "even he would have known where to go next."

Scattered in the trampled grass were spatters of a black stain. Lincoln kneeled and ran his finger through one of the spots, rubbing the gummy transfer between his fingertips.

Ballard kneeled beside him. "This looks like the stuff that was on the knife hilt."

"Why didn't you tell me about that?"

Ballard shrugged. "Thought it could be mud."

"It hasn't rained in weeks."

Ballard squeezed her eyes shut. "Now what?"

Lincoln pointed ahead. "Follow the trail."

The black stains beckoned in the waving, golden grass.

They pushed on. The separate paths converged, and here, the grass was trampled as if a stampede of cattle had cut a clear path of destruction through the field. The ground was pock marked with hundreds of those divots.

The path turned up a rocky incline. The soft earth beneath their feet became a hard boulder, covered in spots by moss and patchy grass. The incline became so steep that they had to bend forward and use the cracks and edges in the rock face as hand and foot holds. Their rubber boots skittered across the surface as they climbed, and Lincoln found several rubber transfers from James' soles. Not one of them hesitated or complained about the difficulty of the chase. Each of the men and women in the search party pushed on, and renewed by the only signs of James Bellman that they'd seen since the broken bush knife, they began to call his name.

"James!"

When they crested the rise, the boulder plateaued. A massive overhang arched over the surface like a tilted hat, as if the rock had been cleaved and tipped. One by one, the last sentries reached the top and fell silent, gazing ahead into the gloom of the shade created by the overhang.

Set deep in the hill, a dark cave gaped like a wound in the earth. The surrounding landscape was bare and rocky. The wind rustled the trees, and a moaning whipped from the cave.

"Ever seen this before?" Ballard asked. "Lincoln?"

He was kneeling and touching the ground. A splash of red adorned the craggy surface.

"No," he said. "Ever seen this?"

"It's blood."

Lincoln pointed ahead to the cave. "It leads there."

"How do you know whatever was bleeding wasn't coming out of there?" Ducard asked.

"You can tell by looking at it which way it was falling," Ballard said. "The amount here indicates pooling. My guess is it's James', and he was hurt. When he got to the top, he lay here a moment, then ran into there."

Lincoln and Ballard walked toward the cave.

"We're going in there?" Lyle looked at his sheriff timidly.

"Lincoln and I will check it out," Ballard said. "The rest of you form up out here. Yell if you see anything."

"Like what?" Lyle asked.

Ballard eyed her deputy and followed Lincoln. The sentries fanned out and faced the cave entrance, eyeing the darkness within.

All light died at the threshold. Lincoln and Ballard clicked on their flashlights. The air was warm and humid, and a stench like decay set them aback.

"Is that decomp?" Ballard said. "Have we found a body?"

Lincoln grimaced and reached behind Ballard where a bloody handprint adorned the cave wall. "Maybe."

Shining his flashlight on the blood trail, Lincoln moved into the darkness. Ballard unholstered her revolver.

They had to watch their step on the uneven floor. A crevice could swallow a boot and break an ankle. A jutting lip could steal their balance and send them tumbling. This labyrinth was something they couldn't have imagined before coming to it. It was an alien world. Beneath the surface, Lumen was unrecognizable. More than that, something deep within them, an instinct, was setting off an alarm. They didn't belong here.

Lincoln halted.

"What is it?" Ballard asked.

Unmoving, shining his light down, he didn't respond.

Ballard's breath hitched. "Did you find him?"

A pause.

"No," Lincoln said.

Ballard moved beside Lincoln. Her flashlight hit something and made a strong glare. They had found the other half of James' bush knife, but neither of them had the desire to claim it.

The blade's jagged, broken tip jutted into the air, its shaft buried in the abdomen of an overturned creature neither of them had ever seen or even dreamed of in their darkest nightmares.

Gleaming like onyx, the creature's black exoskeleton covered a slender body that was bigger than any man. From its body, eight powerful legs curled like fingers in a death grip. Coarse black hair sprouted from its limbs and back like quills. On one end, a jagged stinger curved into the air. On the other end, a maw with dagger-sized teeth lay open in a grimace.

This was what took Lincoln's father. This was what took his wife. This was what took James Bellman.

Ballard gaped in awe and horror. "Have you seen one of these before?"

Terrified, angry, humbled, Lincoln shook his head. "Exo," he said.

"What?"

"It has an exoskeleton. It's an exo." He shrugged. "I have no idea what it is."

He leaned in, peering at the face, finding six beady, glassy eyes staring back at him. He moved around it, and he could have sworn those eyes followed him. Lincoln examined its armored legs and back, an exoskeleton that looked hard as stone. The underbelly, where James had buried his bush knife, looked like leather, a vulnerable spot.

Ballard took out her camera and snapped a picture.

On the other side of the creature, they discovered a blood smear, and the cave dropped abruptly, a hole that opened in the earth. With the dust thick in the air, their lights couldn't penetrate the darkness. Through the gloom, they couldn't see how deep it went.

Lincoln swung his pack off of his back and set it on the ground. "I have rope."

"I don't know if I can let you go down there."

Lincoln stopped rifling through his pack. "With the blood loss, this drop, and these things chasing him, I know he's probably dead, but Elena needs to know. I can't tell her that he's gone if we don't know for sure. I won't."

"He was dragged from here, Lincoln. Dragged."

"Can you look into her eyes and tell her without a doubt that her son is gone?"

A light beamed from the cave entrance. "Ballard." It was Ducard.

"Alain, don't come in here," she said.

"All right, but the sun is getting low. We should head back soon."

Ballard looked to Lincoln with eyes of appeal. "We'll come back tomorrow. I promise."

Lincoln's face burned with rage. "James!" he shouted into the hole. "James!"

Ballard snatched Lincoln's arm. "We have to go."

Then they heard an answer. It was a sound no human could make, a screech that came from deep within the cave and reverberated through the cave walls, surrounding their bodies like electricity and penetrating to the bone.

They froze and gazed into the darkness.

Then they fled. Emerging from the cave, they found the sentries with their rifles leveled.

Ducard lowered his weapon. "What's going on?"

"We have to go," Ballard said. "Now."

The sheriff grabbed Lyle by the shirt and pulled. The sentries fell out one by one, covering the cave until the last man.

The search party raced down the hill and across the Field of the First Families, back through the paths of destruction that the exos had carved into the land. Seeing the diverting trails again, Lincoln remembered there were still at least two more of those things. James, as strong as he was for such a young man, had only taken one. Having seen it, Lincoln wasn't sure a grown man could have done any better.

At the edge of the forest, Lincoln looked across the field and over the rolling hills at the ship that had brought the human race to Lumen hundreds of years ago. Shadows were growing up from the earth as the sun tucked itself behind the mountains and the trees.

"Lincoln," Kennedy Gray called from the path into the forest. "Lincoln, come on!" They weren't waiting for him. The search party was in chaos. People were disappearing into the wild, and it was already plunging into darkness.

"Wait!" Lincoln broke for the trees. "Don't go in there!"

His heart drumming, Lincoln ran up the path behind Kennedy Gray. In a whirlwind of trees and dying light, he followed, knowing that, if he lost them, they would never make it back to the colony. If he didn't stop them, they wouldn't beat nightfall.

"Wait!" Lincoln called.

"Hold!" Gray ordered, and the sentries passed the word up the line. They gathered on the path, doubled over and gasping.

"If we stay on this path, we won't beat sunset," Lincoln said. "We have to go west, through the trees."

"It's getting real dark in here," Alain Ducard said. "We leave this path and we're bound to lose someone."

Everyone looked to Ballard. She looked at Lincoln in that searching way. Lincoln stared straight back. It was her call.

"We go through the trees," she said.

Lincoln clicked on his flashlight and broke into the forest. "Stay within earshot. We won't lose anyone if we can hear each other's voices."

"Everyone sounds off," Ducard growled.

The search party dove into the wild with flashlights beaming in all directions.

They moved through the forest without incident. Lincoln led them around thickets and down deadfall-covered embankments, spotlights at their footsteps in the growing dark.

"Dyson?" Ducard said.

"Here!"

They splashed through brooks with slick, worn rock beds.

"Hall?"

"Right here."

They hacked passage through walls of vines, the trees shuddering with their blows.

"Fowler?"

"Here."

They pushed on until the dusk grew into night in the forest, and the whole world went silent.

"Irving?"

The party stopped. Nothing moved.

"Irving!?"

A breeze swelled through the trees like rising static in their ears. They waited for a response, but none came. In a moment, with the wind reaching a crescendo, only the earth answered Ducard's call, a slight quiver beneath their feet that deceived them into thinking their own legs were shaking, growing into a trembling rumble.

Ballard turned at a powerful squeeze to her shoulder. Lincoln's eyes glistened in the glow of their flashlights.

"We have to move!"

Lincoln pulled Ballard into the darkness, and Ducard and Gray stared in wonder as their guide and sheriff disappeared into the nothing. The sentries followed, the beams from their flashlights casting the whole forest in a disco of dancing lights.

Vaulting over a fallen tree, Lincoln glanced back. A light vanished. He stopped and watched. Then another went out. And another.

The rumbling grew around them, no longer only laying chase behind them, but reaching around like arms closing in an embrace.

Lincoln pushed the men and women forward as they passed the fallen tree. "Keep going!" All they could do, the only thing they could do now, was keep moving.

Lyle was in the middle of the pack, eyes wide in silent screams, laboring from the chase, and Lincoln pulled the young man forward with a strong grasp on his arm. He wasn't going to let go.

More lights disappeared. Screams were cut short. The hairs on the back of Lincoln's neck were rising, the primal sense that something was drawing near.

In the panic, the sentries fired their weapons at nothing. Automatic rifle fire tore through the trees. A magazine clicked empty. Flashlights disappeared. The firing stopped.

They weren't going to make it.

Ahead, the colony's perimeter lights battled the darkness at the edge of the wild. Above, the tree canopy was beginning to open, and the first hints of the aurora peeked through. In another situation, these signs of sanctuary may have given Lincoln hope, but with more flashlights going out around him, the sense that their pursuers were drawing closer, and the world around them beginning to shake so violently they were having trouble staying on their feet, the colony seemed just out of reach.

Lincoln focused on Lyle. At the edge of their salvation, the deputy was beginning to fall to exhaustion. Lincoln pushed him forward.

"Keep moving! You're almost there!"

Something brushed Lincoln's back. It could have been a branch springing back into place. It could have been the wind whipping his shirt as he ran with every ounce of speed he could muster. He knew it was neither of those things.

A few steps later, something punched his shoulder and sent him careening forward.

"Move!"

Then, he experienced a moment of solitude in a silent, breathing world. His heartbeat slowed even as his legs pumped like pistons, and he had a euphoric thought of Shane and Bernie. He thought of Lucy's mischievous smile, of Aeron's disapproving scowl, knowing his brother really only ever wanted the best for him. He thought of Reggie, hoping she'd made it. Then he thought of his wife and swore he heard her voice behind him.

A crushing weight fell onto his shoulders, and Lincoln crumpled. His flashlight clattered on the dirt, and he looked forward to ensure the others were still running. They were, but shadows moved through the trees, closing in on them.

Lincoln rolled onto his back, grasping dirt in the search for his flashlight. The trembling earth grew around him, and then it passed him. All around, there was the sound of cracking trees and snapping limbs. Above him, he heard breathing.

He knew what stood there in the darkness, but he had to see it. His fingers grasped the fallen flashlight, and when he swung its beam above him, he found the majesty of one of those exo creatures rising above him, its front legs raised to deliver a deathblow. Lincoln thought this was when James had seized his opportunity to drive his bush knife into the exo's soft underbelly, but he did not have time to pull his own from its sheath.

As the creature drove its legs down, Lincoln met its eyes.

So did his flashlight's beam.

The exo screeched and jerked away. Its eight legs pounded the ground as it careened into a tree trunk. Its massive armored body cracked the tree like a lightning bolt. Lincoln watched mystified as the creature shook its head and turned back to him, venom dripping from its curved teeth.

When the exo charged, he drove his flashlight's beam into its eyes, sending it scampering back again.

It adapted quickly. It raised a limb in front of its eyes and leaned to charge again.

Automatic rifle fire lit the forest with a strobe effect. Kennedy Gray launched a volley of rounds at the exo's belly. It stumbled, caught itself, then crumpled to the forest floor.

"Go!" Gray said. "Get to the—"

A shadow reached out and snatched him into the darkness.

The wild was coming alive around Lincoln, and he could do nothing for the sentry. The colony was still his only salvation. Alone now, Lincoln ran.

He scanned the forest in front of him with his flashlight and saw more of those creatures than he could count. The light burned their eyes and pushed them away, parting a sea of writhing bodies. They ran into the darkness, but Lincoln had no doubt they were regrouping behind him.

His light cleared the way, and then he saw the edge of the forest and a handful of people gazing in awe.

Lincoln emerged from the trees and glanced back at the seething forest. Just beyond the reach of the colony's perimeter lighting, the shiny, armored limbs of their pursuers shook the trees and pounded the earth. Their arms reached into the light like prisoners clamoring for freedom.

As the remaining search party stood in shocked silence, a hole erupted from the earth only meters away. Another eruption threw dirt into the air on the other side of them. The exos were burrowing under their feet and trying to pull them down where the light couldn't reach.

More sinkholes shot dirt into the air around them, but as the search party huddled in the field, new sinkholes formed farther away from them. Lincoln took note of who was left and found only Ballard, Lyle, and Ducard.

"Kennedy?" Ducard's eyes were pleading. "Kennedy!"

Lincoln snatched the big man's arm. "Don't."

Ducard glared at Lincoln with an intensity he saved only for his most mortal enemies.

"If you move, we die."

A final expulsion of dirt jumped into the air, and then the shaking in the earth pulled back into the wild until the ground steadied once again.

While the search party survivors waited for salvation and the sentries on the colony's perimeter wall searched the trees with spotlights, the entire wild erupted in a shriek of frustrated, tempted loss, an anguished sound that then fell silent.

CHAPTER 4
EXECUTIVE ORDER

One

At the warden's home, Gabe and Mel sat on the living room floor, playing Lore. Gabe was guiding his knight through a cavernous dungeon in search of the Burning Witch Sisters. Mel's priestess followed, healing Gabe's knight when he needed it and casting spells to weaken enemies as they came after him.

Bernie lay on the couch. She was playing too, but her mage was out gathering herbs for potions. In the world of Lore, Bernie was an herbalist and alchemist.

Breathing deeply, she blinked her glassy red eyes, struggling to focus on the brilliant colors of the cards. She didn't feel much like playing right now, but there wasn't much else that could keep her mind off of the setting sun and her overdue father.

Lucy walked through the archway from the kitchen and brushed Bernie's hair back. "Can I get you anything?"

Bernie shook her head ever so slightly.

Lucy turned to her own children. "What about you guys?"

"No thanks, Mom," they said in unison.

It never ceased to amaze Lucy how perceptive children were. When Lucy had told them Lincoln had gone into the wild to look for James, it didn't matter that he'd been out there more than anyone in the colony. It didn't matter that she reassured them everything was going to be okay. They were afraid. All of her attempts to get their minds off of it had failed.

As the day wore on, that anxiety had grown because the truth was, Lucy had felt an increasing unease, and they sensed it. They fed off of it.

She gazed at her husband, who stood in the bay window overlooking the commons. Lucy went to him and wrapped her arms around his chest. She lay her head on his shoulder and felt the rise and fall of his slow breathing.

"It's quiet out there," she said.

"Mmm hmm."

Lucy listened to his steady heartbeat. Aeron took her hands in his, rubbing a knuckle with his thumb.

"He's all right," she said. "He knows the wild better than anyone. I bet he's just late because he found something."

Aeron pulled away and couldn't look at her. He faced her with something like shame. "I shouldn't have let him go," he said.

"Why? There's no one better."

"Because you're probably right. He probably found something."

Lucy's face tightened with confusion. "What do you—"

A knock at the front door interrupted her. Aeron and Lucy froze in each other's stares and then rushed to answer it.

The children looked up from their games.

Lucy tore open the door. At the sight of the person who had come to their home, she deflated, stepped back, and yielded to Aeron.

Sentry Dana Sibley stood on the front steps, out of breath. "Sir. They're back."

Lucy gasped with a hand on her chest. "Thank Lumen."

Aeron glanced at the kids, who were eagerly awaiting more information, and then stepped outside and pulled the door closed behind him.

"Why are they late?" he said.

"They hit some trouble," Sibley said. "Only a few of them made it."

"Is my brother one of them?" When she didn't respond immediately, he grabbed her shoulders. "Is Lincoln one of them!?"

"I don't know. As soon as we saw them come out of the wild, I was ordered to run and get you."

Aeron released her and stepped back, rubbing his stubbly chin. "I'm sorry. Where are they?"

"The east gate."

"Thank you, Sentry." Aeron eyed his curious neighbors who were coming out of their homes and looking on curiously.

"Head on back, and make sure they get their space," the warden said.

She nodded and jogged down the steps.

"And Sentry?"

She turned back. "Sir?"

"Report immediately to your superior for duty assignment. Understand?"

"Yes, sir."

He saw in her eyes she understood she wasn't to speak to anyone else.

Sentry Sibley ran up the street, and he stood still and silent on the steps, processing what it all meant. No matter how he tried to rectify it, one thought was always the result. It was here. The day he'd always dreaded had come.

He went back inside to Lucy's apprehensive, expectant gaze.

"What is it?" she asked.

Aeron glanced to the children in the living room, then back to his wife. "I have to go."

"Go where?"

"The east gate. There was a problem."

"What kind of a problem?"

"I'm not sure."

Bernie was on her feet, a tightness in her demeanor as if she might snap or unravel.

Lucy grabbed the children's coats from the rack on the wall. "We're coming with you."

When Aeron opened his mouth to argue, Lucy stopped him with a raised hand. "We're coming with you." Her determined stare cut through him, and she gathered the children.

"All right," he said. "Let's go."

Gabe and Mel leaped to their feet. Aeron ushered them all outside and followed, closing the door behind him. They hurried down the steps. Some other families on their street were doing the same. They rushed up the road and through the commons where more people had gathered. Word was spreading through the colony. By the time Aeron, Lucy, and the kids arrived at the east gate, hundreds of other colonists had crowded into a crescent of mystified faces.

"Make way!" Aeron pushed through the people with his family in tow. Bodies had compacted so quickly it was already difficult to move forward. They held hands to be sure they didn't lose each other in the throng.

When they made it to the front of the crowd, the gate began to rise with maddening indifference. Its heavy iron gears clinked like a mechanical countdown. Then the crowd gaped upon the four survivors. No one made a sound. Their clothing was filthy and torn. Scratches and

blood slashed their faces and limbs. The worst sight was the look in their traumatized eyes. It told their story. It said they were the only ones left.

It said something out there had claimed the others.

Lincoln moved forward, the limping Alain Ducard leaning on him for support. Sheriff Ballard consoled the vacant-eyed Lyle Albright as they lurched and stumbled through the open gate.

The colonists met them with relentless, scrutinizing gazes and silence.

As the gate clanked closed, Lincoln scanned the crowd, grimacing when he found his brother among them.

The colonists waited, their questions bubbling under the surface. It was in their eyes: *Where are the others?*

"Daddy!" Bernie broke free of Lucy's hold and ran to her father.

He collapsed to one exhausted knee as his daughter leaped into his arms. He ran his fingers through her hair and kissed the side of her head, breathing in her pure scent. He clutched her tiny, fragile body. His precious, innocent daughter.

All he could think of was how she was in mortal danger. They all were.

That was when Lincoln's tears came; holding his daughter, feeling the warmth of her breath against his neck, he felt, not just knew, that he was out of the wild and home, but he was not safe. They perhaps never would be again.

Murmurs circulated among the crowd.

Lincoln rose and walked forward with Bernie clutching his waist. He stood before Aeron, and the warden's pained, glassy eyes peered at him. Aeron regarded his baby brother for a moment, and then Aeron grabbed Lincoln around the back of his neck and pulled Lincoln in for an embrace.

"Are you hurt?" Aeron asked.

"I'll be all right."

Confused voices rose around the brothers.

"Where are the others?"

"Are they lost?"

"Open the gate. They have to be just outside."

"Where's Frederick? Where's my son?"

Aeron let go of Lincoln and raised his hands for the crowd's silence. "Everyone, please! Calm down!"

In spite of his plea, the voices rose into shouting accusations and spitting anger. It wasn't long before almost everyone who had gathered at the east gate was clamoring for answers.

"I know you have questions!" Aeron said. "Please, calm down!"

But it wasn't their warden they were looking to. It was Lincoln. They thought he had the answers because they blamed him for whatever misfortune had befallen the others. If this went on any longer, they were going to tear him apart.

Aeron waved to the nurses who were arriving with their ambulance carts. "Get them out of here!"

With sentries struggling to maintain control, the nurses swept in and took the survivors through the increasingly hostile crowd to the carts, whisking them away to the infirmary.

At Aeron's direction, each of the survivors was given a private room, which was peaceful and isolated from the public, so they didn't have to speak to anyone.

So they couldn't speak to anyone.

Two

Surrounded by angry colonists, Aeron waited at the infirmary's main entrance. He had sent his family home with the promise that they could see Lincoln in the morning. Lucy had protested, but she relented when Aeron made the case that Lincoln and the others needed medical attention and rest.

Some of those in the raging crowd were the families of the missing sentries. Gideon Ford was at the front, urging them forward, stoking their anger. Aeron was once again between his people and the truth. Or at least, that was how Gideon wanted them to see it.

Sentries had formed a perimeter to keep people from rushing inside, and they had cordoned off an access lane for essential personnel. Aeron wasn't sure of the sentries. Nineteen of their own were missing, and he suspected if answers didn't come soon, they would turn on him and force the truth from his mouth.

Yet as they were trained, they held the line until reinforcements arrived. It came in the commanding presence of Captain Ezra Barrow.

The big, non-native soldier marched up the break in the crowd, followed by ten sentries, some of his best and most loyal, carrying full battle gear. They wore white vests, overcoats, and pants, specifically made so they could blend into Vale's perimeter wall. Various armaments rattled from their clips, which secured them to the sentries' uniforms. They held their rifles at the ready instead of securing them in a sling over their shoulder.

Barrow waved two fingers in the air, and two of his men peeled off to fortify the line holding the colonists back.

Barrow's face was hard, blank, and unreadable. Aeron couldn't tell if he was about to receive the man's support or face his wrath. The warden had imagined a scenario in which Barrow supplanted him and took over the colony, but Barrow had always been exceedingly loyal.

The sentries stopped in front of their warden. Barrow took a deep breath, and his broad chest swelled. Aeron thought he heard the man growl on exhale.

"Your sentry service reporting to secure the perimeter for our survivors, Warden."

Barrow spoke deliberately and with a measure of ceremony. A hint of anger surfaced on his face but only for an instant. It was clear to Aeron that even Barrow was conflicted, but the important part was he had chosen duty, and as long as he continued to do so, Aeron could count him as an ally.

"Captain, I'm glad you're here," Aeron said.

"I understand only one of my men returned. Who?"

"Ducard."

Barrow's lip quivered. Still unable to wrap his head around it, he shook his head.

"Well then," Barrow said. "Shall we go talk to our survivors?"

Aeron opened the door and led the way inside. Before the sentries entered, Barrow ordered two more of his men to guard the main entrance.

As they walked through the infirmary, nurses and patients watched them with equal parts curiosity and suspicion. Only moments earlier, this place of healing and wellness had been disrupted by the incoming survivors plowing through the gamut of triage, medical interviews, and placement away from the other patients. The drama that played out was shocking and exciting; however, the warden and a team of elite sentries charging through was ominous of retribution on the way.

Twice more, Barrow commanded a pair of his men to break off and secure a checkpoint along the route to the interior of the hospital.

"Is this really necessary?" Aeron asked as they entered the private wing.

"What?" Barrow said.

"The show of force."

Barrow sneered. "Those people out there are ready to tear your damn throat out for answers. They want nothing more than to come in here and demand them. Yes, it's necessary."

When they reached the private wing, a crash and sounds of metal tumbling on the stone floor made them hurry to the first survivor's room.

Dressed in a white gown, Alain Ducard was trying to tear his intravenous catheter from his arm, and three nurses were struggling with him. A metal tray and medical instruments lay scattered on the floor.

"You're dehydrated," a nurse said. "You have to leave it in. It'll help you feel better."

"You ain't tyin' me down," Ducard growled. He grunted when the IV snapped free, and stomped across the room, pinching the back of his gown closed. "Where are my clothes?"

Barrow charged in. "At ease, Sergeant."

The big man flinched and gaped at his captain. "Sir."

"These people are trying to help you, Alain. You will let them. Understood?"

"Yes, sir."

Barrow turned to leave.

"Sir...Kennedy, he—"

"We will debrief in the morning, Sergeant."

Barrow stared down his sentry with predatory dominance, but something about Ducard's sorrowful expression changed Barrow, and some understanding passed between them.

Barrow's man had returned, but he certainly was not the same man.

Compliant now, Ducard sat on his bed, and the nurses timidly surrounded him.

"Yeah, yeah." He waved at them and lay on the bed.

Aeron had never liked Ducard. He found the sentry crude and intimidating. However, Ducard had lost many of his friends tonight.

On top of everything, Ducard had survived, and that was something sentries didn't do. They were trained to fight to the last man. They either achieved victory in defending their colony, or they died with it. It was a culture of no compromise that Barrow had brought with him when he had come to Lumen, and the idea that Ducard was now a survivor was an insult to his identity.

In the hallway, among a flurry of rushing nurses, Dr. Osman was speeding by with his attention focused on patient charts. He moved with the practiced confidence of having intimate knowledge of his building and possessing keen peripheral vision so as not to run into anything. Aeron caught him before he flew by. The doctor looked simultaneously confused, startled, and annoyed.

"How is everyone?" Aeron asked.

The blank look of surprise evaporated from Dr. Osman's face as he adjusted his attention. "Other than minor lacerations, bruises, and dehydration, they're all fine."

"What about Ducard? He was limping pretty bad on the way in."

"Just a sprain. There's no serious injury here. They'll be free to go tonight."

Dr. Osman turned to continue with his work.

Aeron grabbed his arm. "Just a minute, Doctor."

"I have other patients, Aeron."

"I know, and I'm sorry. It's just that, if we let them leave without addressing the colony, the people out there will eat them alive."

Osman peered at Aeron. "My infirmary isn't a fortress. There are sick and injured people here. This is a place of healing. Those people out there are disruptive and dangerous, and we can't stop patients from leaving if they want to."

"I'm not asking you to defend them or lock them up. I'm just suggesting maybe they should stay overnight for observation. At least they'll get some rest. Just until I figure out how I'm going to handle this. That's all I'm asking. One night."

Osman pursed his lips. "All right. They can stay the night. But tomorrow, you better have handled it. Now please excuse me. My staff here is taking good care of your patients, but I have others I have to see tonight."

The doctor left Aeron before he could say anything else. Osman's quickness stunned the warden. He was not used to being treated with such indifference.

"He's getting the job done," Barrow offered. "You shouldn't take it personally."

Aeron frowned. "Dr. Osman delivered both me and my brother. He was an important adviser for my father, and when I took over, he helped guide me. He's never spoken to me like that before."

"That doctor delivered most of the people in this colony, Aeron." He patted the warden's shoulder. "Come on."

They moved on down the hall, passing Lyle, who lay still on his bed while a nurse tended to him. They passed an empty room, then arrived at Lincoln's room and found Ballard with him. Their nurses were treating them as they sat beside each other on the bed.

Aeron knocked on the doorjamb. "Hey."

"Hey," Lincoln said.

"Nurses," Aeron said, "would you mind giving us some time alone?"

One of them unwrapped a blood pressure monitor from Lincoln's arm and stashed it in a cabinet. The other scribbled some notes on Ballard's chart, and they both left like spirits off to do good elsewhere.

Waving his last pair of sentries to guard the room, Barrow entered with Aeron, and they closed the door.

Lincoln gazed at his brother in suspicion. "Keeping us overnight?"

"As a precaution."

Lincoln craned his neck to look through the window at the people gathered outside. "Sure."

Barrow stood steadfast by the door. Aeron sat in the recliner beside the bed. The old springs groaned. He pressed his fingertips together into a pyramid, like a man about to make a deal.

"You two okay?" Aeron asked.

"That's a stupid question." Ballard glared at him, her icy blue irises swimming in a sea of red.

"Reggie," Lincoln said.

Her glare shot to him. "What? It is."

Aeron nodded. "It was a stupid question. Okay. Tell me what happened."

Lincoln blinked, remembering. "We went to the Field of the First Families. I had to see where Dani last saw James. Found evidence of a struggle."

Aeron leaned forward. "Did you find James' body?"

Lincoln shook his head. "Honestly, I don't think we ever will. I tracked him. The trail ended when we found something else."

"What?"

"The darkness, Aeron. I don't know what else to call it. Lumen's darkness."

"It's an animal, Lincoln."

Lincoln shut his eyes and shook his head. "You didn't see it."

"What did it look like?"

"Black, so black, like the light couldn't touch it. Legs like tree trunks, like it could pound a man into the ground." Lincoln took a deep breath. "It was dead. James had killed it. Most of its body is covered by a thick exoskeleton, but it has a softer underbelly. Ballard took a picture of it."

Aeron, Barrow, and Lincoln looked to her with expectation.

"Now?" she said.

Lincoln touched her hand. "It's okay. They need to see it too. They need to know."

"Know what?" Aeron said.

Barrow cleared his throat. "What we're up against."

Ballard retrieved her camera from the bedside table and handed it to the warden. She shook her head at them. "No," she said. "You need to know how this ends. How it was always going to end because you kept it a secret."

Confused, Aeron peered at her and tumbled the camera in his hands.

"It can be killed," the sentry captain said.

"I don't know that we can win in a fight," Lincoln said. "I don't know if that's the answer. James took one down, but that had to have been pure luck. And they're getting stronger."

Aeron released a long sigh and rubbed his forehead. "How strong?"

"I watched them take men in an instant. They just winked out. Gone. Plucked into the trees or sucked down into the earth. They are everywhere."

"This isn't the end of anything. The survey of the planet found they can't live in our atmosphere. Sooner or later, they will be gone, and until then, we have the wall. We just have to wait them out."

The warden rose to leave.

"You don't get it," Lincoln said. "One of them almost got me. It was on top of me. I was dead. But I had to see it, so I shined my flashlight into its eyes."

Aeron gazed, his full attention locked on his brother.

"The light hurts it," Lincoln said. "No matter what, keep the lights on. That's not going to save us though. Eventually they will get in, and when they do, it will be the end of us."

Aeron's jaw muscles flexed. He noted the haunted look in the eyes of his brother and the sheriff. He judged that, in time, they would be well again.

Time. Time was all they needed.

"Get some rest," Aeron said, and left them all in the hands of Dr. Osman and the Sentry Service.

Three

As the night wore on, the crowd outside the infirmary grew more hostile. To hold the colonists back, sentries strung lines of rope between metal posts they'd pounded into the ground. The people pushed in on those lines like a singular, seething mass, and Captain Barrow pulled more sentries from the wall to hold them back.

When Aeron emerged from the infirmary doors, they were waiting for him. The crowd erupted into accusations of shaking fists, pointing fingers, and raining spit. Their raucous voices crashed against his ears as they fought with each other to be heard. If he didn't stop it, they might start to crawl over each other for him.

Aeron held up a hand, and they fell silent. He breathed deeply, opening his throat and lungs for enough air to project his power and address a body of people he knew didn't want to listen; they wanted to be heard.

"Go home."

"What about the nineteen missing?" an old woman was pushing the rope taut with her fragile, aged hands.

"Twenty," the warden said. "We still haven't accounted for James Bellman."

"The boy is surely dead," said an old man who worked in the marketplace.

"We don't know that." Aeron stepped forward. "And as admirable as your passion is for the people who went missing tonight, as much as I sympathize with what you must be feeling right now, where was your concern for Elena Bellman's son?"

"The people in the infirmary might have answers," another man said.

"Those people in there have been out in the wild every day since James went missing, and they have seen things you all have the luxury of having a wall to protect you from. What have you done? Now, they've had an ordeal, and we won't be able to do anything about that tonight. I will address the colony in the morning. For now, please, go home. Be with your families."

Gideon Ford stood back in the crowd, a crooked smile slashing across his face. No one responded, and then he strode forward and glared at Aeron. "What about the families who are missing sons and daughters tonight, Warden? What will they find when they go home?"

"They will find no sleep, nothing to save them from the sympathy of the people who have already accepted what they never can," said a small voice from the crowd.

Elena Bellman emerged, and the people around her parted as if she were a pariah.

"But they have to look for hope," she said. "And they have to hold onto it."

Everyone froze. Even the sentries did nothing to stop her when she ducked under the rope and stood beside Aeron with a challenging stare.

The night wind whipped through an air of silence.

Gideon couldn't compete with the icon of a grieving mother.

"All right, everyone," he said. "You heard the warden. Let the authorities deal with it. I'm sure we'll all get our answers in the morning." His gaze on Aeron lingered, but he glanced to Mrs. Bellman with kindness, a softness in his aged, folding eyes.

Their zeal sapped, murmurs hummed in the crowd, and one by one, they left the infirmary entrance. When most of them were gone, Elena remained steadfast in front of Aeron, skirt flapping in the breeze, her stone expression unflinching.

"I have to talk to him," she said. "If Lincoln found something, I have to know. I can't go another night, not thinking he might know something."

Aeron bowed his head. "I know you're hurting, Elena, and I wish I could—"

"Don't you do that, Aeron Arokson. Don't you dare. Don't you pretend to empathize with me when what you really feel is your own guilt. You can dismiss me, but the guilt will still be there. It's a lie. You're lying to yourself. Stop hiding things, and tell me what's happened to my son."

"Elena." Aeron sighed. "We don't know anything."

"Stop saying that! You know something, and you're hiding it. Everyone can see, Aeron, and you think we can't take it, but we can. Not knowing is only going to hurt more."

She wiped her eyes with a trembling hand and turned away to regain her composure. When she faced him again, she had a snake's stare. "Answer me," she said. "Is my son alive?"

Aeron reached for her shoulders and she pulled away, her venomous glare persisting.

He sighed. "We don't know."

She shook her head. "Is my son dead? It's okay if he is. You can tell me. I need to know. Even if you just think he's not alive anymore, if you tell me I shouldn't hold onto hope, that will be enough."

Aeron looked into Elena's eyes then, and they resembled cracked dams, threatening to break. He saw her laser focus, her absolute determination that her grief would end here, that she wasn't going home for another night of uncertainty. She was at the mercy of motherhood; it tortured her. Although Aeron pitied her, he couldn't bring himself to release the flood of her tears.

"I won't tell you to give up," he said and looked to the two sentries standing just behind her. "Please escort Mrs. Bellman home."

As their hands grasped her arms, the waters burst forth anyway.

Four

When Aeron opened the front door of his home, he found the house quiet and serene. A certain tranquility accompanied the darkened rooms where loved ones lived when they were safe, accounted for, and resting. For Aeron, home was a sanctuary where, instead of feeling the weight of the entire colony upon him, he could just be a father and a husband. Home was a place with no judgment or expectation. Aeron could enjoy his family and feel like a person instead of the man most responsible for keeping Vale's pillar holding up the sky.

So it was with the feeling of belonging that he closed the front door, pressed his back against it, and simply closed his eyes and breathed. He let the silence permeate and ease his mind. Here, no one was clutching for answers. Here, everyone he loved was safe, and the nightmarish creatures couldn't reach him.

At least, not tonight.

However, with the Warden's Seal pulling heavily around his neck, Aeron never fully escaped his responsibility. In a way, coming home augmented it.

"What's going on out there?"

Aeron opened his eyes. Lucy stood in the dim hallway with her arms crossed. She had that adversarial look on her face like she was mad at him. When he'd sent her home with the children, she'd seen it as an affront to their partnership, and now she wanted to know what she'd missed. The whole colony looked to Aeron for answers, and the truth was he was beholden to her.

He rubbed his haggard face. "Everyone's gone home. Lincoln and the rest are staying at the infirmary. I have the sentries on guard to ensure no one bothers them."

"How long?" she said.

"What?"

"How long are you going to keep them there? Bernie needs her father."

Aeron held up his hands in surrender. "I don't want to fight about this."

She pressed with her stare. "How long?"

"Just tonight. Tomorrow, I'll figure something out. Okay?"

With thin lips, she nodded.

Aeron went to her and buried his face in her chest. She wrapped her arms around him and ran her fingers through his hair.

He released a deep sigh. "The kids okay?"

"Bernie took some consoling, but Mel and Gabe were more curious than anything."

He pulled away and met her gaze. "And you?"

"You know Bernie and Shane are like my own, since their mom passed. I don't want them to lose their father too." Lucy ran her hand over his back. "What about you? What's wrong?"

"You mean other than the nineteen missing colonists?"

"Twenty. But there's something else. I know you. You're faced with a challenge, and you find a way to overcome it. People are missing in the wild? Okay, you find them. But something has you worried. It's not your brother because he's safe now. So what is it?"

"Let's say there was a problem that you inherited and were told it would take care of itself, but it hasn't and it actually has gotten worse, much worse."

"I'd say quit being a baby and fix the problem."

"It isn't that simple. This problem can't be fixed. It can't be lived with, and it's only going to get worse."

She scoffed. "Aeron, you have to give me more here if you want me to help you. What is this really about?"

"The end of our world," Aeron said. "And I don't know if we can stop it."

Lucy pulled away. At arm's distance, she peered at Aeron, seeking the meaning of his words. "The pillar," she said. "Is it damaged? Is the terraforming going to fail? If so, we have to send a message to the other colonies and the central government."

Aeron wiped his face. "They wouldn't come."

"Why not?"

"A failed colony is a huge expense. So is taking on hundreds of thousands of refugees. And there's no accountability. If Lumen goes, none of the other worlds would know. Besides, it would take them months to reach us."

She shook her head in disbelief, or disappointment, or both. "How much time do we have?"

Aeron pulled Sheriff Ballard's camera from his pocket. He'd stopped on the way home and developed the film himself. She looked to him with expectant, confused eyes.

"Not enough." He handed the photograph to her and began his ascent up the stairs where he intended to stand in a warm shower until it got cold.

Lucy looked at the picture. As much as she wanted to, she couldn't look away from the thing that would snatch her children from her. In an instant, with no hesitation, she would give her life for them, but looking at this thing, she understood despair and panic. She knew that, even if she gave her life, it wouldn't save them.

"Close the gates." Lucy dashed to the foot of the stairs. "Lock everything down."

In response, she heard only a deep, unsettling quiet and then the rushing water through the pipes in the walls.

Five

When dawn broke on the next day, Aeron stood on the front steps of Arokson Hall after another sleepless night.

He wrestled with the decision of whether to tell the colony the truth.

The bell tower sounded above him, and Aeron drew a deep breath. He watched over the commons as the bell tolled. In time, people realized the bell was not sounding for routine, and they crossed the field in groups that grew in number until they were a continuous stream of bodies gathering before him. They looked up to him and whispered to each other, and Aeron didn't signal for the bell to cease until he looked out over the field and saw no more colonists answering the call.

When the last strike of the bell rang out across the valley, thousands of people looked to him, and Aeron let the silence linger if only because he wasn't quite sure how to begin. He had never addressed the colony like this. To his knowledge, neither had any warden before him, and the irregularity of it meant the colonists must have known something extraordinary was about to happen. The only respite from that unbearable pressure was knowing there was no turning back.

"Thank you all for coming," Aeron said, his voice filling the open field. "These past days have been hard on all of us, but none more so than the Bellman family. As of last night, nineteen more families now know what it feels like to not know the fate of a loved one.

"First, I'll address the members of the search party who returned to us last night. They are all okay and ready to leave the infirmary. I want you all to respect their privacy and need for recuperation, so I'm going to tell you all we've learned from them. All questions will go through my office, and from now on, questioning these four who returned to us last night about their experiences in the wild without their consent will be punishable by law. I won't have them forced into seclusion by their own people. The dissemination of information is why the warden's office exists, so don't look to them. Look to me.

"Until yesterday, the search party had found no trace of James Bellman. Under new guidance from my brother, the party revisited the original location where Dani Hines said she last saw James. Lincoln discovered a new trail that the party previously missed. They followed it, but the trail went cold and couldn't be pursued farther. In an effort to gather as much information as they could, the party lost track of time, and when they turned back, there wasn't enough daylight to make it to the colony.

"After nightfall, the party was still making its way through the wild, and in the dark, people got lost. Only Sheriff Ballard, Deputy Albright, Sentry Sergeant Ducard, and my brother made it to the main gate. The others are presumed to still be out there.

"Now, as much as I sympathize with the families who are missing loved ones, we have to think of the other families in the colony."

Aeron looked to Captain Barrow and nodded. The captain waved his hand, and a dozen armed sentries burst from the Arokson Hall doors, marched forward, and established a line on the front steps. The crowd began to stir.

"Effective immediately, I am issuing an executive order to place the colony on lockdown. For your own protection, everyone is to remain within the town center. You all are to limit travel within the colony to business. Essential personnel will continue to report to work, and hours at the marketplace will be limited. If anyone leaves our walls, you will not be allowed back in. I have authorized Captain Barrow to use deadly force if anyone is caught trying to enter this colony."

Cries erupted from the crowd.

"Of the missing, alive or dead, we can do no more to help them. They are on their own. But I am confident, with help from sentry actions on the perimeter wall, they will find their way home."

The colonists now were seething, and many of them threatened to advance. The sentries met these people with leveled rifles.

"I know this is difficult to accept, but we have to conserve what we have. Rest assured that, while we will send no more people into the wild, we're not giving up hope. We will do what we can to reclaim our people or at least guide them home."

Aeron's people clamored for him, screaming and reaching with such passion that he feared a force might span the distance between them and pull him in. He hadn't expected a different outcome. Looking upon them, he realized that, other than the sentries' rifles, the only thing that kept them apart was a rift he'd torn in his colony that they would very much like to cross. He knew he had successfully moved the focus away from the returning search party and onto himself.

Everyone was now looking to him for answers, and it was just as he wanted it.

Everyone, that was, except for Elena Bellman, whom Aeron saw leave the gathered colonists and run off across the field toward the infirmary. Aeron could do nothing to stop her because the entire colony stood in his way. He could only retreat into Arokson Hall, lock himself inside, and hope his people would allow him to leave before too long.

Six

Lincoln woke to the static of raised voices in the commons. Warm sunlight beamed through the infirmary room window. Every muscle in his body burned from the adrenaline overdrive of the previous night, and resigned to his confinement, he had slept, the creatures beneath the earth plaguing his restless dreams.

Curious about the noise, he looked to the window. The glare blurred his vision, and he covered his sweaty forehead with a trembling, clammy hand. Even with exhaustion and ache sapping his will to move, he had to see what was going on.

Rolling over and pulling the wool blanket off of his damp torso, the muscles in his back drew tight like tethers on his spine, and he groaned. The tile floor felt cool and refreshing on the soles of his feet, and he sat there on the side of his bed for a moment, eyes closed, breathing, just to be sure he wouldn't get dizzy when he stood.

When he rose, it felt like shards of broken glass twisted in his legs, and he leaned on the cart of electronic equipment beside his bed, waiting for the pain to pass. He couldn't be sure it would, but as he stood there and stretched, his leg muscles loosened. He had never felt so much like age was catching up with him.

He crossed the room and placed his hand on the warm wood of the windowsill. Squinting into the sunlit colony, he saw no one in the marketplace or the streets. Doors to shops and businesses had been left open, and for a moment, he feared the worst, that the exos had found their way into the colony and taken everyone overnight.

Gazing over the commons, he saw his fellow colonists amassing before Arokson Hall, their voices carrying over the empty field like gusting wind through the trees of the wild.

His door burst open, and Lincoln turned with a start. Elena Bellman stood there gasping, running footfalls and jingling metal approaching down the hallway. Elena gaped at Lincoln for a moment, and a pair of hands grabbed her shoulder.

"I'm sorry, sir," a sentry said. "Most of us were called to Arokson Hall. She shouldn't be here. I'm sorry she got by me."

"It's all right," Lincoln said. "Let her stay."

"But my orders—"

"Let her stay, and leave us."

The sentry hesitated but complied. When he was gone, Elena entered Lincoln's room and closed the door.

"Did you know?" she asked.

"Know what?"

"That they were going to call off the search?"

Lincoln nodded. "I figured as much."

"Why?" she breathed. "My son is still out there."

Lincoln hobbled to his bed and sat.

"You know something," Elena said. "Tell me."

He shook his head. "I can't."

"Please." She grasped his arm. "Please, Lincoln. Tell me what you know. I have to know. Is my son alive?"

She looked to him with hopeful eyes, but it occurred to Lincoln that she could simply have been hoping for an end to the uncertainty. If she knew, she could finally begin to grieve.

Even though he knew nothing for sure, had not found James' body, he admitted to himself that he doubted they ever would. As much as he didn't want to give up hope, he didn't want to see his friend hurt anymore. Gazing into the eyes of a suffering mother, Lincoln faced, perhaps for the first time, the fact that James Bellman was very likely dead and gone.

"No."

She was quiet for a moment, and then she collapsed into his arms. He held her for such a time that the strong morning sunlight beaming through his window became a soft glow and, as if in respect for a grieving mother, the whole world went silent.

Seven

Sera sat on a branch high up in the large oak tree that grew in her backyard, camouflaged, yet she felt utterly exposed. Fluttering in the breeze, the leaves shielded her from the world. They wrapped around and isolated her in a comfortable, safe bubble. It was her favorite place to go to be alone.

Now, though, the tree didn't save her from the feeling that the colony's eyes were on her and her family. She wasn't only the sister of a missing boy anymore. That missing boy had caused nineteen other families to know her pain. She wasn't a victim. She was part of a cause, an object of community resentment.

And she didn't blame them.

The leaves rustled below, and Sera wiped her cheeks. Shane pulled himself onto the lowest branch and climbed. All her life, Sera had loved to climb, and she'd become adept at it. She recognized that his footholds were unsteady, his grip uncertain. Instead of watching what he was doing, he was eyeing her with precise concern, a fatal mistake in climbing but also a trait Shane couldn't help. He would never be a good climber.

"Be careful," she said.

He slipped and cried out. The tree limbs crashed, and the leaves shivered and hissed. In the greenery, Sera lost sight of him as he tumbled to the ground with a thud.

She listened a moment.

"Shane?"

He groaned. "I'm okay."

He hoisted himself back up, and when Sera saw him again, she sighed in relief. "Are you hurt?"

"I said I was okay."

She didn't know why, but laughter bubbled in her chest until she couldn't contain it any longer.

"It's not funny," he said.

She forced herself to stop giggling. "It's a little funny." She pointed to a branch. "That one. It's much sturdier."

He eyed her with injured pride. "Thanks."

Sera was quiet for the rest of his ascent. She kept her mouth shut as he missed a limb and took a long way. She stifled more laughter when he slipped and caught himself again. When he teetered on the branch that was adjacent to hers and found his balance, his searching eyes tried to read her.

"What?" she asked.

"Are *you* okay?"

She shrugged. "I don't know. I guess I feel responsible."

He shook his head. "You didn't do anything wrong."

"I get it, but we didn't do anything to help either, and now other people are missing because of it."

Shane released a deep breath and looked away. She saw it in him. The anger. It never frightened her in the sense that he might hurt her, but she feared it all the same. She was scared of Shane hurting himself.

"I'm glad your dad is all right," she said.

"Yeah, well, a lot of good he did."

"You need to talk to him. About what happened."

Shane peered through an opening in the tree cover. "Won't do any good. Nobody will tell us anything. He's no different."

"You have to try. *We* have to try. We can't just sit around anymore and depend on everyone to give us everything and tell us what we need to know. No one will treat us like adults until we start acting like them."

The front door of the house slammed closed, and they heard sounds of someone walking through the kitchen.

"Mom's back," Sera said.

They climbed down. Sera was on the ground and waiting for Shane before he could even see the grass. The instant he hit the earth, Sera moved toward the house, but he caught her arm and stopped her.

"We'll get answers," Shane said. "No matter what it takes, we'll figure it out."

She pulled up one corner of her mouth in a half-hearted smile. "Come on."

They trotted up the stairs to the back door and met Elena in the kitchen. After they closed the back door and shook off the morning cold, Sera's mother looked at them with an utterly blank expression.

"What's happening?" Sera asked her mother.

Elena ignored her and walked into the kitchen.

"Mom?"

Elena meandered to the small dining table, pulled a chair out, sat, and cradled her head.

"Mom?"

Elena stirred from her trance. "Your father, Shane." Her voice quivered. "He's doing well. They're going to let him go home soon."

Sera and Shane shared confused glances.

"Mrs. Bellman, what did my uncle say?"

With empty eyes, Elena gazed at the refrigerator. "I think I'll make a stew for dinner. I'll have to go to the market and pick up a few things. Doesn't stew sound nice? It's getting so cold out. It'll warm us up."

Shane frowned at Sera, who was bewildered with concern. He had to do something.

"Mrs. Bellman," he said, approaching her tentatively, "I'd like to help, but you have to tell me what my uncle said at the town meeting."

She looked at Shane then, the first time she'd met either of their gazes. "You're such a good boy, Shane. Just like your father. He always cared about everyone before himself. Losing your mother changed him. Made him colder. I don't think he stopped caring for people, though. He just started focusing on you kids. I think I understand that now."

Shane went to Sera, leaned into her ear, and whispered. "I think we should call the doctor. Something is wrong."

"Been to the infirmary," Elena said. "Dr. Osman told me I'd just need some time."

"Time for what, Mom?"

Elena looked at her daughter as if she should have known. "Your brother, dear. He's gone."

Stunned, Sera gasped. She took two steps away and collapsed, but Shane caught her. He took her to the couch and laid her down. He kneeled and, with ultimate powerlessness, watched her retreat into a drowning grief.

"What does that mean, Mrs. Bellman?" he called into the kitchen. "Did my dad find him?"

She shook her head. "No. My boy won't have a proper burial."

"Then how do they know he's gone?"

"The warden has called off the search. They're not looking for anyone anymore. Including everyone else who never came back."

Mrs. Bellman was detached from the world in a way Shane just couldn't understand. He glanced at Sera, who grieved in a way that made sense even though she didn't know anything for sure.

Knowing their despair and hurt, the senselessness of it, Shane got red-faced, burning angry.

Eight

At the warden's home, Mel and Bernie sat backward on the couch, looking through the living room window out into the street. Shortly after the noise at Arokson Hall had quieted, an as-yet endless crowd of colonists began streaming through the neighborhood. Mel and Bernie's eyes darted between their neighbors, acquaintances, and friends, many of them clutching each other. Husbands pulled their wives close to their chests or shoulders. Mothers and fathers held their children's hands or, if they were small enough, carried them.

"Must be cold," Bernie said. "They're all hugging to keep warm."

The silence struck the girls as unnatural. No one spoke. None of the children laughed or played. They just pushed forward, exhaustion in their slack, dazed faces.

In that silence, Mel and Bernie felt the tension. Then the armed sentries appeared among the crowd.

"Mom?" Mel called, her attention glued outside. "When's Dad coming home?"

Lucy clinked dishes in the kitchen, cleaning up breakfast. "He has to do a lot of work today, sweetheart. I'm sure he'll be home when he can."

"Okay."

Lucy entered the living room, drying her hands with a dishtowel. "Something wrong?"

"I'm scared," Bernie said.

Lucy rushed forward, hugging her niece. "Don't be scared, sweetheart." She brushed Bernie's gold hair back. "Everything is going to be just fine."

Lucy held Bernie's head to her chest and let a grimace slip just for an instant as she looked outside. She was sure Mel had seen it.

"Are you scared too?" Lucy asked.

Mel nodded, and Lucy pulled her in tight as well, kissing them both on their foreheads.

"My girls. Nothing is going to happen to you. I promise."

"What's going on?" Mel looked to her mother with red eyes. "Why does everyone look so sad? And angry?"

Lucy cocked her head and thought for a moment how to explain it to the girls in a way that would satisfy their curiosity without fueling their fear.

"Do you remember that time we had to ground your brother? Both your brothers? When Gabe and Shane got caught trespassing in the cow pastures and they weren't allowed to go anywhere but school for a month?"

The girls nodded.

"It's a little like that," Lucy said. "There are these new rules, and people are unhappy about them."

"What did the people do to get in trouble?" Bernie asked.

"Nothing, baby. It's more to keep them out of trouble."

While Mel and Bernie frowned in confusion, someone knocked at the front door.

Lucy let the girls go and stood. "Just remember. Everything is going to be all right. I promise."

"Cross your heart?" Bernie said.

"Cross my heart."

Lucy opened the door, carrying the smile the girls put on her face, and when she saw Lincoln standing at the top of the steps, she caught her breath. They embraced.

"How are you?" he asked.

"I'm fine," she said. "How are you?" She pushed him away and looked him from head to toe. "Rough, I'm thinking." With her finger, she traced a cut on his chin, and he pulled away, wincing.

"Been better," Lincoln grunted.

Mel and Bernie came running from the living room and clutched Lincoln's waist.

"Girls!" He wrapped his arms around them.

Bernie looked up to her father with tearful eyes. "I was afraid you were really hurt. They wouldn't let me see you, and they said you were okay, but they wouldn't let me see you, and I didn't believe them when they said you were okay."

Lincoln brushed his daughter's hair back. "Well you can believe me. I'm okay."

Bernie squeezed him tighter.

Her face a wrinkle of confusion, Mel tugged on the back of Lincoln's shirt. "Are you in trouble, Uncle Lincoln?"

Lincoln laughed. "No. Why would you think that?"

"Because you were grounded."

Lincoln looked to Lucy for an explanation, and she shrugged.

"What happened, Dad?" Bernie said.

Lincoln looked to Lucy, who held an expectant gaze, and he glanced down the stairs where Reggie Ballard, Lyle Albright, and Alain Ducard waited with their sentry escorts. Ballard shook her head.

"We just lost track of time, sweetheart. Don't worry. Everything is going to be fine."

Lincoln saw the people walking up the street and fell into a trance. This time of day, most people would be at the market, the commons, or their jobs, but they were returning to their homes en masse. Some of them even wore the bright orange of the pillar workers. Not much would get done today. Lincoln hoped they hadn't lost all desire to work. Vale had to go on.

"You here to take Bernie home?" Lucy asked.

"Yes. I assume you've had enough of her. I know she can be a handful sometimes. In fact, I really owe you for—"

Bernie jabbed Lincoln in the stomach with her elbow, and he grunted. They glared at each other and then giggled.

"Well, sometimes," Lucy said.

Bernie stopped laughing and shot her aunt a laser-focused glare.

Lucy threw her hands into the air as if her niece had pointed a weapon at her. "Just kidding! Go get your things."

Bernie ran into the house and returned with her backpack. "Bye, Mel. Bye, Aunt Lucy. Love you."

"Love you too," Lucy said.

Bernie took Lincoln's hand, and they walked down the steps.

Lincoln glanced over his shoulder and mouthed, "thank you." Lucy simply nodded and went back inside with her daughter. Lincoln's stare lingered on the closed door as he and Bernie joined the surviving search party members at the edge of the street.

Ballard squatted to Bernie's level. "Hey there, Bern. Were you good for your aunt?"

She nodded and squeezed her father's hand. "Yes."

Lincoln nudged her, and she looked up to his expectant gaze and huffed.

"Yes, ma'am, Ms. Ballard."

Ballard laughed. "You call me Reggie, okay?"

She smiled, and Bernie smiled back. Ballard didn't have children, but she'd always been good with them. She preferred them to adults, actually, because kids were pure and definitive evidence that people were mostly good. Either they didn't know any better or meant no harm.

Sentry Dana Sibley approached, and Ballard stood to meet her.

"We have to keep moving," Sibley said.

"You can wait a goddamn minute," Ducard growled, stepping between her and Ballard.

A large sentry who looked like he could challenge Ducard in brute strength came to back up Sibley.

Sibley held up her hand. "I got it, Abel." She focused on Ducard. "I have my orders."

"Private, I outrank you, and I say you can wait."

Sibley blinked. "My orders come straight from Captain Barrow, Sergeant."

"So we *are* under arrest."

Ballard sighed. "Not technically."

"Sure," Ducard said. "Can't very well arrest the sheriff, can you? But we're detained all the same."

"My orders are to take you to your homes and ensure you are secure until Captain Barrow lifts that order."

"You're right," Ducard spat. "We're not under arrest. If we were in jail, we'd at least know when we were getting out."

"It's for your protection," Sibley said.

"It's so we can't talk to anyone." Ducard growled and stomped away.

"Come on," Lincoln said. "I still have to get my son."

Under close scrutiny from the sentries, they merged with the streaming colonists in the street. Bernie wouldn't let her father go, and he certainly didn't mind. Even if he wouldn't have admitted it to himself, her touch offered a comfort he needed. Just yesterday, for the briefest, most intense of moments, he'd thought he'd held his daughter for the last time. Although Lincoln wasn't a sentimental man, today was a gift all the same.

It was slow going with the people in the street, but he didn't mind. He wasn't in a hurry, and as he craned his head toward the sky and closed his eyes to bask in the sunlight, he realized he dreaded nightfall and probably always would. As sure as the sun rose every day, it set every day, and when it did, Lumen ceased being the domain of humans. He supposed it had always been that way. The darkness always belonged to the monsters; even if those monsters existed only in the mind, they existed all the same.

At the stairs to the Bellman home, Lincoln sighed at the door.

"Why did you have Mrs. Bellman watch Shane, Dad?" Bernie asked.

"He was watching the Bellman family, sweetheart. Your brother was helping them."

"They don't need any more help?"

"They need more help now than ever."

Bernie's face twisted in confusion, and Lincoln grinned.

"I know. It doesn't make sense." He looked to Ballard. "Watch her a minute. I don't know how this is going to go. Never do with Shane anymore."

"We'll be here. Won't we?" Ballard turned to Sentry Sibley, who glared at her with a face of stone. Ballard leaned to Ducard and whispered, "They train you guys to be humorless, or does that just happen?"

Ducard didn't laugh.

When Lincoln was almost to the top of the stairs, the door opened. He readied himself for a fight, but the face that met him in the doorway was not tight with hostility, but fraught with grief. Sera looked at Lincoln with vulnerable, hurt eyes.

Lincoln relaxed and took a deep breath. "I'm here for Shane."

"He's not here." She hugged the edge of the door for support. "He went home."

Lincoln nodded. "I see. I'm sorry to bother you. Please tell your mother I stopped by."

"Is it true?" Sera asked. "My brother is dead? I think," she took a deep breath, "I think I need to hear it from you."

Lincoln recognized Sera's expression. For years after he'd lost his wife, he had seen it on his own face every morning when he gazed into the mirror. It was grief without acceptance. She knew and understood what they'd told her, but until she saw it for herself, she wouldn't be able to believe it. Lincoln supposed she never would, and nothing he could do would change that.

"I'm very sorry," he said.

She took another deep breath and released it with a quiver. Lincoln didn't know what else to say. He'd been where she was, but he lacked the ability to help her. That kind of pain was a solitary experience.

"Okay." Sera stepped back. "Thank you." She pressed the door closed.

Lincoln descended the stairs. At the bottom, Ballard's grim face was anything but consoling.

"Goes without saying they're not doing well," she said.

Lincoln shook his head.

"I guess it's good Aeron told the colony that the others may find their way."

"Giving people false hope is the worst good intention."

"If more families were devastated like the Bellmans, this colony would tear itself apart."

Lincoln leaned his head in consideration. "Point taken."

Sibley was glaring at them. "Coming?"

"Sure thing, princess." Ballard charged onward ahead of her sentry escort.

Sibley looked at Lincoln. "What's her deal?"

"She doesn't like you," he said.

"I'm just doing my job."

"You know, I'm hearing that a lot these days. I wouldn't take it personally. Reggie doesn't like most people."

"She likes you," Sibley countered.

Lincoln squinted at her. "What's your point?"

She sneered back. "Most people don't."

He laughed. "Maybe she dislikes me a little less."

Lincoln's was the next home. When they got there, he said goodbye to Lyle and Ducard. To Ballard, he said, "You want to come in for a bit? I'm sure these fine sentries wouldn't mind."

She smiled. "No, I better get home and check on my dad."

He walked up the steps with his daughter and his own personal sentry. Lincoln and Bernie entered their home without saying a word to the sentry, who took a post at the top of the steps. The only communication they shared was a distrustful gaze as Lincoln closed the door behind him.

Bernie ran up the stairs, her backpack jostling from side to side. She stopped halfway and turned back around. "I'm really glad you're okay, Daddy."

"Me too, sweetheart."

Lincoln listened to her excited footfalls across the ceiling as she ran to her room. Thankful to be home, he sighed. The stubble on his chin felt like stone, and some of the cuts on his face still burned. He needed to clean up.

He'd get to that, but he heard Shane in the kitchen. He didn't know if other fathers ever felt afraid about talking to their sons, but he thought they all must at times.

Entering the kitchen, Lincoln found Shane at the counter, assembling several sandwiches.

"You must be starving," Lincoln said.

Shane glared at him and went back to work.

"You know, there's one good thing about calling the search off," Lincoln said. "People can finally grieve. They get to move on."

"That's not what's happening with Sera and Mrs. Bellman."

"It will take time."

Shane tossed a knife into the sink. "Time for what? To accept it?"

"Yes."

"What I don't understand is why everyone wants that. Maybe everyone wants the families to move on so everyone else can move on. Why did they even bother sending out the search party in the first place?"

"Because it was worth trying."

"Then why are we giving up now? James is capable. He can survive on his own. He knows the wild the same as you, the same as you taught me. We could make it out there, and you of all people have to know there's a good chance he's still alive."

Lincoln held up a hand. "You don't understand, Shane. He's gone."

"How do you know?"

"It's hard to explain. Just trust me."

"So we can go on living like it never happened? Move on with our lives? Sera isn't going to be able to do that."

Lincoln reached out to take Shane by his shoulders. "Son, I know this is hard, but—"

Shane pulled away. "No, you don't get it. You might be able to live without knowing. You still don't know what happened to Mom. No one does. That includes me, and don't think it never crossed my mind that you're responsible."

"Shane—"

"It's crazy, Dad, I know, but it's the truth. Maybe you should try it. The truth, my truth, is I can't live without knowing. I *have* to live with not knowing about Mom, but not James."

"I see. You're upset because you feel like we can still do something, but we aren't."

The boy nodded.

"Shane, if you've never trusted anything else I've ever told you before, trust this. There is nothing I or your uncle or anyone else in this world can do to bring James back."

Shane picked up his sandwiches and headed for the stairs. "That's because you believe he's dead, but you don't *know* it." He stomped up the stairs and slammed the door to his bedroom.

Lincoln gazed through the window into his backyard where a single oak tree swayed in the breeze.

Nine

After the streets emptied of colonists, Lincoln went down into his basement where dusty wooden crates with various family artifacts were stacked in precarious towers. The only light came through narrow windows at the tops of the walls, but it was enough to illuminate the herbs hanging on lines strung across the rafters. He picked over dangling floreyfoil leaves until he found some battensoft, which he intended to take upstairs, grind, brew, and drink to help relieve some of his soreness.

It was musty and cold, but he listened to the quiet if only for a moment. In the gloom of the concrete room, he recalled the wild's absolute silence before the exos had come. Out there, it had seemed everything in the world paused to hide from those things, and with the slightest tremble, a muscle twitch in his knee, he felt like the ground might quake at any moment. They would burst through the cement floor, and then they would be on him, raising their great arms into the air in triumph before crashing down.

He accidentally kicked a crate and broke its side. Some framed pictures spilled out. Lincoln had stored these pictures away because it had hurt too much to look at them. He and Haley dancing on their wedding day; Haley holding an infant Shane; Haley covered in yellow splotches from painting the nursery.

"I never asked you what she was like."

Startled, Lincoln whirled around. Bernie was peering at him beneath the staircase handrail, her forehead pressed against the old, warped wood.

"My mother," she said.

With a sigh, Lincoln drew from the picture frames and mementos one particular image bound in a dark brown wood with ornate swirl carvings. Haley in the Field of the First Families with a golden sunset behind her, the wind rippling her dress, her fingertips fighting her golden hair on the plane of her temple. His favorite.

He held it out for Bernie. She hesitated and eyed her father as she crossed the room. She took the frame and examined it, both hands gripping the edges.

"She was very beautiful," Bernie said. "But what was she like?"

Bernie had never questioned him like this. In a way, he had been thankful. Not only did he fear the pain he would feel in talking about the girl's mother, but he also hoped Bernie, never knowing her, might be spared the emotional trauma.

"She made the world better," Lincoln said. "She made *me* better."

Bernie looked up from the picture with a wrinkled brow.

"She asked a lot of questions," he said. "She got me to talk about things. She would ask me things that would have set me off if it were anyone else asking. She was an exception."

Bernie returned her scrutinizing gaze to the picture. "She was your true love."

Lincoln drew a long breath. "She was my exception. When I came home and didn't want to see or talk to anyone, I could talk to her. When I had a secret, she pulled it out of me."

"Why do you keep her down here? Do you want to forget about her?"

Lincoln looked away. "No. I'll never forget."

The girl's face relaxed. "I'm sorry you lost your exception."

Lincoln touched his daughter's cheek. "She gave me two more."

Like gazing at each other across the surface of a lake, they waded in that moment together until boots pounding on the floor upstairs drew their attention.

Lincoln said, "Someone's here."

He went upstairs, Bernie following closely behind him. When they reached the doorway to the kitchen, Aeron stood there with Ballard and Ducard.

"I knocked," Aeron said. "With your detail outside, I figured you had to still be here."

He smiled. Lincoln didn't.

"Uncle Aeron!" Bernie ran past her father into her uncle's arms. He lifted her into the air and set her back on the floor.

"I have to talk to your dad, Bern." Aeron looked into her eyes the way adults patronize children without meaning to. "Can you go upstairs and bug Shane for a bit?"

"Okay."

Ballard ruffled her hair as she ran by. When she was gone, the brothers regarded each other for a long moment.

"I'll just get to the point," Aeron said.

Lincoln nodded. "Please do."

"We have to act fast. I got Ballard and Ducard here because, frankly, you're the only ones I can trust."

"Why?"

"Because you know what's out there."

Lincoln gazed through the window into his backyard. "I've been thinking about that, brother. You knew before we did. How long before did you know?"

Aeron sighed. "Since Dad disappeared."

Lincoln cursed and slammed the counter.

"The day he left, he gave me the Warden's Seal," Aeron said. "He told me there were dangerous things in the wild and that, if anything happened to him, to read his journal. It would explain everything. He said Lumen had a secret, that the people didn't need to be concerned, but the wardens of the colonies had been charged with monitoring it. A week later, Captain Barrow came and said the search was being called off and the warden's seat was mine. Knowing what I knew and that Dad intended for me to lead the colony, I had to accept it. In his journal, he called it a burden. He said no one could know because it was our job to protect them, and if they knew, this planet would be done. Our people would panic and descend into madness, or they would leave this world. Either way, Lumen would be done."

"If these things are native," Ballard said, "we *should* leave."

Aeron scoffed at her. "Do you have any idea how much it costs to put a pillar system on a planet? Once it's in place, do you know the chances of success? Terraforming is an incredibly complex and risky process, and it takes a massive investment of resources. And there are those in power who believe it's not worth it. Every terraformed planet is under intense scrutiny. If we fail at this point, that could be it."

Ducard laughed. "Politics. It's always politics."

Lincoln turned, rage burning in his eyes. "Dad went missing before Haley. You knew we were going out there. Why didn't you stop us?"

"There were laws—"

"To hell with the laws! You can't hide behind them! No more of this 'I'm just doing my job' bullshit! People are dying, Aeron!"

"You know the wild is dangerous. Any number of things can kill a man. How was I supposed to know it was them? I was told the pillars would make this world uninhabitable for them. But when you came back without Haley, I knew. It was too late, but I knew."

Lincoln wiped his mouth and released a frustrated breath. "And you did nothing."

"It was the only reason I had to believe you, Lincoln. Everyone thought you were guilty, and I took the hit for helping you."

Lincoln guffawed. "I guess I ought to be grateful."

Ballard stepped between them with her hands raised. "That's enough!" She stared them both down until they backed off. "There are still breaches in the wall, Lincoln, and we need to stop what happened to your dad, Haley, and James from happening again. I don't know if you've thought about it, but not only can our people get out, but those things can get in."

Lincoln shook his head. "They don't need to go through the wall. They can go under. Or over with the way they can climb."

"Even so." Ballard waved a hand in dismissal. "We have to secure the colony. That's step one."

Lincoln considered it, then nodded. "When?"

"There's still daylight," Ducard said. "Unless you're busy. We can come back later. Maybe tonight, when those things are going door-to-door."

"All right," Lincoln said. "Let me tell my children." Lincoln walked down the hall to the foot of the stairs. "Kids!"

In a moment, Bernie was coming down the steps, and Shane gazed at him from the top landing.

"I have to leave for a while, but I'll be back," Lincoln said. "Shane, watch your sister."

"It isn't like we're going anywhere with that guard out front," the boy said.

"Don't worry about him," Aeron said. "I sent him home. You're the big man now, Shane. We're counting on you."

"What's going on, Dad?" Bernie's face twisted in worry. "You're not going back out there, are you?"

"Don't be scared, sweetheart. Daddy's just going to help your uncle make sure the wall is safe."

Lincoln kissed his daughter on the forehead and looked up to find Shane had already returned to his room. It hurt, but he had to focus on problems he could solve.

"Be good," he said to Bernie and followed the others out the door.

Ten

Lucy's day was dragging. She'd never realized how much school dictated her life. With classes suspended, she'd cleaned the house twice and doted on the children so much they were getting annoyed. Last time she went into Gabe's room, he'd thrown a pillow at her and told her to knock first.

The boy deserved his privacy, and she needed a hobby. When the colony's parents were looking after their own children, she was being overbearing on hers.

For lunch, she had laid out provisions for making sandwiches, and the kids had made their own. They'd had a loaf of bread, some leftover baked ham, canned tomatoes, and pickled onions from a jar she'd found in the back of the pantry and might have been a few years old. She didn't think they'd gone bad, but she figured it wouldn't hurt them. The kids didn't really like pickled onions anyway, and she only ate them to get rid of them.

She picked up the dishes from the dining room table, set the plates and glasses in the sink, and opened the faucet to let the water warm up. The kids had gone through more than half the loaf of bread, and most of the ham was gone. They must have been famished. They'd decimated enough food for two meals.

Strange, she thought.

Lucy went back to the sink, where the water was now steaming. She began scrubbing the dishes as Gabe crashed down the stairs.

"Hey, Mom," he said. "Can I go to the commons and play?"

"I don't think so. I want you and your sister home today."

"But there's nothing to do."

"If you're looking for something to do, I can give you something to do."

"Mom, we've already scrubbed everything except the ceilings, and I'm not scrubbing the ceilings."

Lucy shut off the water and dried her hands with a towel. "What about Lore? Why don't you play some of that?"

"I've played that game to death. I just need to get outside for a bit." He flashed a toothy grin. "Please?"

Lucy supposed the boy was getting as stir crazy as she was. "Fine," she said. "But only for a couple of hours. I want you back in this house by then. Don't make me have to come get you."

"Great! Thanks, Mom!" Gabe ran toward the door and picked up his backpack, which he'd stowed there when he'd come down. It was bursting at the seams.

"Whoa," Lucy said. "What do you have there?"

Gabe's cheeks flushed. "Just some balls and stuff. I don't know what we're going to play, so I'm sort of taking everything just in case."

"Uh huh." Lucy placed her hands on her hips and gazed at her son a moment. She knew he was lying to her. "All right. Remember, don't make me come looking for you."

"Okay." Gabe exploded through the front door and ran down the steps and up the street.

It was just the commons. Where was he going to go?

Eleven

By the time Lincoln, Aeron, Ballard, and Ducard reached the perimeter, the sun waned behind the wall and the quiet wilderness. Walking along the concrete barrier, a shadow slipped over them and into the field like a dark hand reaching for the colony. Without the sun's warmth, the late afternoon temperatures were already falling. A chill crept into Lincoln's chest, and he couldn't be sure if it was a physiological reaction or dread for nightfall.

Ducard hadn't said a word since they left town. None of them had spoken of the previous night because they knew that was how Aeron wanted it. He didn't want to risk the colonists overhearing them any more than he wanted them talking to the colonists directly. Lincoln was learning more than he wanted to know about his brother's predilection toward secrecy. Ducard had lost a good friend, and Lincoln understood how the sentry must have felt.

"Are you all right?" Lincoln asked.

Ducard looked at him suspiciously. "Something's been bugging me. Why did they stop?"

Boots scuffed the concrete at the top of the wall, and Lincoln looked up. Ducard followed his gaze. A sentry paced and eyed them, his rifle resting in his arms like a newborn. He made a clicking sound with his mouth, as if he had something stuck in his molars. He turned toward the wild, pretending not to listen to them.

Ducard lowered his voice. "They could have taken us at the gate, but they didn't."

Ballard shrugged. "The sentries opened up pretty quick."

"So why didn't they come under the wall?" Ducard said.

"It goes down pretty deep," Aeron said.

"They can't tunnel under it?"

"I didn't say that."

Lincoln stopped and gaped at a realization. "They couldn't hear us."

Ballard and Ducard looked at him in confusion.

"They hunt by sound and retreated because they couldn't find us," Lincoln said, continuing along the wall. "They can see, but their vision is only good in darkness. The perimeter lighting blinded the ones on the surface. The others would have pulled us down if they could have found us."

Ducard grunted. "So once we were inside and making noise again, why didn't they come after us?"

"Maybe the wall is like insulation," Ballard said.

Aeron nodded as if he already knew all of this.

"So as long as we stay within the wall, we're okay," Ballard said.

Lincoln shook his head. "I don't think so. I never saw these things before. Either they're getting bolder, or they're getting stronger." Lincoln pointed to the Pillar of Dawn on top of the mountain in the distance, the fading sunlight glinting off the spire like a beacon. "That thing is changing the climate of the world. It was supposed to make Lumen uninhabitable for them, but it doesn't look like it's going that way."

Aeron avoided eye contact and was too quiet, removed from the conversation, like he was trying to hide.

"You know something," Lincoln said.

Aeron sighed. "They've already been inside."

Lincoln, Ballard, and Ducard stopped walking, and Aeron met their wary stares.

"Some cattle went missing from the farmlands. There have been some instances of weird damage to buildings, fencing, things like that. And you know about the problem at the pillar."

Ballard kicked the dirt. "I knew that wasn't vandalism."

Ducard was quiet in thought for a moment. Then he said, "So if they can get in anyway, what are we doing here?"

Aeron glared at the sentry. "Keeping people safe, Alain. Part of that is making them *feel* safe."

The warden continued on. Ballard and Ducard shared a grim glance. Lincoln looked at his brother like he didn't recognize him. After a moment, they followed in silence until they arrived at a pipe extending from the wall and emerging from a ditch.

Lincoln pointed at the pipe. "Here we are."

"A storm drain?" Aeron said.

Lincoln smirked. "When the wall was built, these pipes ensured the colony didn't turn into a lake. It doesn't rain so much anymore."

"But there should be grating to prevent people from going inside."

Lincoln grinned. "Vandalism."

He ducked into the pipe, disappearing into the cavernous gloom and a hollow whispering sound of air passing, echoing trickles of water. Aeron hesitated but followed. When Ballard lowered her head, she looked to Ducard, who was standing several paces back, a wide, fearful look on the big man's face as if the pipe were crawling with revolting creatures.

Ballard scoffed. "Afraid of enclosed spaces?"

"I'm a big guy."

"Maybe you watch the entryway."

Ducard nodded, and Ballard descended into the drain.

The only natural light crept in through the pipe opening, but up ahead, Lincoln was waving a flashlight around, its beam reflecting off of the concrete. Dirt lined the bottom of the tunnel, sediment left behind by torrential downpours, and in some places, weeds sprouted from the accumulated earth.

Ballard joined Lincoln and Aeron in a four-way junction, a small room in the center of the wall where another pipe intersected the one they were in and continued within the wall.

Lincoln aimed his flashlight down the intersecting pipe. "These are overflow. They join the drains together and run through the entire wall as far as I can tell. If you continue on down, it leads to the wild. There's usually a drop-off to ground. Some don't drop too far. Those are the ones we use."

At the entrance to the continuing tunnel, short spokes of steel made for a jagged opening. Aeron touched the stubs of an old grate. The cuts were uneven, but time had worn the metal to a polished smoothness.

"That's what used to keep people from going through, but someone cut the grate a long time ago," Lincoln said.

"I see," Aeron said. "So we just replace this, and we're good."

"No, there are others."

He led Aeron and Ballard out of the drain, and as the wall's shadow grew, he showed them other drains that had been made into passages for the colonists. Little varied except for the place in the wild they led to. Lincoln explained that certain plants and herbs only grew in certain places, and some people even kept gardens in the forest. A long time ago, kids made hideouts out there. Not too deep, but far enough away to feel alone. Others, people who had taken to living in the wilderness, used these passageways to get into town, trade at the marketplace, and taste civilization. They weren't going to be happy to learn their ways in and out had been blocked.

Finally, as the day was growing late, Lincoln took them to another drain, stopping just inside the entrance. He bent to examine the earth, shining his flashlight with a sweeping motion.

"What is it?" Aeron asked.

"Shoe impressions. Someone's been here."

With focused concentration, Lincoln followed the trail down the pipe.

"Maybe someone went out a day or two ago, before I gave the lockdown order," Aeron said.

"I don't think so."

"Why not?"

Lincoln sighed and rubbed his eyes. "Because they didn't come back. And it's strange. There are three unique impressions, but they're small for a man."

"Woman?"

Lincoln cocked his head in contemplation. "Maybe."

He examined the tracks in the dirt until he found a full shoe impression isolated from the others. He shined the light over it and bent to get a closer look. He froze, and after a moment, he reached to the impression almost as if to feel the warmth of a fire he didn't dare touch.

His hand trembled. His chest heaved. His heart pounded. His skin puckered with goose bumps. A cold sweat soaked his back. He stood and compared the sole of his own boots to the impression. It matched his but was several sizes smaller.

"Shane?" Lincoln looked down the tunnel, and then he looked out of the entrance at the darkening sky, the first hints of aurora flickering like phantoms in the atmosphere.

"Shane!"

Only the long, empty pipe answered him with an echo of his own lost voice.

Twelve

When Lincoln hit his front door, calmness washed over him. He knew he would find his son at home, knew Shane would look at him with those resentful eyes, suggesting that his mere presence was a bother. He knew without a doubt they would have years to reconcile.

All of these things Lincoln knew because it couldn't be any other way. It just couldn't.

"Shane?"

Nothing stirred in the house. Silence settled like a fine dust.

Lincoln stormed into the kitchen, knowing his son wouldn't be there but still needing to search everywhere. The faucet dripped, the refrigerator whirred, the tree in the backyard bent in the breeze, taunting him.

He raced up the stairs, taking two steps at a time. "Shane?"

On the second floor, Lincoln heard sobs in Bernie's room, and the sound set him on his heels. He felt the surge of tears, the air leave his lungs, the tremble of despair, and he remembered the feeling of emptiness when he'd lost Haley. Then, it had taken all night to settle on top of him, a weight pinning him to the ground. With his children, it was a sudden impact, like being kicked in the chest.

Lincoln stood at the top of the stairs and moaned, afraid of the door, afraid of his daughter. His body was trying to remedy the anxiety in spite of the fact that it would continue to pour like a waterfall. The floor beneath him began to shake, but it was only his unsteady knees.

He didn't want to move forward, but he had to. Bernie's muffled cries tugged at his paternal heartstrings. For a moment, he forgot his own fears, because he needed to be strong for his daughter. Every day since Haley had disappeared, he'd done the same thing. It was easy to switch his anxiety off because he'd lived that way for years.

He turned the doorknob, and Bernie's weeping stopped. When he opened the door, he saw his daughter curled in the corner of her room, a pillow in her lap for when she needed to scream.

"Daddy," she pleaded, and it was all it took to confirm his worst fears. Shane was gone.

"I'm so sorry," she sobbed. "I'm so sorry."

He rushed to her and wiped the tears from her stained and ruddy cheeks.

"It's going to be okay," Lincoln said. "Everything is going to be okay."

"I'm so sorry. I'm so sorry." She hugged the pillow and rocked her body.

He pulled her to his chest, hushed her, felt her tears soak through his shirt.

"Where is your brother?"

"I'm so sorry."

"Bernie," he said with a voice of stone

She flinched, stopped rocking in his arms, and sniffed a final time.

"Where is your brother?"

"He told me not to say. He said if I told, someone would die."

Lincoln took a deep breath and released it slowly. "No one is going to die, but I need you to tell me where he went. I need to find him so he doesn't get hurt."

"He's not in trouble?"

Lincoln smiled at her. "No, sweetheart. I just want to make sure he's okay."

"Shane said they were going into the wild. He said everyone gave up looking for James Bellman, and they were going to find James and bring him back."

"Who's they? Who went with him?'

She looked at him, a guilty defendant confessing her crimes. "Sera," she said. "And Gabe."

There was a hissing sound at the doorway. Ballard and Ducard stared at him with sorrowful eyes. Aeron had retreated down the hall muttering to himself.

Lincoln turned back to his daughter. "When did they go?"

"Not long after you left earlier."

"It's going to be okay. Everything is going to be okay."

Bernie's tears began streaming again. "You keep saying that, but when grownups say that, everything is *not* going to be okay."

He picked her up, and she sobbed into his shoulder. He carried her to the door, and Ballard and Ducard parted so he stood before Aeron in the hallway. They didn't speak. They didn't need to.

Lincoln and Aeron walked out of the house together into the gathering dusk.

"We have to go get them," Aeron said. "Right now."

"We can't," Lincoln said. "It's nightfall."

"I'm not afraid."

"There's no way to track them."

"Actually, I *am* afraid. I'm afraid for my son."

"Shane knows what to do. He'll keep them safe. He'll keep them quiet."

For the first time in as long as either of the Arokson brothers could remember, they felt like part of the colony again. No longer distinguished by status or reputation, their grief and hopelessness set them once again with their people, who all looked at them with a kind of satisfaction but also a kind of sympathy, a brotherhood that was dying in the wind.

PART TWO
THE WILD

"The first warden of each colony shall be appointed by the central government of Earth and its allied colonies. Each warden thereafter shall be elected by its people in a democratic process designed and instituted by the people."

—Colonization Protocols,
Section 205, Governance and Leadership

CHAPTER 5
THE TRIPLE THREAT

One

Shane had thought of everything.

Swinging on carabiners clipped to the kids' packs, their water bottles sloshed. They had filled the bottles before they left, and the built-in filters would make any running water they found potable. If the filters broke, Shane had thought to bring potassium iodide tablets. They'd pushed through the wild all afternoon and hadn't come across any streams, brooks, or rivers; however, Shane was sure they would. All he had to do was keep guiding Gabe and Sera downhill.

Gabe smacked on one of the ham sandwiches he had packed. Shane had told him to bring some, and when his mom had put out the fixings earlier, it had provided the perfect opportunity.

"The triple threat." He took another bite and spoke with his mouth full. "At it again."

"Maybe it's best if we don't aggro anything while we're out here," Shane said.

Gabe thrust his sandwich into the air like a sword. "The triple threat can ward off any beast, overcome any evil."

Sera rolled her eyes at Shane, and he smiled at her. So far, everything was going great. They'd met up in the commons, gotten by the sentries, and escaped through one of the holes in the wall.

The sandwiches were meant to be eaten today. Shane had brought enough jerky, dried fruits, nuts, and grains to last them a few days.

The first aid kit rattled in Shane's pack. He figured it was knocking against the sewing kit, and he would adjust it the next time they stopped. He didn't know how to use either, but he assumed Sera did. She didn't.

His father had once said the most important thing he could take with him into the wild was knowledge. Shane figured they probably wouldn't need the first aid kit or sewing kit. In fact, the only reason he'd packed them was because his father had once said they were essential.

The hiking boots his father had given him in a shallow attempt to make amends dug into the earth like cleats yet felt like pillows taped to his feet. Whether Shane was too stubborn or the gift inadequate, it wouldn't make Shane forgive his father. They were really nice boots though. They kept his feet dry, and if they did get wet, he had packed extra socks. In the wild, wet feet could be a real problem, his father had said.

He'd also said that the sun could be a real problem, so they had rubbed sunscreen all over. Gabe wasn't aware he still had white globs in the creases of his face. Shane and Sera had both noticed and agreed with a smile not to tell him.

"Wait," Gabe said. "Where's the tent? Who brought the tent? Don't we need a tent?"

Shane grinned and shook his head. "No."

Gabe gaped with concern. "Where are we going to sleep?"

"You'll see."

Gabe looked at Sera and raised an eyebrow. She shrugged and followed Shane into the brush. He was the son of Lincoln Arokson. He had to know what he was doing.

Shane had read Ellis Freeman's weather report in the *First Watch* and knew a storm was coming, so he had packed raincoats for everyone. He also had a waterproof tarpaulin that they could tie up to fashion a shelter. His father had told him about the animals in the wild and said it was safer off of the ground. So Shane had brought rope, and they would anchor themselves to the trunk of a tree high up in its branches.

When night fell, they would have flashlights and a lantern that ran on a fuel cell. He'd brought extra batteries, and they had a lighter to start a fire. If that failed, they had waterproof matches.

They had a pocketknife, a multifunction tool, and a bush knife. They had blankets and gloves so they wouldn't cut their hands doing any strenuous tasks. Shane had brought chemical hand warmer packets in case it got too cold at night.

Shane had thought of everything.

"We've been walking for hours," Sera said. "Maybe we should check the map."

Shane had thought of almost everything.

He cringed at her.

"You have a map, right?" Sera said.

172

With a grim frown, Shane shook his head.

"You're kidding me," Gabe said. "You didn't think to bring the map?"

"I thought of everything else," Shane said, his voice rising into a whine. "Why didn't *you* bring a map?"

"Because this was *your* show. You said you had everything under control and not to worry about anything."

"Yeah, well, that doesn't mean you're just along for the ride. You're going to have to help us out with something other than chewing through all of our food on the first day."

Shane and Gabe were about to attack each other when Sera stepped between them.

"Boys! It's okay. Shane knows where the Field of the First Families is. We can get there and get back without a map. We already talked about this. We search the area, and if we don't find anything, we turn back. If we find something, we follow it. We'll just have to make sure we can find our way back from there."

"Right," Shane said. "Bread crumbs."

Gabe snorted. "Bread crumbs?"

"It's from a fairytale," Shane said. "Hansel and Gretel leave a trail of bread crumbs so they can find—"

"I know the story of Hansel and Gretel." Gabe took a step away and shook his head. "Bread crumbs." He muttered to himself and paced aimlessly.

Sera knew to let it play out.

After a moment, Shane said, "If you're done pouting, we should get going."

Gabe cast a death stare at Shane. Then he grinned.

When they were on the move again, Gabe shot a stiff knuckle into Shane's upper arm. Shane recoiled and rubbed it. Everything was back to normal. This was how the boys made amends.

"There's just one problem about the bread crumbs thing," Sera said.

Shane raised his eyebrows. "Oh?"

"The birds came and ate them, so Hansel and Gretel couldn't use them to find their way home."

Shane laughed. "Well, I guess we're lucky Lumen doesn't have any birds."

Gabe stopped abruptly. "What's that?"

Shane and Sera halted and listened.

Their ears picked up a throbbing hum in the distance, a mechanical sound that was completely alien to the wilderness. As it grew louder, a high-pitched whine and buzz became audible from the hum. It passed overhead, and the kids slapped their hands to their ears and crouched to the ground out of fear that the sky was falling.

The tree canopy shook, but if the wind blew, the kids didn't feel it. Then it was leaving, fading, moving into the distance, and it wasn't long before they couldn't hear it anymore.

They looked at each other with wide eyes.

"What? Was? That?" Gabe said.

For the first time, Shane questioned his dismissal of his father's words when he'd said the most important thing to bring into the wild was knowledge, and for the first time since they'd left the colony, Shane had no idea what something was.

Sera and Gabe stared at him for answers. Shane decided he'd better heed his father's words about the second most important thing to take into the wild; if his knowledge was compromised, he needed to maintain his wits.

"Maybe we should go back," Gabe said.

"No," Shane and Sera said in unison.

"I have to find my brother," Sera said.

Though Shane didn't say it, he was thinking he wouldn't be able to face his father unless he found James. He was in too deep now. Doing what his father couldn't do was the only way he would be allowed back into the colony.

However, what Shane really feared was shame. The same kind of shame his father had faced for as long as the boy could remember.

Shane could not fail.

Two

In the thick of the wild, unlike the colony, the shadows didn't grow long in the failing light. The children learned darkness rose straight from the ground, saturating the world in a blooming void.

The treetops batted away the sun's rays. The shades of gray deepened, and the greens muted. Shane wondered if some great force was sucking the life right out of Lumen.

Sera stopped, her breath labored and deep. She gulped the dwindling water from her bottle. "It's getting dark already."

"Maybe we should make camp soon," Gabe said.

They were right, but Shane had hoped to make it to the Field of the First Families before nightfall. When he looked at the way ahead, hoping

against reason he would see a sign of the field, he could barely see ten meters into the dense vegetation and the great trees striking up like pillars into the sky.

He examined the wild around him. Now that he wasn't focused on pushing forward, the generic sameness of the wild struck him as mystifying. They might as well have been lost in a dense fog. For a moment, he lost confidence in his own navigational abilities. If he were honest with himself, he really couldn't even be sure they were moving in the right direction. For just an instant, he panicked. They could be lost in the wild just like James. For the first time, he considered that, if James could lose his way, so could he. He really could have used that map. Why hadn't he thought to bring it?

Shane tightened the straps on his pack and ran for the nearest tree. The soles of his boots grabbed the bark, and he leaped and grasped the lowest, thickest branch he could find. He pulled himself up and threw one leg over the branch so he was sitting on it, and grinned at Gabe and Sera's amazed faces.

"What are you doing?" Sera asked.

"My father taught us this. He said if we're ever in the wild and aren't sure if we're safe, to climb a tree. He said if we need to wait out the darkness to tie ourselves to the trunk high up."

"I am *not* sleeping in a tree," Gabe said.

Shane shrugged. "Suit yourself. You'll be cold and hungry though." He grinned. "I have the food and blankets."

With a growl, Gabe picked up a stick from the deadfall and threw it at Shane. It whizzed over his shoulder but wasn't close enough for him to even flinch.

"Come on," Sera said. "It'll be fun."

She mounted a low branch and climbed. Once beside Shane, she gazed down at Gabe. "It's just like climbing the oak in my backyard."

"Yeah, times ten," Gabe sulked.

"Trust me," Shane said. "Once you're up here, you'll be more comfortable than you ever could be down there. Up here, there are no rocks to dig into your back, and if it rains, no dirt to turn to mud."

"Yeah, and nothing to catch your fall."

"You won't fall. I promise." Shane offered his hand.

Gabe approached the tree reticently. He took Shane's hand and was pulled up into the tree.

With his arms out to his sides, he balanced on a branch. "Now what?"

Shane reached up to the next branch and pulled himself to his feet. "We climb."

As they'd done all day, Gabe and Sera followed Shane. Gabe cast doubtful glances at Sera as Shane pushed ever higher. It seemed they were bound for the tree's apex. Shane climbed until the forest floor disappeared into a dizzying array of branches and leaves.

"Good enough," he declared. "Hold up a minute."

Shane sat on a limb and removed his pack, and got out some rope and a spare carabiner. He wound the rope around a branch and tied it off, leaving a loop dangling. Then he attached the carabiner and hung his pack from it.

"Both of you, give me your rope, and hang your packs with mine."

Gabe took his rope off of his pack and took Sera's off for her and handed them both to Shane, who hung Gabe's and Sera's pack with his. Then Shane wound one of the ropes around two branches over and over to create a kind of flat platform, a tree stand. When he was finished, there was enough space for all three of them to lie down.

"Genius!" Sera exclaimed.

Gabe still didn't look like he approved, but when Shane invited them up, he came.

As the gray twilight filtering through the tree canopy deepened, the teenagers settled in for the night, unpacking the essentials, like blankets, rolled-up clothing to use as pillows, and the lamp.

Gabe pulled out his Lore playing cards and grinned.

Sera shook her head and smiled. "You're an addict. You need help."

Gabe feigned a hurt expression. "I read creature comforts can be essential to morale when you're roughing it."

"This isn't a camping trip, Gabe," Shane said, trying his best to look serious, channeling his father. "But I guess it can't hurt to have a little fun."

Shane smiled. He put the lamp in the center of the rope platform, and as he dialed up its blue glow, Sera settled in and Gabe dealt the cards.

They didn't play long before the exhaustion of the day caught up with them and they fell asleep.

Three

They woke to a violent, world-ending rumbling. The earth below trembled with such intensity that it might have collapsed and swallowed them whole, Lumen coming for her naughty children.

Shane bolted upright. The tree listed and rattled, its limbs flailing like panicked arms. The whole wild rustled with a seething intake of breath, like someone sucking air through clenched teeth. All the world was static in the darkness.

Their rope tree stand jumped and tossed them into each other. The cool light from the lantern bounced among the trees like a primeval disco.

"What is that!?" Sera screamed. "What is that!?"

Gabe was still asleep, so she slapped him.

"Huh? What? What's going on?"

She clutched his coat. "We're in trouble!"

Shane peered over the edge of their tree stand, and in the deep black of the wild's darkness, streams of iridescent blue raced across the forest floor like meteor showers. The lights moved in pairs, and relentless pounding accompanied the shaking earth.

Sera's fingers dug into Shane's shoulder. "What is that!?"

"I don't know!" he said.

As he stared into the abyss, his eyes discerned bodies writhing in panic, hints of the lantern's light glinting off of slick hide, antlers jutting into the air. There were hundreds of them, rushing like a river.

"Herebors!" Shane yelled.

An alpha male bucked against their tree, cracking the trunk like thunder. Shaved bark and wood-splinter shrapnel rained in the forest. The jolt set Shane off balance, and for an instant, it looked like he was going to recover before he grunted in surprise and fell off the edge into the black below.

"Shane!" Sera screamed.

Gabe leaped for him and grabbed the edge of the rope to use as an anchor. His free hand followed his cousin over the edge, and it purchased nothing but air.

Afraid to look, he lay defeated. The herebor stampede raged on below, and he tried not to think of Shane's body mashed into paste.

The rumbling hooves diminished.

Something powerful grasped his wrist and pulled with such force Gabe thought his arm would pop right off. He slid forward and clenched the rope with his other hand.

"Oh my god, Gabe!" Sera dove and seized his pant legs.

Gabe gaped down into the seething mass of herebors and found a pair of familiar boots swinging in and out of view. He squinted in confusion. Those feet didn't belong. It didn't make any sense.

"Don't let me fall!"

Shane was hanging from the underside of the tree stand, dangling over a chasm of branches and the flow of herebors that would have pummeled him into the earth.

"He's all right!" Gabe looked back at Sera. "He's all right! Hold my legs!"

Her questioning face brightened, and she squeezed his ankles with all of her might.

"Ow! Not so hard!"

"Sorry!"

Gabe and Shane locked their embrace, and then Shane's other hand gripped Gabe's forearm. Shane swung out over the racing herebors, and he looked to Gabe in complete dependence.

"Pull!" Gabe said.

They struggled against gravity. The muscles in Gabe's arms pulled so tight he felt they might snap, but he grit his teeth and tugged until Shane climbed back onto the tree stand, grasping the rope and pulling himself up.

As the last herebors passed below and stormed into the void, a peaceful quiet followed them into the distance. Gasping, the kids fell into each other's exhausted bodies. They took inventory of their bodies.

Then they laughed. They laughed with all of the thrill of near death they'd never experienced, an emotional cocktail of serotonin, endorphins, and adrenaline racing through their veins. They laughed because they made it through this, so they could make it through anything. They laughed as if it were a cosmic joke that Shane could now be dead but wasn't. They laughed until they couldn't remember why they were laughing.

In the not-too-distant darkness, they heard a cough, a snort, and a squealing cry. The trees around them shook, and the muted mewling turned into terrible shrieking that rose into an ear-piercing squelch that faded into a lazy moan.

After a moment of silence during which the kids gazed at each other and didn't dare move, a white-hot scream pierced the air around them and, surely, across the entire valley, if not all of Lumen.

They felt like they would never laugh again. This was the genuine sound of death. They had averted it for now only because it had found something else.

And if the children understood anything about death, it was that its job was never finished.

Four

It was morning, and the world was painted green. The sun cascaded through the tree canopy, pouring sparse rays of light to the forest floor. Sunlight had pushed the darkness back for a time.

Time. What time was it?

Shane jerked upright, his heart again throbbing in his ears. He thought he heard more herebors, but the thumping settled as he realized it was only his own pulse.

He looked up to the sky to gauge how late it was, but he couldn't see the sun's position through the thick canopy. Judging by the pang in his stomach, it was mid-morning.

Shane's movement stirred the others, who cleared their throats and rubbed away the restless sleep in their eyes. They scanned their environment as if they'd hoped it had all been a dream. To dream, of course, they would have had to sleep.

But they hadn't. They had existed somewhere between layers of consciousness where they might have awoken if something stirred, if something approached. However, after hearing death's triumphant declaration, they had heard nothing more the rest of the night.

Gabe groaned. "This must be what old feels like." He massaged the back of his neck.

Shane caught Sera's weary eyes gazing at him. He tried to read her, but she was a blank page. Gabe and Sera assembled the blankets, the clothing they'd used as pillows, the lamp, and the Lore playing cards, which had scattered during the stampede.

Gabe arranged the cards into a stack and thumbed through them. "Aw man. I think some of them are missing." He leaned over the side of their platform. The backs of the Lore playing cards were brown, just like the deadfall on the forest floor. He would never find them all.

He turned back, hopelessness on his face.

Shane tossed Gabe's pack to him. "Come on."

Descending the great tree, they didn't talk about a lot of things. They mostly didn't talk about the herebors, how Shane had almost died, and the sounds of death in the darkness. So fervently they didn't talk about these things that the tension grew in the reddening of their faces when they caught each other's glances and looked away, when one of them breathed to speak but didn't say anything at all, only held the quiet.

The forest looked like a combat zone. The stampeding herebors had torn off every branch up to six meters from the ground, leaving sharp stumps at the trunks and revealing the yellow flesh beneath the bark.

There were gouges from where the herebors' flanks had impacted with incredible force, tufts of fur left behind. A tree leaned on its neighbors, a devastating split shooting up the center of its shaft and then jutting to the side.

"So, uh, how do we get down?" Gabe asked.

There were no branches to climb on anywhere near the ground, and if they jumped from this height, one of them would surely break an ankle.

"I have an idea," Sera said, "but you're not going to like it."

"What is it?" Shane asked.

"I'll lower you two down using the rope over a branch like a pulley."

He wrinkled his brow in confusion. "What about you?"

"I'll climb."

"No way," Gabe said. "It's way too high. If you fall, you'll get hurt."

"I won't fall."

It was clear from the way Shane was looking at Sera that he was contemplating it.

"You can't let her do this," Gabe said.

"She can do it," Shane said. "We can't, which means she has to if we're ever getting out of this tree."

"Tie a rope to this branch, and we'll climb down that way."

"We can't," Shane said.

"Why not?"

"Because," Sera said, "then we lose a rope."

Gabe gave in, and they dropped their packs to the ground, their gear rattling on impact.

Shane tied a rope around Gabe's chest and threw the other end over a branch above them.

Gabe looked at him with frightened eyes. "Don't let me go."

Shane grinned. "It's not far down. I just need to slow your fall really."

He lowered his cousin to the ground without much trouble. When Gabe's feet touched down, he looked up with contempt and untied the knot. Alone, he glanced around in the wilderness, searching for anything that might dash out from behind trees.

"Hurry up, guys," Gabe said.

The rope ascended, and Shane tied it around his own chest. "We have two more ropes."

"We might need them," Sera said. "I can do this."

"I know. I could do it with you."

Sera shook her head. "No, you're a terrible climber. You could hurt yourself."

Disappointed, Shane embraced her. "Be careful."

She kissed him on the cheek and lowered him down. When he was on the ground, he untied the knot, and the rest of the rope coiled down like a dead snake.

Sera was high up in the tree by herself with nothing to help her get down. She studied the tree below. She planned out her course and analyzed how she would move. When she was ready, she swung down on the branch and hung. Then she made the cardinal mistake: she looked down. Her feet dangled with three of her body lengths to spare before the ground.

She regained her composure, found her hand holds and foot holds on the tree trunk, and shimmied over until she could reach out and take them. She grasped the first nub, then took the leap and clutched the second while landing a foot on another stump where a tree limb used to be. She worked her way down, never rushing herself, drowning out the boys' shouted encouragement.

Her route took her in a spiral down the tree trunk, twisting around and back to the side she'd started on, and the boys told her she was close enough to jump.

Sera checked the height and leaped off, twirling in the air for a graceful, balanced landing. She rubbed her hands together and dusted off her sleeves. Shane and Gabe gawked at her with wonder.

"What?"

"Nothing," they said in unison.

"Then let's go."

They each fetched their packs, and while Shane and Sera wound up the ropes, Gabe went off to search for his missing Lore cards.

"Hey, guys!" he said from the other side of the tree. "I found one!"

Shane stopped winding his rope. "Found what?"

"One of the cards."

Shane shook his head as Gabe rustled through more of the deadfall.

"Another one! Aw, it's ruined."

"Gabe, forget about the stupid cards already." Shane went back to work winding up the rope.

Gabe trudged around the tree. "Stupid cards? We've been playing this game since we were kids. You love Lore."

Shane affixed the wrapped rope to his pack. "We're not kids anymore, Gabe."

Without looking back, Shane marched in the direction the herebors had gone.

Sera gave Gabe a sympathetic look. "Come on."

Shane stopped walking.

The fear they felt the previous night as they rocked in the trembling tree returned as if it had never left. Their skin tingled with a fresh adrenaline rush, a flushing heat followed by a tightening chill.

"What is it?" Sera asked with a dreadful sob. "Shane?"

"Look."

Gabe and Sera approached Shane tentatively.

Before the teenagers lay a devastated forest. The wild was typically so thick they couldn't see more than a few meters ahead, but the herebors had cut a tunnel of destruction that led forward a few hundred meters and dove down a slope. Branches lay like dead bodies on a battlefield. Felled trees leaned against their neighbors. One tree had fallen to the ground, its roots splayed into the air like a hand begging for it all to stop. Thousands of divots were set in the forest floor from the pummeling onslaught of powerful legs pumping and thrusting those hulking bodies forward. In the herebors' wake, nothing lived.

Among all of that chaos, dozens of craters pockmarked the landscape like the herebors had run through a silent minefield. In some of those craters, the disturbed earth held pools of red. It was on the trees as if someone had marked them with paint for leveling.

They had heard death. Now they had seen it.

"Okay." Gabe backed away. "Guys, I hate to be the one to keep bringing this up, but it's clearly more dangerous out here than we thought. Maybe we should consider going back. I mean, look at this."

A moment passed before anyone else spoke.

"I'm not going back," Sera said.

"Sera, I'm sorry, but look at this," Gabe pleaded. "Just *look*. Not only are our chances of finding James slim, but what are our chances of surviving out here with stuff like this?" Gabe shoved his hands into his pockets and kicked the deadfall. "What are his chances?"

Shane shot him a glare. "Gabe."

"No, Shane. No." He began pacing. "Back at the colony, I asked you directly, do you know where you're going? And you said yes. I asked you if you knew what's out there? And you said yes. Maybe you thought you did, Shane, but you didn't know about this. If you did and didn't tell us, that would be messed up."

"I told you back at the colony not to come," Shane said. "I said Sera and I needed to do this and that you wouldn't understand. But you insisted that you had my back. You said it's what family did. Now you want to leave? You want to take it back?"

Gabe stopped pacing. His lip quivered, and he shook his head. "I didn't say I want to leave. I said I want to go back. Together. I came because I care about you, and I do have your back."

"We're not going back," Shane said. "If you want to, that means you're leaving." Shane pointed over Gabe's shoulder. "It's that way. Good luck."

Shane surged ahead, following the path the herebors had carved through the forest, leaving Sera and Gabe behind him. Sera was stone faced, and after a quiet moment, she trotted after Shane, her ponytail waving at Gabe as she left.

"I've got your back, but who's got mine, huh!?"

Gabe hated the sight of his friends leaving him.

"We're the Triple Threat! Three of us! Together!"

He hated the thought of being alone in the wild. Because of this reason and no other, he trudged on.

"Guys, wait up!"

Running to catch them, he kept his distance from the craters that pockmarked the earth as if the land had suffered a shelling in a war.

Five

The herebors' trail twisted through the wild and led to a river. Along its banks, huge roots burst from the earth. Trees crowded right up to the edge where they bent over the flat and calm water like they could reach down and sip at their leisure. No doubt the most coveted place for them in all the wild.

At the water's edge, the kids gazed across to the other side. The herebors had plowed straight through, the meager depths of the river posing no obstacle to them. However, for three young people during the onset of winter, the cold water posed a hazard, and it would be reckless of them to attempt to walk through it.

"Great," Sera said. "How are we going to get across?"

Shane scanned up and downstream and saw what he'd hoped for: a fallen tree that spanned the embankments. He pointed. "By using that. You two rest and eat some breakfast."

Having eaten all of his ham sandwiches, Gabe reached into his pack, pulled out a fistful of nuts, and crammed them into his mouth. Sera just wanted to sit for a while.

Despite the obstacle, they'd been fortunate. Their water supplies were exhausted, and if they'd had to go the day without a fresh source of hydration, they would have been in trouble.

Shane took their canteens to the riverbank and lay on the soft moss as he reached over and filled them.

Once the caps were back on and tightened, Shane removed his boots, socks, and pants, and laid them out on the bank. He dipped his toes into the cold river and waded in up to his waist. Shivers stormed up his body as his skin tightened all the way to the back of his skull. He filled his cupped hands, sipped, and pressed his palms to his face. He took his shirt off and hung it on a branch that reached over the bank, and he rubbed the water on his chest and under his arms. Then he dunked his head.

For a moment, all the world was silent and calming in this solitude. Sound died on the water's surface, like a fog for his ears. When he came up, he slicked back his dark hair, slinging water in an arc, droplets gathering at the tip of his nose. Sera was watching him from the bank, her toes dancing in the river.

For a moment, they forgot themselves. The flood of adolescent emotions came and washed everything else away.

Shane took one step toward her, feeling the rocky riverbed with the soles of his feet.

She smiled. "No."

He took another step.

"Don't you even think about it."

When Shane reached for the water, Sera screamed and scrambled to get away. Shane threw two handfuls of the river at her. She screamed again as it splashed across her back and over her shoulder.

Her fingers splayed. She turned with accusatory eyes. "You jerk!"

"Come on in. The water is nice."

"Are you kidding? It's freezing."

"Once you get used to it, it's nice."

Sera huffed in playful frustration, and she glared at him. She approached the bank and sat down to dangle her feet in the river once again.

Shane stepped closer and held out his hand. "Come on."

She eyed him and then kicked water into his face. Shane wiped it away and sputtered it from his lips. She looked pleased.

"Now you're gonna get it," Shane said, and Sera squealed, tearing at the moss to get to her feet, but Shane grabbed her around the waist and pulled her in while she kicked the air and waved her hands like a lunatic.

They fell into the water together, and their whole world became ice. The exhilarating rush of the cold river swept over their bodies, and it seemed, for the first time in their lives, everything made sense. The clarity of the river surrounding them and their warm bodies pressing against each other made them realize it didn't matter what happened to the world as long as they had each other. They could keep each other warm and safe, and no one else in the entire world mattered.

Out here in the wild, it was just them.

They emerged, Sera flipping her golden hair back like a whip. She slapped Shane's pale, boyish chest with both hands, and he laughed. Shane laughed and laughed. Soon, Sera laughed too.

From down the bank, Gabe watched, biting his lip and tossing a stone from one hand to the other. Growling with anger, he chucked the stone at the water, and it skipped, one, two, three times before thumping against the far side and dropping into the river.

Six

Dripping and shivering in their exposed wet undergarments, Shane and Sera returned to the riverbank. Gabe had organized their packs and was tending to a fire he'd built, poking the ashes with a stick. He bit off a piece of jerky and chewed. Shane felt his cousin was devouring their food too quickly, but he decided to let it go.

Silent and disengaged, Gabe stewed in contempt, and Shane and Sera recognized it. He was a smolder waiting for a spark, and neither Shane nor Sera wanted to provide it. The last thing they needed was one of them coming unhinged.

Sera wrapped herself in a blanket and went to hang her clothes in the sunlight to dry. Shane sat beside the fire and warmed his hands. The heat enveloped him. It wouldn't take long to dry off and change.

"Thanks for the fire," Shane said.

"It's my first," Gabe told him.

"It's a good one," Shane said.

Gabe glared at him. "I can do things too."

"I know."

Gabe returned his attention to the fire and fell into silence. Sera sat beside Shane and covered them both with her blanket. For a while, they all gazed into the flames and listened to the snaps and pops, bathing in the warmth until there were only glowing embers.

Gabe cleared his throat and stirred. "So how much farther to the field?"

"Not much," Shane said. "Should be there this afternoon."

"We won't have much time to look around." Gabe stood and slapped the dirt and dried leaves from his pants. "We better get going."

Shane helped Sera up. Still under the blanket, they moved together to their packs to retrieve dry clothing.

Gabe poured his canteen on the fire, and then he went to the river to refill it.

Sera pulled a shirt over her head. "What's wrong with him?"

"He's just jealous."

"Of us?"

Shane nodded.

She tugged her pants over her hips. "I don't think that's it."

Shane jammed a foot into a boot. "You saying he's not?"

"No. Maybe he is. But that's not it. Not all of it anyway."

When Gabe returned and Shane and Sera were dressed, they moved on, following the herebor trail. They crossed using the fallen tree that spanned the embankments and then hiked around an incline that seemed to go up forever. The path dove back down a hill, and after hours of following it, they found another running body of water.

Standing on the familiar embankment, they gazed at the serene, still surface, a mirror for the sky.

"This looks a lot like the other river we crossed a couple of hours ago," Sera said.

Shane crouched on the bank and sighed. "That's because it is."

Gabe picked up a rock and slung it at the water. It skipped across to the other side, making ripples that the slow current bore away.

"Shane," he said, "why are we back at the same river?"

"Because the herebor path led us back around to it."

"You mean we've been going around in a circle!?"

Shane stood and held a hand up to his cousin. "Calm down."

"Don't tell me to calm down. You got us lost!"

Sera stepped toward him with a concerned expression on her face. "We're not lost, Gabe. We can always follow the path back. Bread crumbs, remember?"

"Oh, sure! Then we get to spend another night out here with whatever those things were last night! That makes me feel much better!"

"Is that what's been bothering you?" she said. "You're afraid?"

"Yes," Gabe said. "No."

"Which one?" Shane said.

"I don't know!" Gabe began pacing. "I just thought that...I don't know. Maybe it's stupid, but I just thought that this would all be different."

"Different how?" Shane prodded.

"You know, the three of us. The Triple Threat. Working together, saving James even if we had to sneak around some dungeon and kill some monsters. I just thought there would be more adventure."

"You thought it would be like Lore," Sera said.

"Yeah. Maybe."

"It's going to be all right," she said. "Shane will figure out how to get us to the field, and everything will be fine. Isn't that right, Shane?"

Shane's stare was ice. "You should have stayed."

They gaped at him.

"I told you what it was going to be like, but you didn't believe me. And what? Now that it's not what you thought, you want to call it all off?"

"No!"

"We're going to find that field, Gabe. It doesn't matter how long it takes. It's too late to go back now, and you're not going off on your own. You say you want to be the Triple Threat, then here we are, right now. Don't let your jealousy mess it all up."

"I'm not jealous."

"Of course you are."

"I'm not jealous!" Gabe charged at Shane and tackled him to the ground.

"Stop it!" Sera shrieked.

The boys rolled in an awkward chaos of limbs. They pounded each other's backs and tore at each other's coats, shoved and kicked, struck wildly with eyes clenched shut.

"Stop it!"

They screamed their frustrations, most of which had built up over years during their young lives. They didn't mean most of it, but some of it they did.

"We'll go back!"

Shane and Gabe stilled. Dead leaves and dirt clung to their clothes, faces, and hair. They looked at Sera.

"We'll go back," she said again.

They pushed each other away and stood.

"No, Sera, I can find him," Shane said.

"No you can't!"

He backed away, stunned, hurt.

"No *we* can't," she said. "Look at us. We're fighting each other in the dirt, and we don't even know where we are." Tears filled Sera's eyes. She placed her hand on his chest. "We're kids, Shane. We tried, and we did better than we had any right to, but now it's time to go home.

He looked at her with a pained expression. "Okay." He picked his pack off of the ground and set off.

And so, they turned around, following the herebor trail the way they'd come. Exhausted and without the eagerness of the pursuit, they moved at a slow pace. What did it matter? They effectively had no destination except to cover some ground toward the colony. They would have to stay another night in the wild regardless.

When they arrived at the bend near the foot of the hill where the trail turned back toward the river, Shane stopped at the edge of the path, gazing uphill into the forest.

"What is it?" Sera asked.

He pointed into the trees. "Sunlight."

Gabe slid his pack's straps off of his shoulders and let it fall to the ground. "So?"

"So if the forest is thinning and we can get to high ground, maybe we can get a good look at our surroundings."

"Maybe?"

"If I can see what's around us, I know I can find the Field of the First Families. We have one more night out here anyway, right?" Shane said.

They nodded.

"So let's check this out."

"Okay," Sera said.

"Want to bet?" Gabe said.

"What?"

He grinned. "Your level fifty hunter in Lore."

Shane smiled. "Okay. If I'm right?"

"Anything but my knight."

"I'd never take your main. Your mage?"

"Never liked that class anyway."

They headed uphill. Shane hacked passage with his bush knife, and the terrain wound up and up until it seemed they had to be on top of the world.

Then they were.

The forest opened up on a rocky clearing. Boulders jutted from the earth like icebergs. The sun beamed from above the western horizon, the warmth of its direct light soaking into their bones.

Shane scanned the tree line and breathed a sigh of relief at the sight of the moss-covered, tree-shrouded ship that brought the First Families to Lumen.

"Look." Shane pointed. "The field is just there."

Gabe frowned. "Guess I owe you a mage."

"Nah. Forget about that."

"Okay. But don't think for a second I wouldn't have taken your hunter." Gabe punched his shoulder and then nodded toward the ship. "Is that what I think it is?"

Shane grinned. "It's the ship that brought humanity to Lumen."

"Whoa."

"I heard no one has been there for centuries," Sera said. "They built a fence to keep people out because it wasn't safe. They took what they needed and abandoned it."

From out in the open, Shane had a full view of the sun. He regained his sense of direction, but they were losing precious time and light. Nightfall was on fast approach.

"We can move on a bit, but we'll have to make camp soon," he said.

Reinvigorated by the sighting of the ship and the discovery of the field's location, they charged into the trees on the other side of the clearing and started making their way down the other side of the rise.

It wasn't long before, in the seeping darkness, they made their camp in another tree, and in the cool glow of the lantern, they sat still and quiet, listening to the wild come alive around them. Every sound, every breeze, was an herebor charge or whatever had made those craters and splattered that blood all over the place.

After hours of them flinching at everything, shivering in the plunging temperatures, and clinging to their lamp as if it were their last salvation, they fell asleep, and nothing came.

Seven

In the morning they set off, crunching dried leaves and twigs, charging through the wild like nothing could stop them. Confident they now knew how to survive, their fear diminished, and their youthful delusions of imperviousness returned.

Sera shrieked and fell, clutching her leg, moaning.

Shane rushed to her side. "What's wrong?"

She seethed. "I don't know. I just felt a pain in my ankle like something bit me."

Shane slid up her pants. Two puncture wounds glared like eyes weeping blood. He scanned the brush the way they'd come and found a thorny vine bobbing, taunting him.

A mixture of anxiety and wonder in his eyes, he examined it. "I know what this is." He returned to Sera and placed a hand on her abdomen. "Dad told me about it once. Serpentine vine. If you touch it, it reacts and can wrap around you. Its thorns dig in like hooks. If it gets you, all you can do is cut it off."

"She going to be okay?" Gabe asked.

Shane gazed at Sera with grave concern. "It's poisonous. The thorns have some kind of venom. We have to go back now."

She snatched his wrist. "No! We're too close!"

"Can it kill her?" Gabe asked.

"I don't know," Shane said. "Not if she gets to the infirmary. The poison will make her tired, and she might get a fever. It's like an infection."

Gabe tore off his pack, opened it, and dug in. "Do we have anything in our first aid kits? Think, Shane."

Shane searched his knowledge. Other than disinfectant and dressing, they didn't have anything in their first aid kits. However, a spark ignited in his mind. There were things in the wild that could help.

"Battensoft and floreyfoil," he said.

Gabe retrieved the first aid kit from his pack. "What?"

"If we can find some battensoft, it will help with the inflammation and fever. Dad uses it all the time when he's hurt or sick, and he gives it to the infirmary for them to use. Floreyfoil will help with infection."

"Right," Gabe said. "So we go on and look for battensoft and floreyfoil."

They looked to Sera. It was her call to make.

She nodded. "What do they look like?"

"Floreyfoil has these needles sticking off of it. Battensoft is a pink flower." Shane took off his pack and set it on the ground. "But first, I should disinfect and dress this."

From the first aid kit he pulled a tiny metal flask of alcohol and a roll of cotton fabric. He dumped the disinfectant on her ankle, and she cried out. Then he wrapped it with the cotton.

"Is that okay?" he asked her.

"Yeah."

When he finished, they helped her up and started making their way downhill again. They were slower because Sera was limping and they were scanning the forest floor for weeds, not to mention more serpentine vine.

"Shane?" Sera said.

"Yeah?"

She raised a pointed finger. "Is that bush of needles floreyfoil?"

Shane moved closer to examine it. "Yes!" He ran to it, unfolded his pocketknife, and cut a twig off. "Now we just need a fire."

Sera stopped him. "I'm okay. A little stiff but nothing I can't stand. Let's keep moving and find the other stuff."

Shane nodded, and they continued on. Having seen the ship, they descended the hilltop with the knowledge that they were going the right direction. Having found one of the two plants they needed to treat Sera, they lowered into the wilderness feeling confident in their safety. They beat the foliage and greenery for what felt like hours, cutting through thick, untamed land.

"What I wouldn't give for another herebor stampede right about now," Gabe said.

Sera groaned. "Don't say that."

"Herebors come through here, and I'll just take one of these ropes, throw it around one of their necks, and ride it to the edges of the wild," Gabe said. "Imagine that. Imagine if we were able to ride one back to the colony. Imagine their stupid faces."

"Herebors run through here," Shane said, "and you better get out of the way. I've never seen one up close, but Dad told me once that they can get as big as a house. He said he saw one step on a man before, and he said it killed him and dug his grave at the same time. He said it just kept on going like it didn't even notice."

Gabe's eyes lit up like he thought that was the coolest thing ever. Shane cut through a vine, and then swung his bush knife again and cut through open air. They stepped through the opening onto a trodden path.

Eight

Gabe and Sera had questions, and Shane answered them the best he could. They asked who made the paths, and Shane told them. In the span of a day, they learned that, not only was there wildlife outside of the colony's walls, but there also were people. People had left the colony. The idea sounded asinine and alluring at the same time.

"If you knew," Gabe said with a pained look in his eyes, "why didn't you ever tell us?"

Sera hadn't spoken while Shane explained everything. She'd only given him that stony gaze, which she'd inherited from her mother. It was easy to forget how strong people could be when they'd crumbled and rebuilt themselves.

Shane shrugged. "Dad told me not to tell anyone."

Gabe muttered to the trees.

"Would it have mattered? Would you have honestly cared? You act like it was some big secret."

"There is a whole world out here, and you knew! People should know. They should be told so they can decide whether the walls are what they want. They should know so they can leave if they want."

"It isn't time. It isn't ready. Lumen, I mean. It's dangerous out here. You know that as well as anyone now. Anyway, I don't think your dad wants his colonists to leave."

"My dad knows?"

"Of course he does. Look, I never saw any of this stuff. Dad just told me about it when I was a kid, and he made me promise not to say anything to anyone. Then we just stopped coming out here, and it was like this part of my life was gone. Nothing outside the walls mattered anymore."

"I know that feeling," Sera said. "They drill it into us since birth. Makes you sort of ignore everything over the walls. Gives you blinders. Sometimes I wonder if it has the reverse effect, if it makes some people want to get out more. People want what they can't have."

The kids were quiet, allowing all the revelations of the last day to settle in.

"Let's get to the field," Shane said.

Sera and Gabe followed Shane down the path as it wound through the wild. Sera was beginning to slow significantly. She didn't complain about it, but she winced when she walked now. They had to find the battensoft soon. The floreyfoil would help in the long run, but what she really needed was help with the pain.

When they reached the field, a cool gust greeted them with earthy and floral scents, the smell of rain. The open air felt refreshing, and Shane immediately knew something was wrong.

"Whoa." Gabe gazed at the open land ahead, the waving golden grass.

Sera released a deep breath. "It feels so nice to get out of the forest."

"Look." Shane pointed to the west, the direction of the colony.

Over the trees, dark, swirling clouds amassed like mountains in the sky. They hovered over Lumen as if any moment they might crash down upon the earth.

Gabe whistled. "Haven't seen a storm like that for a while."

"What are we going to do?" Sera asked.

The elegant beauty of Lumen's instability captivated Shane. He was gazing at the fury of a terraforming planet resisting its new climate. It's what nature did. Humans tried to change it, and it fought with everything it had. Men were not gods, and from time to time, they needed to be reminded of their place.

"Shane?" Sera touched his shoulder.

"Find shelter," he said. "We have an hour or so, but by the time that storm gets here, we better be inside somewhere."

A lightning bolt lit up the interior of the clouds, and the sky pulsed. To the north, the Pillar of Dawn stood indifferent, its vortex of gases fanning out across the heavens. As if in response to the storm, an electrical arc shuddered down the tower.

"Come on," Shane said. "This is where Dani last saw James. Let's see what we can find."

They fanned out, the wind rustling the grass and the trees. They stepped carefully on the camouflaged earth, looking for anything, any sign of James. They only found the bending stalks of golden grass and the soft, dark earth.

Gabe veered to the south, heading for the tree line.

Sera walked straight out toward the center of the field, the towering ship looming ahead, gleaming in the bright sunlight that was not yet obscured by the storm. It drew her. It entranced her. She cocked her head to the side as if listening to voices only she could hear, the burning metal a beacon calling her home.

Shane approached behind her, his feet crunching the tall stalks.

"That's the ship that brought us here?" she asked.

"Yeah."

"How far away is it?"

"It's really big. Probably farther than it looks. A kilometer. Maybe two. It's taller than the pillar."

"For serious?"

Shane nodded. "Had to be. It's what brought the pillar here."

Sera scanned the field. She looked back the way they had come. She could see the faint trails they had cut through the tall grass, and they led to the dark opening of the path through the forest, gaping like a mouth. For a moment she despaired.

"Why can't we find anything of James?" she said. "Has it been too long?"

Shane could only return her gaze, and after moment of his silence, she walked away. He followed. Together, they traced the tree line as it curved and headed east, rolling over some rocky cliff faces toward the ship before cutting away and heading out of sight.

A low thrum of thunder rumbled across the sky.

"We should start looking for shelter," Shane said.

Sera's eyes were fixed on her footsteps. "Yeah."

"There might be an overhang or even a cave in those rocky hills over there."

He pointed to the edge of the field where Gabe was heading. As Shane and Sera looked that way, Gabe stopped, turned, and waved. He cupped his hands around his mouth and yelled, "I found something!"

Shane and Sera raced across the field as quickly as Sera could manage.

When they reached Gabe, he was standing in a path that was cut through the field, his amazed eyes cast to the ground at the destroyed grass that lay against the earth, now browning from death.

"Looks like the train came through here," Gabe said.

Shane and Sera looked on in amazement.

"I also found this." Gabe held up a bunch of pink flowers.

"That's it!" Shane extended a hand. "That's battensoft!"

Gabe grinned and handed the flowers to him.

"Let's see where this goes," Shane said. "Then I'll get this stuff ready."

They followed the trail to the rocky hills at the edge of the tree line.

"Maybe herebors," Gabe said.

Shane shook his head and ran his palm over the leveled grass. "Whatever did this was low to the ground. Herebors stand on four long legs."

Clouds passed in front of the sun, casting the whole field in gray shadow.

Sera was wincing.

"Are you okay?" Shane asked.

"Let's keep going," she said.

They could all feel it. They were close, and there was no way Sera was going to stop now.

They followed the path through the field, chased by booming thunder. The temperature plummeted, and when they reached the foot of the rocky hills, their ears popped, the barometric pressure dropping.

They started up the rocky incline, kicking up pebbles and dry earth that no doubt yearned for the rain. For Sera, it was a grueling task, and the boys were there for her, supporting her and urging her along when she needed it.

When they reached the top, it looked like the rock had been sheared right off and laid on its side, creating a large overhang. The craggy, moss-covered surface led back into the forest, down and away.

From the west, they heard a low buzzing, a mechanical churning in the sky. As it drew nearer, it became a whine and hum. When it seemed the sound was going to overtake their whole world, a flying object burst out from over the trees. It flew right over them, leaving a gust of wind in its wake.

"What is that?" Sera asked.

"It's a drone," Gabe said. "That's what we heard the first day."

"They're looking for us," Shane said.

Captivated, they watched the drone bank over the field, level out, head straight for them, and pass overhead again.

It disappeared over the trees toward the west. The whining faded into a buzz and disappeared into the storm.

A drop of cold water landed on Shane's forearm, and he looked to the darkening sky. The forest rustled, as if every tree and plant were trying to free itself from the earth. Another drop spattered on Shane's forehead, and Sera wiped at her cheek. Then they heard the rain approach over the forest like drawing a curtain.

The sky flashed and detonated in a thunderous explosion. The teenagers flinched as Lumen's wrath reverberated in their chests. All at once, without sharing a word, they were running for the overhang. On the far side of the hilltop, the overhang led to a cave that sloped down into the earth, and from it, a whispering, breathing sound erupted like a flow of continuous air. In full retreat from the elements, they didn't dare stop, because their options were simple. They could weather the storm or face the dark earth where at least they might find warmth.

As they entered the cave, Shane pushed back the darkness with the lamp, and the torrents hissed outside.

Nine

The wind and rain pounded the cave opening. Lightning and thunder lashed like cracking whips. The storm had come for them, but they had outsmarted it. The sky darkened to a purple bruise and cracked like breaking bones. Lumen's fury grew.

Shane set his pack down and turned up the brightness on the lantern, casting their shadows onto the rock walls. The lamp's metal base clattered when he set it on the cave floor, kicking dry earth into the musty air. In the blue glow, the fine dust ascended like smoke.

Shivering, Sera wrung out her ponytail and clutched herself. She massaged her leg.

The rain hadn't hit them hard enough that they would need to change clothing, but the ambient temperature had plunged since leaving the sunlit field and entering the dark cave.

"Gabe, hand me a blanket from your pack," Shane said.

Sera's bottom lip trembled. "I'm all right."

Shane took the blanket from Gabe and threw it over Sera's shoulders, smoothing it down her arms and back.

"Can't have anyone getting sick out here," Shane said.

"You sound like my mother."

Shane considered the thought while pulling some kindling from his pack and arranging it into a pyramid on the cave floor. He used a small bottle of fuel and a match to spring the blaze to life.

"Well I am taking care of you." He began preparing the floreyfoil and battensoft by filling a pot from his canteen and hanging it over the fire to boil. Then he went to work grinding the plants and putting them into a metal mug.

Gabe looked out at the raging storm and sighed. "So we're stuck here for a while, huh?"

"Yeah."

The fire was growing and warming their skin.

"Got those Lore cards?" Shane asked Gabe.

"Of course, I do."

Gabe dealt the cards, and Shane dealt nuts and dried fruit. When the water boiled, he poured it into the mug and gave it to Sera to drink. They sat around the firelight snacking and playing Lore while the world outside raged and darkened. For a time, they felt like their old selves. They felt safe in the cave with full bellies and the warmth of a fire where the tempest couldn't reach them. It wasn't long before the storm weakened, and the lightning and thunder diminished, moving on.

The rain persisted, and the cave walls beaded with perspiration. Water trickled in like an unfurling tongue. A stream formed and ran down the slope, around them, and away into the darkness beyond the firelight's reach.

The games lulled, and exhaustion's weight pulled them down. Gabe lay out on a blanket, and having finished her elixir and already feeling better, Sera nestled against Shane's chest. They dozed and entered a place where time had no meaning, somewhere between sleep and consciousness that was deep enough to stretch time like putty.

A screeching cry rattled in Shane's ears, and he jolted awake, his adrenaline surging and bringing him to full alertness. The sound reverberated in his mind, and he thought he must have dreamed it.

Outside, the storm continued. He had no concept of how long he'd been out.

Sera had curled into a ball with her blanket wrapped around her. She breathed deeply and sighed.

Gabe's blanket lay in a crumpled mess. He was gone.

"Gabe?" Shane blinked at the smoldering fire, stirred it with his boot. He threw in another stick. "Gabe?"

"Back here." His voice echoed from deeper in the tunnel. The lamp glowed, and Shane saw a Gabe-shaped cutout in the blue light.

He stood and stretched, aware of a trickling sound from deeper in the cave. The water flowed downward, and just out of the lamp's reach, the ground dropped.

Shane moved deeper into the cave and stood beside Gabe in a pool of collecting water, which was sweeping away the grime of the cave floor. He was holding the lamp out in front of him, revealing the cave floor slipping away into nothingness.

"How deep do you think it goes?" Gabe said.

Shane shook his head. "No idea."

Gabe sighed. "What am I doing here, Shane?"

"What do you mean?"

"I mean, you two have each other. She's here because she has to be. You're here for her. I'm here because I thought it would be fun. It's just that, I see you two sometimes, and I guess I do get a little jealous."

Shane grasped his cousin's shoulder. "For what it's worth, I'm glad you came. You saved my life that first night. And you saved Sera by finding that battensoft."

Gabe chuckled. "That's right, and you owe me."

"I'm sorry about before," Shane said.

"Yeah, me too."

Sera approached, rubbing her eyes. "What are you idiots doing?"

"Nothing," Shane said. "Just seeing where the cave went. How you feeling?"

She narrowed her eyes in surprise. "Good, actually."

"Great. Let's get back to the fire."

As they turned, the stream swelled, and Gabe's foot shot out from under him. He landed with a hollow thud and slipped into the darkness on the slick rock.

Shane lunged for him. "Gabe!"

Gabe grasped Shane's outstretched hand, and they lay interlocked on the cave floor. Shane held the lamp out and saw Gabe's body writhing on the slick surface, dangling over the steep slope.

Sera crawled beside Shane, reaching. Her fingers found Gabe's arm, and the three of them lay on the cave floor, aware they were at a tipping point, teetering over the edge of a cliff. Uncertain of their balance, they froze.

Shane and Sera looked at each other and silently agreed to pull right before the ground slipped beneath them and then gave entirely.

The three of them tumbled down, down into the earth, down into oblivion.

Ten

Their voices echoed like sirens in the rocky cavern. The descent was long enough for them to realize that screaming was doing them no good, but that didn't stop Gabe from carrying on. Just when they felt they would fall forever, the slope leveled out and they tumbled to a stop, gasping, clinging to each other.

Behind them, a rattling sound grew, and a blue light was growing in the cavernous gloom, like a ghost in pursuit. The lamp clattered down the chute and tumbled past them, whipping rooster tails of water into the air. It rolled on its now-battered metal casing until it rested against a rock cleft.

Gabe groaned, his body lying over Shane's chest. With a grunt, Shane pushed him off, and Gabe's legs splashed in the streaming water.

When Shane tried to stand, it felt like he was wearing his pack and it was stuffed full of rocks. When the dizziness passed, he got to his feet and went to Sera.

"Are you all right?"

Blood oozed from a gash on her elbow, but she nodded. "Are you?" She squinted in the gloom. "Oh, Shane, your head."

He hadn't felt it until she mentioned it, but when his fingers went to his temple, he felt the oily tack of blood trickling from a wound on the side of his skull. A surge of electricity flowed up his face. The world faded and then came back again. He wavered and blinked.

Sera moved to help him, but he held a hand up. "I'm okay."

Her palm touched the side of his head, and he expected the spark of agony, but it brought a soothing coolness.

"Great." Gabe stomped water from his boots. "Just great. Now what?" He leaned against the side of the cave for balance. Nursing a knee, he grunted and hobbled back to the chute they'd fallen down. He looked up, and at the top of the dark throat, their fire flickered on the walls.

"What are we going to do?" Gabe cried.

The air in Shane's chest was heavy. "We'll think of something. Just calm down."

"At least we have the lamp," Sera said.

Shane picked it up and examined it, turning it over in his hands, wiggling a loose piece. "We're lucky it still works too."

"Help!" Gabe's voice rang out throughout the cavern. "Help!"

"Quiet!" Shane rushed to his cousin, a surprising pain bursting in his ankle like needles. He grabbed Gabe's sleeve. "Quiet! There's no one to help us. There's no one out there."

Gabe threw Shane off. "Well we gotta do something."

Sera joined them and looked up the tunnel, her eyes icy in the lamplight. "It was so slick coming down."

"This cave must have been natural run-off for the storms that used to come all the time," Shane said. "It must have weathered over the years."

"It's definitely too slick to climb back up," Sera said.

"We could try," Gabe said. "We *have* to try."

"No," Shane said. "We're lucky we didn't get hurt worse coming down the first time."

"Lucky?" Sera said. "Shane, you probably need stitches."

He set the lamp on the rocky floor and started digging in his pockets. "Let's take inventory. What do we have?"

"Everything's up there," Sera said. "I'm lucky I still have my shoes on. I almost took them off before falling asleep."

"There you go," Shane said. "We're lucky."

Even in the darkness, Shane could see Gabe roll his eyes.

"I have my knife, some nuts, and some dried fruit," Shane said. "Gabe?"

"An empty water bottle." He held out a small canteen he'd kept in his pants pocket. Shane took it and leaned against the cave wall where the drop-off was steep. There, the stream made a miniature waterfall, and he filled the canteen.

"This is good," he said. "We have water and food, and we have light. We can't go back up this way. That leaves us with one option."

Gabe groaned.

"We follow the cave."

"You can't be serious," Gabe said.

"I am. This water has to go somewhere, and sometimes these cavern systems run into each other. We could find another tunnel that goes up or an underground river that we could ride out of here."

Gabe scoffed. "Or we could get even more trapped and find ourselves dead."

"Do you have a better idea?"

"As a matter of fact, I do."

Shane flinched, surprised. "Well let's hear it then."

"We wait until the rain stops and the cave dries, and then we climb out."

Sera looked up the chute. "That's actually not a bad idea, Shane. If this wasn't so wet, I might be able to do it."

Shane drew a breath to protest.

"No," Gabe said.

"What?"

"I said no. Ever since we got out here, it's been you two versus me. I'm the odd man out. It wasn't always that way. We're the Triple Threat, a team that can overcome anything. But out here, it's like you don't think I can contribute. I really think, if we just wait, we can climb out of here."

Shane was silent for a moment. "All right. But we might as well see where this goes. If we find a dead end or something else, we come back here. Deal?"

Gabe nodded. "One condition."

"What's that?"

"We get out my way, I want your hunter."

Shane laughed. "Deal."

Eleven

The cave leveled out for a distance. They couldn't be certain about how far they traveled because, in the dark, with the blue spirits of lamplight dashing around the walls and chasing shadows, their concept of space and depth warped. Each step could have been ten. Ten steps could have been none. It didn't help that Gabe's knee and Shane's ankle were locking up like enraged fists.

The floor sloped down again, and it threatened to get too steep to navigate. With the lamp in hand, Shane led Gabe and Sera along the wall, taking half steps like elders concerned about falling and breaking arthritic joints. The stone floors glistened, planes of slippery smooth surfaces like ice sheets in the blue light. The soles of their boots scuffed, and the cavernous echo amplified the sound into a crunching, like a giant chewing on bones.

Shane felt Sera's hot breath on his neck. She clutched his arm as if it were a lifeline, her fingers digging into the spaces between his muscles.

The ground leveled out again, and Sera released his arm. "Was I hurting you?"

"No."

"Sorry." She cast her apologetic eyes downward.

Shane touched her chin and brought her face back up to meet his own. It wasn't regret he saw then, but apprehension and fear. "What's wrong?"

She shook her head. "Nothing."

A screech pierced the darkness, and the unmistakable sound of meat and bones hitting stone followed it.

Shane raised the lantern to find Gabe on his back. "You all right?"

"Just my pride." Gabe groaned and rolled.

Shane offered a hand to help him up. When Gabe was on his feet slapping the moisture off of his backside, they heard the static sound of rushing water. Shane and Gabe shared a glance of mutual revelation, and they charged into the darkness with renewed vigor.

The risk they took negotiating the slick rock seemed for nothing when the tunnel ended. Just ahead, in the lamp's far reach, the cave had collapsed, probably ages ago. The sound of rushing water was nearby, but they could never reach it.

"Dead end." Gabe snapped his fingers. "Guess we're going back."

"No. Wait." Shane was still as he listened. "The water is going somewhere. It's not pooling here."

Gabe shook his head. "So what? It's probably sneaking through a hole or something."

Sera moved closer. "Guys."

"You hear that? It's not a trickle, Gabe. There's an underground river here."

"What good does it do us if we can't get to it?"

Sera trotted to the wall created by the cave-in, and then she had Gabe and Shane's attention. She traced the wall with her hands, looked back with a grin, and then disappeared.

"Sera!"

Shane ran for her, and as he reached the wall, she reappeared, giggling.

"Don't do that," he said. "That's not funny."

"Yeah," she said through her laughter. "It is."

"If you could have seen your face, you'd be laughing too," Gabe said with a grin.

Shane frowned at them, and even as their laughter diminished, he forced the frown to stay put. It became a scowl.

"Oh, come on." Sera pushed his shoulder. "Don't be so serious. You look like your dad when you're serious."

Shane didn't have to force his frown to make a point anymore. The laughter died on its own when Sera realized what she'd said, and in the depths of the cavern, it hadn't felt so quiet, so still, so lonely.

Sera looked at him with pleading eyes. "I'm sorry."

Shane shook his head. "Forget it. What did you find?"

"There's a crack. We should be able to fit through."

"No way," Gabe said. "Uh uh."

"You agreed," Shane said. "This isn't a dead end. We can get through, so we keep going."

Gabe sighed. "Fine."

The fissure in the wall curved, so they wouldn't be able to see the other side until they were within the dark crevice. It slanted unevenly, so they would have to navigate it unbalanced. From top to bottom, the fracture looked like a massive hammer had struck a boulder and broke it in two.

They filed through, shuffling sideways, the quarters so close they could smell the damp stone at the tips of their noses. Jagged rock stabbed like nails against their backs and ribs. Their clothing caught on clefts, and they had to help free each other. The lamp beamed blinding bright but hardly reached behind Shane so Gabe was all but left in the dark. They linked hands, and Shane pulled them deeper and deeper, like clawing through some great animal's bowels.

Just when the fissure squeezed their bodies like a pair of gigantic hands, it opened up, and when it did, the cavern hadn't felt so large.

They entered a great room. The storm water flowed out of the fissure, down a slick slope, and into a fast-moving underground river. Islands of rock jutted from the water, filling the room with the hush of rapids.

Great stalactites and stalagmites reached from the ceiling and floor, some of them connecting, an eternal handshake. Minerals glittered in the lamplight as if the cave were full of jewels and treasures. When Shane waved the lamp around, a pair of voids remained in the wall across the river. Other tunnels joined this room.

"Whoa!" Gabe's jaw hung slack.

"I told you the cave would lead somewhere," Shane said.

Gabe's mouth clicked shut. "But where? Sure, we can keep going, but we don't know where this river or those other tunnels go. We could be lost down here for days."

"Or we could be out in minutes. We have to try, Gabe."

Gabe nodded. "Okay, fine. Where should we go?"

Shane scanned the cavern. There were several tunnels to choose from. He pointed to the left-most tunnel. "That way. That's the direction the river is flowing from, and rivers always flow downhill, so this tunnel might go up."

The kids followed the tunnel. It stretched before them like a giant, fossilized intestine. They continued along the path, Shane and Gabe periodically bickering about when to turn back, until Sera heard something.

"Shhh!" She stilled and waved her hands in their faces. "You hear that?"

She stood between Shane and Gabe with her hands raised, her wide eyes like sapphires in the lamp's glow.

Save for the rushing of the river, there was absolute silence.

"I don't hear anything," Gabe said.

"Shhh! There!"

A breeze flowed through the tunnel. It puffed Sera's hair like flexing fingers. It sounded like a voice, a whisper in the dark. The echoes in the darkness sounded like an intake of air, like holding breath. When it reverberated through the cavern again, it carried with it an unmistakable, low growl, like audible anger, the incarnation of rage on approach.

Then Shane was running, leading a charge with the lantern, back the way they had come. Gabe and Sera had no choice but to follow. They had no choice but to stay in the light.

CHAPTER 6
MARKS IN THE EARTH

One

After the kids' first night in the wild, while they lingered in a guarded doze on a tree stand made of rope, Lincoln and Aeron prepared to go after them.

Since Lincoln had convinced him to wait until first light, Aeron struggled every moment just to remain calm. Lincoln felt the same oppressive weight. They remained strong for each other out of sheer will because they knew they held each other up, the pillars of the house of Arokson.

Lincoln gazed through the window at the gray, milky horizon. It was good enough. By the time they got beyond the wall, the sun would burn the sky like tinder. Every second counted. The trail would cool quickly.

He yanked zippers closed, snapped clips together on his pack, and lifted it onto his back. It was everything he needed.

"Ready?" Aeron asked.

"Are you?"

"Does it matter?"

"No."

Aeron reached for his baby brother, took him by the back of his neck, and pulled him close, pressing their foreheads together. He broke the embrace and turned to walk down the hall.

"Wait." Lincoln clipped the bottom of Aeron's water bottle so it wouldn't swing on the carabiner, tightened his underpack support strap, then turned his brother around and connected the clip that held the over-shoulder straps in front of him.

He slapped Aeron's chest. "You're ready."

In the quiet hallway, they stared at each other, two men choosing the impossible because they couldn't sit around and hope their sons would return.

On the first floor, Lucy stood in the hallway, mid-step, like she had thought about coming upstairs but couldn't decide. She looked at them with small, frightened eyes, Mel and Bernie clinging to her.

Aeron went to his wife and daughter, and Bernie ran to Lincoln. Aeron embraced his family, and Lincoln took Bernie into his arms.

"Don't be afraid," Lincoln said to her. She burrowed her head into his chest, sucking her thumb. She hadn't sucked her thumb in years.

Aeron pulled away from Lucy and fumbled with the collar of his shirt. He bowed his head and pulled the cord around his neck over his ears. The Warden's Seal swung like a pendulum, and for a moment, Lucy refused to take it. Aeron pulled her hand up and let the necklace fall into her palm, closing her fingers on it. Lucy's breath caught, and the sadness broke through for just an instant. Her lips trembling, she squeezed back the tears.

"I've told Captain Barrow that you'll be the interim warden," Aeron said. "He will help you. I don't want to put you in this position, but there's no one else. Be reasonable first, but be strong. Be good. Never compromise the people, but always compromise for the people."

Lucy wrapped her arms around his neck, pulled him close.

"I'll come back, and I'll bring our boy home," he said. "Keep this place together until I do."

Aeron kissed her and Mel and then parted.

"Sweetheart," Lincoln said. "Daddy has to go."

Bernie whined in protest. She clung to his neck, and he had to push her away and set her on the floor. She began to cry and scream, and Lincoln understood he was leaving her utterly alone. She had lost the mother she'd never known, her brother may have already been gone, and now her father was leaving. He understood it, but it was the only way things could be. He'd never felt more powerless.

Lucy looked at Lincoln with hard eyes and embraced his daughter. Bernie continued to cry as Lucy cooed her and escorted her and Mel into the interior of the house.

With piercing, icy eyes, Lucy glared back at the brothers. "Bring them home." It was her first order as warden.

Lincoln opened the front door. Sheriff Ballard stood on the steps with a raised fist about to knock. Ducard stood just behind her, looking out over the quiet street. They each had packs and were ready to go.

Ducard's sentry rifle hung on a single-point sling, chassis across his broad chest, barrel pointed toward the ground.

The brothers stepped outside, looking back one last time at Lucy and the girls, and closed the door.

"You're not coming," Aeron said to Ballard.

"But—"

"No." Aeron's jaw muscles bulged.

"It's all right, Reg," Lincoln said. "We'll be fine." He reached for her hand, felt the electricity between their fingertips, and pulled back.

Reggie looked at him as if he'd hurled an insult.

"I need you both here," Aeron said. "The people need law and order. I've left the Warden's Seal with Lucy. She'll handle the administration. I need you to look out for her. Both of you. People are going to question her. They're going to fault me and use it against her. They're going to challenge her. They'll try to take control."

Ballard crossed her arms. "People?"

"You know who I'm talking about."

Ballard frowned. "In that case..." She swung her pack off of her back and set it down. From it, she pulled gleaming gunmetal. She held the grip of a revolver out to Aeron. "I'm not letting you leave without protection."

She looked at Ducard, and the big man sighed, unhappy but compliant. He grabbed the stock of his rifle and lifted the strap over his head. He held out the weapon, but Aeron and Lincoln just stared at it. Impatient, Ducard stepped forward and shoved it into Lincoln's chest.

"Before I change my mind," the sentry said.

Aeron took the revolver, and Ballard reached back into her pack, producing a handheld radio. "Ernest told me to give this to you. He said he's going to help look. Said you'd understand."

Aeron accepted the radio. "Thanks."

She shook Aeron's hand and hesitated before reaching out and shaking Lincoln's as well. Then she began descending the front steps.

Ducard gazed at the brothers for a long moment, sizing them up. "Good luck." He followed Ballard down to the street.

"I'm not sure we know how to even use these," Aeron called after them.

"It isn't hard," Ballard said.

Ducard cackled. "Point and shoot."

"I'm sorry," Aeron said when the brothers were alone.

"For what?"

"It might be the last time they see us. Sorry you didn't get a better goodbye."

Lincoln glared sideways at him. "Let's go get our kids."

The brothers grimaced at the early dawn light and moved up the street, away from the commons. When they passed the Bellman home, they heard the discord in the silence. Elena appeared at her bedroom window, gray through the glass like a ghost. She locked eyes with them, watching them intently.

Aeron raised a hand.

She faded into the dark interior of her home.

Two

The globe street lamps shut off, and the shadow of dawn towered around them, sunrise beginning to set blaze to the sky. Oranges and reds flowed around cloud cover like apocalyptic magma.

Turning the corner, they discovered why the colony was so silent. At the end of the street, where the wheat fields began, the people waited. They amassed in a group of two dozen, blocking the way. As the brothers approached, news that they were coming spread through the crowd, and they waited in anticipation.

Gideon and Clayton Ford stood at the front.

Gideon sneered. "Morning, Warden."

"Morning. What's this about?"

"It's been a rough few days."

"It has."

"These people are missing family members who are presumed lost in the wild. Then your kids go off and get lost out there too. We figured you wouldn't hold to your own rules, and knew at least Lincoln would find a way out of here."

Aeron peered at him. "What's your point?"

"The point is the same as always. The Arokson family thinks it's above the law, thinks it can do as it pleases."

"So you want to stop us from leaving?"

"On the contrary. We wouldn't stop you from going after your kids. It's your right. We want you to look for the missing sentries."

Aeron looked over each face. In the dim morning light, they appeared unsympathetic and unmoving. They didn't care about their warden's troubles. They only cared about their own. Even in Aeron's time of crisis, they expected everything of him.

"We won't be near where they were lost," he said.

"Doesn't matter. If they're lost, you may cross one of their paths. The people aren't confident you have their interests at heart, only your own. They think, if you find something of their loved ones, you will ignore it in favor of looking for your children. And really, who can blame you? Anyone would understand that. But that's the point, Aeron. You're going out there as a father today, not the warden." Gideon eyed Aeron's neckline.

Aeron nodded. "What do you propose?"

"My son Clayton has agreed to accompany you. He will look for signs of the missing sentries."

Lincoln spat. "No."

Aeron barred his brother with his forearm. "A moment with my brother, Mr. Ford?"

Gideon nodded. "Of course."

Aeron and Lincoln backed away.

"I think we should let him come," Aeron said.

"Why?"

"While we may not need him, having more people who know the wild can't hurt. Plus, it'll keep him out of trouble here."

"This is about you watching your own."

"*Us*, Lincoln. It's about *us*. Our leaving won't go over well, and the Fords have been gunning for us for years."

"You think taking Clay with us is going to stop Gideon?"

"No, but he's got us here. If we leave without Clay, it looks bad. He gains support. If we take him, he's their hero, and the fewer Fords here to start trouble the better."

Lincoln grunted. "Our kids are missing in the wild, and you're playing politics. Fine, but he's your responsibility. Anything goes wrong, that's on you, and you'll have to live with it."

The brothers returned, the sunlight beginning to creep over the horizon and burn their eyes.

"Okay, Clay," Aeron said. "You're with us."

Clay snapped his fingers and threw his pack over his shoulder.

Gideon grinned. "There is one other matter."

"What is it?"

"I noticed you're not wearing the seal. Your interim replacement. Who is it?"

"Lucy will handle the warden's administrative duties. Captain Barrow will continue to monitor the security of the colony until we've returned."

Gideon scratched at an eyebrow. "There's the rub. The curfew, the lockdown, all of it without an explanation, and then you go ahead and nominate another warden while you abandon us. The people feel like you're abusing your authority, powers that you were never elected to carry in the first place. There's no accountability, Aeron, and the people are upset."

Voices of ascent erupted from behind him.

Aeron stared at Gideon in a moment of intense silence. "You question my motives, but let's cut to the chase. You're playing these people." He raised his voice to speak to the crowd. "Everyone, Gideon's only interest is the warden's office. He doesn't care about you. He's using your needs to make you think he does, but it's all just a means to an end. I agree you need transparency. I owe you answers. But everything I've done has been for the benefit of this colony and its people. I know the last few days have been hard, but we can't lose sight of why we're here. The pillar. We have to keep Lumen going. It's almost there, and it depends on you. But unlike Gideon, I don't think you're stupid. I've neglected your intelligence, but I haven't insulted it. I promise I'll return with the truth. If you ever believed in me, I ask you to give me some time. Right now, I have to go find my son, nephew, Sera Bellman, and anyone else if I can. Excuse me."

The people had lapsed into a dazed silence, and when Aeron pushed through them, they parted. Lincoln followed. In time, so did Clay.

When they were clear, Lincoln leaned into Aeron's ear. "Politics?"

"You know the difference between men like Gideon Ford and me? They're better at politics because they care about nothing else. This place could crumble, but as long as he was in charge, as long as he won, he would be happy. That's the dangerous part about it. Men like Gideon inevitably win. They inevitably have the power. Because that's all they care about."

"So why even bother?"

"You want Shane to live in a world where that guy is warden?"

Lincoln was quiet as they continued up the gravel road toward the wheat field, the wall, and the wild beyond. "I want Shane to be able to make it if everything falls apart *because* that guy's warden."

With the colonists watching them move toward the burning daylight, the brothers pushed into the wheat field. Clay's boots crunched the gravel behind them. The wheat stalks rustled, brushing their bodies like affectionate hands.

Lincoln glanced back at Clay. "How much you making on this one?"

Clay's expression didn't change. "This one I'm doing for free."

Lincoln grunted. "I'm sure your sense of satisfaction is enough."

Aeron had the distinct feeling that they were escaping something and taking Clay was the price, but as they neared the wall, it wasn't with a sense of release, of nearing resolution. It was with the growing unease of entering a labyrinth of tree and vine and stone.

Three

Cutting through the darkness of the storm drain with their flashlights, they picked up the kids' trail. Lincoln crouched over Shane's boot impression and swiped his beam of light over it, scrutinizing the treads. He absently rubbed his mouth. He had to face it. Shane was missing, and he couldn't be sure they were going to find him.

"That's a strong print," Aeron said. "Following them should be easier than I thought."

Lincoln shined his light on the concrete pipe around them. "We're contained in here. Nothing to destroy the tracks. But a storm's coming. We're on a clock."

"We should get moving then."

The men walked the remainder of the pipe, sliding into the overflow reservoir, kicking up dry earth and dust. A sentry's boots pounded an iron grate above. Morning light was creeping into the shaft. Crouching into the outlet, they found a straight shot to the other side, a long tube of darkness leading to a circle of light.

At the edge, the dark green of the wild burst forth, the shadows still heavy, and for a moment, Lincoln hesitated.

Clay sneered at him. "You afraid of heights? Or are you just afraid?"

"You don't have to come, Clay," Lincoln said.

"I'm just messing with you. No need to take it personally."

"That's not what he means," Aeron said.

Clay looked between the brothers, mystified. "Why don't you tell me what you mean?"

Aeron motioned with his head. "There's something out there."

Clay laughed, sputtering his lips. "There's lots of things in the wild, Warden. Didn't your brother tell you? Nothing to be afraid of, though." He pushed past Lincoln and crouched at the edge of the pipe, ready to descend. "I swear. You people are so afraid of what you don't know."

"*You* don't know, Clay," Lincoln said. "Tell him, Aeron."

"We've known for a while about the wildlife. It was actually us that put them there," Aeron said. "The First Families brought some species of animals and, when the time was right, released them to see if they could survive. The Dawn forced them to evolve. That isn't at all what we're talking about."

Clay remained still at the end of the pipe, eyeing the brothers.

"When we came here, Lumen had a native species that lived within the planet," Aeron said. "They lived underground where it was warm and dark. We don't know much about them, but at the time, it was assumed the pillars would change the ecosystem so that they would all die off."

"Ain't that illegal?" Clay asked.

"It's the first article in the colonization protocols. If native life is discovered, colonization has to stop immediately."

"So why'd they continue?"

"I don't know. Someone didn't do their job. We didn't find out about this species until we already landed here, installed the pillars, and began building the colonies. It's extremely risky and expensive to begin new colonies. Somebody swept it under the rug."

"I take it the animals didn't die as expected."

"No. In fact, the pillars have made the planet more habitable to them. Or maybe the Dawn forced their evolution. Either way, they're out here, thriving."

Clay eased away from the edge of the pipe. He gazed into the gloom of the wild, evaluating it.

Aeron pointed into the trees. "Our kids are out there. We have to go. You don't. No one would fault you if you stayed."

Clay grinned. "If I stayed, you'd have to pay me to keep quiet. No, I'm off the hook now. We ain't gonna find nothing out here. If what you say is true, the people we're going to look for are gone."

"So why are you coming?" Lincoln asked.

"You said it. Sense of satisfaction."

Clay eased over the edge of the pipe and dropped down to the dark forest floor below.

Four

When all three men were on the ground amid the forest twilight, they searched the bracken for signs of the children. With the soft, untrodden earth under foot and the thick foliage growing like a singular mass, it wouldn't be difficult. It was Clay who whistled for the others, having discovered the void cleaved into the wild by Shane's bush knife and the trampled weeds and ivy, which were already dying in places.

Aeron and Lincoln high-stepped over brush to stand beside Clay, breathing deep the earthy scent. The trail cut into the darkness of the forest floor. Their lungs drew a calming brew of natural air, the wild beckoning. Amid the trees forming a canopy like hands holding up the sky, their fate lay somewhere in the morning mist. Somewhere out there their children were lost, and it didn't cross their minds that they might already be gone, because they couldn't face that idea.

One way or another, they would be with their children soon, and they couldn't move against the weight of such a thought. At the edge of the wild, outside the safety of their home, it wasn't the threat of the darkness that held them in place. It was the fear of what they would find of their children, of knowing the unknown. The only thing that kept Aeron and Lincoln going was the possibility that Shane, Gabe, and Sera were out there and needed them.

"We can stand here all day if you want, but I suggest we get moving." Clay stepped onto the trail. "We're losing daylight." Hiking his pack up on his shoulders, Clay marched into the void, the wilderness shivering around him with his disturbing presence.

Lincoln sighed. "Say it."

Aeron gazed at his brother, wondering how Lincoln had gotten inside his mind. "What if they're already gone?"

Lincoln drew a deep breath and released it. "Then so are we." He stepped forward into the wilderness.

For a moment, Aeron wanted to climb back through the storm drain and return to his colony to salvage what was left. For a moment, he thought it was the smart thing to do. But it was only a short, despicable moment. He couldn't deny the impulses of fatherhood. Even if Gabe was already gone, he had to know for sure, and if he would never know, he might as well disappear into the wild, because he would never be able to move on.

He set off after his brother, and the forest accepted him. It opened its long, amorphous arms and enveloped them all. It wasn't long before he looked back and could find no sign of his home in the deep, thick wild.

Five

Cascades of sunlight broke through the canopy, burning away the mist and revealing the lush green forest floor. The men followed the children's footprints in the soft, dark soil. For the most part, their trail was evident in the way the foliage split apart or lay dead, cast aside.

Occasionally, though, Lincoln had to part the bracken or ivy to find the marks in the earth.

"All I'm saying, Warden, is Lincoln and I know this land. You don't," Clay said to Aeron. "You should head back now before we get too far, before you get hurt."

"Our father taught both of us. Lincoln excelled, but I learned enough."

"Surviving in the wild is more about instinct and quick wits. How long has it been since you've been out here?"

"Out here?" Aeron said. "Never. Our father taught us within the walls."

Clay rolled his eyes.

Lincoln looked up from examining the soil. "What are you really getting at, Clay?"

Aeron waved a hand of dismissal. "It doesn't matter. I won't go back until I find my son. I don't care what's out here."

As Aeron spoke, the plants behind him darkened, shriveled, and drooped. It spread around them in a sweeping arc, a spectacle like the life was draining from the forest. Leaves folded inward on themselves, and limbs fell limp.

Lincoln and Clay dropped to a crouch, and Aeron looked at the plants, confused.

"Get down!" Lincoln whispered.

Aeron dropped, eyes wide and alert. "What is it? What's going on?"

Lincoln's head jerked, scanning the area. His hands gripped the stock of the rifle that hung at his waist.

Clay pinched one of the leaves and inspected it. "Sensitive plants."

Aeron appeared confused. "What?'

"It's their defense mechanism. They do this when something disturbs them. It can set off a chain reaction among them. Something is nearby."

Not far off, something kicked through the bracken and snapped twigs. Clay eyed the rifle.

"Maybe it's the kids," Aeron said.

The thought sent Lincoln shooting up. He scanned over the hedges and found the movement weaving between the trees.

"It isn't the kids." Frowning, he flicked the safety switch on the rifle. The rail-firing mechanism's amplifier hummed with electrical current.

They detected an odor that hadn't been there moments ago. The sickly sweet smell of decomposition crept over them like a cloud, and it repulsed them with a primal warning. The smell informed their instincts that, somewhere nearby, death had recently been at work.

They followed the sensitive plant hedges around a large tree, and when they turned at the perimeter edge, the forest opened wide before them like a great hall with vaulted ceilings.

The wild was completely decimated. Tree branches had been torn away at their trunks. Bushes and shrubs had been ripped from the earth. Vines and ivy plants hung like disconnected umbilical cords.

On the ground, they discovered the source of the movement. A dead herebor lay in the path of destruction, and three small, four-legged animals were feasting. Short, coarse hair struck from their backs like spines, and matted red fur encompassed an otherwise sleek body, which was built for speed and agility, not power.

"Riptens," Lincoln said. "Scavengers and cowards."

Lincoln approached the animals, and one of them looked up from its feast, bearing a bloody snout with hundreds of needle-like teeth. It made a wet, rapid-fire popping sound in its throat that could only be a growl.

"They eat anything," Clay said. "People who live out here are always trying to keep them from their gardens. We should kill them."

Lincoln fired his rifle into the air. In an instant, the amplifier hummed with electrical current, the magnetic rail accelerator zipped, and the round flashed from the muzzle with a punch and crack.

Two of the riptens dashed away into the forest. The third animal flinched but looked like it was going to hold its ground. Then it reluctantly backed away. Before it dove into the thick and disappeared, it glanced back one last time, resentment in its eyes.

Clay scoffed at Lincoln and shook his head.

"You got something to say to me?" Lincoln said.

"I really don't."

"Enough," Aeron said. "We're not out here for you. We're out here to bring people back."

"Speaking of," Clay said, "your kids are lost. Herebors stampeded through here and destroyed everything. Their trail is gone."

Aeron's brow wrinkled. "Stampeded?"

"Something was chasing them," Lincoln said. "No number of riptens would be able to take down an herebor. The question is whether the kids were able to stay out of it."

"Assuming they did, how do we follow them now?"

"The herebors shadowed the kids' path. So we follow the herebors' path."

"Why?"

Lincoln looked at his brother with shimmering eyes. "Because it's all we have to go on."

They put their heads down and carried on, looking for any sign to pick up the kids' trail.

Six

By the time they reached the river, the light was failing. The sky still clutched at day even as twilight crept, but the water flowed like ink, no glimmers on the surface, only darkness below. The sun had fallen from sight, and shadows seeped from the earth, climbing up the tree trunks to the canopy of dark green. Soon, it effectively would be night in the wild.

Lincoln stopped by the riverbank and released a deep breath. "We'll camp here."

"Finally." With a sigh of relief, Clay slipped his pack off of his shoulders and let it fall to the ground in a rattle of clips and punch of canvas. He sought a large rock at the edge of the path and sat down, groaning and unscrewing the cap on his canteen. He tipped it up, and nothing came. Growling, he stomped to the riverbank.

Aeron eyed Lincoln in appeal. "We have to keep going."

"We've been going all day without rest. There's water here, trees, and the river will mask sound. It's a good place."

Aeron bit his lip. "What about the kids? Do they have a good place?"

Lincoln gazed at him sorrowfully. 'We can't move after dark."

"Maybe if we're careful. Maybe if we're quiet."

"Aeron, no."

"Dammit, Lincoln! We can't just stop now!"

"Not so easy, is it?" Clay said, returning from the river with a look of contempt. He sipped from his canteen. "When it's your kids missing. Not so easy to just wait until tomorrow."

Aeron's expression slackened. Lincoln shut his eyes.

"That's right," Clay said. "Now you get it."

Lincoln set his pack down. "That's enough, Clay."

"No, no. This is when our warden learns his family isn't exempt from his own rules."

Lincoln stepped between them. "Let's just make camp."

"You're wrong, Clay," Aeron said, cool and calm. "My family *is* exempt. Because I'm the warden. I make plenty of exceptions for the people in our colony, not just my own. If you don't like it, fine, but you have to accept it."

Clay sneered. "And if I don't?"

"Then I will bury you and yours."

Clay dropped his canteen and rushed at Aeron. "You son of a—"

Lincoln wrapped his arms around Clay's chest and held him back.

"Why do you think I make these exceptions?" Aeron said. "Because I'm a nice guy? Because I can? Because I lack the conviction to make the hard decisions?"

"Aeron," Lincoln said. "Don't."

"I do it for leverage."

Clay stopped struggling against Lincoln and glared at the warden. Across the dead air and dying light, Aeron let the statement sink in. Then he drove it home.

"I know about the drugs. Not just the ones you gather from the wild, but the ones you skim from the infirmary. That summer we had all those deaths from liquid lung and we ran short on morphine? I know that was you. I know your father meets his mistress on the second or third day of every week, depending on how he feels, sometimes both days, usually in the storeroom on the third floor of the fabrication warehouse but sometimes in a field out in the farmlands if the weather is nice. I know she's had to end a third and fourth pregnancy, and neither were her husband's. I know about the resources smuggled out of the colony to people who have left. And I know, after all of these years of people going missing, at least one of those wasn't lost to the wild, and I know where you buried the body. I know everything, and I could use it to end you and your father. If I wanted."

Clay gaped. Lincoln let him go and stepped away. He was shocked too. Clay stood there unrestrained physically but paralyzed by wonder.

"You can't prove any of it," Clay said.

"Some of it, no. Most of it I can. Even so, are you going to take that chance? Why do you think your father has been gunning for the wardenship for so long? Because he wants this power."

Dumbfounded, Clay stared at Aeron.

Aeron grinned. "Now you get it."

The forest darkened, and Clay was silent. For a while, Lincoln watched him for signs of aggression, but he needed to get their tree stand set up. He let Clay be, and for the moment, at least, he kept his distance.

Seven

Lincoln found a tree nearby that would do. Once they started climbing, it wasn't long before the ground was perilously far beneath them.

There was more light in the branches above, but soon that light abandoned them too as night fell.

Neither Aeron nor Clay had protested when Lincoln explained they would be camping in the trees. Lincoln had expected to have to combat his brother over the decision to stop for the night, but after setting Clay right, the fight had left him. Or maybe his capacity for rational thought had returned, and he understood they couldn't help their kids if they were dead.

Just as the kids were doing across the river and up the hill, Lincoln and Clay wrapped the rope around the tree branches to create their bed, and Lincoln instructed Aeron to use another rope to secure their packs.

When their aerial camp was finished, they sat in the tree stand and ate their dinner of jerky and nuts, with dried fruit for dessert.

Lincoln set up a lantern like the kids had, and it glowed between them like a jewel of the night. None of them were willing to invite conversation that would inevitably go bad.

Finally, Clay removed a wad of folded papers from his pack. He unwrapped it, revealing a dried leaf. Aeron stared at him curiously.

"Nod plant," Lincoln said. "To help him sleep."

"I'd brew it, but up here, no fire, no hot water." Clay stuck a piece in his mouth and chewed. A minty aroma filled the air. "I'd offer you some, but I don't want to."

Lincoln shrugged. "Bitter as hell anyway."

In moments, Clay fell asleep, and it was just the brothers in that tree, or as private as it was going to get. For a while, the quiet persisted. The truth neither would have admitted to the other was they enjoyed not fighting and simply being brothers. There was something in the air between them keeping them in tune, and when they weren't fighting it, they felt drawn together and unified, like they were on the same team. They felt like they could take on anything.

Even with these creatures, which they knew were out there somewhere in the wild or beneath it, they could be the exception in spite of Lumen's darkness taking so many others before them, many of whom they regarded as better men.

"It's hard for me to not think about Dad," Aeron said.

"You're worried the same thing is going to happen to us."

Aeron nodded.

"I'd like to tell you we won't die out here. But I don't have that in me. I'll tell you that I think we're more prepared than Dad was, and if we're careful, we will be all right. If we're very lucky, the kids will be too."

"That isn't what I mean."

"What do you mean?"

"Mel and Bernie. Whatever happens out here is going to happen, and I'm sick to death about Gabe, Shane, and Sera, but Mel and Bernie have to grow up no matter what. We had to grow up too fast. I don't want that for them."

Lincoln leaned toward his brother and grasped his shoulder. "After we find Shane, Gabe, and Sera, this isn't over. If we're lucky, Bernie and Mel get to grow up too fast."

Perplexed, Aeron gaped at Lincoln and waited for his little brother to explain, but Lincoln lay back, pulled a blanket over himself, and rolled over.

After a while, Aeron turned down the lamp until it clicked off, and he found himself in a world of surprising darkness. For the first time in his adult life, the warden of Vale looked toward the heavens at night and saw no aurora, nothing.

Eight

Lincoln dreamed of Lumen's night sky. Electrically charged solar particles bombarded the young and fragile atmosphere and created shimmering auroras. He'd grown up with it, and the colonists saw it every night, but it never lost its wonder as far as he was concerned.

The wispy greens and blues and reds like tongues of flame danced in the air like Lumen herself was twirling a dress in the sky, and in the distance, the Pillar of Dawn coughed the endless supply of gases, the occasional bolt of lightning crashing through the clouds and striking the tower.

The aurora was especially distressed on the night Lincoln and Aeron's father, Owen, went missing. Owen burst from the front door of their home, which back then was a modular cabin left over from the original colonization. They hadn't yet built the row homes in the residential district.

Still just a boy, Lincoln looked up from his seated place in the grass surrounded by wooden toys.

"Dad?" he said. "What are the colors in the sky?"

"Not now." Owen hurried toward the main gate.

Aeron, sixteen then, followed their father, launching from the cabin's porch.

"What lights?" Aeron grinned. "I don't see anything. Oh, maybe you're seeing the warning lights. Lumen sometimes warns little boys when they've been bad. She'll snatch you and swallow you up if you don't watch out." Laughing, Aeron trotted off in their father's tracks.

Their mother, Isabel, eased out of the cabin onto the porch and crossed her arms, watching Owen and Aeron in the commons.

"Mom?" the boy said. "What's the aurora?"

She smiled at him. Isabel's smile was unlike any other. Lincoln's mother could beam in such a way that it would light up the person she was looking at. It was contagious. It made everything all right.

She sat next to him in the grass and caressed his cheek. "My Lincoln. Always so curious. It's nothing to be afraid of, dear. It's just the way the sky is."

"But why?"

"You'll learn more when you're a little older."

They watched from afar as Owen met with Trin Bleary's mother, who collapsed into Owen's arms. Isabel's grip tightened on Lincoln's shoulder as Mrs. Bleary wailed and wept. Trin was missing.

Wearing the black face of worry and powerlessness, Jok Anguilaro's father ran to Owen. Jok was also missing. Everyone knew the two teens were together as boyfriend and girlfriend, and even eleven-year-old Lincoln figured out Trin and Jok had likely snuck off together.

A crowd had assembled in the commons. Many of the people were murmuring and shouting.

"Let's not jump to conclusions," Owen said. "Search the compound. If they're in the colony, we'll find them."

By first light, they had found neither Trin nor Jok.

In the commons, Owen put something in Aeron's open hand. Their father then looked long back at their cabin, and as he and two sentries walked toward the main gate, Lincoln saw the Warden's Seal dangling from the necklace that Aeron clutched in his fist. With it, the power to run the colony had passed from Owen to Aeron.

Later that day, as the sun fell behind the mountains, the colony stopped. The farmers stood in the fields. Shop owners came out onto the street in the marketplace. The wrenches craned their heads from the base of the Pillar of Dawn. The sentries took up binoculars on the wall to peer into the horizon.

The sounds of automatic gunfire echoed off of the mountain range and through the valley into the commons where Lincoln played with some schoolmates, and for that thirty seconds they would talk about for years, the gunfire rapped across the sky like a god tapping impatient fingers.

Then it ceased.

Lincoln wanted to go back to playing their game, but everyone else seemed to have lost the desire. Some of the grownups cried, and others consoled them. Isabel came before the bell rang to signal the end of school, and she took Lincoln home. At the cabin, Lincoln heard no bells for the rest of the day. With his father gone, it seemed all of the rules stopped.

Their father did not return by nightfall, nor did he return the next day. Lincoln knew for certain because school had been canceled, and he sat on their cabin's front porch all day, watching the main gate. Days passed, and it wasn't the grownups who stopped to tell him how sorry they were that convinced him he would never see his father again. It was Lumen, herself.

After days of waiting on the porch, Lincoln looked up one night to find only a dark sky. The aurora did not show that night, and Lincoln cried, wishing it would come back, because as long as the colors danced in the night sky, everything was okay and nothing had changed. Yet for the first time in his life, he clearly saw stars, pinpricks of light in an infinite void. He saw a great disk of them, a galaxy of endless possibilities, slashing across the heavens. He saw a bright alien orb that was not the sun, but a moon he hadn't even known existed.

He saw all of it, and he felt small and alone. When Aeron sat with him and was quiet, Lincoln knew in his gut that all of the sibling torment he'd had to face was over. Something terrible had happened, but ironically, terrible events brought people together.

Lincoln and Aeron cried together that night. They mourned until Isabel came out of the cabin and joined them. She pulled them inside. She lifted Lincoln with surprising strength and placed him in his bed where, as far as he could remember, the whole world succumbed to an unimaginable darkness.

Nine

A bright light bled through Lincoln's eyelids and stirred him from his dreams. Opening his eyes, he found an intense glow. He thought Aeron had turned off the lantern. He or Clay could have turned it back on. Then again, this light was green, not blue.

He sat up and rubbed his eyes. The light was in a neighboring tree, and it was pulsing. His adrenaline surged, and he struggled to remain still. He knew what it was, and it wasn't the lantern.

"Hey," Lincoln said with the hoarse voice of sleep. "Hey, wake up."

Aeron and Clay stirred.

"We got trouble. Don't make any sudden movements."

Clay groaned. "What is it?"

"Mollies."

"Shit."

Aeron and Clay sat up, and another green glow illuminated in another neighboring tree. They scanned the trees surrounding them. Three more glowing lights swelled in the night. The wild resembled an enchanted forest with fairies radiating and shimmering. To Aeron, it was majestic and beautiful, but he didn't know any better.

His wide eyes were glassy in the green light. "What are mollies?"

"Mammals. Live in trees. Bioluminescent," Clay said. "Dangerous."

"They aren't carnivores," Lincoln said. "But they're amazingly curious and may try to take our stuff."

Aeron gaped at his brother. "You can get mugged in the wild?"

"Yeah."

"Can't we just scare them away? Fire a shot into the air like you did with those other animals?"

"The riptens?"

"Yeah."

"You don't understand," Lincoln said. "These are *mollies*."

The animals answered when one of them made its eponymous call, a low moan that sounded as if it were crying for someone or something named Molly. Another responded with a questioning whine.

"Molly? Molly?"

"Shhhhh," Lincoln said.

"Molly? Molly?"

One of the green lights moved in the tree and made a declaration. "Molly!"

"No. Stop. Shhh."

The pulsating lights in the opposing trees began to move and circulate, leaping from branch to branch. The animals hooted and grunted and hollered, engaging in a primal dance party.

"Molly! Molly!"

More glowing lights illuminated in the trees and moved among the branches. They joined in the chanting. The pulsating glow was all around them now, a cyclone of light high above the forest floor.

"MOLLY! MOLLY!"

"Quiet!" Lincoln said.

Lincoln glanced to his side and found Aeron aiming the revolver. He was pointing it at Clay, who was surrounded by pulsating mollies.

The glow emanated from their fur-covered chests from which four hairy limbs extended. They moved on all fours, but they stood on their hind legs and made elaborate expressions with their front appendages, which resembled human arms, complete with opposable thumbs. Their heads featured an elongated snout, and each had a prehensile tail, which sprouted from the other end and curled into the air like a question mark.

"Wait!" Lincoln raised his hand in front of Aeron. "Don't. Let them. They're just curious. When they tire of him, they'll go away."

They poked at Clay. They lifted his arms and examined them. They sniffed his hair, chest, and armpits, and licked his face. Through it all, Clay remained perfectly still.

Aeron shifted the revolver in the direction of their packs, where a molly was picking at the ropes.

"Ah, crap," Lincoln said.

The gun cracked the night and silenced the mollies' calls. The ones that had been examining Clay scattered. The bioluminescence dimmed.

The dead molly fell through the branches and landed against on the ground with a sickening thud. The men peered over the edge of their tree stand and watched. After a moment of stillness, its light extinguished.

They returned in much greater numbers. The men were surrounded, and the animals drew nearer, advancing warily but steadily, no doubt coming for more than their stuff this time.

"MOLLY! MOLLY! MOLLY! MOLLY!"

The earth started to rumble, and the trees began to shake. The mollies' glow intensified, and Lincoln understood this was their defense mechanism. He'd always thought their bioluminescence was only so they could find their way in the darkness, but now he understood it would blind the exo creatures.

He was about to see how well it worked.

Their tree trembled. It jumped and bucked, and they struggled to hold on.

A molly lost its grip and fell, crashing through the limbs and impacting the dirt. This one survived the fall, and quickly leaped to its feet. Its focus darted in every direction, and as it bolted, the earth opened and pulled it down, snuffing out its light.

The quaking continued. The mollies were screaming their call now, no longer celebrating their find but dashing about in panic.

"MOLLYMOLLYMOLLYMOLLY!"

The green lights scattered through the trees, the winding cyclone breaking into disorder and chaos.

Another fell. And another. One by one, the creatures beneath the earth shook mollies from the trees like ripened fruit.

Lincoln, Aeron, and Clay clung to their rope platform, but their tree swayed and keeled. It was being uprooted.

"Hold on!" Lincoln said.

Their tree fell and crashed into a neighboring tree with a cacophony of crashing limbs and leaves. The men scattered, thrown in different directions, but each found a place among the tangle of branches and trunks.

The remaining mollies stopped their calls and became still. One by one, their lights dimmed, dissolved, and winked out. The wild was once again quiet and dark, and in moments, the ground settled.

Ten

In the morning, they woke in the branches of a neighboring tree. Their rope stand lay at an angle, and they had their backs against it. The rifle was in Lincoln's lap, and Aeron clutched his revolver.

The men groaned, stretching and massaging muscles that clenched like fists. The tree had been unkind to their aging bodies, which seized in every joint, but the hard bark was not the only culprit. Evident in their red, weary eyes, fatigue had set into their bones. They had spent hours up there in the absolute darkness on high alert, and it wasn't until daylight trickled down into their world again that they felt safe enough to even consider sleep.

Now, however, it was time to move.

"Where's our stuff?" Clay asked.

Lincoln craned his head down. The others followed his gaze. Below, their packs dangled from a creaky branch, swaying in the breeze like a pendulum.

"Thank Lumen for small favors," Aeron said.

Clay grunted. "Yeah, she's a real peach when she's trying to kill you."

The men worked together to unwrap the rope they'd used for their tree stand and climbed down to retrieve their packs.

At the base of the tree, they found the lantern. Aeron picked it up by its wire handle and examined it. Something rattled in the cylinder. He huffed and tossed it back into the deadfall.

"It's broken."

Clay threw his pack onto his shoulders. "What was that about small favors?"

"What are we going to do now?" Aeron asked. "We don't have light."

"We have the day at least," Lincoln said. "And we have our handhelds."

"Lot of good those will do us when those things come back tonight," Clay said.

Lincoln shot him a cold stare.

"It doesn't matter," Aeron said. "We have to get moving. If this changes things and you want to go back, that's fine."

Clay grunted. "Yeah, I bet you'd like that." He brushed past them. "Let's go."

The men took off their boots and pants and waded through the running water, holding their packs over their heads, feeling out the uncertain, rocky river bed with the soles of their bare feet. They shivered in the frigid water. When they were on the other bank, they put their boots and pants back on.

Aeron pointed upstream at the downed tree that spanned the embankments. "Think the kids were smarter than we were just now?"

Lincoln laughed. "Probably."

They followed the herebor trail as it sloped up and around a hill before diving back down into a valley. Already feeling drained by a combination of sleep deprivation and navigating the tough terrain, their bodies labored harder than the previous day, and although Lincoln feared they were exerting themselves too much, he knew Aeron wouldn't allow them to slow down.

At mid-morning, Lincoln stopped at a bend in the herebor trail.

"What is it?" Aeron said.

Lincoln nodded toward the bend, and Clay and Aeron followed his direction. A path into the wilderness had been cleaved.

Aeron cheered. "Yes! They *did* go this way!" He clobbered his brother with an embrace. "Lincoln, you're a genius!"

"All right, all right." Lincoln shrank away at the praise that was unfamiliar to him. "They went north from here. If Shane's taking them to the Field of the First Families, he's too far south."

Aeron cleared his throat and regained his composure. "What makes you think he's taking them there?"

"If you want to find James Bellman, that's where you start. I did." Lincoln pointed at Clay. "So did he."

"The field is only a few hours' walk from the colony," Clay said. "Why would your boy take them such a roundabout way?"

"He has an idea where it is, but he's never been there," Lincoln said. "So they're lost."

"Shane's not lost." Lincoln moved toward the opening in the forest. "He's a kid."

Lincoln led them off of the herebor trail and onto the path of the children.

"Smart," he said.

"What?" Aeron asked.

"Shane took them to high ground to see if he could get a look out over the valley."

Clay snickered. "I told you he was lost."

When Lincoln turned to lay into Clay, they heard a loud pop somewhere in the forest. The men ducked in reflex as if they were under fire.

With wide eyes, Aeron scanned the maze of trees around them. "What was that?"

The men watched for movement. Then another pop sounded behind them, opposite of the first one they'd heard. Closer by, something fell through the branches of a tree, smacking leaves and limbs, exploding when it hit the ground like a miniature artillery round.

Lincoln placed his palm against a nearby tree.

"Is it shaking?" Clay asked.

Lincoln nodded.

"The exos are nocturnal," Aeron said. "It can't be them."

"It isn't," Lincoln said. "These are seeder trees."

"What's that mean?"

As Aeron gaped at his brother, the trees answered his question. A bulbous pod fell from the branches above and hit the crown of Aeron's head. It burst on impact, leaving a stain of brown dust and bits of wooden shrapnel in his hair. Aeron cried out and recoiled.

"Dammit." He sucked air through clenched teeth and touched his head, checking for blood. "What the hell?"

Lincoln and Clay burst into laughter as Aeron brushed the dust from his head and shoulders and inspected the transfer to his hand.

"That's a seed for another tree," Lincoln said. "When the season's right, seeders shake and all drop their seeds. Looks like we're coming through at just the time for it."

"That hurt!" Aeron said.

"It'll sting a bit, but it won't kill you. Let's keep moving."

They restarted ascending the incline, and another seed fell and popped on Clay's back. Lincoln and Aeron cackled. A moment later, a seed fell and popped on Lincoln's head, and the men roared.

It was like the wild was trying to stop their advance with a kind of mortar fire, and it was the most pathetic defense imaginable.

Their voices carried across the wilderness while the seeders continued their harmless assault, raining exploding pods through the forest.

Eleven

When they reached the hilltop, it was mid-afternoon. The forest canopy opened, giving way to blue sky. Craggy rock jutted from the ground, a bald spot on the land, sloping down toward the valley and abruptly ending in a steep cliff.

The men gaped up, blinking in the bright sunlight. Emerging from the shadows of the forest into the sun's warmth washing over their skin and radiating from the boulders below their feet, they felt reinvigorated. They hadn't felt direct sunlight since the morning before, and even that was only the teaser of dawn. Even their bones were starving for it.

Without speaking, they all had the idea that this would be a perfect place to rest. Out on the rock face, they slipped their packs from their shoulders and let them fall to the boulder beneath their feet.

As they lounged, Lincoln's brow wrinkled with deep thought. "Aeron, what was your theory about why the exos never came into the colony?"

"That the wall insulated the sound?"

Lincoln gazed out over the valley. The tip of the ancient spaceship glinted in the late-day sunlight.

"They can't hear through rock," Clay said. "But they live underground. That's ironic."

Lincoln grunted. They ate in silence, and when their break was over, they collected their gear, and Lincoln picked up the kids' trail again on the other side of the clearing.

The entire time they were in the clearing, none of them had bothered to look west at the approaching black sky.

They pushed on through the wild, following the downward slope into the valley. After an hour of creeping through the wild on the kids' trail, something fell in the forest. It was faint but not far off.

Aeron craned his head in attention. "More seeders?"

"No." Clay waved a hand around them at the trees. "These aren't seeders."

Then came another soft impact sound. Another. And another. Soon, the forest all around them was thrumming.

The sky rumbled in the distance.

Lincoln looked up. A drop of water landed on his forehead. Thunder cracked the sky.

"No," Lincoln said. "No!" He took off running, breaking through the thick foliage and disappearing into the wilderness.

Aeron and Clay gawked at each other and then followed.

"What's wrong?" Aeron said. "It's just a storm."

"It's going to wipe out the trail," Clay said.

The wind bore down on the forest. Shadows deepened. The rain hissed. The water broke through the tree ceiling and showered the men. In the chaos, none of them heard the mechanical buzzing until it was roaring in their ears.

An aircraft whooshed overhead.

Moments later, the radio in Aeron's pack squelched and squawked. *"Aeron, are you there?"*

"Wait a second!" Aeron called to the others.

They stopped, and he removed it and held it in his hand. Lincoln and Clay cast questioning stares.

"Ernest is using a drone to look for the kids." Aeron placed the radio in front of his mouth. "I'm here. What is it?"

"I've found them. They're on top of a hill at the southern edge of the Field of the First Families. At the entrance to a cave. It looks like they're taking shelter from the storm."

"That's good."

Lincoln's chest swelled with a realization. "No. It isn't."

And he was running again.

Twelve

By the time the men reached the field, the storm had settled on top of them with all of its oppressive fury. The cold rain stung like ice shards, and wind gusts set them on their heels. The ground shivered along with the rumbling thunder. The swirling black clouds had closed the heavens in a vortex of darkness, cutting their day short.

At the edge of the field, without the benefit of tree cover, the full strength of the deluge slammed into them. Their drenched clothing sapped their body heat, steam rising from their shoulders and backs. Their heaving breaths clouded in the air.

"We have to find shelter!" Clay yelled over the static sound of the storm.

"Where are they?" Aeron asked.

Lincoln scanned the edge of the forest across the field. With the rainfall obscuring his vision, he could barely make out the tree line. After a moment of despair, he found the place where James' trail had gone cold, and he pointed at the rocky incline. "There!"

They broke into a sprint again. The tall grass slapped their bodies like tongues. Lightning cracked the sky in a triplet of flashes that lit the world with a brilliant intensity for just an instant and then plunged it back into darkness with a damning thunderclap. Their boots sank into softening earth, which would soon be mud.

The men worked their way up the slick incline, and at the top, rain hissing on the boulders, they stopped to catch their breath. The water dripped from their eyebrows and poured into their gaping mouths.

Lincoln squinted through the darkness and rain. Light flickered in the cave. "Shane!"

They ran through the overhang and into the cave, and when they stepped out of the rain into that dank space, they felt a sense of physical reprieve at being able to dry their faces. Lincoln dipped his head and whipped his hair back, sending a rooster tail of water to the cave ceiling.

Dying firelight licked the walls. Three packs lay in a row against the wall, and the men set their packs beside them. The kids were nowhere to be seen. Lincoln clicked on his flashlight and cut the darkness with its beam.

"This is where we found the dead one," Lincoln said. "But where is it?"

"Lower forms of insects on other planets have been known to carry off their dead," Clay said.

Lincoln and Aeron looked at him with a mixture of surprise and suspicion.

"What? I can't know things?"

"Shane?" Lincoln called. "Shane!?"

"Gabe!" Aeron shouted. "Sera!"

The only sounds they heard were of their echoing voices in the darkness.

"Where could they have gone?" Aeron asked. "Why would they leave without their packs? Gabe! Shane!"

Lincoln considered it for a moment and then slapped a hand over his brother's mouth. "They wouldn't."

Lincoln took his hand away and followed the darkness deeper into the cave, pushing it back with the beam of his flashlight. The fire's embers popped. His boot splashed in a puddle.

The wall condensation glistened like jewels in the flashlight's beam. As the storm's hiss faded behind them, they heard a trickle of water deeper in the cave. A musty breeze blew from deep within the earth, and Lincoln shivered as it passed over his soaked body. It wasn't far before the cave's floor ran out. He reached the shaft, like a throat, and motioned for Aeron and Clay to join him.

They peered over the precipice, shining their flashlights down into the gloom. The bottom was just out of the beam's reach. The light only touched murky air and motes of dust.

"What do you want to do now, boss?" Clay asked.

Aeron and Clay waited while Lincoln stared into the darkness for a moment, and then he went to work anchoring his rope to the cave floor.

"What are you doing?" Aeron asked.

Clay wiped his face. "He's going down."

Lincoln slipped his harness on and worked the straps into place. "They're not here. They wouldn't go out in that storm. That means they either went down this shaft willingly or were taken."

A sobering look of grim realization passed across Aeron's face, and he nodded. "All right."

Clay was biting his thumbnail. "Someone should stay here."

"You afraid?" Lincoln said.

"No," Clay said. "But if we all go down there and there's a problem, we won't be able to get back up. Someone stays here, he can throw down another rope if necessary."

"He's right," Aeron said.

Lincoln finished looping the rope through his carabiner. "Fine. Aeron, you stay. Clay, you come with me."

"I'm going," Aeron said.

The brothers gazed at each other for a motionless moment.

"Lincoln, if Gabe is down there, I'm getting him. This isn't a discussion. I'll jump down that shaft without a rope if I have to. You know I will."

Lincoln sighed. "Fine. But Clay, if you're not here when we get back—"

Clay put up his hands in surrender. "Where am I going to go with that storm out there?"

Lincoln let his warning glare linger, and then he fit a harness on Aeron and showed him how to use the gear to rappel down.

Flashlight clamped in his teeth, Lincoln stood at the edge of the shaft with his back to the darkness. He leaned backward, looking over his shoulder, and saw the nothing into which he was about to fall.

The anchor held true. Lincoln nodded at his brother and began to feed out the rope and rappel down the shaft.

Getting to the bottom didn't take as long as he'd expected, and when his boots were on level ground, Lincoln used his flashlight to examine the cavern. It went deeper into the cave, farther than his flashlight could reach. The oppressive darkness pushed back on the beam.

Aeron's voice echoed down the shaft. "You all right?"

"Yeah." Lincoln detached his harness and left the rope hanging against the wall. "Come on."

Aeron eased his way down, and Lincoln gave in to the knowledge that, if Aeron fell, he would be able to do nothing. But Aeron didn't fall. He moved deliberately, and his boots soon hit the bottom of the shaft. Lincoln helped Aeron remove his harness, and then two beams of light fought that darkness together. Aeron moved deeper into the cavern, but Lincoln hesitated.

He craned his head up the shaft. "Clay?"

"Yeah?"

"I mean it."

"Okay."

The brothers followed the cavern until their flashlights illuminated what looked like an old cave-in.

"No," Aeron said. "No, no, no!" He rushed to the caved-in wall and slammed it with his fists, sobbing and moaning. After resting his forehead against the rock for a moment, Aeron turned to Lincoln with grievous eyes. "What now? Did they just disappear?"

Cocking his head in wonder, Lincoln passed his flashlight's beam around the walls and ceiling, and then he noticed the trickling water at their feet.

"It isn't pooling. The water."

"So?"

"So it's going somewhere."

At the wall, Lincoln stopped and listened. "Hear that? There's an underground river nearby."

"That's great, but I don't see how it does us any good." Aeron pushed his hair back and cradled his face in his hands.

Lincoln ran his hands over the wall, examining its texture. He followed it until he felt a cool breeze pass through his fingertips. His flashlight illuminated the interior. He had found the fissure.

Aeron lowered his hands from his face and joined him. "Think we can fit?"

"They did." Lincoln squeezed into the crevice and looked back at his brother. "So we have to."

The brothers sidestepped through the fissure, and the sound of rushing water grew louder. The fissure turned inside the cave-in, and Lincoln spotted the opening. When they were through, they entered a dark chamber joining several other tunnels. The storm-fed river rushed through it.

"Where to now?" Aeron asked.

Lincoln was silent.

"I said, where—"

"I heard you." Lincoln swept his flashlight's beam around the chamber, eyeing the adjoining tunnels and gazing into the river's rushing water. "I don't know."

"What do you mean you don't know?"

"I mean I don't know. The kids could have taken any one of these tunnels. For all I know, they jumped into the river and trusted it to carry them out. That's if they weren't taken."

"Well, we can't just stand here."

"I know."

"We have to do something, Lincoln."

"I *know*."

"Maybe we should split up."

There was a moment in which Lincoln thought his brother was actually going to let him think, and then in Aeron's desperation, he started screaming.

"Gabriel! Shane! Sera! Gabriel! Shane! Sera!"

Lincoln tackled his brother and tried to slap his hands over Aeron's mouth, but Aeron resisted and continued with muffled shouts.

"Quiet," Lincoln said. "Think about where we are."

Aeron stilled, and Lincoln scanned the tunnels with his flashlight. Neither of them so much as breathed.

Then they heard a sound echo through the tunnels.

"Shhh!" Lincoln hissed.

They listened. It came again, meandering through the tunnels and growing in volume. In disbelief, they gazed at each other, and utter relief washed over them.

The sound was a human voice.

"It's them," Aeron said.

A light danced in one of the tunnels, and the sound came again.

"Dad! Dad! We're here!"

Lincoln felt like he was breathing for the first time in days.

The kids' footsteps pounded and scuffed on the rocky surface.

"Thank Lumen," Aeron said. "Gabriel! Shane! Sera! We're here!"

Then, *movement*.

Lincoln shined his flashlight into one of the tunnels. Two thick, bony legs jutted from the darkness, the light glimmering on their glossy sheen, and then retreated.

Movement.

Lincoln flicked his flashlight to another tunnel and found more legs, and eyes glared at them with a black lifelessness. It squelched and retreated.

Movement.

The kids were at the mouth of another tunnel, and their smiles were of salvation, but those smiles diminished when they saw Lincoln and Aeron. The kids immediately discerned their fear, and Lincoln held up a hand for them to freeze while he monitored the tunnels.

Stillness.

"Okay, quickly," he whispered. "Come now!"

With their lamp casting a cool glow around the three of them like a protective sphere, Shane, Gabe, and Sera scurried across the room, but there was no time for embrace. Lincoln and Aeron pushed the kids behind them.

Lincoln pointed to the fissure. "Go. Now."

The kids squeezed into the opening. Lincoln and Aeron waited for them to disappear into the cave-in, their blue lamplight illuminating it like a ghostly presence.

When they turned back to the tunnels, two exos were testing the potential for attack, and a third filled another tunnel.

"Move, Aeron. Go."

Aeron followed the kids into the fissure, and when Lincoln was satisfied he'd given his brother enough time to get started and that they wouldn't be on top of each other, he began to ease backward toward the opening.

The exos apparently weren't afraid of his flashlight anymore. One of them emerged completely, its massive body a hulking presence, its eight legs padding delicately over the cavern floor. It recoiled when Lincoln shifted the light but raised a leg in front of its eyes and kept coming. Another emerged, and Lincoln shifted again. The flashlight had a minimal effect, and that was when Lincoln ran.

He hit the fissure hard, tearing a hole in his shoulder. Gritting through the pain, he moved maddeningly slowly through the tight quarters. The sound of the rushing water succumbed to a shrill scream.

The earth shook with the pounding of the exos' legs, and they crashed into the cave-in with such incredible force that the earth around Lincoln moved and threatened to crush him.

The kids and Aeron were shouting for him on the other side, and when he was out, there was time for a quick embrace. Lincoln brushed his son's hair away from his face and, careful of the gash, kissed his forehead.

Shane gaped at his father. "I'm sorry for everything."

"Me too." Lincoln hugged his son, and then he set him back to look at him, his beloved son whom he'd scorned and hurt through his own failings and whom he could not live without. He would make it right. All of it.

"We have to move," Lincoln said.

The sound of the exos filled the chamber now, a rising dull roar of pounding limbs and a chittering, like hundreds of blades dancing over stone surfaces. They pounded on the walls, trying to get through the cave-in, but Lincoln figured, if they could get through solid rock, they would have done so already.

They had to be tunneling around it.

Lincoln and Aeron pushed the kids ahead, and they ran up the cavern as fast as they could until their lights revealed the wall ahead where they'd come down.

"Clay!" Lincoln said. "Clay! They're coming! Pull the kids up!"

At the bottom of the shaft, Lincoln shined his flashlight up and found nothing.

The rope was at their feet, fallen into a coil on the cavern floor.

The roar of tunneling creatures grew.

"Clay!" Aeron said. "What are you doing!? You're killing us!"

Lincoln grabbed two fistfuls of his brother's coat and slammed him against the cave wall.

"He knows, Aeron. He knows."

He released his brother, and realization dawned upon Aeron. "So that's it. We're trapped."

Lincoln stared at his brother in utter loss. "I'm sorry."

"I can make it," Sera said, looking up with determination. She met Lincoln's gaze. "I can make it."

"It's true, Dad," Shane said. "Sera climbs all the time. When we fell, if we couldn't find another way out, she was going to climb up after the storm and get help."

Lincoln looked to Gabe for confirmation.

Gabe shrugged. "It's her thing."

"I was going to wait until it dried." She eyed the shaft around them and picked up one end of the rope from the ground. She tied it around her waist. "But I can make it."

She looked back to Lincoln but didn't wait for his approval. As he nodded consent, she was already sprinting toward the wall and skipping up the stony surface to grasp a ledge that jutted like a shelf. Her legs dangled for just a moment as she looked for her next handhold, and she pulled herself up with surprising speed and agility.

Sera faltered and almost fell once, but she regained her composure and continued her ascent until she reached the top and mantled over the edge.

At the bottom of the shaft, they couldn't even hear themselves cheer because of the violent sound of the exos tunneling around them.

"Okay, tie the rope to something!" Lincoln shouted. "Shane, you go first and make sure the rope is set. Gabe, you're after Shane. Then Aeron."

Sera's face reappeared over the edge. "Okay!"

Lincoln helped Shane find his grip on the rope and sent him up. The boy grunted and heaved. His arm strength was true.

When Shane reached the top, Lincoln motioned for Gabe. The boy grasped the rope and climbed. In moments, he was at the top as well.

Aeron stepped up and eyed his brother.

"Hurry," Lincoln said.

"Maybe you first, little brother."

"We're not arguing about this. Go. Now!"

Aeron leaped and pulled, and when he reached the top of the shaft, the kids screamed. An exo was at the cave entrance. Its front legs were reaching over the edge on the right side.

"Use the lamp!" Aeron said.

Sera threw it at the cave entrance. It clattered and rolled until it filled the cave entrance with bright blue illumination. The exo shrieked and retreated.

"Your flashlights," Aeron said. "The light hurts their eyes."

Shane and Gabe rushed to their packs and retrieved their flashlights. They clicked them on and aimed their beams at the entryway.

Aeron pulled the revolver from his pack, and as he inspected it, the kids screamed again.

He looked up in time to see a black mass hurtling through the air, and it took him to the ground in a flurry of slicing limbs and gnashing teeth.

The exo's weight was crushing Aeron. In reflex, he tried to push it off of him, but it would not yield.

It reeled back, readying its legs to drop like sledgehammers. Aeron pressed the revolver's barrel to its belly and squeezed the trigger, squeezed the trigger, squeezed the trigger.

A warm, viscous goop oozed onto his hand.

The creature screeched and careened off of him. It stumbled into the wall and collapsed, gasping its final breaths.

The kids were frozen in fear.

"Are you okay?" Aeron asked them.

They stared at him.

"Watch the entrance."

Aeron got to his feet and looked for Lincoln, but his brother had not made the ascent yet. He ran to the shaft and could not find Lincoln anywhere. That was when he noticed the rope was shredded near where the exo had taken him to the ground. One of its sharp limbs had severed it.

"Lincoln!" Aeron yelled down the shaft. "Lincoln, are you all right!?"

Shane rushed behind him, and he held the boy back.

"Dad!"

Aeron took Gabe by the shoulders. "Watch the cave opening! Now! Go!"

Aeron looked down the shaft. Lincoln's flashlight clicked on at the bottom.

"You have to go," Lincoln said. "Get the kids out of here."

The brothers gazed at each other in the dim light. The children's screams echoed in the cave shaft. Two more exos were at the entrance.

Aeron couldn't move.

The exos were in the walls. They were breaching the surface outside. There were so many of them that it sounded like a constant rustling of earth, as if Lumen herself were shuddering.

Three exos marched forth from the front of the cave, shielding their eyes with their front legs.

"Dad!" Gabe screamed.

Aeron only heard the exos around them, digging toward the surface, their long legs bursting through the ground like the planet expelling a sickness. Soon, they would be on the children, and Aeron couldn't allow that. They were out of time.

Aeron gazed at his brother one last time, and they reached a silent agreement. Aeron would save the children, and Lincoln wouldn't beg him not to leave.

"Get your packs," Aeron said to the kids.

Shane hesitated.

Gabe pulled him. "Come on."

"But my dad," Shane said.

Gabe tugged harder. "Come on!"

Aeron took one of the dry logs the kids had collected and stowed before the rain had come. He stirred the fire with it and blew on the coals. The glow and heat swelled but didn't quite catch flame.

The exos were still making their way into the cave, blocking their escape and moving with maddening inevitability.

Aeron searched his pack for the camping fuel, and readied himself to douse the end of the log in the accelerant.

He splashed the fuel onto the diminishing fire, and a fireball filled the cave with a pulse of light and heat. The exos squealed and scampered away but did not retreat.

Setting a log aside, Aeron picked up the pile of wood and threw it onto the fire pit. Then he dumped a hearty dose of the fuel onto it, and the fire raised to life once again, burning with an intensity of heat and light that sent the creatures to the entrance of the cave, beyond the lantern, and then out of sight.

"We have to go," Aeron said.

"But my dad!" Shane said.

"Go, Shane!" Lincoln called from the bottom of the shaft. "Go now, son!"

"Dad!"

Aeron removed a shirt from his pack, wrapped it around the end of the last log, and soaked it in the remaining camping fuel. He stomped over to Shane and grabbed his nephew's coat, staring in his eyes with an intensity that he might give any fully grown man. "We have to go."

Aeron pushed Shane toward the entrance, and his nephew began to sob. Aeron thrust the log into the fire, and it caught flame, emitting oppressive light and heat.

At the cave entrance, Shane picked up the lantern. The rain had slowed but hadn't relented. They gray world would only darken until nightfall. They had to leave now while the exos were weak. As the darkness grew, so would their strength.

Aeron led the way out of the cave, holding his torch high and scanning the area with the revolver. The exos weren't in sight, but he could feel them watching from the trees.

Shane held the lantern in one hand and a flashlight in the other, and together, their light repelled the encroaching dusk.

Aeron and the children fled to the incline that descended to the field. Before they began their climb down the muddy, slick rock face, Aeron glanced at the cave. Three exos swept inside. It was too late to save Lincoln, and Aeron knew this was the way it had to be.

Thirteen

Soaked to the point where the falling rain didn't matter anymore, Aeron pushed the children through the wild until nightfall. They had descended the incline into the Field of the First Families and crossed it into the trees on the western edge. With the cloud and tree cover forcing darkness, Aeron listened for the rumble of earth, but every time he thought he heard the exos coming, it was only thunder in the distance.

When he dared not take them any farther, he and Shane climbed a tree and used their remaining rope to make a stand, as Lincoln had taught them. They erected a tarpaulin above to shield them from the rain and each changed into dry clothing.

When the work was done and they were secured for the night, when there was nothing else to do but wait out the darkness, that was when it became unbearable.

Aeron distributed his remaining rations among them, and he chewed on some of his beef jerky. The kids looked at their food as if it were an alien concept.

"How can we eat?" Sera said, bringing her knees to her chest. "How can we pretend nothing happened?"

Shane picked up a strip of the beef and weighed it in his hands. "We have to. There's nothing else we can do." He bit off a piece and chewed.

Aeron watched his nephew. The boy was learning his power was limited. He was learning his existence had value and affected others. He'd lost his father, and nothing could change it.

The boy was growing up. He was losing his naivety. That meant he was also shedding his innocence, and it filled Aeron with incredible sadness.

Gabe didn't touch his food and, instead, quietly cried until he fell asleep. Sera didn't speak for the rest of the night, but at some point, she slept as well. Shane remained deep in thought for a while, but as they all lay down in the darkness and Aeron turned the knob to dim the lantern, he spoke.

"Are you all right?" Shane asked his uncle.

The question caught Aeron off guard, and he had to think about his answer. It occurred to him that, in his intense sadness for his nephew's loss, this tragedy belonged to him too. He knew he'd lost a brother, but until Shane asked the question, he hadn't allowed himself to feel it. As a father and uncle, he'd focused so intensely on keeping the kids safe that he hadn't considered he also was a brother and what that meant.

He nodded to Shane and turned the lantern off.

In the darkness, Aeron waited for winds to blow through or the rain to pick up, and then he wept.

That night was mercifully peaceful.

Fourteen

Aeron woke at dawn. The storm had passed, and the wild had a beautiful, ethereal quality. With bright sunlight filtering through the canopy, the world didn't just look alive. It looked like it was thriving.

The kids still dozed, but he intended to have them moving as soon as it was safe. He went to work collecting their things, and they roused. In time, they were descending the tree and setting their boots on the wet earth.

They took their time, their pace reluctant. Unsure of the path, they kept moving west, but because of the thick canopy above, they could only guess at the sun's position.

Aeron took great care to ensure no harm would befall them in the wild. He stopped them when he thought he heard something rustling in the deadfall, helped them over obstacles like downed trees. He let them rest every hour.

They all sensed that everything that could hurt them was in their wake and wasn't laying chase. The storm had swept it all away.

When the wild broke and gave way to the field outside of Vale's walls, when they knew they were almost home, fatigue set in. It felt as if their bodies had been running off of adrenaline for days, and now it was okay to relax. Their boots grew heavy, as if they'd been filled with cement, and every step sent electric current shooting up their legs and radiating through their torsos.

The gate loomed at the top of the incline that marked Vale's perimeter, and Aeron and the kids admired it. This concrete, metal, and wood bastion of sanctuary, this bulwark, stood against the wild from which they returned. They knew now what it kept out, and it had never looked so welcoming.

"Let's get you home," Aeron said.

They lumbered up the hill, and squinting into the late morning sun, Aeron discerned no sentries manning the gate. He expected a vocal welcome from the guards on the wall, but none came.

As they drew closer to the gate and it towered in front of the sun, Aeron finally saw that the wall was abandoned.

"Maybe they're in between shifts," Shane said.

"Maybe."

When they reached the gate, they stared at it like a puzzle. The wall was unyielding.

Aeron pounded on it. "Hello?" He listened. "Hello!"

Only the silence of the indifferent wild responded.

"Maybe Captain Barrow pulled the sentries off the wall to help in town," Shane said.

"The others, maybe," Aeron said, "but he'd leave someone watching the gate. Barrow knew we could be back any day." Aeron slammed on the gate again. "Hello! We're here!"

His voice echoed over the trees behind them. A wind picked it up and carried it away as if Lumen were sighing with impatience.

"Maybe he didn't expect us to come back at all," Gabe said.

Sera touched his shoulder. "Stop talking like that. Everything is going to be all right."

Grunting in frustration, Aeron pushed off from the gate and gazed up, waiting. No one came. He growled and walked along the base of the wall. Confused, the kids they followed.

The wall curved along the colony's perimeter, and as they continued around the stone monolith, Aeron ran his palm along the concrete and examined the surface as if searching for a seam to peel back and slip through.

"What are you looking for?" Shane asked.

Aeron shifted his gaze down the slope that led away from the wall into the wild. He pointed. "That. Lincoln said the pipe we came out wasn't the only one."

A few meters from the wall, the ground slipped away into a ditch, and when Aeron led them down there, they discovered the opening to another storm drain.

"Let's just hope they never got around to sealing up all of these holes," Aeron said

"What if they did?" Shane asked.

Aeron frowned at his nephew. "They did a really good job building this wall."

He and the kids ducked into the dark tunnel. Their boots sank and slipped in the muck that remained in the drain, and it smelled of washed-away filth.

They reached the grating and found the stubs of old, cut-away bars.

"We're in luck." Aeron said. The place where a grate had once been was open.

He led them into the interchange and up into the pipe to the interior of the wall. When they emerged from the drainpipe, they saw the reason no one had been at the gate. In the center of town, over Vale's modest skyline, a column of smoke rose into the air like a dirty finger.

"Come on." Aeron broke into a sprint toward town.

They crossed the field, entered the commons, and came upon the source of the smoke. Daenuel Market smoldered from an expired blaze. Arokson Hall's bell tower was broken and collapsed to the ground like a discarded hat. The colony was in ruin.

They turned down the road toward the homes and saw walls caved in, doorways busted open, windows smashed.

Then they found a depression right in the middle of the gravel road.

"No," Aeron gasped.

The kids looked on in horror.

They raced up the road to the home of the warden, climbed the steps to the door, and Aeron tried the handle. It turned. The door opened a crack and hit something solid.

"Lucy!" Aeron pushed on the door with all of his strength, and whatever was in the way gave enough that they could slip inside.

A sofa was against the front door, and all manner of furniture, a chair, a mattress, a dresser, blocked the stairwell to the second floor.

"Lucy! Mel! Bernie!"

"Mom!" Gabe called.

Like a panicked, rabid beast, Aeron tore the furniture away from the stairwell. When there was enough space, he and the kids crawled over the barricade and bounded up the stairs.

On the second floor, all of the doors were open except for the master bedroom at the end of the hall.

It opened.

Ballard stood there, her revolver in hand, an intense look of sadness on her face. "You found them. Good."

Lucy pushed Ballard aside, and her eyes gaped at her husband and son. "Oh, thank Lumen!" She ran down the hall and launched into a fierce embrace of her husband and then her son.

"Sera!" Elena Bellman raced to her daughter and pulled her close. "My baby!"

Everyone was bawling.

Ballard tapped her revolver on her thigh. "Where's Lincoln?"

Aeron frowned. "He...he...I had to get the kids out of there. Those things were all around us."

Tears surged in her eyes. "You left him?"

"I...I had to get the kids out of there. I'm sorry."

She took a deep breath and, for a moment, glared at him with an intense hatred. "Is he...?"

Aeron closed his eyes and nodded.

The heat left her face. She wiped her eyes and retreated into the room. A cry from a young girl soon followed as Ballard explained to Bernie what had happened to her father.

The kids were safe. Aeron had fulfilled his promise to his brother. Nothing was right, though; not in the least. There was little that was joyful about this reunion. Instead, it carried a sense of salvage, that in all of the ruin that had befallen them, they had to pull together what they could.

He started down the stairs.

Lucy released Gabe. "Where are you going?"

"I'm going back. I need to be sure."

He plodded another few steps.

"You're not going anywhere," Lucy said.

He stopped and faced her.

"I've seen them. I know what they're capable of," she said. "You have to accept that he's gone. Vale needs you now." She went to him and rested a hand over his heart. "*We* need you."

Aeron exhaled as if gut-punched by anxiety. "What happened?"

Lucy took his hand and started down the stairs.

She led him out to the front steps and pointed north to the mountains. On the ridge, striking into the sky, the pillar stood dormant. No clouds of Dawn rose from its mouth. The sky was a perfect blue in all directions, the most beautiful day Aeron had seen in all his life.

He looked into his wife's haggard eyes. "Tell me everything."

CHAPTER 7
THE STORM

One

When Lincoln and Aeron left the Arokson home to find their children, Lucy clutched the girls, knowing the two most important men in her life were leaving and might not return. Aeron had not shielded her from the dangers of the wild. Overnight, neither of them had even considered sleep, and he had told her everything he knew because she was the warden now. There were no more secrets.

"Aunt Lucy?" Bernie said. "They're coming back, right?"

Lucy's gaze lingered on the closing door. "Yes, sweetheart."

"You promise?"

Lucy blinked the bad thoughts away. "Of course I promise." She forced a smile. "Now let's go make some breakfast."

The girls plodded along behind her into the kitchen in their pajamas and slippers, Mel's ankles emerging from goblin mouths and Bernie's feet kicking pink bunnies, a species she knew only through the storytelling of Lore.

Still wearing her clothes from yesterday, Lucy pinched the front of her button-up shirt and groaned. "Someone needs a bath." She made a show of sniffing her own shirt. "She's stinky."

The girls didn't find it the least bit funny. In silence, they hopped into chairs at the table and stared at the floral centerpiece. Lucy sighed at her inability to amuse her children.

She opened the pantry; her eyes scanned the canned fruits and vegetables, bags of rice, jars of nut butter, bags of flour. An idea curled the corner of her mouth.

"Girls, how about some pancakes?"

"Okay," they droned.

Lucy's mood dimmed, and then another idea occurred to her. "We have chocolate," she sang.

"Okay."

Lucy sighed and pulled the flour from the pantry. She retrieved the butter, eggs, and milk from the refrigerator, and she got a metal mixing bowl from the cabinet over the counter. She poured the ingredients into the bowl and began mixing it with a fork when a sniffle came from the table.

Bernie's face was shiny with smeared tears, and her sweater sleeve was wet with snot.

"Hey," Lucy said, rushing to her niece's side. She rubbed Bernie's back. "It's going to be okay. Everything is going to be fine."

"No it's not!"

Lucy balked, surprised by the sharpness of her niece's voice. "Why do you say that?"

"She's afraid," Mel said. "Jody Patterson said there were monsters in the wild. She's really mean. She said that's what took Aunt Haley away."

At the mention of her mother, Bernie sobbed.

"That's nonsense," Lucy said. "It's just stories people started telling a long time ago to keep kids from misbehaving. That's all."

Mel raised a defiant eyebrow. "Then why do people keep going missing?"

"It's true that the wild is dangerous, and that's why you should never go outside of the walls, but your uncle knows the wild. He knows how to find your brother and cousin. They're going to be all right. Okay?"

Bernie sniffed and nodded.

"Good. Now let me get those pancakes."

Lucy went back to the pantry and grabbed the small box of chocolate from the top shelf. The colony had received it in a shipment from another colony six months ago, and it was all Lucy had been able to get before the rest of the colony learned of it.

She eyed the package with eagerness. "We've been saving this for a special occasion."

She took a piece about the size of her palm out of the box. It was wrapped in wax paper. She set it on the counter and pounded it with a mallet to break it apart, dropped the chocolate chunks into the batter, and stirred.

When the pan on the stovetop was hot, she poured the batter into black-speckled disks that sizzled when they hit the metal. The sweet aroma of melted chocolate filled the kitchen. Lucy lost herself gazing out the window, flipping the pancakes on autopilot. When she had a heaping plate of hot pancakes, she set them on the table.

The girls ate in silence, save for the screeching of their forks on the dishes. Bernie methodically cut her pancakes in straight lines, and when she was finished, she asked to be excused.

"Yes," Lucy said. "Go upstairs and get changed. Wear your school clothes."

"Why?" Bernie asked. "School's canceled."

"Because I have to go to Arokson Hall today, and there's no one to watch you girls. You'll have to come with me."

Bernie plodded down the hallway and up the stairs.

Lucy turned to her daughter. "Are you okay?"

Mel shrugged.

"You know your father and brother are going to be all right."

Mel pushed her plate away and gazed at her mother. She stood from the table. "I'm going to get dressed too." She stopped in the hallway. Her voice was cold, her face blank. "You don't have to lie to us, Mom. We know they're probably not coming back." She offered a grim smile and trotted upstairs.

Lucy took a deep, shaky breath and wiped her hands on a rag. She piled all of the dishes in the sink and opened the faucet. While she waited for the water to get warm, she gazed over the basin and through the window into the backyard. The trees wavered in the early morning sunlight. By now, Lincoln and Aeron would be through the wall and into a labyrinth of greenery that she could only imagine. Aeron had told her not to worry about that. He'd told her she had to be strong.

As the faucet hissed and steam rose from the sink, a torrent of tears burst from deep within her. She cried harder than she had in as long as she could remember, and when she felt the sadness abating, she pushed herself to cry more, because alone in the kitchen, she knew it would be her last chance for a while to be vulnerable.

Two

Ballard and Ducard's boots crunched on the residential district's gravel road. Morning crested the horizon. The dark windows of row homes scrutinized them like soulless eyes set in the disguised faces of giants.

"You think they'll be all right?" Ducard said. "Without us, I mean?"

"They'll be fine. Lincoln knows the wild. All we could have offered was our guns, and I don't think firepower is going to mean much in this fight."

"Then why'd we bother giving them our weapons?"

She flashed her icy irises at him. "Makes me feel better."

"Even so, extra eyes wouldn't have hurt."

"We're needed here." She took a deep breath. "They'll be fine. They'll be fine."

Head down, looking at her own feet, she wouldn't meet Ducard's eyes.

"Are you all right?" he asked.

"Fine." Her glassy eyes glistened in the morning light. "I never told you I'm sorry about Kennedy."

Ducard looked away into the growing dawn. "You're probably right."

"About what?"

"Kennedy was one of our best shots. But it didn't save him. When we were running from those things in the dark, he opened fire. I just put my head down and ran. I ran for my life, but Kennedy, he did his job. It didn't matter how good he was."

She stopped and pulled on his arm. "It mattered. He saved our lives. Because of him, we made it. Because of him, we get a chance."

They continued on and entered the commons. Ducard breathed deep and wiped his eyes. "I miss him."

"I know. I'm sorry."

"Kennedy did what he was supposed to. Sentries are trained to always be ready and, if the time comes, to sacrifice. We *are* the wall. Do you understand? If the wall breaks, we break with it. We ain't supposed to live. We ain't supposed to have another chance unless we earn it. I never owed a debt I couldn't repay. Not sure I know how."

Ballard grasped his shoulder, making him face her. She looked him square in the eyes. "You honor the dead by paying it forward."

"How?"

Regina cocked her head in thought. "I have a feeling that, before too long, we'll both figure that out."

"Until then?"

"We put it off as long as possible."

The cold morning air pricked their skin, but a comforting emotional heat flourished within them as a growing bond of friendship strengthened in the wake of a lost relationship. Perhaps instinctually, they understood that when people died, their loved ones leaned on each other to cope. The alternative was a devastating crumbling of foundations, pillars shattering in a world-ending collapse.

Not all ends were sudden.

"Do me a favor," Ballard said. "Head over to the station and check on Lyle for me. I need to see to my dad."

"All right. I have to check in for duty after. Tonight at Gill's?"

Ballard nodded, and they went their separate ways, knowing consequences would bring them back together before too long to attend to the matter of honoring the dead.

Three

When Lucy pushed open Arokson Hall's heavy doors at the main entrance, the hinges squealed and echoed in the open atrium. The wood floors cracked as she and the girls crossed the lobby. No colonists lined up at the registration window. The lights in the community services office were off. The docket for the courthouse wing was empty. The administration of the colony had effectively shut down, but she couldn't allow that. Lumen was alive because of the pillar. The pillar ran on the colony. The colony worked because of the people. The people worked as a community because of the administration. If the government stopped, the chain reaction might end everything.

"Where is everybody?" Bernie asked.

"I don't know, but we're going to find out," Lucy said.

"Are they in trouble?"

"We'll find that out too."

She and the girls went up the staircase at the back of the atrium and to the second floor. When they arrived at the warden's office, Lucy found Captain Ezra Barrow leaning against the reception desk chatting with Alice. He glared at Lucy with hard, unyielding eyes.

"Good morning, Mrs. Arokson," he said. "I've explained the arrangement to Alice. She's aware you'll be responsible for the warden's administrative duties while I'll continue to ensure our security."

Lucy stopped in front of them with Bernie and Mel by her side.

"Alice, please set my daughter and niece up somewhere. They'll be staying with us today. Then please get me today's agenda and some tea. Anything for you, Captain Barrow?"

"No thank you."

Lucy turned back to Alice. "Please find out where everyone is and bring them in. We have work to do."

Caught off guard, Alice stuttered and fumbled over herself.

"Alice." Lucy held out a hand to steady her. "Nothing changes. We work as if Aeron were here, okay?"

"Okay." She took a deep breath and crouched to the girls. "I have just the spot for you two. You can make it your own. We have lots of toys, even dolls."

Mel rolled her eyes. Bernie stared at her blankly.

"Alice, they're old enough to occupy themselves," Lucy said.

"Yes, Mrs. Arokson." Alice motioned for the girls to follow her.

Mel looked to her mother in appeal but reluctantly complied and walked with Bernie and Alice to an empty office down the hall.

When they were gone, Lucy returned Captain Barrow's stone gaze. "We have some things to talk about."

"We do."

Lucy led Captain Barrow into the warden's office. The arched window behind the desk blazed in the morning sunlight. She hung up her coat on the rack in the corner and stepped around behind the desk, standing with her knuckles pressing the wooden surface. Barrow glanced at her, cleared his throat, and took the chair in front of the desk.

"I think we ought to establish some guidelines," Barrow said. "That way we can be an efficient and effective team. After all, this is only temporary. There's no need for us to get caught up and bogged down in protocol."

"What do you have in mind?"

"Would you like to sit?"

"No."

Barrow cocked his head. "All right. First, Aeron ordered me to ensure the integrity of the colony's security by any means, and typically, he allowed me to use my best judgment in matters concerning security and safety, especially in this kind of time of emergency. Frankly, you have enough to deal with. It's not worth your trouble."

"I'm aware of my husband's hands-off approach, but I'm a little different. While I'm not going to ask you to run everything by me, I do want to know what's happening in Vale."

"Mrs. Arokson, please don't take this the wrong way, but I've already spread my men thin as it is. In addition to keeping our watch on the wall, we're now distributed in the commons, marketplace, and residences, and we're escorting colonists to and from work in the industrial and agricultural districts as well as to the pillar. My men are working double shifts, and they don't have the time to dedicate to a formal report structure, especially since it hasn't been part of their regimen thus far."

Lucy raised a hand. "I'm just asking you to keep me in the loop. If it's something I need to know about, make sure I know."

"But you aren't asking for oversight?"

"I won't be issuing orders, no."

Alice knocked on the door and brought in Lucy's tea.

"Thank you, Alice," Lucy said.

Alice set the mug on the desktop and hurried toward the door.

"Alice," Lucy called after her. "The agenda."

"Oh, I'm sorry, Mrs. Arokson. You'll find it in the top drawer. I'd already set it out for you."

"Good. Thank you."

Alice left and gently closed the door behind her. Lucy stared into her tea. She sat in the warden's chair and cradled the warm mug, inhaling the earthy aroma.

"Speaking of manpower," Barrow said, "there is the issue of my missing men."

"We have to prioritize the colony at this point. You said it yourself. You're already spread thin."

"I know they're dead," Barrow said gravely. "And knowing that makes Aeron and Lincoln's decision to go out there all the more admirable. But that's the point. I know. The people don't. Neither do my men. I can handle them, but you'll need to handle the people."

Lucy pinched her bottom lip and gazed into space, thinking. She nodded. "I'll do what I can, but the best I can do is address them and try to make them understand without creating panic. I'll need to do that anyway."

"Aeron tried to talk to them already. It didn't work. They want transparency, and I think, eventually, they're going to need it."

"Not this." Lucy shook her head. "They can't handle this."

"What choice do we have?"

"If they knew what was out there, they'd tear everything apart."

"What are you saying?"

"I'm saying, if it comes to that, it may be up to you to stop it."

Alice knocked on the door again. "Excuse me, Mrs. Arokson, but Gideon Ford is here to see you."

Lucy squeezed her eyes closed. "Of course he is."

Captain Barrow pursed his thin lips. "Want me to stick around?"

"I can handle him. But don't go far."

Barrow nodded and left the office.

"Send him in, Alice."

Gideon entered, and the atmosphere of the office changed. It wasn't a stench or anything to do with his hygiene, but Lucy sensed a filth in him that raised a barrier in her mind. She'd known through Aeron what Gideon was like, but she'd never been the object of his motivations before. Now that she was in his focus, she wanted to dodge. However, she remained strong. The only way to deal with a man like Gideon was to meet him head on and be stronger so as to deflect him.

Gideon took the seat Captain Barrow had occupied and leered at her. "Mrs. Arokson, I represent a contingent of the people who believe your family continually abuses its status. We are concerned that the administration of our government does not have the colony's best interests at heart. As such, any instability within the colony is a direct threat to the pillar, which is a direct threat to the future of Lumen."

Lucy wasn't about to entertain his conniving political tendencies. "This is about Aeron leaving," she said.

"While our warden leaving during a crisis indicates a lack of commitment, it's merely the latest in a long history of acts that call into question your husband's effectiveness as warden."

"Aeron's leaving isn't him abandoning the colony as warden. He's following his responsibilities as a father."

Gideon stared at her with those aged eyes that, at once, appeared kind and menacing. "Mrs. Arokson, this isn't something you can debate with me. It's the opinion of the people. I'm simply delivering the message."

"I'm sure. So what is it the people want?"

"You must appreciate that we currently have an unelected warden who was put in place by an unelected warden. To remedy the problem and assure the people that their warden has their best interests at heart, perhaps we should hold an election for the office."

Of course he would make his move now. With her son missing, learning the danger they were in, and her husband going out into it, she hadn't seen it coming.

"Aeron will only be gone a day or two," she said. "I'm perfectly capable of administering this office while he's gone."

"Please understand, this isn't an affront to your abilities. I'm sure you're capable in, well, whatever it is that you do. It's merely a question of the legitimacy of the warden's office."

"I see." Lucy's breath burned her own nostrils. "So with Aeron away, you think now is your time to make your play for the wardenship."

Gideon smiled. "I am but a humble servant."

Lucy smiled back. "I understand, Mr. Ford, and thank you for bringing this to my attention. I know you can appreciate that there are some pressing matters to be taken care of, and for now, I'm in the best position to take care of them. I will address the colony in time, so let's pick this up shortly thereafter."

"The people would like to know when. To them, there is no more pressing matter."

"I see. Let's say no later than tomorrow."

"I think it would be best if you addressed them today, Mrs. Arokson. Word that your husband has abandoned us is spreading quickly. The *First Watch* will no doubt have an article tomorrow, and I suggest you get out in front of it."

"Very well. This afternoon then."

Gideon smiled and stood. "Good. I'm glad we could reach mutual agreement. If you don't mind my saying, your grace should serve you well in a leadership role, even if it isn't as warden. Such a gentle and cooperative approach is something I'm not sure your husband ever learned."

Lucy smiled at him as he left the office, and a moment later, Captain Barrow appeared in the doorway.

"Everything all right?"

"Nothing I won't be able to handle," she said. "But do me a favor. Keep an eye on him."

Barrow's eyebrows rose. "Is he a threat to this colony?"

"In a manner of speaking."

"Then yes, ma'am."

Barrow left, and Lucy sat to review the agenda. She had appointments throughout the day, and she had a pretty good idea what most of them were about. Perhaps addressing the colony sooner rather than later was a good idea.

Swiveling in the warden's chair, she faced the window that overlooked the commons. The morning sun was strengthening, and the people of the colony were rising for another day. Come nightfall, she knew, Vale would be a ghost town.

Four

When Ducard opened the door to the jail, the aged wood cracked, the stiff hinges squealed, and the voices of young men arguing carried down the hallway.

"I said shut up!"

"What are you going to do about it?"

Ducard closed the door behind him. The boys quieted. His boots boomed as he approached Lyle, who was standing outside of a cell with his fists clenched.

In the cell, Adam Hathaway gripped the iron bars, his pudgy cheeks squeezing through the opening.

Ducard took a moment to size up the youths. They watched him with something like apprehension, unsure what the big soldier was going to do. He let them squirm and, if he were being honest, enjoyed it.

He sighed. "What's going on, Lyle?"

The flushed color in the deputy's faded into a sickly pallor. "Hi, Sergeant. Nothing I can't handle."

Adam chortled.

Ducard stepped around the deputy, scrutinizing his scrawny, rigid form. When he spotted the swelling around Lyle's red eye, he grabbed the boy's chin and tilted it up so he could see it in the light.

"I can see that. What did he do?"

Adam shrugged. "I warned him."

Ducard glared. "Boy, shut your mouth. Lyle, why's he in the cage?"

"In addition to assaulting an officer of the law, he defaced private property."

"Lose the cop speak." Ducard released Lyle's chin. "What did he do?"

"I caught him at the cemetery, urinating on a headstone."

Ducard flinched and eyed Adam again. "You stupid, boy? I mean, that's got to be one of the dumbest things I've ever heard."

Adam shrugged and lay on his cot.

Ducard blinked in bewilderment and turned back to Lyle. "Whose headstone?"

"Thomas E. Haynes."

"As in 'Thomas E. Haynes School'?"

Lyle hunched his shoulders. "It wasn't just him. It was two other boys. When I told them to stop, they ran. He didn't."

Adam snorted. "Why would I?"

"A lot of this kind of stuff has been going on since the school closed," Lyle said. "Kids are going nuts."

"Let's go outside a minute. You." Ducard jabbed a finger at Adam. "When I come back, I better hear you counting sit-ups. If you did more of that, maybe you'd have a better time with the girls and wouldn't need to cause trouble for attention."

"Whatever."

Ducard raised his eyebrows. "Or maybe you're into the lads."

"Whatever, man."

Ducard guffawed and took Lyle out to the front steps. They sat on the cold concrete, watching the people in the marketplace. Lyle picked a blade of grass from a patch at the edge of the street and twirled it around his index finger.

"Look, you can't let punks like that push you around," Ducard said. "If you want to be sheriff one day, you got to learn to be firm. If they control you, it's over."

"Sheriff Ballard says it's important to be fair and professional."

"Ballard has her way, and it works for her. But people learned to respect her, and it wasn't because of her badge. It was because of how she handled business. You got to train people to respect you."

"How? Are you going to tell me something completely tough guy? Are you going to tell me something about hiding my weaknesses and burying my insecurities?"

Ducard smirked. "No. If there's one thing I've learned from Ballard, it's that you never hide. You put your soft spots out there."

"Won't that leave you open to attack?"

"Maybe. Once you realize it's okay to be afraid and that fear is the only real enemy, you've won, and guys like Adam Hathaway will never be able to touch you, because you'll be more powerful than them."

Lyle frowned. "I don't understand."

"The sheriff stepped into boots that had only ever been filled by men in a town where men, most of them bigger than she was, would have to respect her authority. Do you know how she did that?"

"How?"

"She never let them get to her, and she never told herself that she had to do something a certain way because of the way she was born. She did her job, and she did it good. She stood up for herself. She didn't let them push her around. In time, people stopped seeing her as a woman with a badge. They just saw their sheriff."

"How does that help me?"

"Everyone faces people who just want to hold them down. Some have it harder than others. Point is you got to do what you can do, and in time, people will forget who they thought you were and will see the person you are. Someone to be respected." Ducard paused and was quiet.

"What's wrong?"

"Nothing. Do what I said, and you can be sure you'll get what you want. You'll never feel like you missed out on something because you were afraid. Everyone's got their challenges, some greater than others.

This one is yours." He giggled. "Besides, bust enough skulls like she did, and people will get it pretty quick."

"I wouldn't know where to begin busting skulls."

Ducard stood and squeezed Lyle's shoulder. "You'll figure it out."

He left the boy picking the grass and gazing into the crowds of people he hoped to one day serve and protect.

Five

The old wood floor of Daenuel Hall groaned and creaked under the weight of the growing colonist crowd. The rows of benches were occupied, and while many people mingled in smaller groups, most of the standing room in the aisles and against the walls was filling up. Gideon Ford had no idea of the hall's weight capacity, but he reveled in testing it.

On the stage at the front of the room, Gideon looked over his people. The morning sunshine streamed through the old, rippling windows, and in the spots of bright light and contrasting shadow, he scanned the faces of those loyal to him and found eagerness and excitement for the future.

In them, he'd tapped anger, fear, and dissatisfaction. He'd appealed to their emotions instead of their reason. He'd roused their anxieties. Facts and rational thought didn't matter, only that which evoked visceral reactions.

He'd convinced them the blame for all of their troubles fell on the Arokson dynasty and that he, Gideon Ford, was the only person with the vision to see them and their misfortunes and the only man with the clout to challenge their leadership. Only he, Gideon Ford, could break through the system that had held them down and left them behind. Only he could speak for them.

He had exposed their wounds and given them hope. It was not a general optimism for the future or their power over it. It was a raging idealism that they placed in one man.

And it was working beautifully.

He took a deep breath. His moment of triumph was drawing near. He could feel it. Looking over his followers and supporters, it was undeniable that their movement was a juggernaut that would carry him into the warden's office.

As the last of Gideon's supporters filed in, men at the back of the hall closed the double doors, and nodded to him. The shuffling in the room settled. The last of the popping wood sounds died in the rafters of the vaulted ceiling. Over a hundred pairs of eyes gazed at him.

"Thank you all for coming," he said. "The fact that you are here tells me you already know the first thing I'm going to say. That is, these are dark times."

Murmurs of assent circulated through the crowd. Some people clapped or stomped their feet, a rumble like approaching thunder.

"Vale is a total disaster," Gideon said. "Security is horrible. Our economy is crumbling. It's the worst it's been in years. Colonists come and go through the wall and get lost in the wild. Some, and you may not know this, leave and take valuable resources with them. They take our resources from you and make those of you who already are forced to live in the mods to pay more for less."

The people growled and stomped.

"The sentries have turned inward and aimed their weapons at you. The school is closed, and your children are sitting at home. People can't get the medicines they need because our warden allowed the central government to reduce our supply. The warden sends our food and other resources to other colonies that can't provide for themselves, and we can't really afford to do that. It's all killing us. Now, nineteen of us are missing, and our warden has no intention of searching for them," Gideon said. "Worse, he has abused the power of the Sentry Service and restricted us from looking for our loved ones, and he's done this under the guise of concern for our wellbeing."

"It's not right!" someone cried.

"The warden's lying to us!"

"We should throw him in jail!"

The people growled with affirmation.

Gideon held up a hand for silence, and the crowd obliged. "That's right. You're being lied to, and you're right to question whether your leadership supports you. You know why? I'm going to tell you why. You may have heard the rumors. Well, they're all true."

Gasps and whispers circulated through the crowd.

"This morning, the lying Aeron and Lincoln Arokson left the colony. They went to find their foolish children who snuck through the unsecure and unsafe wall late yesterday."

The people swelled into a din of angry voices.

Gideon put his hands up. "Please. Please settle down."

They quieted.

"I've sent my son Clayton along with them to help find their children, and I convinced them to look for the missing sentries as well. I'm confident they will return with some of our people. However, we have to question our warden's hypocrisy. More than that, we have to question his commitment. During this dark time, he chose to abandon us."

"So who is running the warden's office now?" a man in the back asked.

"Aeron's wife, Lucy, is the interim warden."

"But she isn't elected," someone else said.

"No, she isn't," Gideon said. "If you recall, neither was Aeron. We have an unelected warden put in place by an unelected warden. This isn't how the First Families envisioned our government."

The people clamored for answers, spat their anger. They crawled over each other to appeal to Gideon, their surrogate for justice. He raised his hands, and they settled once again.

"I went to see Mrs. Arokson this morning, and she agreed to a proper election. You all will be able to re-elect Aeron if you choose, or another candidate."

"I nominate Gideon Ford for warden of Vale!" someone cried.

"You should run, Gideon!" another said.

The crowd roared its approval.

Gideon held up his hands for silence, and at his command, the room quieted again. They waited expectantly.

"If that is the will of the people," he said, "then how can I refuse?"

Daenuel Hall erupted in cheers, and Gideon Ford stepped forward into his followers' waiting arms.

Six

As soon as Sheriff Ballard opened the front door to her home, she recognized the deep quiet. Her breath hitched at the thought that her father was already gone and had died alone.

She moved swiftly but quietly down the hallway toward the bedroom, turned the handle gently, and entered. In the gloom, a figure sat on her father's bed.

"Good morning," Doctor Osman whispered.

The doctor removed the stethoscope from his ears and flipped the cable over the back of his neck. He laid the blanket back over her father's chest and eased off of the bed. He pulled Reggie into the hallway and closed the door, leaving her father in peace.

She gazed at him apprehensively. "How is he?"

Dr. Osman sighed. "Soon."

The word stole Reggie's breath. She bit her lip so hard she tasted copper, but it stopped the tears.

Dr. Osman rested a hand on her shoulder. "With everything that is happening, with all the demand of your job, I'd like to take him to the infirmary. We can keep him comfortable there, make sure someone is with him at all times."

Ballard shook her head. "He wants to be here. He made me promise."

"Reggie, I mean this with the utmost respect, and I speak now as a friend, not a doctor, but have you considered your father wanted to be here because he thought you would be here with him?"

She blinked at him. "He hasn't said anything to me about that."

"People in his position tend to come to terms with it before anyone else. He knows you'll have to let him go soon, and he knows you're needed elsewhere, but given the state of things, wouldn't you rather him be in compassionate company instead of being alone?"

"It isn't about what I want. It's about what he wants."

Osman's eyebrows arched. "Are you sure?" He let the question linger a moment. "He was awake about an hour ago. He spoke."

"What did he say?"

"He asked about you. He asked where you were. I told you you were out all night helping others, and he was glad. He was proud."

"That tells you he wants to be at the infirmary?"

"It tells me he's accepted what's happening to him. It tells me that he's ready to let go."

Pacing the hallway aimlessly, Ballard thought about it. Through the living room window, the morning sun caught her eye, and she thought of Lincoln. He had been by his mother's side when she died of this terrible condition. He had been alone with her when Isabel Arokson took her final agonizing breath.

Reggie didn't want it to be like that for her, and she knew her father didn't either.

"Okay," she said, "but if he protests even once, he stays. Understand?"

Dr. Osman gave her a warm, compassionate smile. "He won't."

Ballard looked Dr. Osman in the eye. She imagined she held a fire there and that it would drive home her point, but Dr. Osman had seen that look hundreds of times before. He knew what came next. The fire in Ballard would burn out and give way to something else.

Soon.

Seven

As Sergeant Ducard crossed the south fields, the wind whipped the heat from his body, and a shudder crawled up his spine. He hiked his coat up around his neck and blew into his cupped hands. Morning was the worst time of day. It was always the coldest, and something about being in a remote part of the colony, the loneliness and solitude of it, made the cold that much more unbearable.

Captain Barrow had gotten word to him that he was to report for duty first thing. The weird thing was the captain wanted to meet along the southern part of the wall.

He ascended the staircase to the top of the wall. Barrow faced the wild with his hands clasped behind his back, peering into the trees with intense discipline.

At the top of the stairs, sentries Sibley and Able leered at Ducard. Able grinned in a way that suggested the sentry was pleased, that maybe he thought Alain was going to get what he deserved.

Glaring at him sideways, Ducard muttered, "What are you looking at?" He brushed by and snapped to attention. "Sir, Sergeant Ducard reporting as ordered."

"At ease, Alain."

Ducard relaxed and glanced at the other two sentries, who were watching him with great interest. Ducard detected a measure of resentment in Sibley's eyes. Able sneered and whispered something to her. She nodded.

"Leave us, sentries," Barrow said.

They gawked at him, simultaneously surprised and offended.

"Now."

They scurried down the staircase, and at the bottom, began their long march across the south field. Barrow leaned on the inner wall and watched them go.

"They think you're in trouble," he said when they were out of earshot.

Ducard drew a deep breath. "Am I, sir?"

"Yes, sergeant. Yes, you are."

The sentry closed his eyes. He knew it. Because he hadn't fought to the last man, because he ran when he should have made a stand, because everyone else died but him, because he lived, he had disgraced the Sentry Service.

"We all are," Barrow said. "We're all in for some serious trouble."

Ducard's eyes shot open, and he grunted. "Gotcha."

Barrow shifted his weight. "I never got a chance to properly debrief you. I want you to tell me what happened out there. I want you to tell me what you saw, how they move and fight, what their organizational and strategic capabilities are. Everything."

Ducard leaned on the wall beside the captain. "You think we can fight them."

"I think we don't have a choice."

While Ducard told the story, Barrow stared straight ahead at the center of Vale in the distance. Ducard told him about the exos' ability to tunnel underground, how they moved through the trees with amazing speed and agility. He told the captain about their weak spots underneath and their strong points everywhere else, about their sensitivity to light, and how it seemed they had some kind of hive mind because of how organized they were and how they moved as a singular mass instead of individual soldiers.

When Ducard was finished, Barrow was silent. His stoic expression hadn't changed even as Ducard felt increasingly nauseated. Then the captain nodded.

"I have good news and bad news," he said. "The good news is I'm promoting you to lieutenant. Gray was my most trusted sentry, and losing him was a big blow. I need someone else I can count on, and you're that man. I know he was your friend, so I want you to understand you are not filling his boots. No one can. You earned this distinction and responsibility. It is an achievement on its own merits, and in recognition of your bravery in the wild, you deserve it."

The news hit Ducard like blow to his chest. "All due respect, I don't feel like it, sir."

"Why not?"

"I lived. You trained us to fight to the last man. I should have died. It was my duty to die." He shook his head. "I'm a disgrace."

"You saved three people, Alain. They wouldn't have made it without you."

"I ran."

"I'm glad you did. Look, it was a terrible situation all around. None of you knew what you were walking into, and for that, the blame is my own. I personally thank you for living and not putting another soul on my conscience. I'm going to need you in the days ahead. We all will."

Ducard met his captain's gaze and found something in it that lit a fire within him that he thought had extinguished for good. It was the look of absolute confidence and determination. Barrow had no doubt about Ducard's ability or value. He believed, so Ducard believed.

"All right," Ducard said. "Thank you, sir. What's the bad news?"

"The bad news is I'm assigning you here today, alone. I trust you not to speak about your experiences in the wild, but if it's all the same, you should probably stick to yourself for the time being."

"What about those things out there? They ain't gonna wait."

"Plans are in motion, and you need to trust that it's best for the colony. There's a process, and we need to follow it. Anyway, I don't think it will be too long before I need to call on you."

Ducard nodded, and Barrow stood and made his way to the staircase.

"What am I going to do out here all day?" Ducard asked. "There isn't even anyone to talk to."

"That's the point." Barrow smirked. "And anyway, all things considered, it's a good day for some target practice."

"You know about that, huh?"

"I know everything, Lieutenant." Barrow trotted down the stairs and began the walk across the field toward town.

For the first time since he returned from the wild, Alain Ducard's mind lingered on something other than grief and shame. "Lieutenant."

Eight

From the mountain, the valley stretched before Ellis and Ernest Freeman to the horizon in every direction, an endless landscape of green mystery. Surrounded by the wild, the colony below wrestled with the colossal weight of Lumen's nature, struggling to hold back the life they had given to it. The wilderness encroached upon them. In a matter of centuries, they had transformed the planet from a frozen wasteland into a hospitable garden, but even as the ground sprouted life, it came for them, the monster clutching for its maker.

"Can't see it yet, but we got a storm coming," Ellis said, looking out toward the west.

Ernest crouched and examined the hole the wrenches had dug. In the exposed dirt, a thick metal pipe had cracked, the seam jutting into the air. A yellow ribbon lay slack in the dirt. It read: DANGER—HIGH VOLTAGE.

"Take a look at the break in the metal." Ernest pointed. "It's like something impacted it, but the way the pipe peaks instead of sags suggests the force came from below."

Ellis bent over and grimaced. "Earthquake?"

"Maybe. If the earth shifted just so, sure. You said the pillar created a tremor the other night?"

"Yes, but the system didn't detect this fault until early this morning before sunup."

"Maybe after it was damaged the signal didn't decay enough for the system to think anything was wrong until this morning. Maybe the weight of the dirt around it finally pushed it enough to fault."

Ellis hummed in consideration. "When I asked you to come up here and look at this, I was hoping for something more definite from you. There are other things."

"Like what?"

"Well, this is only one of three faults. Thankfully, the pillar's redundant connection to Vale is redundant, so the system rerouted without a hitch. But there are more like this. Other than that, some trees have fallen on the compound wall. We're taking care of them now. It's strange. Winds were calm last night. All of that can be fixed, but what really bothers me is that some of the men said they felt tremors in the power plant last night. The reactor is fine, but if it sustains any damage, it could shut itself down. Although Lumen has tectonic plates, the geological survey was thorough. They chose this location for a reason. We just don't have earthquakes. That said, when they put this colony here, they were applying conventional knowledge to an alien world. Maybe the plates are shifting and we're experiencing earthquakes, which is a possibility as the planet's core becomes more active, or something else is happening. Either way, the pillar is in danger."

Ernest scanned the dirt, imagining the power line running through the earth, down the mountain, toward the colony. "Where does this line go?"

"Substation relay down the hill. Utility building housing various sensor equipment. Used to pull water up from an underground glacier, I think." Ellis searched his brother's face. "Why?"

Ernest walked to the other side of the hole and peered over the edge of a cliff. Below, trees and overgrowth enshrouded an ancient building with wooden sides and a corrugated metal roof.

"You check it?" Ernest asked.

"No. Most of the equipment in there is obsolete. It's little more than a tool shed now."

"Let me guess. It houses an old, powerful drill, and you still send enough current through there that it could run."

Ellis' eyes narrowed. "Well, yes. The power goes through to the colony, but there's no need to decommission it. Why?"

"I need to see it."

The men followed the slope of the mountain around to where the grade was passable. Eventually, the brothers made it to the utility building. It was little more than a shack, emerging from the side of the mountain like some kind of surfacing corpse. A wooden bridge between the building exterior wall and the rocky cliff made a level walking surface. It was rotten in places, fallen into disrepair from neglect and disuse, and as the brothers crossed, it creaked and swayed, threatening to send them tumbling to the rocks below.

On the far side, they found shrapnel of a door lying in the grass. It had blown outward and disintegrated into fine shards of wood.

"Something explode?" Ernest said.

Ellis' astonished eyes gaped. "I have no idea."

"There's no charring or any other indication of heat. An arc blast would have set fire to the whole building, not to mention the surrounding trees."

Ernest entered the building, and as his eyes adjusted to the darkness, his chest heaved. There, in the center of the structure, the old drill lay in pieces. Machine parts and lengths of hose were strewn around the place like the guts of some eviscerated robot. The ground where the drill bit would have been was a void. Before Ellis and Ernest, a great hole opened in the earth.

Ellis clutched his brother's shoulder. "What in the world?"

Ernest gaped. "We have to tell the warden."

"He's out there looking for the kids."

"I mean Lucy. She has to know about this."

"What are we even going to tell her happened here?"

"I know what I'm going to say. I think she can tell us exactly what happened here."

The Freeman brothers left the utility building and got off of that mountain as quickly as they could.

Nine

Captain Barrow entered the warden's office. The sun was setting on the first full day after Lincoln and Aeron had left for the wild. He had spent more time with the colonists than ever before. He had resolved disputes between them and his sentries before they got too heated, apologized for the necessary military presence, and he had learned two things: the people were beginning to fall apart, and he could never be a warden. Civilians were just too complicated.

Alice escorted him in, and he was surprised to find Ellis and Ernest Freeman with the warden.

Sensing the discord, Alice's eyes darted between Barrow and Lucy.

There were no pleasantries in Lucy's hard face. "Please leave us, Alice."

"Of course. If you need anything, I'm right outside." She closed the door gently behind her.

"I thought you summoned me for a private meeting," Barrow said.

"This is a private meeting. Between the four of us." Lucy gestured to the third chair in front of her desk. "Please sit."

Barrow took his place. The brothers gazed at him impishly. He intimidated them, and he took some satisfaction in that.

"I've called you all here because it's time to stop the secrets," Lucy said. "Secrets are why we're here, and secrets are why it's possible that everything we've built could fall apart." She let that sink in. "It's time we're open with each other because it's the only way we're going to make it. Ellis, you start."

He shifted in his chair and cleared his throat. "From the beginning?"

"Yes. Tell Captain Barrow everything you've told me."

"Okay. Five days ago, we had a hiccup at the pillar. We didn't know what happened until the men found a low voltage line had been damaged. We repaired it. Then last night we had a few more damaged lines. These transmit power to the colony. Some trees fell down onto the compound wall, and the men reported tremors in the reactor."

"We didn't see any power outages," Barrow said in confusion.

"The pillar's reactor supplies power to the colony. It has to generate an enormous amount of energy to jump start Lumen's core, so we just patch into that and use a fraction of a percent of the energy it generates. It has redundancies for its redundancies. Power rerouted without a problem."

Ernest leaned forward. "Let's rewind a bit. A few days ago, Aeron came to me with a problem. Some cattle had gone missing. I repurposed a drone to look for the cattle's tracking chips, which emit a short-range radio signal. It's how they keep track of them. Long story short, I found them. They were outside of the colony walls. And they were underground."

Ellis jumped forward to cut his brother off. "Then today, with the disrupted lines, Ernest and I found that a utility building had been ransacked. The building housed a coring drill that used to be used to tap into an underground glacier for water. Captain, it looked like something had come out of that hole."

Barrow dug at his eyes and grimaced.

Lucy folded her hands on her desk. She allowed her gaze to linger on him, a request for permission. He consented with a nod.

"Aeron only told me yesterday, but he's known since his father left the seal with him," she said. "All of the wardens have kept this secret, and they did it because they expected the problem to go away. Lumen wasn't a dead planet when we landed on it. There was a native species that lived underground. The expectation was that, as we changed Lumen's atmosphere and environment, they would die off. But they've become stronger. As we've charged the planet's core and it's grown hotter, it's pushed them closer to the surface."

The Freeman brothers gaped at her.

"This is what we're dealing with," Lucy said and set a picture on her desk. "Sheriff Ballard took a picture of a dead one that the search party found. That's what came out of your hole."

Ernest reached forward and Lucy handed the photo to him. Though horrified, he examined the image with the objectivity of a scientist.

"It looks like it has an exoskeleton," he said. "It looks insectoid."

Lucy nodded. "Lincoln called them 'exos.'"

"On other planets, certain insects have been known to be drawn by electromagnetic fields. The core heat pushing them to the surface is a good theory, but maybe the EM field is drawing them up, and maybe the pillar, generating all of that electricity, is drawing them too."

"Great," Ellis said. "It isn't like we can just turn off the pillar."

"Why not?" Barrow asked.

"Atmosphere isn't finished."

Lucy steepled her fingertips. "If we were to turn it off, how long would we have?"

"Before Lumen becomes inhospitable again?"

"Yes."

"Without the electromagnetic field, Lumen's star would blast the atmosphere away. I really don't know how long it would take, but it could be months or years."

Ernest tilted his head, shrugging it off. "Well that isn't so bad. Time to figure out a solution."

"Oh, no, no, no," Ellis said. "It would take a while to reset all of our progress, but we would see the effects almost immediately. Superstorms, rapid climate change, natural and ecological disasters the likes of which this world has never seen. And that's being conservative. A hospitable environment is a precarious balance, and without the pillars, we are shoved off. The civilization we've built would be unsustainable within a few weeks. All life that has evolved here would die. We wouldn't last long enough to see Lumen return to the way it was."

Barrow rubbed his face and sighed. "I'm hearing that we need to protect the pillar at all costs."

Lucy took a deep breath and leaned onto her desktop. "I need you to do whatever it takes to ensure the pillar is safe. Take all of your men there if you have to."

"What about the colony?" Barrow asked.

"The colony isn't threatened right now. The pillar is."

"Unless I'm mistaken," Barrow said, "Ernest just said these exo things have been inside the walls."

Lucy held up a hand. "We'll deal with it if it comes to that. For now, we need to be concerned with the pillar. The pillar goes, it all goes. Understood?"

Barrow nodded. "People are going to see something is going on. They're going to be curious."

"I'm going to tell them."

The captain raised his eyebrows. "You think that's wise?"

"No," Lucy said. "But we don't have a choice."

They each sat back in their chairs, gazing into nothing, an impossible weight descending onto their shoulders.

Ten

The Arokson Hall bell tower tolled with Lucy standing on the steps beneath it. She wanted to be out front when people arrived. She wanted to portray transparency and honesty, and she wanted to eliminate the barrier her husband had created.

That's why she'd instructed the sentries to stay away. They were watching, but they weren't to be visible to the colonists. Her colonists.

With questioning, expectant stares, they amassed before her. Some of them expressed disdain or irritation about being summoned. Some of them whispered inquiries about what they already knew. Some of them looked at her with perplexed expressions, unaware Lucy was their acting warden.

At the sight of her people, a trembling overcame her. Lucy had never addressed more than a classroom of children in all her life. Here were adult men and women who had suffered and sacrificed for their colony

and this world. Regardless of the fact that Gideon Ford had manipulated their grievances, they were unhappy with the general state of affairs. Now she understood the scrutiny Aeron had faced every day, and she would have to bear it and play this right.

She raised a hand, and the bell silenced. Lucy scanned over her people who had filled the commons. By their sheer number, she guessed the homes, market, school, infirmary, and every other building and facility in the town center had emptied. She would be able to reach as many ears as possible this way. The rest would have to hear it secondhand.

Gideon emerged from the throng, wearing a hard expression as if he was trying to figure her out. People around him asked questions and looked to him for answers, but he zeroed in on her. Lucy hadn't expected his presence to affect her, but it struck her confidence.

She cleared her throat. "Thank you all for coming. By now, I'm sure many of you are aware my husband has left Vale in search of our son, nephew, and Sera Bellman, who snuck out last evening. I know it appears as though he is violating his own rules. But that is because, for some time now, this office has been lying to you."

Murmurs stirred in the congregation. Lucy held up her hands for silence, and they obliged.

"Last night, I learned of some disturbing truths my husband said I needed to know if I was going to lead. He said you could not know if you were to follow. But I think the time for secrecy has passed, and I think to not disclose the truth to you now would be immoral.

"There is native life here on Lumen. We have known about it since the beginning, and it was assumed the Pillars of Dawn would make this world uninhabitable for them. We were wrong. They have thrived.

"We now face a hostile species threatening our home and our mission of finishing this world. And you need to know about this threat for two reasons. First, we are not looking for the missing sentries because we know them to be dead."

Voices shot from the crowd. Some of them, family members of those sentries, cried out.

"My deepest condolences to the families of these men and women. The night the survivors of the search party returned, they were attacked by these creatures. Only Sheriff Ballard, Deputy Lyle Albright, Alain Ducard, and Lincoln Arokson survived.

"I tell you this because of the next thing you need to know. My husband and brother-in-law left the colony because they believed our children to be still alive, and they did not want to risk more colonists' lives to search for them. Certainly, any parent here must understand they could not leave their children to the wild. They had to go."

The people loosened. They stopped whispering and gaped. Some of them teared up. Couples joined hands and embraced. She had them now.

"When they return, and I expect that to be soon, we will ensure no one else is lost. Until then, we have to carry on. We have to ensure the pillar finishes its work, and that can only happen if we work together. Now, questions?"

The crowd erupted, and as Lucy pleaded for order, Gideon stepped forward. Now the fight for her people's support would begin.

"Mrs. Arokson," he said, "considering these revelations, how can we trust you are telling us everything? What assurances do we have that you are being transparent?"

The crowd rumbled with support. Their cries persisted, and Lucy locked eyes with him. She saw the truth of his intentions, and he sneered. He didn't care that she knew. He made no attempt to hide it anymore, and that was how Lucy knew this was the moment he was choosing to make his move.

Gideon silenced the crowd with a wave of his hand. "Mrs. Arokson, you are an unelected warden appointed by an unelected warden. How can the people trust in a leader that they haven't elected? With all due respect, I think everyone is aware of your history of breaking the law for your family's benefit. It's corruption, plain and simple. Furthermore, by your own admission, the office of the warden has been lying to its people for some time. If what you say is true, since the establishment of Vale! Your apparent honesty is admirable, but as my daddy said, a liar is never so untrustworthy as when he claims to be coming clean. I think it's time we rectify the mistakes of the past. It's time the people get to speak. It's time we have someone who truly represents their interests."

Gideon smiled as the crowd roared behind him. People clapped and reached out to pat his shoulder and shake his hand. All the while, he glared at Lucy. He'd made his move, and now it was her turn. There was only one thing for her to do.

The crowd settled, expecting a response, and Lucy intended to give them one they wouldn't forget.

"Mr. Ford, everyone, let me be clear," she said. "Our pillar hasn't finished its work. If it doesn't finish, Lumen will quickly become uninhabitable for us. There is a hostile native species here, and it wants all of us, our husbands, wives, mothers, fathers, and children, dead so it can take its planet back. We have no idea what they're capable of, but we do know that we are in a precarious position. I have no interest in petty politics. That is my husband's game, and that's your game. It isn't mine."

She removed the Warden's Seal from around her neck. She clenched the cord and dangled it in front of the crowd. The blank gold face beamed, a circle of fire like a star hanging from Lucy's hand.

"As soon I learned what we were facing, I knew you all had to know so we could work together. It's the only way we're going to make it. It's the only way Lumen's going to make it. That's what I want. I want to live. I want this world to live."

Lucy tossed the Warden's Seal into the dirt between her and Gideon.

"If this is all you want, take it. It's yours. I'm not going to fight you in petty politics. I've got a colony and a people to save, and it's not worth sacrificing over selfish ambition. If you think it is, there it is. It's yours. You can have it."

Hundreds of eyes glared at the shining circle lying in the dirt. Moments passed where the only sound was the rustling wind. Across the space and time, Lucy felt Gideon's desire to bend down and rescue the seal from the dirt, but he couldn't. He knew that, if he did, he would confirm everything Lucy had said about him.

In front of the people who gave him power, Lucy had neutered him. She had offered him the thing he desired more than anything, and he couldn't take it because, if he did, the power it held would evaporate.

Gideon had surrounded Lucy in her tower, giving her only the choice to surrender. He'd had no idea that she'd be willing to burn the whole thing down.

Lucy gazed out at her people. They weren't lost in the allure of the Warden's Seal anymore. They weren't cheering for Gideon. They were watching her, waiting to see what she was going to do, listening to what she was going to say. Her, not him.

She took a deep breath and relaxed. Her trembling finally settled. "Right, then. Effective immediately, there is no more curfew. No more lockdown. You all are free to do as you please because we're all in this together." She glanced at the Seal. "There's a storm coming tonight. Go be with your families. Stay inside. Be safe. Take care of each other."

Lucy exited the stage of Arokson Hall's steps to an utterly silent crowd. Ernest and Ellis Freeman brought Bernie and Mel, and they and Captain Barrow accompanied her into the building. Barrow closed the doors behind them, and they stood in the lobby, reeling from the experience.

"Aunt Lucy!" Bernie leaped into an embrace. "You were great!"

"Good job, Mom," Mel said.

Ernest smiled at her. "Lucy, you're one of the most manipulative, political people I know, and I mean that in the best possible way. I had no idea you would play that so honestly."

"It's all politics, Ernest. All of it," Lucy said. "Even when it isn't."

Still leaning against the door, Barrow frowned at her. His soldier's glare bore into her. "Do you think that was wise?"

She nodded in affirmation to herself. "It had to be done. One thing my husband never understood. It's not about how good you look. It's about how bad the other guy looks. Ultimately, people don't want the best person for the job. They just don't want the worst person for the job."

"Let's just hope it doesn't have unintentional consequences."

"We'll fix Aeron's reputation when he gets back."

"That isn't what I mean," Barrow said. "People can get crazy without effective leadership. Let's hope they still see you as a leader, because I won't be able to help you tonight. I have to take Ellis to the Pillar. You ought to stay here."

There was a knock at the door. When no one else moved, Lucy opened it.

With flushed cheeks and watery eyes, Elena Bellman and Dani Hines stood in the doorway. Elena presented the Warden's Seal to Lucy.

"What are you doing here, Elena?" Lucy said.

"You said for people to be with their families."

Lucy flinched. She accepted the Seal and embraced Elena and Dani.

"Please, come in," she said.

In the quiet Arokson Hall lobby, Elena Bellman and Dani Hines wept, and it brought everyone together.

Eleven

Many things came naturally to Sheriff Regina Ballard. Letting go of the ones she loved wasn't one of those things.

Though, she was getting used to raising a glass of shine to her lips.

"What are you doing?"

Ballard turned in her barstool, the shot glass shaking in her fingertips. Ducard stood beside her in the increasingly crowded Gill's Still. The sheriff looked over the place. She didn't know when all of these people had gotten there. It seemed like she blinked and Gill's had filled up. She was sure that, only moments ago, the place had been empty.

"I said, what are you doing?" Ducard's face was twisted, but it had a natural look to it. The man scowled a lot. This was just what he looked like, as if his displeasure was carved in stone.

Ballard shrugged and went back to her shine. Ducard slapped it out of her hand. The glass tumbled on the bar top, and Gill was there to catch it before it fell to the floor and shattered, before it got the attention of everyone in the place.

"You're completely blasted."

Ballard leaned on the bar top and sulked. "Oh? Mission accomplished then."

"You can't let people see you like this."

"Who cares?"

The sentry grabbed a fistful of Ballard's shirt and pulled her up to her feet, but she was dead weight. "What the hell is wrong with you?"

The sheriff grasped his wrist and twisted the big man's arm, pinning him to the bar top.

Ducard growled and groaned. "Damn, Reg! Okay! Let go!"

She released him and stumbled backward. Catching herself, she straightened her uniform and observed the patrons of Gill's gaping at her. Another night she might have spoken to them and offered some kind of reassurance. Tonight, though, she simply wiped her mouth and returned to the stool.

Rolling his shoulder, Ducard took the seat next to her. "Tell me what's going on."

"My dad's gone."

Ducard signaled to Gill for two more glasses of shine. "Damn. I'm sorry. When?"

"This afternoon. Osman took him this morning. He said he was close and that, with my being away so much, it wasn't right for him to be alone." Ballard rubbed her eyes. "I agreed. He never woke up when they took him. A few hours later, someone came and told me."

"Reggie, I'm so sorry."

Ballard looked at Ducard for the first time that evening, and her face was empty, bereft of any spirit or vitality, pale like the weathered and beaten concrete of Vale's perimeter wall. The grief manifested in a sickness, and Ducard could do nothing for her.

Gill arrived with the shine, and then, like the best barmen, left without a word.

"Well, we knew it was coming." She picked up her glass. "Osman told me my dad would be one of the last, as if that would be some consolation."

"One of the last what?"

"To die of liquid lung. He was sixteenth gen. We're seventeenth. There aren't many sixteens left, except for those whose families beat it in earlier generations. Apparently, there's a map of it, the family trees. They know everyone who's left and who may get it. There aren't many."

In the corner, Gideon was surrounded by a handful of his most loyal supporters. The men and women at the table erupted in laughter.

Ballard eyed them. "Unfortunately *that* family beat it two gens ago. One of the first. Why is it those who deserve to live die, and those who deserve to die live?"

"Hey," Ducard said. "You can't talk like that."

"Why not?"

"Because you're the goddamn sheriff. You're supposed to be the good guy."

Ballard returned her attention to her shine and sighed. "I think the time for good guys is coming to an end."

Ducard was silent while Ballard sipped her shine. He picked his up, gulped it all, and slammed the glass down on the bar, exhaling the burn like fire. "You can't worry about him now. He's the warden's problem. We have bigger problems."

Ballard blinked lazily. "Oh?"

"Seems Lucy saw fit to tell everyone about those exo things, so now everyone knows."

"That's a problem?"

"Yes, it's a big damn problem. This place is going to implode, and we can't be distracted. We have to be ready for them if they come."

"I've got news for you, Alain." Ballard drained her shine and set her glass on the bar. "It doesn't matter. The sentries can't protect this colony from them. If they want in, they're getting in."

Ballard rose on unsteady legs and stumbled toward the door with a disgusted look on her face as if everything in the world were an insult to her.

Without saying goodbye, she left Gill's to the din of voices that had turned it into a place she could no longer stand. In a way, the worst offender had been her friend who had pulled her hurt from her heart and to the surface.

Into the cold and darkening world, she waded in a liquid haze. Whether she was disoriented from the loss or the shine, she didn't know.

Twelve

The earth shook under the march of hundreds of feet. Sentries moved en masse through the industrial district's gravel streets. Personnel in the fabrication plants and storage warehouses watched in awe as the sentries passed by with slung rifles, machine guns, and various other armaments suitable for a battlefield. Spare magazines and hand grenades rattled on their body armor. The soldiers said nothing, but their determined eyes set in grim faces told the colonists that the sentries were ready for war, they were willing to fight for Vale's survival, and they would die to preserve all life on Lumen.

In the late afternoon hours, they hit the train platform and lined up along its edge. Captain Barrow didn't have to utter the command for them to stand at attention. His sentries did it anyway, and as he looked over his men and women of the Sentry Service, he nodded his approval of their conduct. With his sentries fit, trim, and steadfast, if the exos came tonight, they would break upon the wall like waves against a cliff. His sentries were ready for anything.

The train thundered into the station and halted. A set of doors parted, and Ducard stood there to greet his captain.

"You guys need a lift?"

Barrow stepped aboard. "Lieutenant."

"I don't know if I'll ever get used to that."

"You will."

Instructed not to leave the captain's side, Ellis followed and stared uncertainly at the big sentry.

"Ain't gonna bite." Ducard pointed a thumb at Barrow. "He says I can't."

"Reassuring."

Ducard grinned. Ellis took a seat, and every train car filled with sentries methodically securing space on the benches or standing and gripping a handhold, which hung from the ceiling. With everyone aboard, the train lurched toward the pillar.

Fighting the shimmy and sway of a moving train, Ducard staggered to meet Barrow in the aisle. "Did you pull everyone off the wall?" he asked.

"Yes. At Ernest Freeman's suggestion, we turned off the perimeter lighting. He said the electricity could draw them to the colony. Everything else nonessential was powered down, and we have a small force in the commons. If they attack, we expect them to come for the pillar since they've already hit it a couple of times that we know of. Three hundred sentries in one focused location ought to be a hard perimeter to crack."

Barrow accepted a rifle from a sentry and handed it to Ducard. He ejected the magazine and inspected the rounds.

Ellis cleared his throat. "So, Captain, if these exo creatures do attack the pillar tonight, what's the plan?"

"We make a wall, and we fight."

The sentries in the car stomped and rumbled their approval.

Ellis glanced around, checking for scrutiny. "Like the Battle of Thermopylae. If you'll recall, that didn't end well."

Ducard slapped the rifle magazine back in. "The battle of what?"

"You know," Ellis said. "The three hundred Spartans."

Ducard's perplexed expression persisted while the train knocked and banged.

"Seriously?" Ellis said. "Captain, how can your men not know one of the most notorious battles in military history?"

Ducard stabbed a finger at him. "Hey, we're trained to fight for your wussy asses, not to read history."

Barrow clapped Ducard's shoulder and smiled. "He's got a point. Now that you're an officer, you may want to study up on some military strategy. Flex that brain muscle along with all the rest."

"Maybe he's been compensating," Ellis mumbled.

Ducard shot him a glare. "What was that?"

"Nothing!" Ellis put his hands up. "Don't shoot!"

"I wouldn't waste a bullet. I'd just tear your arms off and beat you with them."

"Relax, Alain. He's just joking around," Barrow said. "To your point, Ellis, the Spartans may have all died at Thermopylae, but they saved the other Greeks so they could pull back and fend off the Persians later. Their heroics and sacrifice boosted the morale of the Greek army. The glory, in fact, lives on even today on the other side of the galaxy. My men should be so lucky."

A grim expression befell Barrow's face, and he gazed into nothing, recalling either memory of past battles or premonitions of his glorious future.

"Captain?" Ducard said. "Are we the Spartans in this scenario?"

Barrow blinked at his lieutenant, amazed. "Don't be a fool. The Spartans were the greatest soldiers to ever live. You all are pukes until you prove otherwise."

The sentries in the car erupted with cheers at this. Ellis shot a questioning glance around, unsure why they approved of being called "pukes."

Ducard narrowed his brow at Ellis. "What? You don't get the 'pukes' thing?"

"You didn't get the Spartan thing?"

Ducard rolled his eyes and walked toward the front of the car, as far away as he could get from them. "It's gonna be a long night."

The train lumbered up the side of the mountain and reached the peak as the approaching storm joined the expansive clouds of the pillar's Dawn.

Thirteen

Under gray skies, Reggie rocked in the commons' swing set alone. The temperature was dropping, and she shivered from the sickness of too much shine. She had delayed it as long as she could, but it was time to go home.

This morning, when Dr. Osman had taken her father, Ballard had known an empty house would be difficult to adjust to. Now that he was gone, she didn't know if she would be able to bear it.

She walked the lonely road that connected the commons to the residential district, gravel crunching underfoot, the globed streetlamps haloed in a soft mist, and only she disturbed the silent night's peace.

The whole world, it seemed, was holding its breath.

Turning onto her street, a gust of wind blew, but she didn't feel it tear through her flesh. With the numbing agent of her grief, she didn't feel much of anything.

Reaching her house, Ballard looked up from the ground and discerned a shadow rocking in one of her porch chairs. There were no lights on in the house or its exterior to illuminate the shape, but it stood and grasped the column over the railing. She regarded it for a moment before it leaned into the waning daylight, which illuminated the kind face of Dr. Terrance Osman.

"Here to make a house call?" Ballard asked.

With piercing blue eyes, Osman gazed at her, evaluating. The doctor nodded. "I've been waiting for you a while." He put a mug on the railing and poured a liquid from a dented and scuffed metal canister.

"Sorry. Had I known I was going to have company, I would have been here." Ballard walked up the steps to her home and sat in one of her chairs. The thought of shine made her feel the urge to retch. "I think I've had enough for one day."

Osman grunted. "Not of this you haven't. This will make you feel better."

"How'd you know?"

He offered the mug to Ballard. "I'm a doctor."

It was warm and smelled earthy and herbal. She held it up to the light and found it had a green tint to it.

She smiled. "Lincoln's tea."

"Mmm hmm."

Ballard took a deep breath of the aroma. "He's usually the source of my headaches, not the cure for them." She sipped the tea, and it tingled on her lips.

Osman threw back his own mug. "I still think of him as that troubled boy who lost his father too early. Now he's a troubled man whose losses keep mounting. Losing loved ones changes you."

"Yes." Ballard cradled the mug with both hands. "It does."

She could already feel the tea working in her gut, filling her belly with warmth, sticking to the inside of her ribcage with a comforting glow that calmed and soothed her.

"A lot of people in this colony have lost people," she said. "Life on Lumen has gotten easier, but it's still a hard life."

Osman sighed. "It is. But people are soft. You might think that, if you harden up, grief will just bounce right off of you, but it won't. It gets inside, and if you harden up, it'll never get out. It'll just eat away at you like a sickness."

"So I'm supposed to open up, is that it?"

"It will help. Leaning on loved ones and friends helps."

"I won't get over it."

"You'll never get over it, no."

"So what am I supposed to do?"

"Embrace it. Grief isn't sadness. Sadness is the result of grief handled improperly. Grief is knowledge that a part of your life is over, but how you handle that is up to you. You can dwell on it and drown in it. Or you can accept it and use it. You can use it to do something great."

"How?"

"Your father was always a part of you, and he is a part of you still. He no longer has needs of his own. Harness the strength he gave you in his life to focus on your life now. When you're ready, use it for good. It's an energy. Energy can't be extinguished, only transformed. It will either burn you up, or you can use it as fuel to drive you."

"That's awfully spiritual for a doctor."

"If you prefer, I can prescribe chemicals that will physically alter the function of your brain and help you deal with this, but in all of the grief counseling I've done as this colony's medical professional, I've learned that dealing with people on a spiritual and emotional level is just as important as medical or surgical precision. The illusion many doctors have is that they're fixing their patients. The truth is I can't fix you. I can only help you fix yourself. That's the same for whether you skin your knee, catch a virus, or lose someone you love. You can lean on me. I can support you. I can make you numb or strengthen you. But it's up to you to put yourself back together, Reggie."

They rocked together in the graying world, sipping their tea. Her father was gone, and while everyone else was worried about the pillar and the exos, all she knew was that there was no one else in the world to call her a child.

"And maybe yet," Osman said. "Maybe there's more room in your life now."

Reggie peered at him. "What do you mean?"

"It's none of my business, but it seems to me Lincoln is of particular concern to you."

"You're right, Dr. Osman. It's none of your business."

"If I may, your defensiveness suggests he's more than an ordinary colonist to you."

"So you're a psychologist now too?"

"Please, we all wear many hats here. I may dabble. My point is, if you want to help him, if you want to stop him from being so reckless, you can't do it through law. You have to give him a real reason."

"His kids aren't enough?"

"Children are one thing. A father will give everything to them. But for others, you tend to hold something back because it's more of a symbiotic relationship."

When Dr. Osman saw that he'd gotten Reggie thinking, he stood. "I should get going." He started down the steps.

"So soon?"

He stopped and turned back to her. "The longer I stay, the longer you'll resist going in that house. Do yourself a favor. Go in there, and get some rest. You'll feel better in the morning."

"Doctor's orders?"

"Yes, in fact. Good night, Reggie."

"'Night, Dr. Osman."

Dr. Osman walked up the street toward his own home, and Reggie watched the gray world plunge deeper into the darkness and cold. Before too long, she looked at her front door, evaluating it, considering it. Then she pushed back in her chair and went to sleep on her front porch, even though the chill was already setting into her bones.

In the west, lightning pulsed within black clouds, and thunder rolled across the sky.

Fourteen

In the glow of dim lamplight, Lucy brushed Bernie's golden hair. Quiet and still, Mel lay in her bed with her blankets pulled up over her head.

Rain pounded the window, and lightning flashed outside. The storm had come.

"I know it's been very hard," Lucy said. "It'll all be over soon. Your fathers will come back with your brothers and Sera, and we'll figure this whole mess out."

Neither of the girls responded. Bernie stared at the wall, only moving with each gentle tug of the brush through her hair. Lucy fingered the tines of the brush, and evaluated her. Nothing. The girl was blank and unresponsive.

She set the brush on the nightstand, and Bernie crawled into bed with Mel. Lucy pulled the blanket over them and waited for them to settle in. Their innocence radiated like a light, and it warmed her maternal soul. However, Lucy despaired at the thought that, even as she watched them, they were hardening. As children grew, they took shape into people, and sometimes their experiences distorted and mutated them into bitter, resentful beings. Lucy feared the thought that these sweet girls could grow into such people because of the hardships they endured now.

She would do anything to protect them, but she didn't know if she could save them from that.

"Everything all right?" a voice asked from behind her.

Startled, Lucy turned and found Ernest standing in the doorway. She switched off the lamp on the nightstand, and as she crossed the room, a gust of wind sent a torrent of rain against the house.

"Storm's still going strong," Lucy said.

"We have a warm home and a roof to weather it," Ernest said. "Thanks to you."

She raised a hand in dismissal. "It's no problem. You all can stay here anytime."

Ernest laughed politely. "That's not what I meant."

"What did you mean?"

"I meant Vale was spinning out of control, and you leveled her out. You pulled it all back together. You did that."

"Yeah, well, hopefully it lasts, though I doubt it will. Gideon will find another way."

"You're missing the point, Lucy. You gave us tonight. Tonight, those girls can sleep soundly in that bed, and we can cherish their innocence for one more day. None of that was certain this morning."

Lucy blinked away tears. "Well, that's something I guess." She wiped her eyes. "Dani and Elena are settled in?"

"Already asleep."

She felt the first pull of exhaustion. She rubbed her eyes, and Ernest squeezed her arm.

"It's time you get some rest," he said. "You were right."

She raised her eyes to his. "About what?"

"This nightmare will be over soon."

With a smile, she humored his attempt to console her as she'd done for the girls, but she knew better. There was still a chance they didn't.

As she breathed to speak, a gunshot cracked the night. Its report echoed across the colony.

Lucy raced to the window and scanned the darkness outside. The street in front of her home was empty. Her neighbors' lights came on.

Mel bolted up in the bed with wide eyes. "What's going on?"

"I don't know." Lucy moved toward the door. "Stay here."

"Mom, don't leave us."

Lucy rushed to them. She touched their faces. "It's going to be okay. I'll be right back."

On the way to the door, she met Ernest's concerned gaze.

"Stay with them," she said. "No matter what. Keep them safe."

Ernest nodded, and as Lucy charged into the hall, he followed her to meet Elena outside of the guest bedroom. He tried the same reassuring tactic with her. Lucy didn't have time to see if it worked.

She ran out into the night. Raindrops, cold and hard, pelted her face and chest. Her nightgown flapped behind her like a cape. Most of the homes on her street were illuminated now. Some of her neighbors were coming out of their front doors.

"Stay inside," she told them.

They stood firm, neither complying nor protesting. She didn't have time to argue.

She rushed toward the commons, the direction in which she thought the gunshot had come. The psychedelic aurora above was a thick river of red tonight, but the darkness of the storm was overtaking it.

Two figures stood in the field in front of Arokson Hall. Another figure lay on the ground. As she neared, she discovered it was Sherriff Ballard and Deputy Albright standing. On the ground, Adam Hathaway lay still, a red splotch on his chest as if the aurora had leaked onto him.

Ballard was hugging Lyle, and she held a revolver. Hers was still in its holster on her hip.

Chest heaving, Lucy's panicked eyes begged the question. "What happened?"

"I caught him running from Milly's shop in the marketplace," Lyle said. "I think he'd broken in and stolen something. I yelled for him to stop, but he just kept running, so I chased him. He just wouldn't listen. He wouldn't stop. He wouldn't listen to me!"

With Lyle sobbing into her chest, the sheriff frowned at Lucy. Adam's blood was staining the grass around him, and as it pooled, the storm strengthened. It peppered the collecting crimson, and reality set in.

A young boy was dead. Deputy Lyle Albright had killed him.

Gray figures in the downpour, people charged across the field and encroached the scene of the shooting. They gaped and whispered, waited and watched. They looked to Lucy for answers.

She had none.

Gideon emerged, a grin of renewed fervor on his face. "Take him."

At his word, half a dozen men advanced, clamoring for Lyle.

"No," Lucy commanded, and still they came.

Ballard raised her weapon. "This is an officer of the law. You're not taking him anywhere."

The growing crowd retorted with spitting shouts. Gideon held up his hand and they quieted.

"Surely you understand, Sheriff, that the people want answers for what happened here," he said.

Ballard cocked her head at Gideon. "And you'll get them with due process."

"So you'll investigate," Gideon said. "That isn't good enough. We want answers now."

The angry mob advanced. Ballard's hand tensed and trembled. The sickness of the shine still coursed through her veins, weakening her, clouding her mind. She drew back the revolver's hammer.

Lucy stepped in front of her with her hands raised. "Enough!" She eyed the sheriff. "Put the gun down, Reggie."

Ballard flinched with betrayal. "I've got this, Luce."

"I know you do. But maybe it's time we try not pointing fingers and guns at each other."

Ballard lowered her revolver. The men and women who were coming for Lyle relaxed and backed away to give Lucy some space.

"Now is a time to come together. So let's come together." Lucy looked to the sky and held her hands out to collect some of the rain. "But maybe we ought to do it inside."

"She's right," Gideon said. "Let's take this to Daenuel Hall."

Voices of ascent murmured in the crowd, and Gideon led them toward the marketplace.

Ballard put Lyle's weapon into her waistband. "Do you really think we need to do this now?"

"I really don't think we have a choice," Lucy said.

As the mass of people moved across the commons, the world went silent except for the hush of the falling rain and a boom in the western sky. Above, black clouds devoured the aurora.

Fifteen

The storm pounded on Daenuel Hall's old wooden roof. Even indoors, the rain hissed like a constant intake of breath through clenched teeth. The humidity and temperature skyrocketed and made the room feel like the air was swelling.

Lightning flashes and thunder cracks served as reminders that Lumen was either indifferent to the plight of humanity or choosing just the right time to strike.

The floor and benches cracked and groaned as people filed in and took seats. Puddles formed at their feet from their dripping clothing. Shuffling feet squealed wet soles on the solid wood.

At the front of the room on the small stage, Gideon raised his hands for attention. "I now call to order this meeting of the people of Vale. We assemble tonight as an inquisition of justice."

The colonists in attendance quieted and fixed their scrutinizing stares on Lucy, who along with Ballard and Lyle, were standing beside Gideon on the stage.

"In question of our leadership," Gideon said, "we, the people, grieve tonight as one of our own was unceremoniously taken from us. As a people, we draw the line. Enough is enough."

Those in attendance stomped and cheered. Without surprise, Lucy watched them clamor and spit. These people, her people, were angry and felt overlooked, neglected, forgotten. Gideon had recognized that long ago. All he'd had to do was harness and focus it, and they'd thanked him for giving direction to their voices.

Ballard stepped forward. "What are you doing, Gideon?"

Lucy grabbed her arm and pulled her back. "Lyle's not on trial tonight. I am."

The sheriff gaped as the realization set in. "That's why you intervened. I was only making it worse. It was exactly what he wanted."

Lucy nodded. "It's a game. This is a game to him, and now we have to play it."

Gideon pointed a finger at Lucy. "Mrs. Arokson, under your leadership, a child has been slain. It's because of the failed policies of your administration, a party that has demonstrated time and time again that it believes some people are better than others, that sows inequality and stands in contempt of justice, that we suffer this heavy toll."

The people in the hall roared. They threw fists into the air and accosted her with their accusatory stares. They were a force, and she had to reckon with them.

She waited for a measure of quiet. "What Lyle did tonight is what any one of you would do, especially under these extreme circumstances. He felt threatened, and he defended himself."

Gideon chuckled. "So you're saying that Lyle, being a deputy of the sheriff, not only had the right to use lethal force but that he was justified in doing so?"

"What I'm saying, Mr. Ford, is had one of our people respected the authority of the law, this tragedy might not have happened."

He sneered. "Perhaps you would like to explain that to Adam's parents, Mr. and Mrs. Hathaway."

Two men ushered the grieving parents to the front of the room. Simple people who worked the farmland and lived in the mods, the Hathaways were meager even in stature. Sobbing, Mrs. Hathaway buried her face in her husband's chest, and he looked out at the people with timid, bovine eyes.

"Our boy was a good boy," Mr. Hathaway said. "He never hurt nobody, even though people like your nephew hurt him."

This was a trap. Lucy couldn't get defensive, and she knew it.

"I'm truly sorry for your loss," she said.

"They don't want your sympathy," Gideon said. "They want their son back."

Something about the way his face appeared so relaxed and content, the smugness just beneath the facade, triggered a rage in Lucy. Confident and comfortable, he blinked lazily and breathed slowly, as if he were a stone cliff face and she were an incoming wave, powerless to influence the tide, breaking into infinite pieces upon collision.

"You scum," she breathed, and she knew it was over.

"What was that?" Gideon said.

"These poor people should be at the infirmary with their son, not here helping you further your agenda."

Gideon smiled. "Mrs. Arokson, they asked me if they could be here."

"That's right," Mr. Hathaway said. "We don't want any more of our sons and daughters to die. You and yours need to pay for what you done."

"Mrs. Arokson," Gideon said, "because of your carelessness, your favoritism, your crookedness, we, the people, strip you of the Warden's Seal. Sheriff Ballard, remove it from her. She doesn't deserve it. She is a disgrace to it. And then place her in a jail cell."

The people cheered and chanted, fists beating the air.

Uncertain, Ballard looked to Lucy. The shouting voices crashed upon their ears. The sheriff couldn't move.

"Sheriff," Gideon said. "Need I remind you that you serve the people, not the Arokson family?"

"It's okay," Lucy said to her.

Ballard let go of Lyle, who slunk away. She took a step and eyed the hypnotizing gold circle at the base of Lucy's throat, the ring of fire, the reflection of light.

She drew her weapon on Gideon. "I don't think so."

Lucy reached out to her. "Reggie, no!"

The people in Daenuel Hall erupted. They were so loud that nobody heard the wind and rain build outside, but when the lightning struck the power distribution node that served the marketplace, and when it exploded, the whole building rocked with the shockwave, and everyone fell into silence with the darkness.

Warm, wet, sticky bodies writhed in the confusion. Voices and the storm beating on the building created a cacophony so that no one could establish order. Blindly, they found the door at the back of the room, filing outside into the horrible storm and leaving the suffocating air of Daenuel Hall.

Sixteen

In the pillar's control room, Ellis Freeman scrutinized the screens that cycled between satellite imagery, radar, lidar, and scrolling data feeds. They were giving him a splitting headache, but it was better than conversing with Captain Barrow.

Barrow wasn't much for casual talk. Whenever Ellis tried to discuss something, the captain looked at him like he was an alien life form. Barrow wasn't a scientist. He was a soldier. So it wasn't with fascination that he analyzed Ellis. It was with consideration of elimination.

Barrow paced in the back of the room, and a portable radio squawked on his hip. He raised it. "Say again, over."

"There was an accident down in the colony, sir. A sheriff's deputy shot a boy. People are pretty worked up."

Barrow sighed. "Copy." Then he was still.

"Maybe they could use some help down there," Ellis said before he could think better of it.

"If the whole colony burned tonight, the only thing I'd do is tell you to turn off the exterior lights up here because we'd have plenty of light from the fire. That is to say they can go to hell for all I care. My mission is to protect this pillar and ensure it finishes its job. With essential personnel quartering up here and enough supplies, the colony is little more than a parasite as far as I'm concerned."

"Does the warden know you feel this way?"

"She told me to feel this way."

"It's just that my brother is down there, and with most of you all up here, there's no one down there to keep them all safe."

"Just do your job."

Mumbling, Ellis adjusted some of the data feeds. He looked over his shoulder. He didn't think Barrow had heard him, but that stare might have killed him regardless. With arms crossed, Barrow glared at Ellis with a violent heat akin to the blazing sun, and Ellis had to turn away.

The pillar trembled.

"What was that?" Barrow looked up at the ceiling as if it had all of the answers.

Ellis' fingers danced on the console. "I don't know."

"What do you mean you don't know?"

"I'm running diagnostics. It's going to take a minute."

That was when the gunfire started. The popping of rifles and screams came through the static of the radio.

"Contact! We've got contact!"

Barrow moved toward the door, putting the radio to his mouth. "Alpha, Bravo, Charlie, Delta, form up on your perimeter positions and fortify. Do you copy?" The radio's static persisted. "Report." He unholstered the pistol from his thigh and pointed the radio's quivering antenna at Ellis. "Stay here."

The captain dashed from the control room. Stunned, Ellis' fingers rapped on his console like the rapid fire of the machine guns outside. The data stream reported multiple power failures at hubs just outside of the perimeter wall. Ellis watched in horror as cascading faults tripped through the network. The system prompted action with blinking red messages. Even though it didn't spell it out for Ellis, he knew he was witnessing catastrophic failure.

The pillar shuddered.

His hands raced over the controls, and the damage reports flooded his screen faster than he could process them.

"Come on. Come on."

In the data stream, he found the core's status. He selected it, and it expanded on the screen in green text. The core was online and fully functional, its containment integrity one hundred percent. Ellis breathed a sigh of relief and moved the data stream aside, replacing it on the wall with surveillance feeds from the exterior compound.

Helpless, he watched through the sheets of rainfall as sentries in formation fired into the wild, streaks of darkness dashing across the screen and taking them one at a time.

Seventeen

With his rifle in hand, Alain Ducard sprinted for the perimeter. Two trees lay toppled on the pillar's wall, and another was coming down, cracking like thunder. Sentries fired into the darkness, and the darkness reached out and snatched them away.

"Fall back!" Ducard cried.

The rain pelted his face as he dashed across the open compound. His fellow sentries fired panicked streams of ammunition into the wild. Muzzle flashes illuminated the trees and the writhing black forms. Machine guns galloped with disciplined, controlled bursts. More trees fell, and Ducard was unsure if it was the exos or the sentries' armaments that shattered them.

"Fall back into the light!"

The pillar rumbled again, and the compound's exterior lighting dimmed. Darkness prevailed. Above, the swirl of Dawn merged with the storm clouds and shut out all cosmic light. The surface of the mountain became the exos' domain.

Still sprinting for the wall, Ducard saw his fellow sentries disappear, the exos pouncing from the trees and taking his brothers in arms into the sky like the hands of night. Ducard raised his rifle to fire, but the exos dashed in and out faster than he could fix his aim on them.

The sentries had formed an impenetrable wall as they were trained, but the exos were picking that wall apart piece by piece.

"Fall b—!"

The ground trembled beneath his feet and lifted him toward the sky. He tumbled off of the bulging dirt, his rifle rattling over the ground.

The world stopped. The persistent gunfire and screams faded. His own breaths were static. He rolled in the cold mud.

The first of them breached the surface, and Ducard saw it more as a void in the rainfall than a physical body. Its legs arched and grasped with grace and power, articulating like a dancer entering a stage. The oily, armored exoskeleton shimmered. Its black eyes fixed on him. They were still.

Ducard sought his rifle but couldn't find it. The exo stared at him, but it wasn't moving. He didn't want to provoke it, but he rose to his feet.

The exo undulated, breathing through its jagged jaws.

When he was upright, Ducard knew the creature would not allow him to move. He spotted the rifle to his right. He had to risk it.

He pivoted, dashed, and immediately heard and felt the thrum of the powerful legs on the earth, the hiss of the falling rain on its exoskeleton.

It skittered to a halt between him and the rifle. Ducard slipped in the muck and slammed onto his back, his breath ejecting from his chest. It waited as he struggled to his feet. Then it was on him, raising its powerful front legs into the air and bringing them down like sledgehammers.

In reflex, Ducard leaned in and caught the exo's bony, armored legs before they crashed down, and he pushed with all of his might. For a moment, the big man and the exo were locked. He grunted and looked into those eyes and the dripping fangs. It snapped at him, its breath a repulsive stink like a gas that stole his strength.

Retractable claws like scythes extended from the ends of its limbs.

Ducard's muscles quivered like taut ropes threatening to snap. His arms and legs started to give, and he pushed back, refusing the massive exo. He grunted and snorted, willing fresh oxygen and adrenaline into his limbs.

He sank to his ankles in the mud.

The sentry was the wall. He would brace the wall. He would not break. He would stand his ground and stop anything that tried to cross him.

But Ducard was not a wall. He was only a man.

The exo threw him off, and he tumbled onto his back. When he looked up, it was already over him, raising its legs once again for a deathblow.

He reached for his sidearm and heard its report. For an instant, he thought he'd accidentally squeezed the trigger on the draw, but the gunshots continued, and the exo flinched again and again until it listed and keeled, stumbling and struggling to stay upright.

The shooting stopped, and the exo faltered. Black blood oozed from gaping holes in its side. Turning toward the tower bridge, it found its assailant. It shrieked and charged.

Captain Barrow unloaded his weapon into the thriving mass of legs, and it jerked, tumbled, and slid to a stop before his feet.

Ducard looked to his captain. "Thanks."

In one swift motion, Barrow ejected his sidearm's magazine and replaced it. "On your feet, Sentry."

He offered Ducard a hand, and the sentry took it. They ran to the wall line, but as they approached, the last shots from the eastern perimeter died in the night.

Reports echoed from the north and south. From the west, nothing.

Ducard and Barrow stopped in the courtyard. The captain held up his radio, a beaming red indicator hovering in the darkness. In his hand, Barrow held cries for help and salvation.

"Sir, the wall's broken," Ducard said. "We have to fall back."

Barrow glared at him, struggling with it, the ideal of fighting to the last. "It's our duty, Lieutenant."

"Our duty is to Ellis now."

Barrow contemplated it. Then he nodded, and they abandoned their men. They retreated into the pillar and huddled in the control room, watching the perimeter surveillance as a tide of explosions, screams, and earth-quaking impacts rose and then receded in the silent night.

Eighteen

The tremor rolled down the mountain, across the valley, and into the heart of the colony, shattering windows, cracking foundations, splintering wooden structures, and toppling the people who were exiting Daenuel Hall.

On the mountain, the pillar stood illuminated under the dark, swirling cloud of atmospheric Dawn, burning the night like a sword of fire.

The earth rumbled as if a god slammed a gavel, and the pillar's light extinguished.

The colony fell to darkness.

The people cried out, and the wild answered. A piercing shriek filled ears and penetrated minds. It emanated from all directions. The scream was so crushing, so demoralizing, that many of the colonists fell to their knees and clapped their hands to their heads to block out the sound.

A moment of stillness followed. Frozen by fear, the people stood amassed in the marketplace street, the storm whipping them with wind and beating them with rain. So mystified were they by the darkened pillar and the alien cry that the storm's oppressive weight wasn't enough to move them, because they didn't know where to go.

An exo thudded across Daenuel Hall's rooftop and rested its hulking form on the edge, perched and presiding over the people in the street. The rain striking its armored shell glimmered like a halo at the edge of darkness. It commanded a void so black and deep that only by the physical presence in the rain was it visible.

The colonists gasped and recoiled.

"Nobody move," Lucy said.

Confused voices broke the silence.

"Quiet!"

Ballard raised her revolver at the exo. "I've got a shot."

"Save it, Reg. It's not alone."

The people gaped at the creature on the rooftop, watching, waiting. Only the rainfall marked the passage of time.

Then the first bolt of darkness struck over the street and took one of the colonists. It cut through the rain like a singing blade and landed with grace. When it swept the colonist away in a flurry of flailing limbs, it flew into the night as if it had wings.

Before they knew what was happening, another came. And another.

"Run!" Lucy screamed.

The people scattered. Some of them dashed into alleyways. Some of them sprinted back toward Daenuel Hall. The majority of them fled up the street in a flowing mass toward the commons.

On the run, Ballard opened fire with her revolver, hitting targets on rooftops. Most of her bullets ricocheted off of the creatures' exoskeletons, sending sparks into the night. One of her rounds struck true in the soft underbelly meat, though, and the exo squealed and keeled off of the building, crashing to the ground in a symphony of knocking bone.

She flipped open the cylinder and despaired at the eight empty holes. "I'm out!"

"Use mine," Lyle said.

"Save your bullets for when we really need them," Lucy said.

An exo swept in and stole a woman from beside her.

Still surging up the street, Ballard saw the woman disappear into the storm. "And now doesn't qualify as a time for needing them?"

Lucy met her gaze. "It's going to get worse."

People were all over, splashing through the mud and gravel, and the darkness was picking them like crops for the reaping. The exos lunged from rooftops on either side of the street, crashed onto them, and leapt to the rooftops on the other side of the street.

The fleeing colonists could still hear the victims' screams as the exos took them over the marketplace buildings and away.

At the commons, Lucy pointed to Arokson Hall. "There! Go!"

The flood of people streamed toward the residential district, while Lucy, Lyle, and Ballard crossed the field. Moving voids dashed over the rooftops and skittered through the rain, taking more people. Lucy's colonists were being slaughtered.

On the mountaintop, the pillar flashed with artillery and tracer rounds dashing into the night. Explosions and machine gun fire rapped across the sky. Somewhere within the colony, sentries opened up their defenses. Syncopated rifle fire crackled, waned, and then died in a pathetic sound of a lone sentry making a last stand.

As Lucy, Lyle, and Ballard raced up the front steps of Arokson Hall, the ground shook. The dirt at the base of the entry bulged and broke. Black limbs emerged. They closed the door just before the exo surfaced.

In the atrium, Ballard, Lucy, and Lyle were quiet as the exo scurried up the building facade and onto the roof, knocking and creaking the wood. They watched. They listened.

With a trembling hand, Lyle wiped his drenched face and smoothed his hair back. "Are we safe?"

"For now." Ballard removed her coat and dropped it to the floor.

"This is all my fault," he said. "If I hadn't shot Adam, everyone would have been in their homes."

Lyle began openly weeping, and Ballard embraced him.

"We just need to be quiet," she said. "We can wait them out."

Lucy was searching the reception desk and the column that struck to the ceiling. "We're not staying long."

Ballard pulled away from Lyle. "What do you mean?"

"I'm going to ring the dinner bell."

Ballard stood dripping in the atrium as she processed Lucy's plan. "You're going to turn on the bell tower."

"Yes."

"Why?"

"Our people are dying. We need to do something."

Ballard's hand tightened around Lyle's revolver. "I don't think I can let you do that."

Lucy stopped searching for the tower control and eyed Ballard's shooting hand. She measured her approach to the sheriff, looking her square in the eye.

Outside, people were screaming. The earth rumbled as exos tunneled nearby. One of them scampered down the side of Arokson Hall and galloped off to continue the conquest.

"Regina, we have to do this," Lucy said. "I'm acting warden, and you're the sheriff. It's our duty to help our people."

"The same people who were willing to take the seal from you at the expense of each other?"

Lucy's shoulders sagged, and her eyes drooped. "Please. It's the only way we can get home. It's the only way we can get to the girls. We have to keep them safe."

"They have Ernest and Elena."

Lucy took a deep breath. Tears flooded her eyes. "I can't stay here not knowing if they're okay. I have to get to them. They might be all I have."

Ballard relaxed. "All right. But if we're going to do something stupid, let's at least be smart about it. Are there any portable lamps or flashlights here?"

Lucy's face swelled with hope. "In the maintenance closet. Under the stairs." She pointed to the back of the atrium.

Ballard jogged to the closet. The door was locked, so she kicked it open. Several lamps and flashlights sat on a shelf. She ripped some cords from the head of a mop and tied the lamps together. Then she returned with a flashlight for Lucy and Lyle and went to the door.

"The moment you turn that on," she said, "be ready."

Lyle and Lucy nodded.

Lucy hovered over the switch for the bell tower, closed her eyes, counted to three, and then activated it.

The bell tower sang, filling the colony with its sweet, triumphant voice.

Ballard cracked open the door and tossed the lamps out like a grenade. They tumbled in the grass and illuminated the front of the building in cool blue light.

Somewhere outside, exos cried. One of them pounded up the exterior wall of Arokson Hall and across the roof.

"Move!" Ballard said.

They ran out into the commons, the beams of their flashlights cutting through the sheets of rain and obliterating darkness. As the bell tolled above, the earth beneath them trembled. Ballard picked up the lamp cluster as one of the exos emerged from the darkness to take them and redirected itself away from the light. Another tried the same attack. It squelched and leaped away. An exo flew out of the darkness and balled up as it entered the light. It tumbled over their heads and rolled away.

They dashed across the commons, and when they were at the edge, they looked back to Arokson Hall's bell tower. A vortex of darkness amassed and rose into the night, descending upon the building. It ripped the bell tower down and tore Arokson Hall asunder in a great whirlwind of crashing debris and dying musical tones.

While they stood there gaping at the expiration of a dream that was Vale, Lyle leaped from their presence, plucked into the air by a hand of darkness.

"No!" Ballard raised her weapon and fired at anything, everything. She didn't care if she hit Lyle. It would have been better than whatever they were going to do to him.

But Lyle was already gone, and that realization set in as the revolver's trigger clicked, its rail engaged, but no bullet fired.

Lucy tugged on Ballard's arm. "We have to keep going!"

They sprinted up the street, the ground still rumbling beneath them. The darkened homes looked like an apocalyptic warzone. Gaping holes opened siding, jagged glass framed broken windows, and some homes had collapsed entirely, flattened and demolished.

As they entered the front door of Lucy's house, several exos breached the surface outside. Lucy shut the door with her back against it.

They were still. They breathed.

Footsteps padded down the hall. Mel latched onto her right thigh. Bernie wrapped her arms around the other.

Lucy stroked their hair. "Be quiet. It's going to be all right, girls. It's going to be all right." She couldn't stop her voice from quivering.

Ernest, Elena, and Dani emerged from the kitchen, their amazed, wild eyes glassy in the blue lamplight.

An exo pounded up the side of the Arokson house. They jerked toward the sound but saw nothing in the darkness. Lucy held her breath and clutched the girls.

She despaired. She had led them to her home.

More pounding rolled over the roof. Bernie began to hyperventilate and sob, but Lucy clamped a hand over her mouth and hushed her.

Lucy kept the girls close, easing to the bay window in the living room. Holding her breath, she looked out.

The exo breathed at the window, a snort fogging the glass.

At once brutish and graceful, a spiny limb dangled just outside. As if playing with them, it stabbed the exterior facade, a talon bursting through insulation and drywall, tore a thick, vertical hole, and it pulled away and up onto the roof, thumping and scratching. Then it shrieked and leaped off of the house onto the street below, a black shape moving into darkness.

"Is it gone?" Bernie asked.

"Yes," Lucy said. "It's gone."

Colonists' screams pierced the night. Her people were still dying. At least she'd gotten to the girls. Maybe she'd given some of the others a chance too.

"Is it going to come back?" Mel asked.

"As long as we stay quiet, we'll be all right."

Ernest pressed a palm to the hardwood beneath his feet. "We should get off the ground floor."

Silently, they ascended the stairs. Ernest and Ballard placed furniture in front of the door and staircase. In Lucy's bedroom, they waited out the darkness until the screaming stopped, until the storm passed, until sunrise came and shined upon a whole new world.

CHAPTER 8
DAWNBREAKER

One

The exos were right on top of him. They stomped around in the cave above, searching, hunting. He didn't think they could count or that they knew for sure he was still there, but he didn't doubt for a moment they were going to find him.

"Okay, okay, okay," he whispered as he inventoried his resources. The only thing he had was the flashlight. If he turned it on, they would certainly know he was there. If he saved it for the eventuality that they would find him, it could only hold them off for so long. He needed to make them think he was more powerful than he was. He needed to scare them away so they didn't come back.

He screwed off the bottom off of the flashlight, and the string of batteries fell into his hand. Ernest had made these things from studying the pillar's technology. They were like miniature versions of the pillar's core, stable and safe unless they were punctured or misused. Then they could release their energy with incredible power that would be neither stable nor safe.

He had no idea what he was doing, but he had to do something.

The exos screeched and snorted. Rocks and dust fell down the shaft into his eyes.

Holding his breath, he detached the wires connecting the batteries to the contacts inside the flashlight. He bit the jacket off the ends of each and revealed frayed cabling. Then he reattached the cables to the opposite contacts, and with a spark, the flashlight illuminated with an intensity far beyond its normal capacity.

"Oh!" he said.

The exos squealed above and rushed to the top of the shaft. They glared down at him and hissed. He shoved the batteries back into the flashlight and screwed the cap back on. It grew burning hot in his hand.

The exos started to descend.

He threw the light up the shaft. Glowing orange, it tumbled end over end and hit one of the exos in the face. For a moment, it danced precariously, balanced in the air just before gravity snatched it.

Then it exploded like a hand grenade, illuminating the cavern with the light and heat of a miniature sun.

The exos screamed and retreated.

Darkness returned.

Lincoln was safe for now.

Two

For an immeasurable amount of time, there was only the darkness. Blind to the physical world, reality elongated, stretched thin like elastic, and then a sound like a clap or a bang would echo from some distant corner of the labyrinth, or the earth would tremble, and everything would snap back into place.

The sound of breathing was amplified. It was too loud, too dangerous. Awareness and alertness lasted moments before succumbing again to the depths of isolation.

The pain had evaporated like a mist. Numbness set in. The void offered comfort to the loneliness. Oblivion came in waves. Panic came only once, maybe twice.

After passing through the veil of madness, after living on the edge of fear that the exos would come from the darkness, and after that never happened, a gold dawn broke and cast its rays down the cave's throat.

Lincoln struggled to stand, and searing pain returned to his head. Daylight was his salvation. Having thought he would never see it again, he didn't intend to squander this chance.

Swimming in disorientation, he bit his forearm to bring the world into clarity. He clawed at the rock, searching for any handhold he could find. It was pointless. He had gotten to his feet, though, and that was something.

Facing his dire situation, he pressed his back against the cool cavern wall. He had nothing to lose.

He swallowed, and the lining of his throat stuck to itself. He knew where he could find water.

Leaning against the earthen cave walls, he hobbled into the darkness' waiting arms, and its embrace was cold.

Three

Although getting through the fissure was harder than he had thought it would be, he managed. He couldn't decide if the exos' pounding had shifted earth and narrowed the opening or if his head wound had affected his dexterity.

He emerged into the room that joined the passageways with the underground river. The sound of rushing water filled his ears. The cool air flowing through the chamber gave him chills. The fear arose in a surge. In an instant, he expected them to be on him, but after every moment the exos did not attack, he grew more accustomed to the anxiety. He was not becoming comfortable; he was adapting.

As he kneeled for the river, part of him resisted. It had taken so much strength of will to stand, and he didn't want that to be in vain if he sat by the river and couldn't get back up. Yet the rushing water tempted him, and he instinctually moved toward it, his animal sense of desperation taking over.

The incredible shooting in his head lessened to a throbbing as he lay on the ground beside the river, and he breathed until the pain subsided.

In a cupped palm, he raised the cold water to his mouth and sipped. He did this several times until he pulled his body closer to the edge and dunked his whole head, the rushing river burning the open wound on his forehead.

Submerged, he sensed that one of the exos was watching him, and he expected to be pulled away at any moment, clawing at the rock, but he was letting go of that fear.

After he had his fill of water, he faced the fact that he had to keep moving. Crossing the river was out of the question, so that left only two options. He could go left, the direction the kids had gone, or he could go right, which meant ascending an incline. Water took the path of least resistance and inevitably made its way out, so he decided he would follow its lead and go left.

Movement was arduous, his progress slow. He trudged onward because he had no other choice.

For a while, he shuffled down the tunnel, the touch of the cave wall offering the only sensory data he could use for any kind of orientation. Fortunately, the tunnel went only one direction.

Dunking his head had been unwise. He was beginning to shiver. Hypothermia would kill him faster than dehydration. One of the most important factors of survival in the wild was staying dry. He knew all of this.

There was a moment when he realized he had gone too far down the tunnel. Enough time had passed and he had expended too much energy that he couldn't turn back even if he had to.

Wooziness crept in and overwhelmed him. The void was returning, the world folding in on him, the earthen walls of the cave closing around him, burying him alive.

When he realized he could see light at the end of the tunnel, all measure of despair vanished.

When he tried to run, he fell. His cries echoed around the cave, but there was nothing and no one to hear them.

Or so he thought.

Four

He lay on the ground groaning for so long he almost fell asleep. When he realized he was beginning to return to that oblivion, he jerked awake. His head thrummed now, but he had to get into that light. Before he succumbed to unconsciousness, he had to find a way out of the exos' domain. Then, and only then, could he rest.

He committed the remainder of his strength to the act of standing, and when he was up, he looked at the light again to ensure he wasn't hallucinating.

He felt the same compulsion to move as he'd felt at the river. It wasn't only a necessity of survival that he had reasoned. It was something deep within his instincts. He had to get out of the darkness. Until he was in the light, his life was in danger.

So he moved one step at a time. The tunnel turned up, and he pushed on. He pushed on, and on.

Lincoln shuffled and hopped, stumbled and caught himself, using every ounce of fight he had left to get into the light.

Finally, he emerged from the tunnel, and the sight stole the pain and disorientation.

The ship that had brought the First Families to Lumen towered above him. The wild had claimed portions of the exterior with vines and moss and growth. Trees rose alongside it, curving around the hull in possession. The ship was one with the landscape now.

With the bright sunlight, the pain in his head grew, but he didn't care. He marveled at the ship of his heritage, the carrier of dreams.

Painted on its hull in giant white letters, the ship bore its name: *Dawnbreaker.*

It drew his attention so fiercely and so long that, if the dark figure watching him from the airlock hadn't made a sound, it could have silently killed him, and he may never have even known.

Five

Lincoln stepped through the airlock into an alien world of gleaming metal surfaces. Edges like knives and curves both precise and natural, the ship appeared untouched for millennia yet impervious to age.

A fire crackled in the center of the room, casting a golden glow, leaving deep shadows in the corners. Various containers presumably filled with rainwater were scattered around the room. A recently killed ripten carcass lay on the floor, its head cocked stiffly back as if crying to the heavens, its dead eyes greeting him, a clean disembowelment incision running down its abdomen.

Leaning on the boy for support, Lincoln's astonished stare lingered on the animal.

"How did you...?"

"Kill it?"

"Yes."

James grinned. "They're greedy, and they're not good at being able to tell when something's dead or pretending to be dead."

They moved farther into the air lock, and James helped set Lincoln by the fire. Getting to the floor was excruciating, but he felt some contentment in knowing he wouldn't have to move for a while. He was safe and could get comfortable with the fire beginning to reach his bones and melt the ice that had formed there.

"You've been here this whole time?" Lincoln asked.

James nodded. "Is Dani okay?"

"She made it. She's fine."

Tears flooded the boy's eyes. "Thank Lumen."

In the airlock, everything was dark and dormant. Computer panels lined the walls, and they had hundreds of glass squares of various sizes that he presumed once were illuminated. Hooks held shreds of fabric that must have once been space suits but had disintegrated over time. Exposed piping above probably held ancient cabling. A door at the far end had a small porthole window that looked into darkness.

"I couldn't get in any farther," James said. "Inner door's locked. Nothing works. The power's dead. The outer door is open, but I can get it mostly closed for nighttime when they come out. They crawl all over the ship. It's like it attracts them."

Lincoln fixed his eyes on the young man. A slash cut across his chest from his shoulder to his ribs, and around the wound, his crimson-stained shirt hung in tatters. His pants at one of his knees was torn and bloodied. His skin was blackened with filth.

"What happened to you?" Lincoln asked.

James limped to the port door and gazed out into the wild. "Lumen's become such a beautiful place. I can't imagine the change you've seen in your lifetime. I just thought I'd show Dani something nice. I'd been out here a dozen times before, and I'd never thought there was anything that could hurt us. Then those things came, and she and I got split up. I got lost and had to fight one of them. I think I killed it."

"Yeah, kid. Yeah, you did."

"I ended up in a cave, and I fell, as I imagine you did too. Hurt my leg pretty bad. I was stuck in that hole for a while before I came to the same conclusion you probably came to. I had to move or I was going to die. So I followed the tunnel, ended up here. I immediately knew what I was looking at. I'd looked over the field at this thing in the distance so many times, but I never had the courage to come. They always said it was dangerous to get close to it, but I didn't have a choice."

James sat beside the fire and handed Lincoln a metal cylinder filled with water.

"You tear pieces off the ship to catch rainwater?" Lincoln asked.

James nodded. "I haven't been able to move fast enough to risk getting back to the colony. I figured I would be healthy enough to move soon. Either that or someone would come. In a way I think I knew." The flames danced in James' glassy eyes. "I knew you wouldn't give up. I knew you wouldn't stop looking for me."

Lincoln held his breath. James looked to him expectantly.

"Your mom," Lincoln said. "She's been so worried, but she was never going to give up. I think she kept everyone going."

James nodded as if this made all the sense in the world. "She's strong. I can't wait to see her and Sera."

"Your sister actually came looking for you."

James' eyes screamed in alarm.

"It's okay." Lincoln raised his hands. "She's fine. She, Shane, and my nephew Gabriel snuck out, but we found them. We brought them back."

"We?" James said. "You didn't come out here alone. Where are the others?"

"Gone."

"Gone?"

Lincoln closed his eyes with the shame of it. "We didn't come to find you, James. We came to find my son and nephew and your sister."

James was quiet while he processed. "You gave up, but they didn't."

Lincoln nodded. "We stopped looking a couple days ago. I'm sorry."

"But if you're here now, that means you don't know if Sera made it back."

"They had Aeron with them, and—"

"You don't know!" James said. "We have to get back."

"James," Lincoln said, "I can't move like this."

"You can't expect me to stay here now." James paused a moment, head bowed, shadows dancing on his face. "Maybe I ought to leave you like you left me."

Without speaking the contempt his face bore, James stood and went outside.

Lincoln struggled to his feet and hobbled toward the door. "We can leave at first light tomorrow."

When Lincoln was at the door, he found James frozen, staring to the north. Something was wrong.

"What is it?"

James wouldn't respond.

Lincoln eased out of the port, and when he was beside James, he saw it, the Pillar of Dawn, standing monolithic on the mountain, clear as a sword in sunlight, not a cloud in the sky.

"We go together," Lincoln said.

"I can help you if you help me," James said.

Through the miles of crisp air, under the bluest of skies, the dormant pillar was now either a bastion of victorious atmospheric stability or the blackest of omens. Either Lumen was now a stable planet, or the pillar had suffered a catastrophic accident that could threaten their entire world. They couldn't know which until they made it home.

"Yeah."

They set off across the field, leaving the fire in the ship to burn itself out.

PART THREE
THE COLONY

"We are not the sword. We are the shield. We are not death. We are life, the line of the light's farthest reach. If we are crossed, we will oblige death with the edges of our swords, the darkness in our light."

—The Sentry Service Handbook,
Article 100, an Introduction

CHAPTER 9
BRACE THE WALL

One

After the final cracks of gunfire diminished, Ellis Freeman sobbed in the sanctuary of the pillar's darkened control room, the still heart of his dormant giant. He wept not only for the loss of human life. Ellis mourned the death of his pillar and the implications of its demise; all life on Lumen would perish.

In time, he succumbed to sleep, and soon thereafter, so did Ducard. Sometime in the early morning hours, Captain Barrow left them.

When Ducard and Ellis woke in the icy glow of a lantern, they had no concept of how many hours had passed, only that the captain was gone. Fighting the ache of spent adrenaline, they searched the control room for him. Hatch doors squealed on stubborn hinges as they ventured into the pillar's darkened corridors, whispering his name like screams in the dark. Hanging chains twinkled in the chilly air. Their footsteps on the metal grating sounded like bones grinding on blades. The industrial complex was devoid of any warmth or life. Then the daylight streamed through a window, signaling salvation, as temporary as they knew it to be.

They pushed open the pillar's metal outer door, and the sunlight blinded them. Breaking over the horizon, it set the world ablaze. As with all agonies, they coped, and they found Captain Barrow on his knees in the muddy compound, overlooking the valley and the colony, pieces of it still smoldering, smoke columns reaching toward the perfectly blue sky, and the burning sun beaming its judgmental gaze.

Around the yard, trees lay flattened, not from the torrents of rain and wind, but from a great storm nonetheless. Fencing was rolled and folded in piles of twisted metal. A utility building had crumbled, the walls folded inward and the roof lay on the ground. The earth itself had shattered, cracks tearing the topsoil in erratic paths.

The wild encroached through holes punched in the perimeter wall. Scorch marks from artillery scarred concrete. Some of the stone had fallen inward, hammered to dust by the exos' enormous strength.

Except for the ruin, the landscape was barren. No bodies, nothing remained of the workers or the sentries who had fought and died for the pillar. The compound had been picked clean, like scavenging meat from bones.

Ellis gasped. "My goddess."

"They took their dead." Barrow bowed his head. "And ours."

Tears welled in Ellis' amazed eyes. "Why?"

Ducard's boots clanked on the walkway's metal grating as he crossed the expanse of the chasm. Once lit by the glow of energy and crackling electrical arcs, it now was black oblivion, and he could swear the exos were down there, watching and waiting, reveling in their conquest.

The sentry descended the stairs and approached his captain with a disapproving frown. "Get up."

Barrow's eyes fixed on the blinding sun, and he was still.

Ducard clutched the captain's arm and pulled. "I said on your feet."

Standing, Barrow threw off Ducard's powerful grip, sheer will of practiced dominance outmatching brute strength. His relentless glare burned as if his eyes had captured the sun's fury and now wielded its power.

Ducard stood his ground. "We have to move, sir."

"Mission's over, Lieutenant. We failed."

"No. We lost the pillar, but we saved Ellis. He can get it working again. Isn't that right, Ellis?"

The engineer blinked and rubbed his forehead. "I, uh, I'd need to assess the damage, but with some time and a whole lot of—"

"He can get it working again," Ducard said. "For now, we've got a new mission. Come nightfall, there's people down there gonna need our help. We gotta figure out how to protect them, whoever's left. We gotta stop those things or kill as many of them as we can. And then we gotta find a way to survive."

"It doesn't matter," Barrow said. "They'll just come back tonight. And the next night. And the next."

The captain pulled his sidearm from the holster on his thigh and examined it. "I've killed men who believed in something greater. I fought beside men willing to die because they were told to. Or because I told them to. I've seen darkness, and I've paid everything but the ultimate price. I've never seen anything like this. It comes relentlessly. It kills mercilessly. It's the darkness erasing the light. It isn't evil. I've seen evil. I've *been* evil. This is natural, and it's the most terrifying thing I've ever seen."

He tossed his weapon to the ground and turned back toward the strengthening sun. "We're all going to die."

"Pick up your weapon, Captain," Ducard said. "Pick up. Your weapon."

Barrow shook his head. "Son, we trained to be impenetrable. For years, we waited for something to fight here, thinking it would never come. It finally did, and we were ready. I made sure of it. That was my job. Even so, it overcame us, and now there's no one left. We can't fight this thing, and that's all we know how to do. There's nothing more for us but to wait for nightfall and let it take us."

Ducard picked up Barrow's sidearm and offered it to him. "We are not the sword."

Barrow looked at the weapon as if it were breaking his heart. "We are the shield."

"We may be broken, there may be holes in us, but we ain't done yet."

Barrow met his gaze. "We should have given our lives last night, Lieutenant."

"Maybe. But like I said, we still have Ellis, and as long as we have him, the pillar's got a chance." Ducard placed Barrow's sidearm into his hand. "We can't repay our debt to those who died last night, but there are others we can pay it forward to. The wall still stands."

Barrow held Ducard's gaze. He searched the lieutenant for weakness, cracks in his resolve. He found none.

Captain Barrow accepted his sidearm and returned it to his holster. "All right, then. Brace the wall, Lieutenant."

"Yes, sir."

Ducard led; Ellis and Barrow followed. Save for the platform awning's shattered windows and a fractured concrete column, the train station appeared untouched. They descended into the tunnel and took the stairway up to the platform between the tracks where they encountered their first problem: No train.

"It should be here," Ellis said, limping up the concrete concourse. "No one was allowed to leave. Your orders, Captain."

Barrow grimaced. "Maybe some of the workers tried to escape with it."

Ducard looked into the distance. The tracks sloped down the mountain and disappeared around a bend, the wall enclosing it all of the way. "We were going to have to hoof it anyway," he said. "No power." He looked to Ellis who was wincing at the pain in his knee. "Think you can make it?"

"Do I have a choice?"

Ducard shrugged. "I could piggy-back you."

"No, then. I'll be all right."

"There's a lot of ground to cover," Barrow said. "We have to make the center of town before nightfall. Well before it. Every minute counts. You can't slow us down."

Ellis grimaced and sat on the platform edge. He lowered himself onto the tracks. "Then we better get moving."

They set off down the mountain, quickly disappearing between the towering walls that provided safe passage as long as daylight held the shadows at bay.

Two

Homes were crumbling. Shattered glass glittered in the morning sunlight. Red smears glistened on grass and gravel. The air smelled of burning wood from a smoldering fire in the heart of the colony.

Lucy wept in the street, and Aeron embraced her. They held each other up. If not for the mutual support, they would have collapsed like everything else.

It was over. Everything was over. They felt it in their bones.

Ballard, Elena, the kids, and Ernest Freeman descended the steps and gaped at the destruction. They'd survived the night by hiding, remaining silent, and fighting despair. Now each of them looked upon their home and realized the nightmares they'd endured were nothing compared to this. Their new reality overwhelmed them.

"What now?" Ballard asked, her shaken resolve audible in a vocal quiver.

Lucy took a deep breath and wiped her eyes. "We have to look for survivors. There have to be others."

"And then what?" a voice called from a home that appeared untouched by the carnage. Eyeing them with hard disdain, Gideon Ford emerged through the front door. "What is the point? You've lied to us. You've misled us. And do you see the cost?"

Then there was Clay, coming out of the house to help his father down the stairs. Several other men and women were behind them.

"I've lied?" Aeron said. "*Me*? Your son left us to die."

Aeron advanced, his body tensing and shimmering with rage, fists balling into weapons.

Gideon hobbled toward them on the gravel road. "He did no such thing!"

Ballard grabbed Aeron's arm and pulled him back.

"We were down there," Aeron said. "When we came back, he was gone, and the rope had fallen."

"I heard something outside," Clay said. "When I went to check it out, those things started coming up all over the place. I had to get out of there. I'm sorry, but I thought it meant you all were already gone. I don't know what happened to the rope. Glad you made it."

"Let go of me." Aeron jerked away from Ballard. "Children, Clay. *Children.* You abandoned children."

Ballard wrapped her arms around Aeron's chest. "There's been enough of this for one day."

"Lincoln! My brother! He's dead because of you!"

"I'm sorry," Clay said.

"No you're not! You only ever wanted him gone!"

Ballard pulled. "Dammit, that's enough, Aeron!"

He broke from her hold, spun, and punched the sheriff in the mouth.

She stumbled and toppled to the gravel. Gaping at him in surprise, a look that Aeron returned, she touched her lip and examined the blood on her fingertip. Then she stood, and she glared.

Aeron held his hands up. "Reg, I'm s—"

She hit him back with everything she had, and Aeron reeled from the blow.

"You don't think I want this asshole dead too!?"

"That's enough!" Lucy leaped between them. "Those things did enough to tear this colony apart. We don't need to help them."

Her face had flushed, but the color was draining. She gulped and settled herself.

"Now," she said. "We have about ten hours of daylight. We have to try. We have to survive."

Aeron moved like he was going to run at Clay again. Lucy pushed her husband back. She grabbed a fistful of his shirt, and he gazed at her in amazement. In the wake of tragedy, something inside Lucy had flourished. She imposed on him a strength of will that he couldn't deny. As her fierce blue eyes tore into him, he had no choice but to yield.

"I know," she whispered to him. "I *know.* But now is not the time." She let him go and faced the others. "Gideon, take your people and do a door-to-door search. See who's left."

Gideon raised a pointed finger. "What makes you think you can—"

"Just do it. I'm going to take everyone else to Arokson Hall. Our pillar's down, but we're not the only one. The other colonies may be able to send help. We may be able to contact them with the radio."

"The power is down," Ernest said.

"The radio has a battery backup." She turned to Gideon. "Do your job." She stormed away toward Arokson Hall. The others followed.

Aeron rubbed his jaw and eyed Ballard. "Sorry."

She held her sleeve to her split lip. "It's okay. I'm with you, but Lucy's right. There will be a time for justice, but it isn't right now."

Aeron glared at the backs of the Fords walking the other way along the street. "Yeah."

Confident their time would come, Ballard and Aeron left them to do whatever it was they were going to do.

Three

The concrete walls towered over Ducard, Barrow, and Ellis, and above those barriers, the trees reached across the tracks and almost touched limbs. A channel of shadow held dominion over their pathway to the colony, and their only path was through.

In the absence of direct sunlight, the impending winter bit into their flesh. Ellis ran a finger over one of the frosty rails. Their skin tightened; their muscles trembled. For all of their resolve, they couldn't be sure if they shook from the chill or fear that this place was now friendly to the exo creatures.

The trees swayed in the morning breeze, and the sentries paused. They assessed the threat of every movement even though, if something came, they only had Barrow's sidearm for defense.

Limping ahead, Ellis called back, "Every minute counts, sentries."

Barrow's gaze hardened.

Ducard laughed and clapped him on the shoulder. "He's been waiting to use that against you. He's right, though. We're okay during the day, and even we can't be alert all the time. We should save it."

Barrow rubbed his mouth. "You're right. I'm on edge. I didn't sleep last night."

"I'm sorry I did."

"No, it's good you did. At least one of us is rested. It's going to be a long day and an even longer night."

The group continued on the tracks. The rocks and gravel crunched between the rails and ties. In the clear, still morning, companions walking along tracks and wilderness, it would have been a beautiful day if not for the calamity of the previous night.

Ducard and Barrow maintained their distance behind Ellis for no particular reason. If for nothing else, they had silently agreed to let the engineer lead for a while so he wouldn't have to feel the pressure of keeping pace. Consideration for others was not a part of their training, but the sentries were human after all.

It was Ducard who broke the silence. "Why'd you come here, Captain?"

"What do you mean?"

"I mean what made you decide this world and not another? For that matter, why the Sentry Service?"

"Well, why did you?"

"I was born here."

"Yes, but why did you choose to be a sentry instead of working in the quarry with your uncle? Or, if that question answers itself, why not be a farmer or a fabricator or a business owner? Or an engineer like our friend Ellis here?"

"I don't know. Is 'I like guns' good enough?"

Barrow laughed. "You want to know why I left the military for a security guard's job."

"Yeah."

"The men talk."

"Yeah."

"I think the prevailing theory is I'm here because I did something disgraceful, and it was either this or discharge."

"Was it?"

"No."

Ducard gazing in anticipation, and Barrow ignored him, continuing on the tracks.

"So what was it?" Ducard said.

Barrow searched his feet as if they held the answer. "Not every world is like Lumen. Some are so rife with political instability that they erupt into civil war. Some worlds that have finished developing push back against the rest of us. The answer is always the same, and I just got tired of it all. With the skills I had, there weren't many options. I suppose defending people instead of attacking them felt more right."

Ducard nodded. "But why Lumen?"

"It was as good as any other."

"You chose it?"

"No. I was placed."

Ducard grinned.

"What?" Barrow said.

"You ever think things happen for a reason?"

"Yes. All the time. And that reason is either I made something happen or I didn't stop it."

"I think there's always a reason."

Barrow sighed. "I've seen a lot of people die, Ducard. Most of them have died for no reason at all."

"That you know of."

Ellis stopped walking.

"Hey, Hobbles," Ducard called. "Every minute."

"Look," Ellis said.

Up the tracks, around a bend, the earth was disturbed. The rails twisted and jutted into the air. Dirt and gravel mounded from a powerful impact. A long, jagged crack in one of the walls beckoned like a finger of destruction.

"Goddess," Ellis said.

"Would you stop that?" Ducard said. "You people talk about Lumen like it's some kind of all-powerful being."

Ellis flinched. "What if it is?"

"Then she's a spiteful bitch."

"Wrath," Barrow said.

"What?" Ducard said.

"Whether it's Lumen or something else, it wouldn't be the first time people have suffered at the wrath of a higher power."

"I thought you said you didn't believe in things happening for a reason."

"When a child throws a tantrum because it doesn't get its way, that's not a reason." Barrow started walking again. "Come on."

As they approached, the crack in the wall led to a hole and, just a bit farther, the train, derailed and resting on its side. The chassis crumpled, like the hand of a god had descended from the sky, grasped it, and squeezed.

Ducard cupped his mouth. "Hello?" He turned to Ellis. "Stay here. We'll check it out."

Gripping pipes and axles, the sentries climbed the train's undercarriage and pulled themselves onto the side of the rear car. They got to their feet and investigated the wreckage, the metal booming hollow under their boots.

"Hello!?" Ducard called. "Is anyone there?"

There was no response. Measuring the destruction in shattered glass and fractured metal, the sentries walked the train's length. Ducard ducked his head inside an opening, peering into the shadowy corners. Careful to avoid the razor shards that remained in the window's frame, he leaped down through the opening and landed inside.

The hollow interior was caked in dust and filth from the crash. Earth and rock had invaded. The twisted metal of handholds and railings, the bunched-up carpeting like a dead tongue, loosened seats that had tumbled after the bolts that had secured them shattered, it all gave the environment a sense of the natural instead of the manmade. Ducard felt as if he were inside a deceased giant beast.

Barrow rested his hands on his hips and scrutinized the train's interior from above. "It's almost like the train got hit with artillery."

Ducard exhaled through puckered lips. "I think that's basically what happened here."

The sentry shook his head in awe, and then something shiny caught his eye. He crawled over dislodged seats and swung on a pole that miraculously was still straight and sturdy. In some dirt that had poured through a busted window, a sentry's sidearm lay discarded. He picked it up and examined it.

"Empty."

"What did you find?"

"A sidearm."

"Sentries were on board?"

"Looks like." Ducard tucked the weapon into his own holster and mounted his way back up out of the train car. Barrow helped him up through the opening.

"If some of our men were here," Barrow said, "maybe they made it."

"Or those things took them," Ducard said. "Either way, they deserted their posts and left the others to die."

"So did we, Lieutenant."

Ducard nodded with a grim expression. Having found nothing of any certainty, they leaped to the gravel below and started their return to Ellis.

"I don't get it," Ducard said.

"What?" Barrow said.

"They don't leave any bodies. It's like the people just vanished."

"It's like the darkness just came and took them."

When they got back to Ellis, he stared at them expectantly. "Well?

Barrow shook his head. Ellis frowned.

The haunting thought burrowed into each of their minds. From all they'd seen of the exo creatures, it was like the planet itself was coming for them. It was like Lumen was eradicating a sickness, which would make humanity the disease.

"Let's keep moving," Ellis said.

They set off again along the tracks, passing the train like an empty tomb. Too disturbed for words, they paid their respects with silence.

Four

The air in the warden's office had chilled. With no power transmitting from the pillar to the colony, winter's fingers peeled away the layers of insulation and reached inside. Head in hands, leaning on the desk, Lucy was too tired to pull her coat up around her neck.

"Anything yet?" she asked.

Brow furrowed in concentration, Ernest fiddled with the radio. "No. Something's not right."

He'd removed the metal frame on the back of the case and was shining a flashlight into its interior, inspecting the components and circuit board. The unit had plenty of juice flowing from its battery, and its signal light indicated that the satellite was passing overhead. As best as Ernest could, he had visually inspected the cable that ran from the radio to the dish mounted on the outside facade, and everything appeared intact.

"Was it damaged in the storm?" Lucy asked.

"I don't think so."

Ballard leaned on the warden's creaky desk. "Can't you, uh, boost the power or something?"

Ernest sighed. "That's not how this works." He stood from behind the unit and clicked off his flashlight. "The satellite is in range. We're sending a signal. I don't see anything that would indicate signal degradation so that they aren't receiving clearly. I don't see anything wrong on our end. It all appears in perfect working condition. Try it again."

Lucy pulled the microphone to her mouth. "This is Vale to Horizon. Is anyone there? Please respond, over."

They waited, but only a hiss of static came out of the speaker.

"Vale to Horizon. Please respond, over."

In all of the times a warden had radioed another warden, it wasn't uncommon to receive no response. For various reasons, the receiving warden could be out of the office, but his assistant would respond. Even so, considering the circumstances, getting nothing back from Horizon was disconcerting.

"Why isn't it working?" Ballard asked.

"It's working," Ernest said.

"Then why aren't we getting anything back?"

"Our radio is fine. Either they're not able to respond, or..."

"Or no one is there," Lucy said.

While the radio hissed, they looked to each other for answers. The meaning was clear: Horizon wasn't responding because they couldn't. Lumen's end went beyond Vale. The exos commanded the entire planet, from its core to every inch of its surface.

"Could they have gotten hit too?" Ballard asked.

Lucy shook her head. "I don't know." She set the microphone on the desktop. "I think we have to operate under the assumption that they did."

Ballard cursed and stalked around the room. She wiped her face and craned her head toward the ceiling as if to speak to the heavens. "So what now?"

Ernest looked at Lucy expectantly.

She looked to her husband. "Aeron?"

He stood at the window, hand pressed against the frame, chewing the inside of his cheek. He gazed at the row homes across the commons where Gideon and Clay, along with a growing crowd of surviving colonists, emerged from one of the residences with a woman and her eight-year-old son, who were no doubt thanking them for saving their lives.

Five

The tracks opened onto the colony farmlands. Gazing over the rolling hills of crops, Ellis, Ducard, and Barrow breathed as if for the first time. The enclosed path down the mountain had been suffocating them, and they hadn't even known it. With the land opening wide and the sun climbing into the sky, they once again entered the colony and the good graces of daylight.

In the direct view of Lumen's star, warmth trickled into their bones. To the west, the lake glittered. The golden wheat fields swayed in a persistent breeze, a world seething with the life they had given it. For a time, it seemed the grateful planet was giving back to them, but now they knew it had been only biding its time.

Barrow stopped and stared at the lake.

"What is it?" Ducard asked.

"We need water."

Ducard frowned at the lake and squinted at the sun's position in the sky. "There's no time."

"Remember what I said. It's going to be a long day and an even longer night. We need water."

Barrow left the tracks and waded into the field, the wheat stalks giving and reacting to his presence.

Ellis raised his eyebrows. "I could stand to splash my face and wet my whistle."

Ducard glared.

Ellis put his hands up. "I'm not choosing sides. I just don't see much of a point in running from Marathon to Athens just to die when we get there."

"What?"

"Greek mythology."

Ducard's scowl persisted, but his expression changed from disapproval to confusion.

"Read a book," Ellis said.

The engineer followed Captain Barrow into the field, and after a derisive grunt, Ducard plunged into the wheat too.

They traversed the fine rows in the golden landscape. The wheat stems brushed their fingertips. The breeze carried the organic scent of the blossomed kernels, ready for harvest.

The wheat field broke onto a plain of crops that had been reaped not long ago. The men stepped carefully between the sharp chaff that emerged from the damp soil. The scent of manure was strong.

It wasn't long before they reached the banks of the shimmering lake. Barrow kneeled and sipped from cupped hands. Ellis removed his boots and rolled up his pants. Hooting, he ventured into the frigid water. True to his word, he splashed his face and ran his wet fingers over his pale, bald head. Droplets hung like icicles on his trimmed, snowy beard. Ducard quietly filled a canteen, but even he couldn't deny the water was recharging his body and spirits. They all smiled, a swell of happiness emerging from their despair.

The fishing boat emerged from behind a peninsula of thick reed grass. Capsized and drifting, it meandered in front of the men, rocking with the gentle lapping of the water. Like the ghost that it was, it hovered into the nearby bank, landing with an earthen thud and a pathetic whine of strained wood that bowed under the boat's own weight.

The moment spoiled, Ellis got out of the water and put his boots back on. Ducard finished filling his canteen. Shaken by the sense that there was no happiness left for them, that Lumen would corrupt even the simplest joys, they headed southeast to rejoin the tracks.

When they came upon the first depression in the earth, they knew they would never be free of Lumen's oppression. There were walls throughout their entire world, and they were bigger and more effective than anything man could ever build. The reminder was ever present that, though humans had discovered this planet and attempted to make a home of it, Lumen was not theirs to rule. It never was.

Ellis kneeled and dug his fingers into the disturbed soil. The harvested wheat remnants were scattered when the exo had exploded from the earth.

"So far from town?" he said. "What would make them surface out here?"

"I'm done trying to understand them," Ducard said. "None of this makes any damned sense."

Hands on his hips, Barrow shook his head. "I don't think they're at war with us so much as they're reacting to us." He sighed. "Let's keep moving."

Ahead, they passed more depressions, each one adding to their dread. The exos' impossible numbers, and the odds stacked against them, only grew.

Farther south, they reached the edge of the livestock pens. A section of fencing had exploded outward. Fractured and splintered wood planks lay like casualties in the path of destruction. Nearby, in the shade of a tree, a single cow chewed and looked at the humans dumbly, indifferent, perhaps expecting the men to lead it home. A splatter of red adorned its broad side, but the blood was not its own.

"Where is the rest of the herd?" Ellis asked.

Neither Ducard nor Barrow answered.

On the other side of the pasture, they left the muddy fields and rejoined the tracks. In a way, the railroad now felt like safe passage across a hostile and alien landscape. Although the wall may have still stood, they had no illusions that the wild had retaken their home. The farmland was lost to them, and as the industrial district station emerged ahead, none of them spoke of the fear they shared.

They didn't speak of it all of the way into town.

Six

Daenuel Market was a ruin of ashen remains. Some time in the night, a fire had consumed it, taking the stalls of harvested crops, the butcher shop and its refrigerated meat stores, and the cubicles of handmade goods, clothing, and crafts. A blackened monument, Gill's distiller stuck out through the smoldering rubble that once housed it. The bones of structures lay defeated in the balding gravel street. Smoke poured from their bodies like final breaths amid the dying flames crackling in the wreckage.

Dazed and silent, the dozens of colony survivors walked between the rows of charred and collapsed structures. Within the nest of twisted building materials, they found recognizable artifacts—a refrigerator, the legs of an overturned stool, a perfect and intact drinking glass gray from smoke, a doll with a ruined face.

"What are we going to do now?" Gideon said. "No food. No resources. It's all gone."

Aeron picked through the burned remains of the building that had housed a cafe on the first floor and the office of the *First Watch* newspaper on the second. He found a ceramic mug and tipped it over to pour out the ash and dust.

Lucy watched her husband for a moment, waiting for him to return to his leadership role. When she decided he wasn't going to, she sighed. "Calm down, Gideon. We're going to figure something out."

"Don't patronize me," he said with a phlegmy growl.

"We're alive," Ernest said. "And that's something."

"But for how long? How long are we going to last with no food, no resources, no help, and only daylight to live by?"

The other survivors, the ones who were still scared and angry and looking to Gideon for leadership, nodded along with him. After all of this, all of the despair, Gideon still commanded their loyalty, and he wasn't doing anyone any good.

Farther down the street, the sheriff's office and jail still stood, untouched by the flames.

"At least there's still justice," Ballard said. Nobody responded. She didn't care. Having lost everyone who mattered to her, the structure that housed law was simply a shell to her.

Gabriel began to cry, resting his head on Sera's shoulder. Blank-faced and silent, the girls were latched onto Shane. The children were traumatized, and Lucy could do nothing for them.

Clay approached from up the street, toward the far end of the marketplace. His mouth was a thin line, his face grave and white, save for the smears of smoke on his cheeks and forehead. He ran his fingers through his hair. "It's everything. It's all gone."

Lucy closed her eyes, bowed her head, and released a deep breath.

Clay stepped through the haze in the air. "There's nothing left for us here."

Aeron let the ceramic mug roll off of his fingers and crack in the gravel, and he turned his back on the colonists, meandering silently up the street. The colonists followed because the only thing they knew for sure was that they needed to stay together. They trailed him to the edge of the commons.

"Aeron," Lucy said.

He wouldn't turn.

"Aeron."

They walked through the playground haunted by echoes of children's laughter and ghost stirrings in the swings. They crossed the open field. They watched him lean against the fallen clock tower for support and rest his head. When he sat on the steps of Arokson Hall and faced them, they kept their distance.

In Aeron's face, they saw the ruin of the colony. Aged, haggard, defeated, wiped clean, destroyed, he gazed out upon Vale and now saw the world as it was, not as it could have been.

Unaware that Lucy approached, he recoiled at her touch, and when she sat beside him and cradled him, he fell into her breast and wept for his monumental failure, which had stamped out so much life and ended a world.

Seven

Acknowledging the end meant different things to different people, and they each bore different weights of it. For all of Aeron's strength of will and resilience, it had torn his identity to pieces to realize Lumen was lost. He didn't know who he was if he wasn't building the future, and unlike the others, he didn't have the luxury of blaming the creatures. He knew he was responsible.

For the children, it meant a lot of confusion. They didn't understand what was happening, the hopelessness of it. They didn't know how they felt or how they *should* feel. They very much felt the sorrow, but they didn't know that this grief would last forever.

Gideon Ford had lost everything, but everything for him wasn't much. He lamented the fall of their civilization because, without it, he felt insignificant, and he feared nothing more than obscurity and powerlessness, the ultimate natural state of humanity, the fact that, in all of the universe's vastness, a human being was indistinguishable from an atom of a grain of sand in an ocean. Despite his years, Gideon was now learning any idea they'd ever been in control of their fate, that they could birth life to a world, was an illusion.

Sheriff Ballard mourned the loss of the colony and all of its people, of course. At one time in her life, Vale was everything to her. However, the loss she truly mourned was for her father, for her deputy, and for the man she might have loved. She only knew now that, after so many years of hardening herself, of rejecting vulnerability, she craved that connection like any other, and now that was gone.

It was very different for Lucy. She lamented for the losses the others felt. Her heart broke for them, but she was lucky. Most of her family was still here. The end hadn't changed much for her because she could still take care of them. For Lucy, the stakes were higher now, the risks greater, but she had to save them. To her, they were everything.

In the commons, before Arokson Hall, she persuaded them all to persevere, to fight.

"I know it looks hopeless," she said. "But we can't give up. Not now, not ever. I'm not going to give you some rallying speech about the darkness winning if you give up. I'm not going to try to inspire you. What I am going to do is tell you that there's no stopping. You probably feel like you want to just sit and wait for nightfall for those things to take you. That's one option. But there's still someone or something here you care about. There's still a reason to try. There's still a reason to live."

Aeron jumped to his feet. Everyone looked to him with expectation that he would support Lucy and take over for her, reciting his own allocution.

"She's right," he said.

He stood still, everyone waiting for him to continue, but instead, he sprinted through the group of survivors and leaped on top of Clay, raining fists.

Lucy reached for her husband. "No, Aeron!"

Aeron pushed her off, and Clay gained leverage, flipping him over and forcing a knee into his chest. Clay landed several blows before Ballard barred her arm across his throat and pulled. She lifted him from the ground, threatening to break his neck if he didn't comply, and he clutched at her hold.

Aeron got to his feet and charged, tackling both Clay and Ballard. His fingers clamped around Clay's throat. Clay's hands grasped for his face, thumbs reaching for his eyeballs. A set of knuckles pounded the sides of his ribs, but Aeron was too close for Clay to strike with any force. Aeron had the power now, and he felt Clay's strength slipping through his fingers. The man's face reddened and then darkened to a deep purple as if the pressure was going to make his head pop.

A gunshot cracked the sky and stopped time.

With Aeron distracted, Clay shoved the warden off of him and lay coughing and struggling for air.

A tendril of smoke rising from his sidearm's barrel, Captain Barrow approached. "I have a limited supply of those, so it pains me to use one so foolishly. But you fools need to stop what you're doing."

The survivors gaped in awe, their reality shattering. They weren't the only ones left, and if these men had made it through the battle at the pillar, maybe others did too. The sight of Barrow, Ducard, and Ellis filled them with hope, and even a small drop of it washed away the dread and sadness they'd wallowed in since the dead of night. Such was the nature of the human spirit; it didn't take much light to push back the darkness.

Everyone came together then. The group welcomed Ducard and Ellis as one of their own. The Freeman brothers embraced. Ducard shook Ballard's hand as partners who'd each done their best to bring their people through alive. Barrow watched from the outskirts and then found Lucy.

He approached and loomed over her, surveying the group. "Is this everyone?"

"Near as we can tell." Lucy shook her head. Even she couldn't believe it. "We've searched the homes and all of the public spaces. I don't think there's anyone else left."

"You're sure?"

"We called out. Someone would have heard us."

Barrow's face flushed with anger. "There have to be others."

Ernest's pants squawked with a burst of static. Everyone looked at him for answers, and he gaped back with the same confused expression. His pants made the noise again, and he searched his pockets, finding his handheld radio. He held it out with an expression of wonder.

"Is anyone there?" the voice on the radio said.

"Lincoln?" Aeron said.

Ernest held the radio to his mouth. "Lincoln? Is that you?"

"Yeah. We're at the main gate. Why isn't anyone on watch?"

"We?"

"Just open up."

A moment passed where everyone registered this revelation in their minds, and then they raced across the field, through the ruined town, and to the main gate. Having not eaten or slept, most of them doubled over out of breath, but were nonetheless electric with anticipation.

Ducard and Barrow climbed the stairs to the controls on top of the wall and cranked the rotary levers to raise the gate.

As the metal gears clanked, two pairs of legs became visible, and in moments, the door was up. Filthy and bloodied, Lincoln and James limped into the colony, finally home.

"Oh my goddess!" Elena raced to her son and took him in her arms. She touched his face to ensure he was real. "I never gave up hope. Nobody gave up hope."

James eyed Lincoln, who was embracing his brother and kids.

"I'm sorry," Aeron said to Lincoln. "For leaving you."

"I would have done the same."

Aeron flinched. "Why didn't you radio sooner?"

"Nobody else needed to go out there." Lincoln surveyed the colony, saw the gray haze lingering over the marketplace and the broken tower where Arokson Hall's bell once stood. "What happened?"

Lucy ran a hand through her fiery red hair and blew air through pale, puckered lips. "Those things attacked the colony last night. The pillar is down. Most of us are gone. We looked everywhere. This is everyone." Lucy motioned with her hand to the dozens of remaining colonists.

Lincoln looked to the falling sun in the west. "We don't have much time."

Barrow rubbed his square jaw. "I know a place."

CHAPTER 10
NIGHTFALL

One

After the pillar fell, the infirmary's backup generators failed, and its halls darkened. Set apart and isolated from the marketplace, the quiet building stood untouched by the blaze and forgotten by the exos that patrolled the conquered colony.

The refuge of the sick, injured, and dying waited for Lincoln and Aeron. They found it sealed. Aeron slapped the access control panel on the wall, but with no power, the motorized doors remained tightly closed.

Lincoln shook his head.

"What?" Aeron said. "It should have a backup."

The younger brother dug his fingers into the crevice between the doors. "We'll have to do this the old-fashioned way."

The muscles in Lincoln's arms and shoulders bulged, his back stiffened. He grit his teeth. The gears resisted but ultimately gave with a snap and grind of stripping metal. The doors parted and slid into the frame.

The brothers stood before the inky darkness of the infirmary's reception area.

Lincoln outstretched his arm in invitation. "After you."

"It's pretty dark. How do we know there aren't any of them in there?"

"You could have stayed with the others. I know what we need and where to find it."

"No." Aeron took a deep breath. "You need my help."

"What makes you say that?"

"Because I'm your big brother. Now get in there."

Lincoln smirked and entered the gloom, his flashlight illuminating the darkened corners. Dust motes floated in the air. He swept the beam over the vacant waiting area. Most of the wooden chairs were flush against the wall, some toppled. Shattered glass twinkled on the concrete floor. At the receptionist's desk, jagged shards emerged from the window frame like crystalline teeth.

Aeron gaped. "What happened here?"

"Same thing that happened everywhere else."

Lincoln pushed on the swinging door to the treatment area. It knocked against a solid barrier.

"Someone had to block this door," Lincoln said.

Aeron and Lincoln dug in and pushed with all of their strength. A blue light crept around the edge of the door. The barrier squealed as metal dragged on the stone floor, and they squeezed through the opening they'd managed to create.

On the other side, they found the cool blue glow of a battery-powered lantern in the center of the room. Two silhouettes stood around a gurney among a graveyard of toppled beds and tables. One of the shadows picked up the lamp and thrust it toward Aeron and Lincoln.

"My goddess." Pale in the blue light, Milly's wrinkled brow arched as if seeing the brothers gave her so much hope it hurt.

"Who is it?" Dr. Osman squeezed an air bag valve mask that was helping Milly's husband Richard breathe.

Richard lay on a gurney, covered in several layers of white blankets. He was still, but his chest rose and fell as Dr. Osman pumped oxygen into his lungs.

"I'll be," Osman said. "I thought for sure everyone was gone."

Aeron scanned the room. "What happened?"

"When the lights went out, everyone panicked." Osman squeezed the air bag. "Our backups must have been neglected because the emergency power and lighting never kicked on like it should have. Most of the infirmary staff ran out to see what was happening." He squeezed the bag again. "They never came back. After a while, most of the patients got up on their own and left. When we heard the first screams at the far end of the commons, everyone else was gone. Everyone except for Milly and Richard here. He can't be moved."

"And we stayed." Milly looked to Osman with glassy eyes. "You stayed."

He helped Richard breathe. "Any self-respecting doctor would. It's nothing."

"It's heroic," Aeron said.

Osman frowned and glanced around at his desolate treatment room. "Maybe heroism isn't enough anymore. What's going on out there?"

"Lumen has native life," Lincoln said. "And now it wants its planet back."

"What do you mean? Like aliens?"

"No. In this case, we're the aliens.'

Dr. Osman continued to squeeze the bag and watch the rise and fall of Richard's chest. The man was dying from liquid lung. He would be the last to succumb to it. It wouldn't be long now, and Osman knew better than anyone in that room that there was nothing he or anyone could do to stop death from taking Richard. It was always going to be necessary for so many people to die from drowning in their own liquefied lungs. The terrible condition developed because Richard's generation wasn't adapted to breathing Lumen's developing atmosphere. However, it was always supposed to herald Lumen's life-sustaining maturity. They'd come so tragically close only for Lumen to be just another dream, one that they had unwittingly ruined.

Osman looked to Lincoln and ran a finger over his own brow. "What happened to your head?"

"I fell down a hole."

The doctor frowned. "I better take a look."

"We don't have time. A few of us are a bit banged up. We came for medication and first aid supplies. Then we have to move."

Osman eyed Lincoln. "Milly, would you take over?"

She reached for the air bladder with shaking hands.

With confident eyes and a steady voice, Osman stilled her hands. "Just count to five, squeeze, and repeat. Breathing is so easy we do it and don't even know it. Just do that for him. I'll be back in a minute."

Taking the bag, she exhaled in a quiver. In their happiest times, she never dreamed of this moment, but she'd known it would come. Having taken care of him since Dr. Osman delivered the diagnosis months ago, Milly had had time to prepare. She knew exactly what was going to happen to her husband, and as much as she'd dreaded it, there was no going back.

Maneuvering between fallen tables and gurneys, Dr. Osman led Aeron and Lincoln across the room. He righted a bed and patted the mattress, and Lincoln sat down. Osman studied Lincoln's head wound with a flashlight. There was some swelling and bruising. It had closed on its own, so it wouldn't need stitching.

"Any sensitivity to bright lights?" Osman asked.

"Just when you shove them in my face."

"Any nausea or dizziness?"

Lincoln pushed Osman's flashlight aside and blinked away the spots in his vision. "I'm fine."

The doctor turned off his light. "The good news is you don't have a concussion. Normally, I'd tell you to rest as much as you can, but my guess is you're going to insist that you can't. Luckily, an anonymous benefactor supplied the infirmary with some of the best herbal anti-inflammatories available on any planet. It will help with the swelling, but you'll need to take it easy."

"We'll need some for James and Shane too. And bandages and antiseptic. Also, Sera got into some serpentine vine. Shane got her some battensoft and floreyfoil pretty quickly, but she should get some antibiotics to be sure."

Osman nodded. "I'll be right back." He went to the back of the treatment room, the light from his flashlight leading the way like a ghost, and disappeared through a door.

"At least your head isn't broken," Aeron said.

Lincoln grunted. "That remains to be seen. He didn't say what the bad news was."

Aeron's eyes narrowed. "What bad news?"

"The stuff he's going to get me is called 'robby root.'"

"So?"

"It's going to make us high as the aurora."

Aeron laughed as Osman burst through the door at the back of the room. The doctor stopped and stared at Milly and Richard.

Milly's gaze remained on her husband. "It was time."

Lincoln hopped off of the bed. The men looked on, their hearts breaking.

"He didn't have much left." She ran her palm over his wispy, thin hair, touched his aged face, a face that had once been full and strong. "He wouldn't have wanted us to stand around here while there's people who need help. He was a hard man. He was always tough on me. But his heart was always in the right place. The last thing he ever wanted was to be a burden. He said so. I just couldn't let him go until now."

She let the air bag valve mask fall and bounce on the concrete floor.

In silence, they waited for the moment when Richard would struggle to breathe. They anticipated the moment when his body would convulse.

He never did.

Milly allowed her beloved husband to go, and in peace, he departed.

Two

After covering Richard's body, Aeron and Lincoln led Milly and Dr. Osman from the infirmary into waning daylight. As they moved through the marketplace ruins, Milly wept. Dr. Osman carried a large bag full of medical supplies and turned back to his infirmary, knowing that it might as well burn too. He would never again help the sick or injured there. Everything he needed was now in his bag, and if he needed more than what he had, there would be nothing he could do.

They met the others at the toppled tower of Arokson Hall. While Aeron and Lincoln had gone to the infirmary, Barrow had led everyone else in a search for resources. They had collected enough food and water for days. On Barrow's instruction, everyone had gone back to their homes and taken three changes of clothing. When they left their homes, they all had the sense it was for the last time.

When the colonists were together again, they welcomed Milly and Dr. Osman. They exchanged greetings and handshakes, sympathy for Richard, and expressions of gratefulness that they were alive. The doctor tended to the injured.

Through it all, the sun had continued its descent in the sky. Their time was burning away, but all of this preparation and consolation was necessary. If for nothing else, they needed it to cope. Strength came not of willpower alone. It needed to be fed through human connection and ritual.

Barrow scowled. "Is this everyone?"

"We've searched all the residential district," Ballard said. "It's safe to say no one's hiding in the commons or the marketplace. And curfew means no one was at work in the industrial district or farmlands." She sighed. "I think this is everyone."

Lucy let her husband go and stepped away from him. She stood up straight. "This is everyone."

"How can we be sure?" Aeron said.

"Because we have to get moving," Lincoln said. "If there's anyone else left, they're on their own for at least the night."

"Wait," Ballard said. "Where's Gideon and Clay?"

"They didn't come back with you?" Aeron said.

Ballard shook her head.

"Then they're on their own," Lincoln said. "We can't wait any longer. They wouldn't wait for us, and we know that for a fact."

Captain Barrow scanned the crowd. His last charge added up to only dozens of people. They all were looking to him to protect them, but he knew that, when it would come to it, all he would be able to do would be to lay down in front of them to buy them some time. He wasn't their leader or their protector. He was their shepherd, taking them to a safe place to hide, but they couldn't hide forever. They needed another solution, and it wasn't something Barrow could give them. Time would be his only gift, and it was incredibly finite.

Barrow looked at Lucy, and she nodded her consent.

"All right," he said. "Let's go."

The colonists crossed the commons and funneled into the train station. They moved onto the tracks and followed them for such a time that the sun became perilously low in the sky.

When they arrived at the industrial district, Lincoln measured the distance between the horizon and the sun as one hand's width.

As they walked in the shadows of the industrial district's bleak and gray warehouses and facilities, no one asked what they were doing there. None of the colonists questioned their leadership. Demoralized by the carnage and loss, they followed because there was nowhere else to go and no one else to trust. Facing the end of everything, they sealed the rifts that had divided them; they joined the seams of humanity. The last colonists of Lumen united for self-preservation. They settled all old quarrels, or at least put them aside, because of an instinctual understanding that, if they didn't work together now, none of them would make it.

Barrow led them onto the desolate gravel road, which cut between abandoned warehouses and factories. The smelting chimneys were dormant. Exhaust vents were silent. The muted stone and gray metal complexes had never felt so devoid of life.

They came to the edge of the district where stone met crop and farmland covered the distance to the perimeter wall. Then they entered the field. Curious, Ellis watched the colonists wade through the tall grass.

Ducard gave him an impatient wave. "Come on, Mr. Greek history."

Ellis huffed with frustration and dove in.

Out in the field, a small wooded area grew. The sentries led the colonists into the trees, which sheltered them from the sunlight. In the unsettling darkness, the world grew quiet, but it wasn't long before they broke through to a clearing and were looking at a complex of fencing surrounding a concrete building. Plain, muted gray stone, it looked like any other utility building only larger. Being the pillar's keeper, Ellis knew it wasn't one of his buildings.

"What is this place?" he asked.

"I knew you guys had a headquarters," Ballard said, "but I never knew where it was."

"That was the point," Barrow said.

Ellis breathed to speak, but Ducard raised a finger and cut him off. "Don't start with the questions. Just take it for what it is."

Ellis' brow narrowed. "And what's that?"

"A gift," Ballard said.

They pushed into the compound. The perimeter fencing appeared intact. Ducard approached a security gate and tapped five digits on a keypad. The door buzzed and popped open. He smirked at Ellis. "The not knowing is just burning you up, isn't it? Okay, fine. Go ahead. Ask."

"How is there power here?"

"We're not on the grid." Barrow pointed to the top of the building. "Solar panels on the roof."

"Why not use the pillar's power?" Ellis asked. "The core has plenty to spare."

"Not anymore."

Ellis frowned as they walked on to the building's main entrance, a heavy metal door set into the side of the building, and Ducard tried the same entry routine. This time, nothing happened.

"What the hell?" He tried again, but it wouldn't unlock.

Barrow pushed Ducard aside. "Let me try." He input his credentials three times, and when it wouldn't open, he slammed the door. "Dammit!"

"Can you get it open, Ellis?" Ducard asked.

The engineer gaped. "What do you expect me to do? Science it open? I have no idea, but Ernest may have a trick or two."

The other Freeman brother stepped forward, his eyes roaming over the controls. "Let me see." He pulled a screwdriver from his pocket and twirled it in his fingers before attacking the device's screws.

"Tonight, we'll have power and running water," Barrow said. "The walls and entrances are reinforced. There are weapons and ammo. We'll be able to stay here a while."

"You will?" a voice said from the roof.

Backlit by the oncoming dusk, a silhouette presided over them. Gideon Ford leaned over the edge with a smug smile.

"Mr. Ford, let us in," Barrow said.

"World's changed, Captain. You're not in charge anymore."

A look of murderous intent crossed Barrow's face.

"Please, Gideon." Lucy motioned to the colonists behind her. "There are a lot of innocent people who need someplace safe for the night."

"I know there are a lot of you down there, and I'm sorry. I really am. If I let you all in, then we have a lot of people we need to look out for, and now, we have to look out for ourselves. That's just the way it is."

"There's nothing in this world anymore that anyone owns," Lincoln said. "It all belongs to them now."

Gideon's eyes narrowed. "I let you in, you do what we say. That includes you, Aeron, and you, Lincoln. The colony is over. We're starting a new one, and I will be its warden."

The remaining colonists who had supported Gideon before the exos attacked rumbled with agreement.

"No," Aeron said.

"What we have here is a classic case of the haves and have-nots," Gideon said. "This is non-negotiable. If you want in, you'll have to abide by my rules."

Aeron and Gideon glared at each other, a standoff that put the once usurper on the high ground. As much as Aeron hated to admit it, Gideon was right. He had the power now.

"Take a moment and discuss it if you like," Gideon said. "We're not going anywhere."

Lucy tugged on Aeron's arm and motioned with her other hand for Lincoln and Barrow to join them out of earshot from the other colonists.

"We can't give in to him," Lincoln said.

Barrow nodded. "I agree."

"I don't see any other choice," Aeron said.

Gideon eyed the western horizon. The sun was beginning to kiss the treetops. "If you aren't going to agree to my terms, I suggest you all find somewhere else quick."

"Okay," Lucy said.

"No," Lincoln said. "We'll go somewhere else."

"Lincoln, there is nowhere else." Lucy looked up to Gideon. "We agree to your terms."

Gideon's grin stretched across his face, and he retreated from the rooftop edge. A moment later, the security door buzzed and popped open for them.

"Why does it feel like we're surrendering?" Lincoln asked.

"Because we are," Aeron said.

They entered the sentry headquarters building, and when the door closed behind them, the locks re-engaged.

Three

The colonists shuffled into the facility. Before them stretched an atrium of stone and metal gleaming in harsh floodlights mounted high up on the walls. A staircase led to a second-floor walkway, which circled the room. Up there, three sentries established a perimeter.

On their right, Marco Tamland gazed down upon them. With his soft, boyish features, his appearance was not threatening, but being a new recruit, his unsteady hands could cause trouble. Barrow had expected Marco to fail, but despite being a coward who wasn't particularly good at fighting, he was likeable. For the most part, the sentries had taken to him like a loveable pet that was in their care, and Marco never seemed to mind.

On their left, Brent Helmsworth had been a pretty face until he'd gone one word too far with Ducard. To his credit, Helmsworth didn't back down from a fight, but he'd never looked the same after Ducard was finished with him. His nose was crooked and jutted like a bird's beak, and the flesh on his bones appeared to have hardened.

At the back, with his mounted SAW machine gun, Abel Livingston was the guy who had pulled Ducard off of Helmsworth, and it had torn a rift in the sentries' relationship. Ducard had seen it as Abel siding with Helmsworth. Helmsworth had seen it as Abel saving his life. This other big, imposing sentry leered at them from behind the sights of his weapon. He looked eager to turn the atrium into a shooting gallery.

On the main floor, with Gideon and Clay approaching, a fourth sentry emerged from the shadows at the back of the room.

Save for the sidearm in her thigh holster, Dana Sibley was unarmed. A woman who was out to prove something, she continually asserted her authority, even though she didn't officially have any. She'd been trying to climb the ladder for years, but Barrow had held her down because she hadn't yet learned leaders didn't have ambition to lead. They simply led.

Gideon raised his hands to his side like their savior. "Welcome! I apologize for the security measures, but we couldn't be sure of your intent. As you'll come to learn, the safety of my people is of the utmost importance." Gideon signaled to his sentries with a wave of his hand, and they raised their rifles. "For this reason, we'll have to take proper precautions for now."

Sibley met her captain's gaze. She smiled at the twist of fate. "Surrender your weapon."

"Absolutely not," Barrow said.

"Now, Captain Barrow," Gideon said. "Remember the terms of our agreement. If you don't plan to comply with our rules, you're wasting your own time. It's going to be dark soon. You're welcome to find someplace else."

Barrow stared Gideon down. "If you had any brains, you would let us help defend this place."

"There's no need for insults, Captain, but as you'll see, you all will be perfectly safe." He meandered around the room. "Your new warden, that's me, has seen to every detail here. We have food and water, and we have sufficient defense against the creatures from the earth, the ones our previous wardens lied to us about. But you all are refugees, and we are happy to take you in, even though there are some among you who wish us harm. I recognize a need for us to work together in the long term, but for now, we have it all handled."

Barrow would not yield. It simply wasn't in him. He glared at Gideon with a tightness like a compressed spring. Ducard, Lincoln, and the other survivors watched the sentry captain to see if he would attack. If he did, they would have no choice but to follow, and likely everyone would die.

Knowing this, Ballard removed her revolver from its holster and held it out, considering it. "We don't have a choice." She offered it to Sibley, and the sentry accepted it.

"That a girl," Sibley said. "Smart."

"Aww, hell." Ducard shoved his empty sidearm into Sibley's chest, and the force pushed her off her balance. She offered a curt, sarcastic bow.

Finally, Barrow complied and surrendered his weapon.

"Good," Gideon said. "I can already tell this is going to work out. Now, everyone, leave your bags with these sentries."

"Why?" Lincoln said.

"Because we will pool resources. You will share anything that could benefit the colony. No individual will be permitted to have their own resources. It's called equality. The haves give you shelter. The have-nots pay for it with provisions. Society benefits."

"Sounds like the haves taking everything they can to me," Lincoln said.

Gideon sneered and motioned with his hands for them to remove their packs and place them on the floor. The colonists hesitated but ultimately complied, leaving dozens of bags full of food, water, clothing, and other provisions on the floor.

"Good," Gideon said. "Now follow Clay. He'll show you to your quarters."

Clay led them deeper into the facility and down a long corridor. Various nondescript passages led off of the hallway, some into darkness, but some doors were closed and locked. At the end, Gideon opened a door into a locker room in which a dozen or so other colonists were already hunkered down. They gazed at the newcomers with a defeated, bovine stare.

Clay motioned them in with a hostile arm gesture. "In you go."

"This is stupid," Lincoln said as he and the other colonists funneled into the room. "What are we supposed to do if they get in here? We're backed into a corner."

"Well, then you better hope they don't get in here." After everyone was inside, Clay backed out with a leering smile. "Goodnight."

The door closed and locked with a boom.

Four

There was a damp coldness to the locker room. In the failing evening sunlight, the concrete walls shimmered with moisture. The gray metal lockers bit with chill upon touch. Exhalation fogged the air. Scattered and sitting on the floor, the colonists' body heat leached into the stone.

Huddled together to fight the freeze, heartache presided over the quiet room.

Barrow, Ducard, Ernest, and Ellis were working on the door, but they weren't getting anywhere.

Lincoln lay against a wall, Bernie asleep on his chest. Beside them, Shane and Sera dozed on each other. Brushing Bernie's hair behind her ear, Lincoln regarded her. He loved her so much it broke his heart that he couldn't change their predicament.

He grasped Shane's shoulder, and the boy stirred.

"I need your help," Lincoln whispered.

Shane blinked away sleep and looked to his father with weary eyes. "What is it?"

"I can't do this alone."

"Do what?"

Lincoln brushed Bernie's hair with his fingertips. "If anything happens to me, you need to take care of your sister."

"Of course I will."

Lincoln stared into his son's boyish, soft eyes. He looked at Shane as he would any man, hard and unyielding, as equals. He knew Shane wasn't ready.

"I'm not a good person, Shane. But I've tried to be. I've been hard on you your whole life. I asked you to grow up too fast, and I'm sorry for that. But we're out of time. You need to be a man now. For her. Can you do that?"

Shane wanted to look away from his father's eyes. He wanted to refuse. It would have been more comfortable to say he couldn't do it. Instead, he took a deep breath and then nodded.

"If something happens tonight, it's going to happen fast," Lincoln said. "These people, they're looking to your aunt and uncle and me for help. I have to do what I can for them, but you don't. It comes to it, you leave me, and don't make your uncle drag you away this time. You go, and you take your sister and Sera somewhere safe. Understand?"

Shane's eyes glistened. He looked at Lincoln with a haunted expression, as if saying it had invoked the possibility.

"Understand?"

"Yes, but—"

"You'll go if it comes to it, and you won't hesitate. To do what I got to do, I got to know you and your sister will be okay."

A tear fell over Shane's eyelid. He brushed it away. "Okay, Dad. I will."

"Okay then."

Bernie groaned in protest as Lincoln lifted her and placed her beside Shane.

"Go to your brother now," he said. "Go on."

She curled under Shane's arm, and Lincoln stood.

"Where are you going?" Shane asked.

"To see to the others. Stay here."

When Lincoln walked away, Shane felt the weight of his two girls. He wanted to go after his father. He wanted to help. But he didn't dare move and disturb Sera and Bernie. For now, they were free of the fear and despair, and he had no right to steal that from them.

Five

Lucy and Aeron sat across from each other between rows of lockers. Gabe was asleep on a nearby bench, and Mel had fallen into a slumber in Lucy's lap.

For a while, cherishing every breath, they watched their children doze until it became apparent to Lucy that they were using their children as a way to avoid each other. They hadn't made eye contact since they arrived.

Lucy's hand fell on the Warden's Seal beneath her shirt. She'd forgotten the circle of metal hung there. It felt heavy around her neck, and looking at her husband, she thought he looked lost without it.

Careful not to disturb her daughter, she brushed her hair back and pulled the necklace over her head. She held the medallion in her palm, offering it to Aeron.

He glanced at it and gazed deep into her eyes. He stared at her for such a time that Lucy's hand grew heavy, and she wondered if his intention was to leave it hanging until she tired and relented.

"Take it," she said.

"No."

"It's yours."

"It's meaningless." Aeron sighed and stared into his folded hands, which he rested in his lap. "When my father gave that to me, he said, even though he was giving it to me, it wasn't mine. He said I'd have to earn it. He said the seal tends to end up with the person who deserves it, the right person."

Aeron took Lucy's hand in both of his and kissed her knuckles with a tenderness he hadn't shown her in a long time. She felt a melting inside of her, some part of her being recalling what it was like to experience human connection, to indulge in self-fulfilling love, to feel for another person and know the feeling was returned.

"I'm sorry," she said.

Aeron narrowed his brow. "For what?"

"All these years, I tried to support you as best I could. But I wasn't always that. I know now that I've been unfair to you. I thought you picked the job over us, but I know now it was the job pulling you away and that you didn't have a choice in the matter."

Aeron frowned at the thought and breathed with a heaviness of acknowledgement. Then he looked into her eyes with purpose. "I love you, Lucy. I always will. But this colony, this dream, was never about us." He looked to his sleeping children. "It was about them. Their future. You have been the best partner in that a guy could ever want. For that, I thank you."

He closed her fingers around the medallion and sat back.

She examined the seal's shiny surface. In the dim light, the golden circle shined from the ambient light. She ran a thumb over its smooth, worn face. Then she set it down on the concrete floor. Brushing Mel's hair with her fingertips, she exhaled as if she'd thrown off a great weight.

"I just want to keep them safe," she said. "I just want to be a good mom."

"That's what makes you perfect for the job." Aeron stood. "I'm going to go look around."

"For what?"

He kissed her on the forehead. "Anything."

When he turned to leave, she grabbed his arm and pulled him back. They kissed, and it made every one of their kisses that had come before irrelevant. It was a kiss of love, of understanding, of appreciation, of acknowledgement that neither of them could have gotten there without the other, of encouragement, and of goodbye. After all, they knew their luck would eventually run out, and one of their kisses would be the last.

Lucy let him go into the growing gloom, and she shoved the seal away from her, ringing across the floor.

Six

The sunlight poured through the windows in a deep shade of red. The blue lantern cast a cold glow onto the concrete walls and metal lockers like a sheet of ice. Nightfall approached.

In the lockers, Lincoln found many personal effects. He found a lot of clothing, and he dealt coats to the colonists to use as blankets. He found some pictures of loved ones, some of whom he knew to be gone. He also found one half-full bottle of shine.

It felt cool in his hands, the clear liquor sparkling like diamonds.

"Don't even think about it." Ballard sauntered down the aisle of lockers. She had that look on her face that Lincoln couldn't read. She appeared simultaneously attentive and indifferent.

"We could use it as a fuel to get a fire started," Lincoln said. "We just need something to burn."

Ballard leaned against the lockers, crossing her arms. "I'm sure that's what you were thinking." She eyed him with a curiosity he'd not seen in some time.

Lincoln's eyes were drawn to her body. Although she wasn't a curvy woman, something in the way she carried herself appealed to him. He was attracted to her, of course, but he liked even more the way she held up no barriers, her courage, her strength. She was who she was, and she wasn't going to apologize for it.

"What are you doing?" she asked.

"Looking for anything we can use."

"Anything in particular?"

"A weapon would be nice."

She shook her head. "Never going to find one. Barrow's meticulous about tracking the sentry firearms. He keeps all of them logged, organized, and locked away, and he shares all of the registration information with me, down to the serial number. He's thorough."

Lincoln put the shine back into the locker. "So you're telling me I'm wasting my time."

"I wouldn't say you're wasting it. We're not going anywhere."

She reached into the locker, took the shine, and unscrewed the cap. "Cheers." She raised the bottle and took a modest pull.

"Reggie, I'm not sure now is a good time."

She breathed the burn from her mouth. "I'm not on duty." She squinted and coughed. "I don't think this is Gill's. I think it's already making me blind." She blinked away tears and passed the bottle.

Lincoln gazed at it, considering taking a sip. One drink wouldn't hurt anything, but he also knew it wouldn't help. Once it touched his lips, he would just want more. He put the bottle into the locker and respectfully pressed the door closed.

"I was sorry to hear about your father," he said.

She shrugged and cast her eyes down. "He wouldn't have made it through all this anyway."

"No, he wouldn't, but knowing that doesn't make it any easier." He waited for her to raise her eyes and meet his. "I'm sorry I wasn't there."

She shook her head as if that was the most ridiculous thing to say, and she smoothed her hair back and waved to brush him off. "It's fine."

"I mean it. We all had to go through it, but we shouldn't have had to go through it alone."

Ballard fixed her eyes on him and was quiet. He couldn't read her expression. She was breathing hard.

"I know there's more to this," she said. "There's going to be an after, I mean."

Lincoln smirked. "Don't tell me you're getting hopelessly hopeful on me."

"I'm just saying, if we make it through tonight, I know there's going to be more than just making it. I plan to see to that."

"Don't go making promises you can't keep."

She straightened up, moved in, and wrapped her hands around the back of his neck. "You know I always keep my promises."

Their moment was simultaneously pleasant and torturous. Frozen in place, feeling the pull of attraction, they regarded each other, locked in a battle of expectation and unknown intent.

That was when something pounded the concrete beneath their feet, rattling the metal lockers and sending the nearby wooden bench sliding across the floor.

Seven

With Reggie in tow, Lincoln ran through the panicking crowd, waving his arms in the air like a madman.

"Quiet," he pleaded. "If they can't hear us, they can't find us."

Each blow to the concrete foundation triggered a wave of screams and cries.

BOOM

Mothers and fathers embraced their children.

BOOM

Couples young and old clutched each other for comfort.

BOOM

Locked in that room with no escape, they all knew that, if the exos broke through the floor, they would be taken.

Lincoln picked up the lantern, held it up like a beacon, and hushed them.

"Quiet!" he whispered fiercely. "Stay calm. Don't move."

BOOM

Another blow rattled the metal lockers and sent shivers through their bones, but the people remained silent and still. If they cried, they cried into the chest of a loved one. They clamped hands over mouths. They bit their forearms. They took any measure they could to stifle their rising hysteria.

BOOM

BOOM

BOOM

The floor and walls cracked. Dust fell from the ceiling. Windows shattered, and the colonists resisted the urge to pick the shards from their hair.

The creatures struck the floor again and again. Through it all, Lincoln held their beacon of hope, the lantern's blue light, their source of comfort and strength.

The exos were moving now, either testing the concrete or searching for their lost prey. As they tunneled beneath the floor, the building trembled with the disturbance of its foundation. Lincoln held the lamp up and clenched his eyes, like everyone, willing the creatures to leave. With the silence holding, the rumbling earth settled, and they were gone.

Lucy clutched her sobbing daughter. "How did they find us so quickly?"

"Maybe they've been there all day long," Shane said. "Deep enough so we didn't know but close enough to follow us."

Lincoln set the lantern on the floor. "They hunt by sound. I thought this concrete would insulate us, but maybe we were too loud."

Aeron pointed to the ceiling. "Or maybe they did something to attract them."

Emerging from a trance of realization, Ernest shot to his feet. "I know!"

The people hushed him.

"I know," Ernest whispered. "We first encountered them near the Field of the First Families."

Ernest had everyone's attention, but the engineer retreated into his thoughts once more.

Lincoln made a circular motion with his hand. "And?"

Ernest pressed his fingers against his forehead as if the strain of his intelligence caused him pain. "That ship's core is still generating energy. We then encountered them at the pillar, which also was generating a lot of energy. Namely, electromagnetic energy. And now they're here, the only source of electromagnetic energy left in the valley."

"James and I were at the ship," Lincoln said. "It didn't have any power."

"The system may be down, but I assure you the core is very much still active."

Aeron gaped. "I don't understand."

"These things are not unlike insects, which have been known to be drawn to EM fields."

Ellis grunted as he struggled to stand. "It's true. To run the pillar, I had to study the biology and ecosystems of other worlds. Insects play a very important role in an ecosystem, but they can be pests. On some worlds, ants, for example, would infiltrate electrical equipment, like air conditioners, and damage their sensitive components. It was discovered that they were drawn to the electromagnetic field."

Ducard was staring dumbly. "What's an ant?"

Ellis rubbed his eyes. "Seriously, Ducard. Read a book."

"All right," Lincoln said. "That's not helping."

"I was just kidding," Ducard said. "I know what an ent is."

Lucy kissed Mel's forehead and passed her off to Gabe. She stood and eyed the Freeman brothers. "If you're right, how do we get them to go away?"

"I'm not sure it will get them to go away," Ernest said. "But—"

"If we cut the power," Ellis said, "we turn off the EM field, and we stop attracting them."

Lincoln paced the room.

"What is it, brother?" Aeron asked. "We learned something here."

"Yeah," Lincoln said. "If we want to stop attracting them, all we have to do is turn off all of our lights."

Eight

Night fell. The building's perimeter lighting leaked through the windows. Shane and Gabe had carried a bench to the wall, and they were standing on it to look out at the trees beyond the clearing. Exos darted behind the cover of foliage, and the bushes and branches trembled at their presence.

Aeron tapped at the door and kept his voice to a whisper. "Hello?"

"That isn't going to work," Lincoln said.

Aeron shot a sharp glare at his brother. "How do you know?"

"Because they're not out there."

Automatic gunfire thrummed overhead.

Ducard eyed the ceiling. "They're on the roof."

"Idiots," Lincoln said. "They're just calling more of them."

Aeron beat on the door.

"Stop that!" Lincoln said.

"They're shooting guns on the roof, Lincoln. You think my knocking on a door is going to bring more of those things here? We have to do something."

"Maybe, but you're not going to get through that door."

"You're both right," Lucy said. "We have to do something. So what do we do?"

"We could check these lockers for something useful," Aeron said.

"Lincoln already looked," Ballard said.

"We had regular inspections and strict regulations," Barrow said. "Isn't that right, Ducard?"

The sentry tilted his head. "Just because you inspected us doesn't mean we weren't hiding anything, but no, we probably wouldn't find anything useful."

"Why don't we go out the windows?" Shane said.

"Ernest," Aeron said, "is there any way to cut the power from here?"

The engineer shook his head. "I'd need access to the main panelboard."

"Couldn't you overload the circuits or something?" Ducard asked.

Ellis laughed. "That's cute."

"No, everything here is downstream. Power flows one way," Ernest said.

Shane cleared his throat. "Guys, why don't we go out the windows?"

"If we could establish enough leverage, we might be able to pry that door open," Ernest said.

"It won't work," Ellis said. "That door's too strong."

Ernest shot his brother a spiteful look. "Are there any tools in here?"

Ducard shook his head. "No, just our uniforms and soaps and stuff. Like Captain Barrow said, we were under pretty strict regulations."

Shane shuffled closer and raised his hand. "Guys, hey."

"There's got to be another way out of here," Lucy said.

"Hey."

"We already checked the door to the gym," Ballard said. "Locked up tight."

"Listen to me!" Shane said.

Everyone silenced and turned their attention to Shane, and he immediately regretted it.

Lincoln scowled. "Keep your voice down."

"I tried, but you all kept ignoring me."

"What is it, Shane?" Lucy asked.

Now that he had their attention, Shane's nerves were on fire. His body tingled, and sweat broke through his pores. His heart pounded. "I was just thinking that, if there's no other way, we could go out the windows."

The colonists erupted at the ridiculous notion.

"We're safer in here than out there."

"I'm not going outside."

"He's just a kid. He doesn't know any better."

Lincoln's expression relaxed, but it was still serious. "It's a good idea."

The people fell silent.

"We don't all need to go." Lincoln placed a hand on Shane's shoulder. "It's a good idea, son."

He stepped over to the windows and examined them. It would be a tight fit, but he could make it.

Aeron approached his brother. "There's got to be another way."

"There isn't. You know it."

"Daddy!" Bernie ran to her father and leaped.

Lincoln caught her. "It's okay, sweetheart. I'll be in the light the whole time. I'll be safe."

"Don't go." Her voice was small, defeated, and afraid.

He pulled her close and wrapped his arms around her. The heat from her tears penetrated his shirt. He pushed her away and looked into her eyes.

"I'm coming back," he said. "I made it before. I'll make it again."

Ballard eased up beside him. "You sure about this?"

More gunfire thrummed through the night.

"Yeah. If we don't stop them, this place will get overwhelmed."

Ballard nodded, and Ducard assumed a position to lift Lincoln up.

Barrow's eyes were stern. "You hit that ground, you move fast. Turn right, and cut around the exterior of the building. There's a ladder to the roof. It's up off the ground a ways, but you should be able to make it." He reached around into his rear waistband. "Take this." He handed Lincoln a semi-automatic pistol.

Ducard's eyes grew wide. "Where did you get that?"

One side of Barrow's mouth lifted, which was as close to a smile as the man ever seemed to get. "You all weren't as good at hiding things in here as you thought."

Lincoln weighed the weapon in his hand and looked at Barrow doubtfully. "Thanks." He kissed his daughter on the forehead and embraced his son.

Shane's eyes were downcast. "It's my idea. I should come with you."

Lincoln gripped his son's arm and smiled at the boy. "I'll be right back."

He stepped onto the bench. Ducard interlocked his fingers, and Lincoln put his boot into the sentry's hands. The window lock was tight and rusted, but it popped open. When Ducard felt Lincoln begin to pull himself up, he assisted.

In an instant, Lincoln was gone.

Nine

When Lincoln hit the ground, his feet shot out from under him. Lying in the grass and willing air to fill his lungs, the earth started to rumble, but his limbs wouldn't move.

"You have to get up!" Aeron hissed down from the window. "Go!"

Lincoln gasped and sat up. Dirt gushed like a geyser around him. He remained still, hoping the exos wouldn't be able to find him. Another sinkhole erupted to his left.

Aeron was right. He had to move. The exos were triangulating his position.

"Move, brother! Go!"

The ground jumped and rolled in waves.

As Lincoln got to his feet, the world fell beneath him. Damp soil sprayed into the air like mist, flowed around him, and on top of him, delivering its crushing weight. It squeezed the air from his chest and pulled him down, down, down.

Lumen was swallowing him whole.

Lincoln clawed, his muscles twisting like taut ropes. He fought with everything he had. He even fought the urge to scream because he knew it would only damn him.

The earth stopped sucking him down. He was still. Nothing took his legs. The ground had collapsed from the exos' digging, but they had not yet found him. His primal sense of danger blazed in his mind, assaulting him with the knowledge that the exos lurked beneath, they were hunting him, and they were close.

Another sinkhole erupted behind him, raining dirt and rock on his head.

Fear fueled him to climb and dig the loosened soil. He kicked, thrashed, and twisted his body to get free.

Voices carried through the window above. He heard the hollow clank of metal striking metal. He heard the soft thudding of dozens of feet pounding concrete.

Lincoln's family and friends were trying to draw the exos' attention.

As he reached the surface and pulled himself upright, the loosened earth behind him disappeared in a vortex of grinding limbs like a violent machine.

Aeron's voice returned. "Move!"

Lincoln ran. The surface exploded around him like a warzone. The damp soil showered him and filled each breath with the scent of earth. Shockwaves from the exos' powerful, digging legs set him off balance.

He looked back. A collapsing trench drew a line in pursuit, and it was gaining on him. Lincoln was losing solid ground.

At the corner of the building, he leaned on the facade to navigate the turn. The structure was vibrating like a tuning fork.

The ladder was up ahead. He pushed with everything he had left. His lungs burned, and his heart pounded. The first hollow pang of exhaustion bloomed in his chest.

Measuring his steps, he approached the wall, and his panic disappeared. The world quieted and slowed. His mind retreated into isolation. He didn't think about the crushing weight of being buried alive or the claws and teeth that could tear through his flesh and bone. There was only the ladder and him, him and the ladder, a connection that they shared, a connection he intended to make.

He leaped and stretched and soared, and when he hit the wall, his fingers curled around the cool metal of the bottom ladder rung. He squeezed as if he would never let go.

Lincoln hung there in disbelief, and the world rushed back to him in all of its earth-churning fury, like a tornado of rocks and soil.

Beneath him, the exos hit the building's foundation and tore the ground asunder. A crushing vortex surfaced. The rumbling was now a chittering as their sharp, bony limbs sheared through dirt and stone like scythes cutting through earth.

When Lincoln reached for the next rung, one of those limbs reached into the light, retracted its claw, and struck his leg. It knocked him from his position and he dangled with one hand on the ladder. He gazed down into that darkness again and saw snapping, dagger-like teeth at the line between light and dark.

Another limb came from the hole, and Lincoln lifted as it swung for him.

He had to go. They could play this game all night, but gravity worked against him.

Lincoln's free hand grasped the ladder's second rung. Hugging the wall, he found new leverage, and his other hand gripped the third rung. Then he reached the fourth, and the fifth, and soon, he was looking down at the hole from a place where the creatures could not reach him. All of their thrashing and gnashing was meaningless across the expanse of light. They squelched and vanished, the earth collapsing to cover their tracks.

On the roof, Lincoln took a moment on his hands and knees to collect himself. Across the rooftop of electrical equipment and solar panels, he spotted the sentries still firing their weapons into the trees, cracking the night sky in every direction, a beacon for the exos.

He pulled the pistol from his waistband. He flicked the safety off, and the amplifier heated up and hummed. It was ready to do what it was made for. It was ready to take lives, and so was Lincoln, if he needed to.

Dana Sibley's body rocked with her rifle's recoil as she fired deliberate shots that punched the tree line and missed every dark shape that dashed through the greenery. She ejected her empty magazine and pulled another from her belt.

Lincoln placed the barrel of the pistol at the base of her skull, and she froze with the magazine in her hand.

"Don't bother," Lincoln said. "Put it down. Order them to put theirs down too."

"But we're keeping them at bay."

"No," Lincoln said. "The lights are keeping them at bay. The shooting is just pissing them off."

Lincoln applied pressure.

She grunted with disgust and frustration. "Cease fire!"

"What?" Abel Livingston spun with hard, angry eyes.

"Cease fire!"

Standing next to each other at a corner of the roof, Marco Tamland and Brent Helmsworth stopped shooting. Upon seeing Lincoln, Helmsworth swallowed and lowered his rifle to his side. Tamland raised his, but Sibley shook her head. Helmsworth grabbed the other sentry's rifle barrel and forced it downward.

"Put your guns down," Lincoln said.

"We're defending this building," Helmsworth said. "We're defending you."

"No." Lincoln moved behind Sibley to use her as a shield. "You're putting your guns down."

"Do it," Sibley said.

They reluctantly complied, dropping their weapons to the asphalt rooftop.

"Good," Lincoln said. "Now we go inside."

"What about them?" Tamland asked.

"The lights will handle them. You've just been wasting bullets up here. Let's go."

Lincoln pushed Sibley away but kept the pistol trained on her. The sentries led him to the roof-access door, and they entered and began their descent. When Lincoln closed the door, the tree line calmed, and the shaking earth stopped. As long as the lights shined, they would be at a stalemate. However, the exos would continue to amass their forces outside as long as the electricity was on. Eventually, their numbers would grow large enough that they would overcome the facility one way or another.

Ten

Lincoln and the sentries exited the stairwell into the second floor hallway. The metal door squealed on dry hinges, and the old wooden floor cracked beneath them. The atrium opened to one side, and down below, over the railing, Lincoln saw the door they came in. Opposite the railing, doors to offices lined the wall. Hooded lamps hung from the ceiling on long black cords.

An exo tunneled below, shaking the building. Lincoln and the sentries steadied themselves on the walls and railing and waited for it to pass. When it did, Lincoln motioned them forward with his pistol.

At the end of the hallway, they turned into an open room. The sentries had stored all of the colonists' belongings here in a large, unorganized pile. Their backs to the door, setting canned and preserved food aside, Gideon and Clay were taking inventory.

When the sentries stomped in, Gideon looked at them with a curious expression. "Why aren't you on the roof? Why has the shooting stopped?"

Lincoln entered with his pistol still aimed at the back of Sibley's head, and then it made sense to Gideon.

The old man scoffed and slammed an aluminum can onto the floor. "What are you doing, Lincoln? These sentries are our only line of defense."

Lincoln pushed Sibley toward the other sentries and trained his pistol on Gideon.

"All that gunfire was just attracting more of them," he said.

Gideon's eyes narrowed. "How would you know?"

Sensing an oncoming understanding, Lincoln lowered his weapon. "That first night we escaped them, they could have taken us outside the wall, but they didn't. They hunt by sound, Gideon. That's how they're able to find us while underground and in the dark. They can hear us."

Gideon's face darkened. "If that's true, that gun you got in your hand will make quite a ruckus if you fire it. Without anyone to defend the perimeter, I might opt to wager that you wouldn't—"

Lincoln fired a round through the window behind Gideon. The crack of its report reverberated through the room, and the weapon's amplifier zipped and hummed again, ready to launch another bullet.

The sentries froze. Bewildered, they looked to the window. When they returned their attention to Lincoln, they found the black eye of the pistol's barrel staring at them again.

Lincoln cracked a smile. "One can't hurt. Now let's go get the rest of our people."

Another exo tunneled below and shook the building.

"All right," Gideon said. "What's the plan, Lincoln?"

"To stop them from doing that." Lincoln motioned with his pistol for everyone to lead the way from the room, and they complied.

In the hallway, Gideon said, "You know I was just locking everyone in for their safety. It was nothing personal."

"I'm sure you thought so," Lincoln said.

On the first floor, Sentry Sibley jingled a set of keys and opened the locker room's heavy door. Barrow was the first out and took the keys from her. She shied away from his judgmental gaze.

Their eyes full of wonder and awe, as if confronting a new world, the colonists filled the atrium. Each colonist milled about, unsure what to do or say but bathe in the plentiful light and relative safety.

Bernie and Shane emerged from the crowd, and Lincoln embraced them. Aeron and Lucy joined the reunion.

Lucy placed a hand on his chest. "We didn't know if you made it. Then we heard the shooting stop and knew it was you."

Lincoln's eyes searched the crowd, his focus elsewhere. "It wasn't exactly smooth, but I got it done."

Captain Barrow reached for a handshake.

Lincoln handed the pistol back to him. "I think it's better that you have it. I'm no good with it."

Lucy clapped. "All right. Where's Ernest?"

The engineer raised a hand. "I'm here." He emerged between a tightly knit group of colonists who were sharing their relief at being out of the cold locker room.

"Good," Lucy said. "Barrow, take us to the power source."

Gideon's hands shot out in a questioning expression. "Why do you want to go to the power source?"

Lucy waved in dismissal. "Because we're going to turn it off."

"Why would you do such a thing!?"

Ernest cleared his throat. "Insects have been known to be attracted to electromagnetic fields, and we've seen that behavior—"

"The electricity is attracting them," Lincoln said.

Gideon's confused expression persisted. "But we have lights because of the electricity."

Ducard grunted. "Don't tell me you're afraid of the dark."

As another exo tunneled below, Lincoln held up a hand. Everyone quieted while the building shuddered and then stilled as the creature continued on.

Lincoln lowered his hand. "They're not going to stop that. We think if we turn off the power and stay quiet, we can make it through the night."

"You think?" Gideon raised a finger and stepped forward. "It would be stupid to give up something we know is working to benefit us for something we aren't sure will!"

BOOM

The building shook with an impact.

Lucy motioned to Ducard and pointed to Gideon. "Shut him up."

The sentry grabbed the old man, slapping a hand over his mouth and twisting an arm behind his back. Clay and Abel moved to intervene but stopped when Barrow raised his weapon. The people were so quiet that the only thing breaking the silence was the hum of the pistol's amplifier.

"It's the best chance we've got right now," Lucy whispered to Gideon. "I know we've never agreed on much, but the simple fact of the matter is, every minute that power source is on, more of them come. Every shot we fire, more of them come. Everything we do just makes them stronger. All the while, they're looking for a way in, disturbing the foundation, and sooner or later, they're going to bring this building down on top of us. If we don't turn off the power, we won't make it through the night. They'll get so strong that they'll find a way in."

Breathing through his nose over Ducard's fingers, Gideon nodded, and the sentry let him go. Barrow lowered his weapon, and the tension in the atrium eased.

Barrow led Ernest toward the back of the atrium, and Lucy followed, giving instructions to Ducard to watch them. She didn't need to specify whom she was talking about.

Lincoln found who he'd been looking for in the colonist crowd. Reggie stared at him with a hard, frightened expression. He smiled at her, and her look didn't change. When he narrowed his eyes to question what was wrong, she shook her head and turned away.

Mystified, Lincoln left to join the others who were going to pull the power.

Eleven

Barrow led Ernest, Lucy, and Lincoln to the back of the atrium and down a hallway across from the locker room. Most of sentry headquarters was utilitarian, devoid of any personality or luxury that went beyond military practicality. This part was bare bones. The wooden studs were exposed, there was no insulation, and black cabling snaked across the floor, up the walls, and into the ceiling.

It was the heart of the building, and it wasn't meant to be seen.

Ernest whistled. "I guess whoever set this place up never heard of workmanship."

"What do you mean?" Lucy asked.

"Look over here." Ernest pointed at a cluster of cabling on the floor. "Some extra slack is never a bad thing, but wind and tie it up so it doesn't get tangled. And over here," he drew their attention to the central heating unit, "the main access panel is affixed by two bolts instead of four. And over here—"

Barrow pinched the bridge of his nose. "Could we stop scrutinizing the condition of my building, please?"

Ernest stopped mid-breath, his finger still in the air to make his point. "Of course." He lowered his hand. "Apologies, Captain."

"Apology accepted. Now kill my building."

Ernest laughed. "This guy. He makes jokes." The engineer examined a metal panel in the wall and went to a shelf to don safety glasses and a pair of insulated gloves. Then he rummaged through the toolbox in the corner and pulled out a wrench.

"Tell me how this works," Lucy said.

"It's pretty simple really. This is the battery storage unit for the solar panels on the roof. I just have to unplug it."

"Not that. The electromagnetic thing."

Ernest started turning a bolt on the side of the panel. "If you pass an electric current through a wire, it generates an electromagnetic field. Electricity is running throughout this building to energize lights and other equipment, so this entire building is basically one big electromagnet. If we stop the flow of power, we turn off the electromagnetic field, which is the thing that's attracting them."

"How sure are you about this?" Lucy said.

"I'm a scientist. It's a theory."

"How sure?"

"Fifty-fifty." Ernest smirked at her. "It either will work, or it won't."

Barrow crossed his arms. "Once it's off, can it be turned back on?"

"Of course. We'd just have to plug it back in."

"So if we're wrong, no harm done," Lucy said.

"If you think there would be no harm when hundreds of bloodthirsty creatures charge across an open field, rip the top off this building, and tear to pieces everyone who's left and we hold dear, then yes, no harm done," Lincoln said.

Lucy hitched a breath. Barrow's face was unreadable.

Ernest finished removing the panel covering and set it on the floor. "I hate to add to the morbidity, but before that, we have to consider that I could electrocute myself here, kill you three in the arc blast, and set fire to the building."

"Good," Lucy said. "I was starting to think this was too easy and it had to be a trick."

"Jokes all around tonight," Ernest said. "Have you people lost your minds? We could be dead in minutes."

Barrow grabbed a hard hat from the shelf, put it on Ernest's head, and patted it down. "We're going to be fine. This is going to work."

Ernest adjusted the hard hat and challenged the captain with his gaze. "How do you know?"

"Because I'm not a scientist." Barrow returned to Lucy and Lincoln. "Now do it."

Ernest took a deep breath. "Are we sure?"

The concrete foundation trembled as an exo tunneled beneath them.

"If we don't, they're going to bring the whole building down," Lincoln said.

Lucy nodded. "Pull the plug."

Ernest faced the panel. "You all may want to take a few steps back."

They took a position near the doorway.

Ernest pressed a red button, which made a cracking sound, and the whole world plunged into darkness. People in the atrium cried out. Red emergency lighting kicked in, and then Ernest yanked a cable from the panel, cutting those lights off as well. Electricity snapped and a spark flew across the darkened room.

Silence settled over them like a blanket. They hadn't even known the hum of electrical current had surrounded them, and when it was gone, the quiet carried an unmistakable dread into their hearts.

No one made a sound. All was still. In the maddening darkness, they waited for death to come.

"Do you think it worked?" Ernest whispered.

Around the facility, the world erupted in a piercing scream that punched through the walls, their ears, and their minds.

Twelve

The aurora cast a green glow through the facility's windows. The fluorescent haze filled the rooms and corridors with the intensity of a full moon. The people were at peace, huddled in the atrium hallway, quiet and still, embracing each other. There were no tears, no lamentations or prayers, only whispers to the young and the afraid that everything was going to be all right.

With the perimeter lights off, the exos stalked the night, emerging from the tree line with a level of care approaching reticence. Shining in the aurora's light, the hulking black masses eased forward, rustling branches and stalks of grass but keeping low. Their advances were deliberate yet tempered. They took their time. They had all night.

They roamed in patterns that resembled organized patrol routes. They stomped by windows, making their clicking sounds and knocking their bony joints together. When they neared, a noxious stench like decay penetrated the facility. They pounded up the walls and thundered on the rooftop, establishing a perch of dominance.

As they surrounded the colonists, Barrow led his sentries, Lincoln, Ballard, and Aeron up to the second floor. They passed offices and training rooms in a darkened hallway until they reached a locked door at the end. Barrow inserted a key into the lock and swung the door wide open.

They stood in the threshold to a pitch-black room. The aurora couldn't penetrate it because there were no windows.

Barrow clicked on his flashlight and stepped inside. The others followed suit.

Cool cones of blue light dashed around the room. It was utilitarian and sterile. No decorations hung on the plain walls. The desk was tidy and bare. A pair of chairs stood before it just like in the warden's office.

"Usually, if you see this place, you screwed up," Ducard said. "Now I think we're just screwed."

"Is this your office?" Aeron asked Barrow.

"This is where I conduct business when necessary, yes."

"Why'd you bring us here?" Lincoln said.

Barrow beckoned and led them to the back of the room where another locked door was set into the wall. He turned another key in another lock, and the door slid into a pocket. Inside, gunmetal gleamed in the flashlight beams.

Ducard rubbed his hands and marched inside. He hefted a light machine gun with a belt of bullets and cast a crooked smile at the others.

Barrow emerged from the room with a rifle in each fist. "These are for you." He shoved them at Lincoln and Aeron.

They gazed at them as if they were foreign objects.

"But, Captain," Lincoln said, "I didn't get you anything."

Aeron scrutinized Barrow in astonishment. "What's going on?"

"In time," Barrow said. He went back into the room and brought out two more rifles. One he gave to Ballard, and he offered the other to Dana Sibley. She reached for it, and Barrow yanked it away.

"We can't afford not to trust each other now," he said. "You refused to follow my orders. What's more, you abandoned your post at the pillar, and you may have caused the deaths of your brothers and sisters."

"Wait a minute." Ducard stomped out of the armory with a rifle slung over each shoulder, belts of bullets crossing over his chest, and the machine gun under his arm. "They were at the pillar?"

"Yes," Barrow said. "And they tried to escape on the train."

Ducard cursed and rattled as he tromped back in to collect more treasures. Barrow pressed her with his patience. They all knew he wasn't going to let it go. Sentries Livingston, Helmsworth, and Tamland held their cold, stone stares, neither challenging nor humiliated, but apparently unaffected. Sibley, though, cast her eyes down in shame. As their leader, she felt the responsibility for what they'd done.

"We told ourselves we were saving them, some of the wrenches," she said. "They were loading up on the train, and we couldn't stop them, so we went with them. To protect them. That's what we told ourselves. But when the train got hit and people started disappearing, we ran."

"We were only trying to—" Helmsworth tried to explain.

"It doesn't matter, Brent!" Sibley cut him down with her glare. "We ran. Sentries don't run. We brace the wall."

Her eyes lingered on him until he couldn't bear her anymore and looked away.

"As those things picked people out of the train, we just ran for it," she said. "I don't know if it was the storm or what, but the creatures couldn't hear or see us. We looked back, but there was nothing we could do. We hoofed it down the mountain, scared out of our minds all night that they'd come and take us, but they never did."

"Yeah," Ducard said. "They had plenty to go around elsewhere."

"So we came back here and holed up until Gideon and the others came. He told us they were all that was left and he'd taken charge. We just re-established the order we were used to and tried to carry on."

Barrow studied her. To the others, it appeared as if he were evaluating her resolve, gauging the truth in her story. The truth was he believed her because, if he could run, any one of them could.

He held out the rifle. "You have to understand now there will be no more running. We're the last line, and we'll hold it. You owe a debt. We all do. If it comes to it, I expect you to pay it. For them." Barrow nodded to Lincoln, Aeron, and Ballard.

An understanding flared within Sibley that accepting the weapon meant acknowledging its responsibility. She took it.

Ducard thundered out of the room with two rifles for Helmsworth and Tamland. For Abel Livingston, he had a light machine gun. Ducard offered it, and the other big sentry accepted it with a grin.

Barrow stood back and observed them all. Armed now, they were a small squad. Out there, exposed, they wouldn't cover much of a perimeter, but if they could control the environment, like the Spartans at Thermopylae, the numbers didn't need to add up. If it came to that, they were enough. They had to be. They were all that was left.

After loading up some wooden crates with weapons, ammunition, and ordnance, they exited the armory, and on the way down the hallway, Lincoln joined Barrow ahead of the others.

"Can we count on them?" he asked.

Barrow glanced back over his shoulder at his sentries and returned. "I don't know that it particularly matters, Lincoln."

"Then what was that all about?"

Barrow's expression was somewhere between a grimace and a smile. "Getting everyone on the same page."

"What page is that?"

"Would you die if it meant your family would have a better chance?"

"Yes."

"That one."

Lincoln slowed as he considered Barrow's words, and the captain went on ahead. He was certain the old soldier wasn't being fatalist, but it concerned Lincoln that Barrow was so grave. No one knew the chances, but if anyone had an idea, it was Captain Barrow.

Ballard caught up to him. "What's wrong?"

He shook his head. "Nothing. Everything's great. How are you?"

"Smart ass." She sneered at him. "You know we're going to make it through tonight, right?"

"Yeah."

In solemnity, like a funeral procession, they rattled down the stairs into the atrium with enough weapons for an army.

Thirteen

Ducard peered through his rifle's scope, which was set to night vision. He could see the exos about the clearing before the tree line. Their rigid, armored limbs hooked on bulbous joints, like arthritic fingers, narrowing into earth-churning scythes. The slender abdomen and thorax flowed with the grace of water. The serpentine tail hoisted its stinger into the air. The elongated head jutted into a flat snout, like a shield for the maw. Ducard even could make out the spine-like hairs on the leathery underbelly, and he shivered with the sense that they were crawling all over his flesh.

He lowered his weapon and held his breath, stifling the urge to vomit. "Just looking at these things makes me hate living. How could something like this even exist?"

Lincoln was leaning against the wall and watching them through another window. "Maybe they weren't always this way. Maybe the Dawn forced them to evolve. Humanity has been in control of its evolution since before we left Earth. It's made us weak. These things had to fight to survive."

"You saying they're angry?"

Outside, one of the exos bumped into the chain-link fence, casually reached up with its front legs, and tore the fence down as if it were newspaper.

Lincoln slid down the wall into a sitting position. "I'm saying they're here now, and we don't matter much anymore."

From the interior of the room, Barrow's pale face frowned down at him. "We still matter. Before this is over, you'll see that. Even if they take us all, we matter more than they ever will."

Lincoln grunted. "Why do you say that?"

"Because we're here. We came to Lumen. We escaped the fate the universe handed to us. We were born in the light of a dying star. From the beginning, our days were numbered. There was a time that was ours, and nature would have had that be all. But we beat it. We won. Humanity is greater than these things, and I intend to show them every ounce of that greatness. I'll make them believers. I'll make a believer out of you too."

"We are the shield," Ducard said.

A flashlight beam swept the floor, and the sound of boot falls on the concrete approached from the atrium. Appearing exhausted and defeated, Aeron and Ballard entered the room.

Aeron took a seat on the floor next to his brother. "About ten to the west."

"Twelve to the south," Ballard said.

Ducard left his riflescope and turned from the window. "I counted only a handful to the east."

"And to the north?" Aeron asked

Lincoln rubbed his neck. "Thirty."

Aeron's hand went to his forehead, and he blew through puckered lips. "What are we going to do?"

Barrow walked to Ducard's window and peered outside. "We're going to hold out until dawn, but if it comes to it, we're going to choke them to death."

Ballard's bewildered eyes flashed with aurora light. "What does that mean?"

"Typically, we fight in a perimeter," Barrow said. "But when the perimeter is compromised, we retreat and find a wall to put our backs against. Here, they can come at us from four directions. If we had enough sentries, I would order a defense in stages. We would hold the perimeter as long as we could, and then we would fall back to the wall. We don't have the manpower, so we're going to fortify the south wall and wait. If they come at us, it'll be down the atrium, and we can focus fire on the choke point."

"Sounds like a last stand," Ballard said.

Barrow left the window and faced her. "It is."

"One problem," Aeron said. "These people aren't soldiers. They're farmers and businessmen and wrenches. They aren't going to be any help if it comes to that."

Barrow fixed Aeron with an icy stare. "You ever hear the expression, 'the chain is only as strong as its weakest link'?"

"Yes."

"We don't use chains to build walls. We just need bodies."

"You mean to arm these people?"

"No. But I expect everyone to do their job when it's time for them to do it."

With no hostility, Barrow held Aeron's challenging stare. The captain waited for Aeron's protest, but none came. Deep down, Aeron understood their plight and the necessities for survival, but he was unwilling to accept it.

Moving silently over the concrete floor, Barrow left the room like an apparition.

"Lincoln, he's going to get people killed," Aeron said.

"It's a race now," Lincoln said. "We have to adapt. Whoever adapts faster wins." Lincoln stood. "He means to save as many people as possible."

Aeron appealed to Ballard and Ducard.

Ballard adjusted the rifle strap over her shoulder. "This is what it's come to."

Ducard frowned and slid to the floor. "Yeah."

Lincoln followed Barrow into the atrium. He stopped the captain, and they whispered a conversation. Aeron watched with disapproval, reeling from the realization of their desperation's depths. He couldn't control this situation, and the reality that Barrow had already embraced was that none of them were in control anymore, not while the exos stalked the yard outside the facility. Until the sun rose, they had no choice but to prepare, wait, and hope nobody did anything stupid.

Fourteen

When Aeron came out of that room, the expectant colonists were waiting for him. They watched his every move and scrutinized his every expression. He didn't have the heart to lie to or deceive them. He couldn't shield them from the realities of this world anymore. They were innocents, but for all Aeron knew, Lumen's wrath was going to tear down their walls and take them anyway. If they were lucky, they would live long enough to be recruited into the Sentry Service for one last mission.

Lucy met him just beyond the door, Gideon at her heels. Barrow was directing Lincoln, Ballard, Ducard, and the other sentries at the back of the atrium, setting up a firing line.

Everything was happening too fast.

Lucy's eyes were fearful. "What is going on? Barrow wouldn't talk to me."

Aeron sighed. "He doesn't answer to us anymore."

Gideon pushed forward, his beady eyes blazing. "What does that mean?"

"It means he's taken control."

"And you just let him?"

"It isn't like that anymore, Gideon. We're all in this together now. Don't you get that?"

Gideon crossed his arms. "I just want the right person making the right calls. That's all."

"Are you saying I finally have your support?"

Gideon sneered. "Not exactly, but if it's between you and a guy who's liable to shoot without thinking things through, I'd take my chances with you."

"Good. Then you'll be happy to know that I agree with him."

Lucy touched his arm. "You do?"

"The plan is to fortify the building and ready for an attack that we hope will never come if we don't give them a reason to come in here."

Lucy's eyes widened. "But there's only a handful of sentries. They can't expect to hold off all of those things if they attack."

"We'll be armed too."

Lucy shook her head. "Aeron, we aren't soldiers."

"I know."

"So does that mean he isn't considering turning the power back on?" Gideon asked.

"No. The power stays off."

"But the lights would keep them away."

"On the surface, yes, but they dig underground. It would only be a matter of time."

"So we go to the roof."

"The power stays off."

Gideon threw his hands up and stormed off.

Aeron looked to Lucy, and he was terrified. She saw it, and she pulled him into her embrace.

"We won't let them get in," he said. "No matter what."

"I know."

"I love you."

She pulled away and took his face in her hands. "I know that too."

Aeron kissed her then, and it was sweet and loving but, ultimately, forced and ritualistic. When he left her and walked toward the back of the atrium to help with preparations, Lucy bridged the distance with her horrified eyes and stripped soul, which reached out for him to come back. She knew it was futile. That connection could never be severed, but it could never impose such a physical force. It could only endure across space and time, and no matter what, it would, because they'd been through so much, and it had.

Yet for each of them, there was a moment when the full measure of their desperation set in, and this one was hers.

Fifteen

When Bernie's father returned to her, she didn't like the way he looked. He was frowning a lot. Even when he smiled at her, she could tell a frown was underneath.

He picked her up in his warm, strong arms. The gun was strapped over his shoulder, and it brushed against her leg. The metal was cold, and she didn't like it.

"Are you afraid?" he asked.

She dutifully shook her head.

"Good. There's nothing to be afraid of. Everything is going to be all right."

Bernie wondered if this was what growing up felt like. She wondered if being an adult meant knowing when someone was lying. She didn't question whether she would grow up. She knew times were tough, and she knew that many people had died, though she never questioned her own mortality. She had her father and her brother and a group of soldiers to protect her. The night was going to be long, but she expected to make it to tomorrow. To Bernie, there would always be a tomorrow.

One of the sentries came over. It was the big one that she thought was kind of funny even though she couldn't say why. His smile was a lie too.

"Hey, Bern," Ducard said. "Everything going all right? You keeping an eye on your aunt?"

She gazed at him, unsure how to answer.

Ducard laughed. It was a funny laugh. It sounded like it normally would be loud, but he was having a hard time keeping it quiet.

"It's okay," he said. "I'm going to need your dad. Is that okay?"

Bernie continued to gawk at him.

"Give me a minute," Lincoln said.

"Barrow said—"

"He can wait. This is worth it. Don't you have anyone you'd like to say anything to?"

The big sentry was quiet, his eyebrows pushing together in thought. "Yeah. As a matter of fact, I do. Thanks, Lincoln. You're a good man. I'm sorry I never saw that before."

"It's all right," Lincoln said. "Now go on."

The big, funny sentry went to the old guy who walked with a limp and exchanged a few words. She couldn't hear them, but she could tell that their faces weren't lies. The old man was crying. So was the big, funny sentry. They hugged, and then Sheriff Ballard came and took the big, funny sentry away.

"You know I love you, right?" Bernie's father said to her.

"Of course, Daddy. I love you too."

His smile wasn't a lie anymore. He pulled her to his shoulder and squeezed her just enough for her to feel safe. She wrapped her arms around his neck and breathed deep his earthy scent, which wasn't a particularly pleasant aroma, but she knew it well. It smelled of home. It smelled of safety.

Then he was pushing her away, and she didn't want to leave his arms. She squeezed his neck and whimpered to let him know she just wanted another minute.

"You have to let go now, sweetheart," he said. "I love you."

"No," Bernie said. "No."

"Yes," her father said. "You have to stay with your aunt, and you have to do what she says."

He stood from her and kissed her Aunt Lucy on the cheek.

"Look out for her," he said.

"You know I will."

Shane was there. Bernie didn't understand where Shane had come from, but he also had a gun like her father.

"Remember your promise," Lincoln said to Shane.

She didn't understand. She didn't understand any of it. Why was Shane being so nice? And why was he holding her so close?

It never crossed Bernie's mind that she could die tonight, but as her father left her, she had an overwhelming feeling of sorrow she couldn't comprehend.

A sense from deep within her being told her that she would not see him again, and it manifested in tears. Her aunt pulled her close and pressed her face to her abdomen where she let Bernie cry until she fell asleep.

Sixteen

The colonists were secured in the locker room. The sentries, Lincoln, Aeron, Ballard, and Clay had formed their firing line in the atrium. At Captain Barrow's direction, they erected their armaments to kill anything that came down that hallway. They each had high-powered, rail-fired automatic rifles with magazines in reserve. At opposite ends of the firing line, Alain Ducard and Abel Livingston manned machine guns mounted on bipods. At Lincoln's suggestion, they stocked themselves with flashbang grenades, which produced such bright flashes and concussive blasts they would surely stun the exos; although, Barrow wasn't ready to give explosives to untrained colonists, so he only issued them to the sentries. To compensate, Barrow had mounted tactical flashlights to the frames of their rifles.

Once they were ready, they waited. Only the night and the silence came for them. No more exos climbed the building's facade or on the roof. The earth hadn't trembled in hours. The colonists hadn't smelled the exos' foul odor. If they hadn't known better, they might have thought it was a pleasant night. Time wore on. They settled in.

Clay yawned. "I don't get it. They know we're in here. They could come in if they want. Why aren't they?"

"They know we're armed," Lincoln said. "And they know we have light. They can wait us out. They have all the time in the world."

"Until the sun comes up."

"Then we have until sundown, and round and round we go."

"They can't be that smart."

"You're right. It's embarrassing how they've beaten us."

"Quiet," Barrow hissed. "It doesn't matter. We're here. They're there. It's their move."

Silence permeated the atrium. The men and women on the firing line stared at the front door, waiting, watching. Their breathing hitched at every creak in the old wooden frame and every breeze that brushed against the building facade. Greasy from sweat, their palms stuck to their weapon grips, and their knuckles and joints ached from stiffness.

Ballard rubbed drowsiness from her eyes. "Captain, how do you do this? Every day, all day, you just watch the wild for something that may never come."

"We don't distract ourselves with unnecessary conversation. We stay focused. And we remember that we're always a blink away from missing something that could save lives."

The firing line fell silent again. The aurora washed the atrium in the green light, and the only movement from anyone was the inspection of a magazine or amp indicator. The only sounds were the rattle of equipment and shuffling of feet.

Sibley rolled her sore neck. "Hey, Ducard. What are you going to do if we make it through this?"

"Why?" He raised an eyebrow at her. "You asking me out?"

"Sure. Let's go down to Gill's, have some drinks, and maybe you can rub this crick out of my neck while we watch the skylights from the farmlands. Real romantic stuff."

"There's something I ought to tell you," Ducard said. "Kennedy was more than my best friend."

"Oh," Sibley said and paused. "Oh!"

Barrow's whisper was a scream. "Quiet! All of you! It doesn't matter. Do you not understand the gravity of this situation?"

"They understand," Aeron said. "They're just nervous."

"Lives depend on us. Not just our lives, but the lives of the people in that locker room. They entrusted us to get them through this night. I understand you're tired, but remember that, if we fail here, it's over. If we take our eyes off of that door for even a second, it could be the opportunity they need to—"

Barrow disappeared. His rifle clattered on the floor. Somewhere, he was growling.

Everyone gaped at the exo that was ascending the wall behind them with Barrow upside down and flailing in its grip. Its powerful limbs danced over the wood and grasped the surface, climbing toward the second floor.

"Ducard, Livingston, watch the door!" Lincoln said. "Everyone else, fire!"

The rifles cracked in syncopated rhythm. Rounds skipped off of the creature's armored hide. The sentries fired in controlled bursts. The untrained colonists rocked from the recoil. Their volley accomplished nothing.

Barrow got his sidearm from its holster and did his best to still himself as the exo jerked and swung his body. Timing it just right, he pumped two rounds into its underbelly.

The creature stopped its ascent and tensed. The limb holding Barrow relaxed, and he plummeted to the floor. The exo's grip faltered. It slid and caught itself for a delicate moment. Then it too came crashing down.

Aeron leaped forward. "Barrow!"

As the hulking body hurtled to the floor, the captain rolled out of the way before it crushed him in an earth shattering impact of bony armor and razor limbs.

The air smelled of burning metal and a noxious gas-like ammonia coming from the creature's body.

With their rifles trained, the sentries established a perimeter around the exo. Sibley kicked one of its legs, but it didn't react.

Lincoln and Aeron rushed to Barrow. Gasping, the captain was sitting on the floor and gazing in awe at the creature's body.

Aeron shook Barrow's shoulders. "Are you all right?"

The captain looked at him with bewildered eyes. "You could have hit me."

"You were dead either way," Aeron said. "We had to try."

"You're welcome," Lincoln said.

Barrow searched the room. "Where did it come from?"

Above them, another exo crept down the wall from the second floor.

Lincoln pointed. "There!"

They opened fire. It raised a thick, rigid limb in front of its gnashing mandibles and started to retreat. Lincoln hit it with his tactical flashlight.

It shrieked and fell to the floor onto its back, thrashing its legs. Moving as a unit, the sentries hurried into a better position and fired into the vulnerable spot. The legs slowed and stilled.

Sibley frowned at the corpse. "They're already inside."

"How?" Aeron said.

Lincoln blinked. "The roof access door. They must have gotten it open."

"Hey," Ducard said. "We got more trouble."

"What is it?" Barrow said.

Ducard pointed toward the atrium. "Look."

The main entryway, which had been lighted by the aurora, was now darkened by exos covering the windows in their ascent up the facade. They cast shadows onto the floor and walls. An army of writhing silhouettes was making its move.

The front of the building rumbled, and then the entire wall crumbled in a bone-rattling crash. Dust rolled forward like a wave. The machine guns opened up, and their low thrum kicked inside chest cavities. Shrieks of multiple exos pierced their ears. In the haze, dark shapes dashed from wall to wall.

The machine guns rumbled the very air, stretching the fabric of reality tight.

"Open fire!" Barrow yelled.

Then a torrent from the rifles shattered it. The world pounded in a syncopated rhythm.

The atrium became a ruin of crumbled brick and splintered wood covered in the haze of battle. Several of the exos lay like open, dead hands.

Lincoln slapped a new magazine in. "The good news is the machine guns are punching through their exoskeletons. The bad news is this is probably a diversion for them to sweep down on top of us."

"How can they be so coordinated!?" Sibley asked.

The machine guns perforated the remaining walls, decimating an exo in a blaze of triumphant impacts and shockwaves. The weapons severed one of the creature's limbs, and it toppled end over end in the air and then stuck in the ground outside like a javelin.

Ducard's weapon clicked and wouldn't fire. "Dammit!"

"What is it?" Barrow asked.

"Overheated. Barrel's fried."

At the other end of the line, Abel engaged another exo at the front door with a hailstorm of bullets, and then a dark mass swept in and took him away. Still clutching his machine gun's trigger in a death grip, high-caliber rounds rained down and eviscerated Marco Tamland and Brent Helmsworth. They cried out, slumped, and went limp in their places on the line.

In shock, the others hesitated. Another black streak stole Dana Sibley. Slapping against the wall as her captor ascended, she pulled her sidearm and fired straight up. Her shots ricocheted without effect, and without interrupting its escape, one of the exo's legs curled around her throat and crushed her neck. Sibley's sidearm clattered on the concrete floor, and the exo spirited her away like a doll.

Barrow saw it all falling apart, so he triggered the fuse on three flashbang grenades and tossed them into the center of the room.

"Get down!"

He pulled Ballard to the ground, and Ducard jumped beside them. Lincoln jumped on top of his brother and covered his ears.

Everything went ringing white.

Seventeen

In the locker room, most of the colonists languished as they listened to the unfolding battle. Some of them pleaded with no one in particular. Others whispered prayers. The exos were pushing against their last line of defense, a final wall, and if it gave, there would be nothing to stop them from wiping the rest of the human race from Lumen's surface.

Gideon Ford believed there was another way. He stood at the ready for his chance to act. He waited, seemingly detached from the fear that gripped everyone else. The truth was, fear squeezed Gideon harder than anyone else. It always had, and it would never let him go.

Lucy stood with her back to the door. The dozens of colonists had become refugees, and they were all looking to her for answers. As the machine gun fire pounded, they begged her with their eyes, and she had nothing for them.

Gideon eased forward, his focus on that door. The answer to all of their problems was beyond that door, and only he had the wisdom to act. If he could make it to that door, he could save them all. It called to him. The yearning to be revered called to him. It would only take one heroic deed.

Milly touched his wrist, her old face twisted in a shrewd expression of scrutiny. "Where do you think you're going?"

He shook her off and glared at her. She challenged him with her inquisitive expression.

"Don't you worry about a thing," he said to her, and to Gideon's credit, he truly meant it.

Then the human screams started, and people descended into panic and sobs. A moment later, the flashbang grenades detonated in the atrium, and everything went silent; the colonists in the locker room froze.

In reflex, Ernest took hold of Lucy's arm and pulled her away from the door. They didn't know what the battle stopping could mean, but if their wall had fallen, if their people had failed, the exos could pound on that door at any moment.

And then what? What would they do?

Ernest's astonished eyes were full of wonder. "That was the grenades," he said. "Barrow said he would only use them as a last resort."

"Are we going to check if they're all right?" someone asked.

"They're gone," someone else said. "It's all over."

"Quiet!" Lucy hissed.

For an eternal moment, there was only silence. Only the slanting glow of the aurora moved in that room. Then they heard the cries, the exos squealing in pain, not in triumph.

Lucy heard voices, coughing and speaking. Her people were still alive; their wall still held. The knowledge allowed a breath to leave her chest, and she hadn't even known she was holding it.

This was Gideon's chance. He was going to prove he was right all along. His aged body found the capacity to run. He broke for the door.

Lucy screamed, "Gideon! No!"

He threw it open.

Eighteen

The ringing in their ears became a persistent exo scream. The disorientation from the concussive blast cleared. Their senses were returning. The first one to hit with full force was fear. It moved them before they were ready to stand, and they stumbled over the debris of a broken wall.

Screeching in pain, writhing exos littered the atrium. Limbs curling into the air, they lay on their backs in heaps of bullet-chewed and blast-shattered concrete, wood splinters, and glass shards. With little energy, they kicked to roll and get upright once more, but their motions were exhausted, as if hovering at the fringes of consciousness.

Lincoln crawled to his rifle, raised it, and checked the room. He wavered. He couldn't have hit anything in his dizzied state. Luckily, no exos were above or at the obliterated doorway. Outside, they shrieked in the wilderness. They'd pulled back, but they hadn't gone far.

He stood and shuffled into the atrium. Ballard joined him. She eyed him with a measure of concern, although it was barely perceptible in the slight tremble of her bottom lip, the glassy sheen in her eyes.

"You all right?" she asked.

"Yeah."

She drew her revolver.

Laboring for breath, Lincoln nodded. "Yeah."

Without another word, Lincoln and Ballard went to each squirming exo and ended them with all of the ceremony of hammering nails.

When the job was done, the sheriff sniffed and wiped her bloody nose. Her face was a smear of grime and crimson streaks, the paint of war.

"I think we can relax for the moment," she said.

Lincoln counted the bodies. They had killed about a quarter of the exos they'd observed, but they didn't know how many of them they hadn't counted or how many of them the battle had attracted. By contrast, they'd lost half of their firepower.

Ducard was up. He tossed his broken machine gun into rubble. Then he picked up Livingston's machine gun and blew dust from it. The amp hummed and whined. It still worked.

A fast-moving object caught Lincoln's eye. Gideon Ford was running along the south wall.

Ernest was in pursuit. "Stop him!"

Barrow and Aeron leaped into action to chase them into the utility room.

Ernest screamed, "Don't touch—"

An electrical arc blast snapped. The lights in the building surged and then dimmed. The air smelled of ozone and burned flesh.

By the time Ballard and Lincoln could react, there was already a wavering orange light in the utility room and black smoke billowing into the hallway.

Nineteen

In the utility room a gray haze obscured Ballard's and Lincoln's vision. Breathing burned their throats and chests. They called for Barrow, Aeron, and Ernest. They called for Gideon. No one answered.

In the back of the room, the battery unit was humming. Sparks erupted from it in fountains. At its base, a fire poured waves of heat and blinding light. Ballard and Lincoln shielded their eyes and found a burning body.

A hand grasped Lincoln's ankle. Captain Barrow had been blown across the room almost clear through the doorway.

He was swallowing and croaking. "We have to get back on the line."

Barrow's right arm and shoulder were charred and smoking. Pieces of shrapnel had embedded in his chest and torn through his shirt like the claws of a predator. And he was missing a boot.

Shane was at the door. He gasped.

Lincoln eyed his son. "Get Dr. Osman."

Shane nodded and ran for the locker room.

Barrow was trying to sit up. "We have to—"

Lincoln held him down. "We're all right. We have men on the line. We're getting the doctor. You're gonna be okay."

Barrow looked at him with a dazed but curious expression.

Ballard returned from a deeper part of the smoke-filled room. "I found Ernest." She grimaced. "He's dead."

Her eyes burned with tears.

"And Lincoln, I found—"

"I know."

Dr. Osman arrived with his bag and kneeled beside Barrow. He visually inspected the captain's injuries and checked his vital signs. After performing his assessment, he unzipped his bag and prepared a syringe filled with precious morphine, and he eyed Lincoln as he administered it.

With the drug given, Osman pulled Lincoln into the hallway. The others were pouring out of the locker room and filling the atrium. Lucy and Ellis gazed at Lincoln with expectation. He couldn't face them right now.

"He's dying," the doctor whispered. "I gave him morphine for the pain, but there's nothing I can do for him. My guess is the shock has destroyed his organs as the current traveled through his chest. He won't last long."

Lincoln took a deep breath. "Can we move him?"

Osman pushed his glasses up on his nose and wiped sweat from his brow. "It might kill him."

"You said he's dying."

Osman's eyes narrowed. "Lincoln, there's no need for him to suffer."

After a long moment, Lincoln nodded his understanding. He looked to Ballard, who was waiting in the doorway.

"Do it," Lincoln said.

She unholstered her pistol. Cognizant of the snapping flames and the noxious air, she entered the utility room solemnly. She stood beside the captain and aimed her weapon.

Barrow pushed it aside. "Get that thing away from me."

Lincoln watched from the doorway. "You're suffering. Let us help you."

Barrow laughed, and even as he coughed blood into his hand, he laughed.

"I'm not the one who needs help. You are." Barrow groaned as he tried to stand.

"Don't," Ballard said.

He glared at her. "Help me up."

She threw his good arm over her shoulder and helped him get to his feet.

Barrow wavered and breathed deeply. "Use me," he gasped. "If I'm going to die, use me. Make my death mean something."

"Are you sure?" Lincoln asked.

"Remember what I said about building walls?"

"You just need bodies."

"Yes." He leaned on Ballard. "Now help me get out of here before we all burn to death."

Lincoln and Ballard helped Barrow into the dim hallway where they found everyone who was left gazing at them with expectation.

Twenty

As Ballard carried the seething and groaning Captain Barrow into the atrium, Lincoln approached Clay and Ellis. Pale and taut, their expressions made it apparent that they already knew what Lincoln was going to tell them. They already knew their worst fears had materialized, but it was a reality to which they were unwilling to surrender. They stood in anticipation as if hanging onto the edge of a cliff, waiting for words to sap their remaining strength and send them into the pull of gravity.

Lincoln couldn't look at them. Despite his disdain for Clay, his friendship with Ellis, the heavy weight of the grief they'd already felt, none of it mattered. Loss was loss.

"They..." Lincoln closed his eyes. "I'm sorry."

Ellis drew a deep breath and nodded his understanding. He turned away to deal with his sadness in as much privacy as he could find.

Clay's stare persisted. "No." His denial was intonated like a question. "No."

"Yes. I'm sorry."

"No." Clay backed away, paced back and forth. "No."

"We tried. But your father wouldn't—"

Clay shot a glare at Lincoln and fixed it like hooks burrowing into skin. "Shut up."

Lincoln sighed in frustration. There was nothing he could do. Clay glared hard at him and then he stormed off.

Even as he was aware that everyone was watching him, Lincoln wallowed in loneliness. His brother was gone, and he struggled to comprehend the meaning of it. A piece of himself had been sucked into a void. His big brother was gone. It didn't matter that they'd grown apart in adulthood. Being a brother to an older, wiser man had been part of Lincoln's identity. He'd always known Aeron would be there for him regardless of everything else. Now that was gone. His big brother was gone.

Then there was Lucy. Her face was tight, her breathing unsteady. She looked at him hard, a gaze that resembled anger more than despair, and it frightened him.

"Was it them? Or is he in there?" She nodded at the utility room.

"He's in there."

Lucy moved to rush into the fire, but Lincoln caught her, his strong arms wrapping around her waist.

"Let me go, Lincoln."

"He's gone."

"Let me go!"

"He's gone!"

She relented, and Lincoln pulled her into an embrace. She trembled and sobbed.

"He's gone. I'm sorry. He's gone. I'm sorry." He whispered it to her over and over.

Together, they grieved. Everyone respected it and gave them the space they deserved.

Ballard eased Barrow onto the firing line. The captain stretched across his body and tried to retrieve his sidearm from the holster on his thigh. He couldn't reach it, so Ballard handed it to him. He gripped it, the weapon bringing him a sense of security. He clutched it to his chest like a beloved ornament. It belonged in his hand, and he breathed, at ease for the first time in hours.

Ducard laid down his machine gun and stood.

Barrow grabbed his arm. "Sentry." His pain cracked the facade of his projected strength. "Hold your position."

Ducard gazed down at his captain, a man whose animus once burned in his eyes now looked innocent in his frailty.

"There's gonna be a time for dying." Ducard breathed. "But it ain't right now."

The captain nodded and let go of his lieutenant. Ducard marched across the atrium and wrapped his arms around Ellis. The old scientist struggled, but Ducard's powerful grip forced him into stillness.

Ellis relented, collapsing in Ducard's arms, and a sob cracked his lips.

"It's okay," Ducard whispered into his ear. "It's okay."

Everyone watched in astonishment as Ducard showed his friend compassion, keeping him from falling to his knees so he wouldn't have to weep alone.

"We don't have time for this," Barrow said.

"We make time for this," Ballard said.

"My clock is ticking, Reggie."

Although his face didn't change, the uncertainty in his eyes frightened her.

An exo tunneled beneath the floor and rumbled the whole structure. The dread of the facility's imminent collapse returned.

Lucy pulled away from Lincoln's embrace. She watched a man bred for combat hold his grieving friend. Ducard and Ellis could use each other until the dying of the night. She lamented her inability to give them that. Aeron was gone. Whether she liked it or not, she was their leader now, and she had get them through this.

"We have to go," she said.

Lincoln rubbed his exhausted, grief-stricken face. He looked at Barrow, who coughed up more blood, and returned to Lucy's expectant gaze.

"I have an idea," he said.

Lumen help him. He had an idea.

Twenty-One

The billowing smoke roiled from the utility room and spiraled to the atrium ceiling where it gathered into an inverted pool of darkness. The burning odor already stifled their lungs, and it wouldn't be long before the noxious fumes started to suffocate them. Facing the exposure of the cold night, the heat already warmed their backs like a friendly hand leaning in for a push.

"I don't understand." Bernie trembled with the flood of emotions, frustration, fear, even anger. "I don't understand why it has to be you."

Lincoln gazed into his daughter's beautiful eyes. "Because I can make it."

Her innocent face twisted in exasperated rage that might have otherwise been endearing if not for the circumstances.

"Make someone else go," she pleaded.

He pulled her to his chest, and her small fists beat against his shoulders.

"Make someone else go, Daddy!"

He stroked her hair and breathed in her pure scent. "I never told you, but you look like your mother. You asked me what she was like, but you're such a reflection of her. Remember that."

Bernie's sobs grew. In her childish innocence, she never questioned that she would live, but she always feared, every time her father left her, it would be the last time she'd see him. She could tell from the way he was acting he thought it too.

Lincoln squeezed her into his memory and then pushed her into Lucy's arms. The girl clawed at her father's arms, but he forced her away, and Lucy took her, whispering and hushing in soothing tones that only mothers, the good ones, can make.

Bernie would be okay.

He moved on to Shane. Holding Sera, the boy drew a deep breath and raised his chin. He was not yet a man, but he had the stubborn mind of one, and the fierce capacity to love. Lincoln thought everything they'd been through had changed Shane, but no, his son had always been this way, strong, compassionate, caring, excess zeal that would no doubt become overbearance if he ever had the opportunity to hold something as Lincoln had held him.

"And you," Lincoln said. "I did my best, but you turned out like me anyway. Sorry about that."

The father and son shared a smirk, and it might have been the first thing they'd shared in as long as either of them could remember. Lincoln embraced him and Sera. He kissed her on the cheek.

"Be good," he said to his son. "Be better than me. Take care of your sister."

Shane's face contorted in emotional anguish, and tears flowed from his eyes. "Okay, Dad."

For a moment, Shane's shame showed through, and he feared his father would tell him to stop crying. Instead, Lincoln pressed his hand to his son's cheek, and his fingertips slid away like the wind.

Lincoln moved on to Reggie. They regarded each other across a short distance that felt like an impossible expanse.

"Why don't I take this one?" she said.

Lincoln shook his head. "These are your people." He squeezed her forearm. "Don't you try and put them off on me. You gotta get them to safety."

She hugged him fiercely. "Be careful."

"I think that ship has sailed."

They pulled apart, and she nodded. "Then come back," she said.

"I will."

"You better."

Captain Barrow was leaning against the rubble of the wall that used to be the front doorway. His pallid, moist skin resembled melting wax, and his chest was rising and falling in great gasps.

"Are you ready?" Lincoln asked.

Barrow licked his dry, cracked lips and nodded. They had to hurry. Barrow didn't have much time.

Lincoln slung Barrow's good arm over his shoulder and helped him to the opening.

"Good luck," Reggie said.

"You too," Lincoln said as they stood before the dimly lit yard. There was no sign of the exos, but they were no doubt watching, waiting.

Lincoln drew a deep, settling breath. "I'm sorry about this."

"Don't be," Barrow said. "I am your shield, and you are using me as I was intended."

He looked Lincoln in the eye, and it struck Lincoln how Barrow's irises already appeared faded and gray, as if they were a gauge of his life force and most of it had already drained.

"Just be sure and survive," Barrow said. "I don't like partial victories."

"You might have to get over it."

"I guess I'll take what I can get."

The men crossed the threshold of the broken wall and stepped onto the concrete landing outside. Barrow stopped and breathed, collecting himself. He looked aged and weary, and every movement caused him immense pain. He rose and straightened, his face twisting in agony held back by determination.

Their feet set down on soft earth, and Barrow pulled Lincoln with surprising force.

"Move!"

They ran east along the exterior wall. Lincoln monitored Barrow for failing strength, but the captain's pace quickened. They were almost to the building's corner before they felt the rumbling in the deep.

The men broke beyond the end of the building and kept running for the tree line. Their legs pumped, and they rocked and reeled with adrenaline-fueled energy.

It wasn't long before Barrow began to feel heavier to Lincoln, and he began to wheeze and fade. Before they could reach the trees, Barrow's legs gave, and he crumpled.

He lay on his back, gasping, hand clutching his chest. "Leave me."

Lincoln reached for him. "Get up."

The sentry fought him weakly. "Get out of here."

"On your feet."

"Go!" Barrow raised his weapon at Lincoln. His eyes surged with life again. Lincoln knew he wouldn't pull the trigger. There was no threat in him, only adamance.

The shaking in the earth grew as the exos honed in on their position.

Screams and cries came from the front of the building as the colonists ran for their lives. Barrow and Lincoln saw them cross the yard. At the front, Ducard tossed several flashbang grenades into the tree line, and flashlights and lamps illuminated among the people as they charged.

"Lincoln," Barrow pleaded. "Go."

"Thank you."

Lincoln ran.

Twenty-Two

Shane fled across the open yard, remembering to help the others and ensure they kept moving. He helped a mother carrying her daughter. He helped a middle-aged man with a limp. He helped a little boy who didn't seem to have anyone.

He remembered his promise to take care of Bernie, and she was right with him. His fist balled the back of her shirt, and she clutched the waistband of his pants. Sera held her other hand.

He glanced to the east and saw Barrow fall, saw his father hesitate. The earth sprayed into the air as exos approached.

The perimeter lights flickered and failed, plunging their world into darkness.

By the grace of the aurora's haze, he watched his father run back toward the building, and then slide to a halt when one of the exos breached the surface and cut him off.

The last of the colonists passed Shane, Sera, and Bernie.

"Go with Sera," he said to his sister.

Sera's eyes electrified. "What?"

Bernie sputtered. "But—"

"Bern, go!"

He cast off his sister's grip and pushed her into Sera's arms. "Go!"

Sera's horrified face faded as she clutched Bernie and ran with her into the trees to follow the others, disappearing into the thick.

Shane ran with everything he had.

Twenty-Three

The exo's hulking form rose into the air with all of its majestic strength and power. It swelled in the open air. Its jaws dripped viscous white saliva and snapped as if it were already devouring him.

Though futile, Lincoln raised his rifle. Bullets would do him no good, and as if the creature knew, it snorted, which sounded almost like laughter. Lincoln's hand slid down his weapon's barrel and clicked on the tactical flashlight. The creature squealed and recoiled. Enraged, it shook its head and careened in disorientation. Then it raised a limb to block its eyes and marched forward, determined.

It bore down on him, advancing a step at a time like a ticking clock. The trembling in the earth intensified. The others were right beneath him and all around him, closing on him like a hand.

The exo in front of him raised its tail into the air, readying to strike, posing like a dancer prepared for the music to begin.

Automatic gunfire rattled the night.

The exo shrieked and canted to the side. It scurried away and tried to dive into the earth, but more automatic gunfire tore into its soft spot and scattered its black innards. Its body seized, and it crumpled, bony joints knocking like a pile of rocks, and was still.

Glowing like a spiritual form, Shane stood before his father. He was trembling. The lamp clipped onto his belt illuminated the area around them, keeping the creatures on the surface at bay.

Lincoln gaped at him in amazement. "What are you doing?"

Gasping, Shane approached with wild eyes. "I couldn't do nothing."

Behind Lincoln, Barrow lay motionless, mercifully dead, but the exos hadn't taken him. The earth surged beneath Shane and his father.

"Come on," Lincoln said. "We have to move."

Shane helped his father up, and they broke for the burning building. The earth knocked and crashed as the exos pursued them like a chain of detonating dynamite.

At the ladder to the roof, Lincoln helped Shane get started climbing, and when there was room, he leaped and pulled himself up with all of his might.

The earth opened, and two exos emerged.

Lincoln planted a foot on the bottom rung. "Keep going!"

His voice failed in the torrent of crashing stone and shredding earth. The exos chittered on the surface and set legs against the wall, beginning to scale the facade in chase.

Heaving oxygen and wired with adrenaline, Lincoln and Shane pulled themselves onto the roof, but the exos were already gripping the edge.

Lincoln clutched his rifle. "We've got one chance, Shane. When they get to the top, we should have a shot."

Shane was staring back at his father in fear like the child he was.

"Okay?" Lincoln squeezed Shane's shoulder. "I can't do this myself."

Shane blinked and nodded. "Okay."

Father and the son readied their weapons. The exos pulled themselves up, glaring with their bulbous onyx eyes. When they reached the top, their long legs and arched bodies gave Lincoln and Shane a line of sight to their abdomens.

The rifles cracked and sizzled like electrical whips. Rounds sparked on the exos' armored legs, but in the hailstorm of bullets, some of them struck true, punching through the leathery bellies, which popped and expelled the black life force all over the rooftop.

The exos squelched. One of them curled into a ball, rolled onto its back, and opened its long limbs in the release of dying. The other stumbled and fell off of the edge, hurtling to the ground and impacting with a solid thud.

The father and son looked at each other's shocked, amazed faces and cried out in celebration.

Shane continued to leap, while Lincoln scanned their surroundings.

"It's not over," he said. "We aren't safe." He kneeled and pressed his palm to the rooftop. It was hot. He ran to the edge. The yard was illuminated in an orange glow. The blaze shattered windows and cast enough light to keep the exos at bay, but it wouldn't be long before it consumed the building.

Smoke rose in wispy columns around them. It thickened until it burned their eyes and squeezed their chests.

Shane coughed on the smoke. "What now, Dad?"

Lincoln looked to his son with reverence.

"What now?"

Lincoln embraced him. "Same as before. I'll go down and lead them away. You run for the others."

"No."

"Shane, it's the only way one of us makes it."

"If I leave you now, what was the point of coming back for you?"

"We can't stay up here."

The building trembled. The rooftop cracked like jagged lines on an eggshell.

They ran to the side of the building and looked over the edge. The earth around the perimeter was churning.

"They're going to bring the building down," Lincoln said.

The shaking intensified, and the building started to crumble. Hundreds of fractures formed on the outer face, and whole cinderblocks tumbled to the ground. The rooftop's flat plane tilted, tossing and shattering solar panels and electrical equipment. Asphalt dust exploded into the air. Smoke slithered through volcanic vents.

Lincoln held out his hand. "Come here!"

Shane ran to his father and wrapped his arms around his chest.

"Hold on!"

Lincoln gripped the edge of the building. A great rift opened in the roof, and flames licked the open air. The rooftop inclined until Lincoln was more holding on than standing. Their boots scuffed the hard asphalt, frantically trying to find purchase.

The shaking reached a crescendo, and the building's exterior walls folded. Lincoln held on as long as he could. The ground beneath the structure caved, and the building submerged.

Lincoln and Shane dangled in a world of dirty gray and black air. Then his hold gave, and they slid toward an abyss of flames.

Twenty-Four

In the woods, the exos pierced the night with their rage screams and murder lust. All around the colonists, the creatures shook tree limbs like prisoners. They ripped down whole trees. Nothing stood in their relentless pursuit. While lamps and flashlights held surface creatures at bay, the exos tore the earth asunder, tunneling beneath, thundering with inevitability.

At the line of the light's farthest reach, Ducard ushered his people forward. The lamps attached to every fifth colonist cast a haunting blue glow in the trees, and shadows danced among them like a wild disco ghost party.

Ducard hoisted his machine gun barrel into the air. "Keep moving!" He slapped shoulders and backs, urging his colonists onward. He radiated strength where weakness and fear would have consumed them. With or without their last sentry, they would have run for their lives, but with him, they found the resolve to move together and combine all of their lamps and flashlights, creating a singular torch of luminance.

Eyes wide and wired, Lucy pointed into the treetop behind Ducard. "Look out!"

The sentry wheeled, and with legs splayed like a star of darkness, an exo descended upon him.

Ducard fired with one hand, spraying bullets into the heavens. The exo balled and slammed into the ground, tumbling and coming to a rest at his feet. Chest heaving, he resisted the urge to kick it.

Lucy grabbed his arm and pulled him forward. "Come on."

Wanting something more, a deeper vengeance perhaps, Ducard reluctantly pulled away from the creature and followed the hazy, slotted orb of colonial light. He dashed through the shrouded trees, sensing the exos right behind him, shifting through the limbs and branches like wind. He resisted the urge to fire blindly into the darkness.

The colonists burst into the open field. They poured forth like a single entity of light, an ethereal being entering a new plane of existence. The way forward was clear. The surface exos stopped at the tree line, but the ground jumped and rolled as the others continued their pursuit.

Behind them, the blaze illuminated the sky in a false dawn.

The last to break free from the woods, Ducard spun around, firing his machine gun into the trees, punching holes in bark and bone. As the last sentry, he would fight to his death.

"I..."

He would kill these creatures to give his people a chance.

"...am..."

His weapon flashed and bucked, and he thought of Kennedy, who had died so the others could live.

"...the shield!"

Everything was a circle, and it was his turn to honor the dead.

The machine gun roared. Alight with singed edges, tree trunk shrapnel exploded into the night. Exos shielded themselves in vain as Ducard's rounds pierced their armor. They had dared to cross him, and now he would show them the darkness in his light.

He felt it; the collective spirit of his fallen brothers imbued him with their strength, and facing the exo torrent, he punched through their advances. They broke upon him like water against a wall.

However, his strength was finite, his ammunition limited. The machine gun lit up the dark no more. Only steam rose from its glowing orange barrel.

Heaving for breath, Ducard let his weapon fall to the ground. It rattled and clanked like a bundle of scrap metal.

Enough. He had done enough. He had cleared his shame, earned back his pride.

He fell to his knees and waited. Soon, they would come. He felt it in the prickles on his skin, a primal sense telling him to flee, but there was nowhere for him to go.

He pitched forward and grasped the dirt. He wanted to feel the earth stir, to know they were coming, to sense the end, and fight it to his very last. But the great trembling beneath him quieted and calmed. In a bizarre act of desperation he couldn't understand, his fingers dug into the ground as if to seek them out.

Across the field, a scream pierced the night.

Most of the colonists were on a course toward the wall. No, that wasn't right. He saw the shapes of exos on the surface. They were herding his people, backing them into a corner from which there would be no escape, no more fleeing.

To the left, an orb of light had separated from the main group and broke for the industrial district. Ducard discerned four humans, and they were standing still in the field.

His work was not yet finished. He slung the machine gun over his shoulder, drew his sidearm, and ran for them.

As he neared, the ground woke, shuddering, a warning to stay away.

Not a chance in hell.

Twenty-Five

Dani raced across the field alone. She knew she was going to die this time. On the night she had run from these creatures through the wild all the way from the Field of the First Families to the sanctuary of Vale, it had surely been sheer luck. So it was with a measure of satisfaction that, when she looked over her shoulder and saw the large glow of the remaining colonists moving away from her, she considered that, because she wasn't going to make it, maybe they would. And somewhere in all of those panicked people was James.

Her James. She'd lost him again. This time, she was the one who was all alone.

She pumped her arms and legs, tearing through that field. Ahead, in the gloom, a fleeing form emerged. Something in the darkness must have heard her silent pleas, because she was no longer alone.

Milly drove her aged body to its limit. Dani recognized it in the way she favored one of her legs and in her hunched, exhausted posture.

"Milly!" Dani called, a note of relief audible in her voice. "Milly, it's me. It's Dani."

The old woman turned, her face haggard and white. She gasped for air. "They're right behind us, dear! Keep running!"

Dani caught her and wrapped her arms around the woman's frail figure.

Milly pushed her away.

Behind them, with the backdrop of the colonists' light, the hulking forms of the creatures in silhouette rocked to and fro, lumbering in relentless pursuit.

"I don't think we can outrun them!" Dani said.

Milly grabbed the girl's shirt. "You don't have to outrun them." She pushed Dani forward. "Just me."

Dani's face tightened in horror. They weren't meant to survive together, but Dani couldn't leave her.

Between their terrified gasps, a voice called after them. The trembling below intensified, the exos closing in.

In front of the exos' wavering silhouettes, a human form emerged. Dr. Osman entered their light. "We have to keep going!"

"Leave me," Milly gasped.

A look of heartbreak crossed Osman's face. "No, we don't give up on ourselves. We don't give up on each other."

Wincing, Milly nodded. "You're too stubborn, Terrance. Let's go if we're going to go."

They pushed on across the field. The persistent quake ceased growing, but it remained, the exos nipping at their heels. They hit a stride where the pain and exhaustion grew no more. In that equilibrium, hope emerged, and the light of their lamp touched the concrete walls of the industrial district. Under the green aurora, rooftops glowed with a skyline of salvation.

"We're almost there," Osman said. "I can see it."

"Stop!" a voice called from behind them.

Another sprinting figure emerged from the darkness. It was not as tall as Dr. Osman, but it was broader, more solid, stronger.

James grasped Dani's arm. "Stop. I mean it. Stop!"

She struggled against him. They were so close. She could see the end of the field and the gravel road, but his powerful embrace enclosed her. He lifted her into the air and shushed into her ear. She relented. She was still in his arms.

Osman and Milly were leaving the light, and she wanted to run to them to keep them in its range, but James wasn't going to let her.

"Stay still," James whispered

In the light, the exos on the surface couldn't reach them. If they made no sound, the exos under the ground couldn't locate them.

The doctor turned back and saw the young couple, and he realized what James was doing. He stopped and pulled Milly close. They suppressed every cry of terror. They willed their legs to stop shaking, waiting for the tide of creatures to pass James and Dani. They waited to be spared or taken.

Across the field, the other fleeing colonists were screaming and continuing to sprint toward the wall. The black alien shapes of the exos danced in the blue lamplight. Somewhere not so deep down, Dani hoped the creatures would go after the others. In the face of their terror, they were so quiet that she thought they deserved to be rewarded.

For a moment, the earth stilled. The darkness receded, ceasing the blow of its frigid breath across the backs of their necks.

Gunshots rang out across the night. Muzzle flashes illuminated the exo silhouettes in syncopated rhythm. The creatures ceased their slow march and turned toward the last of Vale's guardians. Lieutenant Alain Ducard was engaging them.

For a moment, they thought they would be spared. For a moment, they faced a future where they might escape this horror. However, when Osman and Milly took steps toward the industrial district, the shaking in the ground returned with such ferocity they almost tumbled off of their feet. James squeezed Dani, and she understood to be still and silent as the earth opened and first took Dr. Osman, then Milly. In an instant, with the slightest mistake, the two of them were gone, erased from Lumen's surface, leaving only depressions in the dirt.

James and Dani held each other as the earth quaked around them. They dared not move even as the shaking diminished, even as Ducard fired his weapon and stomped away into the darkness, even as they found themselves alone, trembling in the cold night under a hazy aurora that had turned red without them noticing.

Twenty-Six

Every time the fleeing colonists ran toward the industrial district, an exo surfaced, splayed its massive limbs, and hissed, forcing them in a different direction. With a cluster of lamps thrust forward, Ballard tried to put them on a path to safety, but the exos had other plans. In spite of the strongest light the humans could muster, the creatures held their ground. Ballard had to keep her people moving, so she had to continually alter their route and face the realization that they were being herded toward Vale's perimeter.

At the wall, their road ended.

Ballard cut north, and an exo breached the surface. Gravel exploded into her face and rattled on the lamp cluster. She turned south. A creature leaped from the darkness and thundered when it landed. She slid to a stop within the exo's striking distance, but it seemed content simply blocking her route of escape. Scuffling backward, she got to her feet and joined the other colonists against the perimeter wall. Exos closed in from all directions. Several of them dangled from the top of the wall, descending like hands of dark gods. They encroached on the light, squeezing it, snuffing it out.

Ballard thrust her lamp cluster at them. They recoiled but continued their slow, inevitable advance.

It was over. They had nowhere else to go. Built to keep the wild out of Vale, the wall was now their prison, and the new wardens were coming to deliver their death sentences.

Ballard closed her eyes. She thought about Lincoln. She hoped he had made it, and if not, she hoped that some part of them would find each other again in whatever awaited beyond the darkness, for in spite of everything, she believed there was more to existence.

Lucy squeezed her shoulder. "You have any shots left?"

"Yes. One."

Lucy extended a hand in request for the lamp cluster. With grave concern, Ballard passed it to her.

"What are you doing?" Ballard said.

"This."

Lucy reeled back and pitched the lamps at the exos that were encroaching from the north. They snatched the cluster from the air and held it up like a trophy.

"Shoot!" Lucy said.

Ballard cracked a smile. She raised her revolver. She steadied. She fired.

That final round cracked out of the barrel and punched a hole in the lamps, which sizzled, sparked, and exploded. The chemicals in the lamps ignited like napalm, engulfing several of the creatures in a liquid flow like lava. Blazing, those exos screamed and raced through their ranks, setting alight others in their force. The fire spread. Its light grew. Through flame, a path emerged.

"Go!" Lucy screamed.

Ballard broke into a sprint and turned to ensure the others followed right when something thudded in the grass to her left. It took her an instant to discern what it was.

"Everyone, get down!" She dove into the gravel. The rest of the colonists followed her lead.

Ducard's flashbang grenade erupted in brilliant, concussive light. Ballard wasted no time getting her people to their feet. Ducard fought his way through the exo ranks that were still standing. The creatures facing him down, he used his machine gun to parry their attacks, expose their bellies, and fire his sidearm into their weak spots. He ran through the field of squirming and burning exos, his brutality rivaling theirs. Ducard batted them away like lesser beings. He ended any creature standing between him and his people. Ducard's brilliant advance never slowed as he dodged exos that attempted to pounce on him and killed the ones he needed to.

Finally, drenched in the exos' black blood, he stood before them. His people gaped.

"Let's go!" he said.

Ballard led them north through the field of patchy flames. The heat cooked their skin and singed their hair, but they pressed through it, shielding themselves as best as they could. A shrieking, burning exo crossed their path and disappeared into the smoke. Another leaped from the wall and slammed into the ground, shooting sparks in swirling fountains into the air. Ducard charged, shoved his machine gun's frame into the creature's jaws, and fired his last rounds into its abdomen, rolling its dead body away. Finally, they found a drain.

"In here!" Ballard called.

As the colonists funneled into the wall interior, the exos changed their tactics. Instead of boxing the colonists in, they started picking people off, snatching them from the arms of loved ones and carrying them into the dirty night air. Ballard and Ducard waited at the opening, raising lamps into the air, but even combined with the ambient firelight, it wasn't enough to ward off the rabid creatures. The trickling loss of human life continued.

With the final colonists in the tunnel, Ballard and Ducard ducked inside.

A flaming exo charged from the smoke and grasped the end of the pipe. Its powerful limbs beat upon the concrete, and dust fell from the ceiling. It wrestled and tore. Cracks formed, but the structure held. It screamed into the pipe, its mandibles gnashing even as it succumbed to the fire and fell into stillness, a burning ball of bone.

Once inside, Lucy yelled for her people's attention, but the colonists split directions.

"No!" Lucy shouted. "Stay together!"

The walls trembled with enraged exos trying to break in.

"It's okay," Ballard said. "I'll go north. You go south. Meet in the marketplace at first light."

Lucy reluctantly agreed and waited for Ballard to head down her tunnel before following her own group.

The colonists knew dawn broke when their world stopped shaking.

CHAPTER 11
DOMINION

One

Wispy smoke columns drifted toward a bruised sky. The earth smoldered. Lumen's sun breached the horizon and cast the treetops in golden light.

Dawn.

A coughing fit gripped Shane's body, and he doubled over onto the dirt. When the sentry headquarters building had collapsed, the fiery rift had filled in with the loosened soil, snuffing out the flames.

Lincoln wheezed on the filthy air. "Guess we're lucky."

Shane spat gray mucous onto the ashen ground. "How do you figure?"

"If they hadn't collapsed the building and smothered the fire, we would have burned to death."

"Sera's always asking me where I get my cheerfulness." Shane lay on the inclined rooftop, and his laugh turned into another coughing fit.

"What's funny?"

"I used to get mad when she told me how much like you I was. But here we are."

"Here we are."

Lincoln climbed the incline to the edge of the collapsed structure. He looked out over the yard, squinting into the early dawn light, and found the place they had left Captain Barrow's body. There was only a depression now, loose dirt filling the void of a sinkhole.

Shane joined his father. "Do you think anyone else made it?"

"They made it."

"How do you know?"

A breeze blew across the wreckage and left fresh air in its wake, sparing them from the smoke if only for a moment.

"Because when they took your grandfather, I felt it. When they took your mom, I felt that too." Lincoln grasped his son's shoulder and gazed into his eyes. "What do you feel about Sera?"

Shane searched himself, whatever part of his being that had bonded with her, and felt that the connection had not been severed. That was enough.

"She's alive," he said.

Expecting this would please his father, Shane appealed to him with eyes of boyish vigor, gleaming like jewels in a blackened face, but Lincoln's frown persisted, gazing into the expiring darkness.

"We should get going," Shane said.

Lincoln gazed at his son's blackened face, and then he embraced him. "We can take a minute."

They stood there on top of the ruins of the sentry headquarters, smoke rising around them, their whole world ended, and they held each other up.

"Okay," Lincoln said.

They slid down the leaning building exterior onto the ground. Lincoln tested it with the heel of his charred boot. He reached up to receive Shane.

As they crossed the yard into the dark woods, Shane's resolve faltered.

"Dad?"

"What is it?"

"What if we're wrong?"

Lincoln paused. Nothing about his stone expression changed except for his pallid, thin lips, which withdrew between his teeth.

With no weight, he put his hand on the boy's back. "Keep moving."

Two

Forging south within the wall, Lucy, Ducard, Elena, Sera, Bernie, Mel, and Gabe periodically encountered a shaft and looked up to find a grated drain allowing checkered aurora light through. The space between each opening became their only measurement for time and distance. Hours passed, and they trudged on and on. The whole time, their only view through those wrought iron grates was the red, hazy aurora.

Fighting despair, Lucy kept them moving. She held up a lamp like a torch, penetrating the veil of night ahead.

Sera carrying Bernie and Ducard hauling Mel, they marched in silence. Having escaped the immediacy of the threat, they all reeled from the emotional aftermath. So few of them were left, and because the survivors had split, they couldn't be sure who was still alive.

Lucy, though, never faltered. As their emotions threatened to steal their hearts, she was their beacon of strength. Even as exhaustion set into their bones, she pulled them onward. Seeing her unfazed charged them in a way that kept them moving. She was the only reason they didn't despair in the darkness. She was their hope for another day and their faith that their loved ones still lived.

They reached a point of equilibrium where, at least for a time, their wells of mourning ran dry, and in the darkness, they soldiered on.

"I'm sorry about Captain Barrow," Sera said to Ducard. "He seemed like a good man."

"No, he wasn't. But he did some good. I hope that was enough for him."

After hours of walking, they had passed so many grates that nobody was looking up anymore. Dazed, they moved until forward momentum wasn't even a thought; their bodies simply carried on regardless of will. Consciousness retreated into a void beneath a protective surface where it could rest until it was needed.

Lucy stopped in one of the intersections. Blinking, she pointed toward the sky. "It's tomorrow. We made it."

The aurora had vanished and been replaced by a purple and reddish sky, as if, with enough sacrifice paid, daylight had seeped from their loss.

"We need to go a little farther, just to be sure."

Lucy led them until sunlight poured through the grates above. She slid down into the next junction and splashed into a shallow pool of rainwater. She gazed through the pipe that led to open daylight. Instead of feeling like sanctuary lay ahead, she felt only growing dread because she knew Lumen continued to turn and that the sun was burning across the sky toward the horizon.

Laboring for breath, Lucy motioned with a weak hand. "This way."

They exited the pipe into morning. The light burned their eyes. The icy air sprouted thorns in their lungs. A stinging breeze clawed their faces.

And they loved every second of it.

Ducard recognized where they were. There was something about the way the wall curved and the distance between the wall and the wild. He squinted toward town, and the distance over the harvested farmland seemed right.

The sentry breathed a pleasant sigh. "Thank you, Kennedy."

The others gaped at him.

He motioned with the tilt of his head and hiked up the kid on his hip. "Come on."

With their boots crunching the frosted grass, they followed him along the base of the wall to a staircase that led to the upper walkway. There, they found the southern-most lookout post for the sentries, and Ducard uncovered a rifle and a cache of ammunition that had been stashed away under a heavy brown blanket. He brandished it with a grin.

"I don't understand," Lucy said. "Why hide a rifle? You all were issued weapons."

Ducard inspected the gun. "We made some changes to this one. Bored holes into her barrel and amped her down some. She might not punch like the others, but this baby's quiet as a whisper. It was a game Kennedy liked to play. Target practice, basically. But really, the game was Kennedy showing everyone up. He could be real cocky sometimes."

"Didn't you have a firing range in the headquarters?"

"Yeah."

"So why didn't you use it?"

He tilted his head, thinking. "Too many rules."

She nodded. "Let's get back to town. The others might already be there."

Lucy led the way down the stairs. With the girls asleep in their arms, Sera and Ducard stayed at the top of the wall, gazing over the farmland. The fires at the center of Vale had burned out, and despite the missing bell tower, its skyline looked almost normal at this distance.

"I'm worried about her," Sera said.

"Luce?" Ducard said. "She's tough as nails. She'll be all right."

"She lost her husband. And we don't know about Lincoln or...or Shane. She's acting like she's unaffected, but she's hurt."

"How do you know?"

"She has to be." The young girl eyed the sentry. "We need her."

With Bernie squirming, Sera stepped down the stairs into the harvested farmland, leaving Ducard to ponder by himself on the wall, a state to which he'd been trained for and grown accustomed to years ago.

The girl in his arms stirred. "Hi," he said. "Look who's awake. Think you're up for a walk?"

Mel laid her head back on his shoulder.

He sighed. "That's okay. Go on back to sleep."

As Lucy drew farther away, he grew more anxious because Sera had planted a worrying thought in his mind. Sera was right. They needed Lucy to get through this. She was smart and strong, and more than anything, they could trust her.

Ducard hurried after them. With his undying loyalty, he would be there for Lucy. He would protect her. He would die for her if it came to it.

After everything, he believed she was more important than he was. Her life mattered more. She wielded more power and influence over the surviving colonists. If anyone had a chance of getting their people to safety, it was Lucy.

She was their warden, and that's what wardens did.

Three

Seated at the edge of the farmlands' train station platform, Ellis looked north at the dormant pillar on the mountain range. The cold wind tore across his face, but he didn't care.

It was all over. They weren't going to get the Dawn flowing again. The planet's core would slow its churning, and the electromagnetic field that protected Lumen from its star's radiation would fail. The only uncertainty was how long they would survive and whether it would be the exos or natural forces that took them. They were one and the same anyway.

Boots scuffed behind him. "I said I wanted to be alone," Ellis said over his shoulder.

Clay sat on the platform edge beside him, chewing on a blade of grass. "Sorry, friend. That's not a luxury anyone gets anymore."

Ellis leered. "Oh. You. What do you want?"

"A fistful of nod and the opportunity to use it, but I don't think that's coming anytime soon."

"No, I meant, why are you here?"

"I know."

Clay went on chewing and staring at the pillar. Ellis couldn't remember ever wanting to hit anyone before, but he wanted to drive his fist into Clay's throat. He wasn't just a classic asshole. He was an exceptional one. Why did someone like him get to live while Ernest didn't? It wasn't right.

Clay stood. "Time to go."

"What's the point?"

"I'm not sure there is one. Why does everything have to have a point? Sure, I thought about walking out into the wild at dusk and letting them take me. But I'd rather not. Besides, I don't want to do those things any favors. By not moving, we're doing them favors, so let's go."

"I don't want to live in this world if my brother isn't in it."

"I lost my father."

"You still don't get it. There are more important things in this world than you."

"No, there aren't," Clay said. "That's what it's all about. You asked me why I'm here, and the reason is I need you. I hate to admit it, but I do. If anyone else were up here, I'd still be walking to town, but without you, we aren't going to make it."

Ellis' shoulders sagged. "The pillar is dead, and even if we could get it back online, those creatures would come for it again. It's all over."

Clay shook his head. "You're smart as hell but also dumb as rocks."

"What does that mean?"

"It means you won't have to worry about living in this world without your brother. Because we're not going to live in this world."

Ellis gaped at Clay. The asshole had saved them.

The scuffs of Ballard's boots ascended the stairs. "You two coming?"

"I know what we have to do," Ellis said.

"Okay," Ballard said.

Ellis jumped up and hobbled to the stairs. "Let's meet the others in town. I'll explain there."

Confused, Ballard looked to Clay, who shrugged, and they followed Ellis into the station below.

Four

James stood at a second-floor window that was caked in grease and grime. He and Dani had taken refuge in the fabrication plant. Though daylight bore upon the land now, they stayed. As far as they knew, they had nowhere left to go.

"Do you think there's anyone left?" Dani was wrapped in an oily blanket, sitting on the concrete floor, huddled beneath a table. Her face was smeared with tears.

"I don't know."

Outside, the gray, industrial landscape was desolate and still. Depressions pockmarked the gravel road. Across the way, a loader remained burrowed into the side of a building; a wheelbarrow lay on its

side, its rocky contents spilled into a rare patch of grass; stores of metal rods in wooden bins had been toppled. On the roof, an amputated smokestack held its breath.

Dani was drawing ghost shapes in the concrete with her finger. "I can't get their faces out of my head."

"Whose?"

"Milly's and Dr. Osman's. They looked like they knew what was coming and were okay with it."

"I doubt that."

"Maybe not okay with it, but at peace with it, and I think I know why."

"Why?"

"They had each other. In that moment, they had someone to hold onto. They weren't alone." She started scratching the floor. "Don't leave me, okay? I don't want to be alone."

James looked at her with utter heartbreak. He went to her and took her in his arms. "Even if you asked me to, I wouldn't."

Dani sobbed, and James rocked her.

"Whatever happens, it'll happen to both of us. Together."

In that time of great sorrow, James and Dani were bound by a connection they couldn't sever if they wanted to. Although the exos had tried to separate them through force and despair, their spirit persevered.

James held her for such a time that she quieted. All was silent in the fabrication plant. In the absence of the whirring and grinding machinery, the great metal warehouses would have amplified every sound, but there were none to be heard.

As the young lovers consoled each other and bordered on the edge of slumber, a noise woke them. Outside, a syncopated crunching approached. Feet on gravel.

James ran to the window, hands splayed on the frame, and he cried out in joy.

Five

Lucy cut through the last alleyway between homes, and Arokson Hall came into view. She stopped to scan the length of the crumbled bell tower, which lay in the lawn. She had hoped to find the others already there, but the commons were desolate. A cringe cracked her thin mouth, and she broke into a sprint across the field.

Ducard emerged from the dark alley. "Lucy, wait!"

A hand slapped his shoulder. "Come on," Sera said, chasing Lucy.

Ducard looked back to Elena and Gabe, who nodded wearily. "I got her," he said.

They raced after Lucy. Ducard ran with Mel in one hand and his silenced rifle in the other, covering Lucy's blind spots and corners. In the daylight, they assumed they were safe, but they were making a lot of noise as they stomped across the commons. If the exos were active at all during the day, they would have no trouble tracking the remaining survivors.

At the ruins of Arokson Hall, Sera gasped for air, her weary body lacking nourishment and sleep and beginning to show in her gaunt cheeks. She set Bernie down.

"Where is everyone?" she asked.

Ducard set Mel down in the grass and slumped against the bell tower with his rifle between his knees. "They should be here."

Gabe arrived with Elena. "Maybe they just got held up somewhere," he said.

The tension in Sera's chest had grown too taut. She trembled with the anxiety of not knowing. The feeling overwhelmed her, and she had to find Shane. She had to find him now.

"Shane!" Sera ran into the field and craned to the heavens. "Shane!"

Elena went after her. At her mother's touch, Sera collapsed to her knees, sobbing.

"It's all right, dear," Elena said, soothing her daughter. "It's all right."

"What if it's not?"

"She's right," Ducard said.

Lucy hissed. "Alain."

"What? We don't know anything, and while we sit here, the sun's burning out. We're all thinking it. What if we're the only ones?"

Lucy fixed him with a stony gaze. "What choice do we have? We wait."

The big man rocked in acknowledgement. His body felt like a bag of water, and in truth, he craved rest more than anything.

Gabe collapsed beside him. "Is there anything to eat?"

Ducard opened a pocket in his jacket and tossed the boy a stick of dried beef. Gabe accepted it and chewed. Ducard gave him an exhausted wink.

Sera released her mother and slipped from her embrace. The tears had stopped, and she lay in the grass.

Elena leaned over her. "I know the pain you're feeling. I feel it too. You're not alone." She noticed Sera's palm was flat on the ground. "What are you doing?"

"Listening."

"For what?"

"Them."

In that moment, when the world faded to a haze and the burning sun darkened behind closed eyelids, Sera heard the creatures that had brought her so much ruin. She heard a faint tremble in the earth, a low frequency that was imperceptible to humans except for in that trance-like state between consciousness and dreams. It was growing louder.

"We're here!" a voice called. "Here!"

Sera sprang up. The others were running across the field.

Ballard, Clay, and Ellis.

That was all. So few of them were left.

Lucy looked at Ballard with something like wonder. The two women met in front of the decapitated Arokson Hall. Unsure what to do, they regarded each other at arms' length, and then Ballard drew Lucy in for an embrace.

The sheriff pulled away and looked Lucy in the eye. "Where's Shane?"

"I thought he was with you."

"Lincoln?"

She shook her head.

With the realization that James and Dani were still missing, Elena fell to her knees.

Their reunion's tidings were sullen. Lucy had lost her husband, brother, and nephew. Sera had lost her brother, and she had lost the boy she'd fallen in love with.

In Sera's youth, she knew she would not love again, even if she were permitted the time to live without fear of the darkness beneath their feet.

Six

As soon as they were reunited, Lucy split them up again. She sent the fragile ones to search homes for food and water. Ducard would keep them safe. The other survivors, the ones who had demonstrated more resilience, she sent to the jailhouse. It was still morning, but they had to prepare for nightfall. The jail was the most fortified structure still standing, and there they would hide, quiet as ghosts, and wait for daybreak.

Even though she delegated all of this, she didn't believe they were going to make it. If someone had asked her, she would have said they were going to see tomorrow. She would have even thought she was being truthful. But she was giving them something to do because it was the only way she could think of to stay the hand of despair.

She walked through the ruined Arokson Hall. Portions of the roof had been ripped away, and blue sky shone through the holes. A fine dust had settled, a mixture of ash and wind-blown dirt. Lumen was already beginning to take this abandoned place.

The stairs creaked, and the wood on the second floor groaned. The walls slanted in places, and she worried the whole building might collapse. The window at the end of the hallway cast diffuse light, guiding her and showing her it was safe.

She leaned over the railing and observed the desolate lobby. She was alone.

The door to the warden's office stuck in its frame. She struggled to get it open, and eventually, it popped and allowed her entry.

She meandered into the warden's office, looking at everything and nothing, and it occurred to her that maybe she'd been cut deepest of all. She knew her suspicion was correct when the thought had no effect on her. She felt no anxiety, no grief. In her detachment, it meant about as much to her as a key sticking into a lock when she was in no particular hurry or a sock that was turned ever so slightly so as to be inconveniently uncomfortable.

Her fingertips danced on the old desk as she rounded it, and she picked up the toppled chair. Her boots crunched broken glass, and she sat and gazed through the shattered window that offered a view over the commons, the residential district, the train station, and Daenuel Market, or its ashen remains.

From here, she could see no one. No pillar workers were making their way across the commons to the train. No children were walking to school. No one was going to the marketplace to get this morning's fresh produce.

All she had was the moaning wind cutting across the jagged edges of glass. That's all Vale was now.

A chill crept up her arms, and her heartbeat quickened. Something sucked the oxygen out of the room. A sob ascended her throat, but she bit it back until she could no longer resist the pressure.

When her armor cracked, her full measure of grief burst forth. She tried to plug the holes, but more fissures formed until she had no choice but to get out of its way.

"Luce?"

Startled, she turned. A blurry shape stood in the doorway. She wiped her eyes, but her vision didn't clear. It was a shadow, like a black stain in physical space, a being of darkness, and its form frightened her.

"Luce, it's me."

Another silhouette filled the doorway, but it was shorter and narrower. After a pause, it dashed toward her.

She leaped to her feet, and the shape wrapped itself around her and wouldn't let go. Then she saw the eyes that she would know anywhere.

Lucy gasped. "Shane!"

Lincoln's boots thundered across the room, and he took her in a strong, warm embrace.

"Where's everyone else?" Shane asked.

Lucy's mind stalled, and she felt Lincoln's warm hands on her face, thumbs brushing away the tears and leaving black smears on her cheeks.

"Where's Bernie?" Lincoln said. "Gabe? Mel?"

"They're all right," she said. "They're all okay. We lost a lot of people last night, but our family is alive."

Lincoln breathed a sigh of relief.

"What about Sera?" Shane asked.

"She's okay too." Lucy offered him a smile. "It doesn't matter though. There are so few of us left. We won't last the night. And even if we do, there's nowhere we can go that they won't find us."

Lincoln frowned at her. While it saddened him to see her despair, it heartened him to know, of everyone left, she would show him such vulnerability. She would never admit it to anyone else.

"Let's go find the others," he said.

He left the room, and looking at Lucy questioningly, Shane followed his father. It took immense strength of will for her to overcome her despair and go after them.

But she did. She always had, and she sure as hell wasn't going to let it stop her now.

Seven

Bernie sat on the remnants of Gill's porch and watched Sheriff Ballard at the jailhouse. Ballard caught her, and she smiled, offering an enthusiastic wave.

With her father and brother away and her aunt doing other things, the sheriff had become another adult friend to her. Bernie liked the sheriff. She liked the way Ballard made her feel safe, like she would never be alone, like she would always have a protector or shield against the world.

The little girl felt these things, but what she didn't know, what she couldn't understand for another decade or two, was that she was right. Reggie would never leave her. She had these people who would never under their own volition leave her.

Thinking about her uncle, that idea made it more painful when they did.

Sheriff Ballard, Clay, and Sera were hauling mattresses from the infirmary and nailing them to the walls. Bernie's Aunt Lucy had told them that they would have to be as quiet as possible and that putting soft things on the floors and walls would help them stay hidden from the exos.

Gabe was seated on the bottom step at Gill's, digging in the ashen dirt with a burned stick. "You want to play a game? I have my Lore cards."

Mel picked at the dead skin around her thumbnail. "Why do you even still have those?"

"I dunno. I thought we could use some fun."

She scowled. "Kids' stuff."

Footsteps crunched on the gravel street. Bernie stood and gripped a charred and broken pillar, which used to support an awning. There were five faces, two of which were blackened and filthy. Her aunt smiled for the first time in days.

"Dad?" Bernie descended the stairs and stood gaping in the street. A gasp overcame her. "Daddy!?"

Her father's filthy lips parted and revealed his white teeth, and even though she was exhausted and hungry, she ran to him with everything she had left. She needed to feel his strong arms, his warm kisses on her forehead. She needed to know he was real.

Sera came out of the jailhouse, preoccupied with getting another mattress from the pile in the street, and when she saw the approaching human forms, she reeled with immediate recognition. Her heart climbed into her throat, and she clutched the railing to steady herself.

Then she was running up the street and screaming. "Shane!"

Lincoln received his daughter in a loving embrace, and it was everything Bernie had dreamed in her waking state. A weight drained from her as he lifted her and kissed her forehead, leaving a black splotch.

"Hey, Bern."

"Hi, Daddy."

Sera fell into Shane's chest. "I thought I'd lost you."

"Me too."

Ballard and Clay rushed out of the jailhouse and stood on the front steps.

The sheriff gaped. "Thank Lumen."

"Yeah," Clay said. "Joy."

Despite Clay's gloominess, Ballard observed the reunion with an expression flooded with pain, happiness, hope, and fear.

"Go on," he said to her. "You know you want to."

A tear leaped from one of Ballard's eyes. She caught and brushed it away, giving Clay a shrewd glare. She walked into the street, and Clay reluctantly followed. She approached Lincoln with reticence and couldn't resist embracing him.

"I'm glad you made it," she said.

"I'm glad you're all right too."

They pulled apart and eyed each other, both clearly containing their utter glee in knowing the other was alive and well.

The sheriff cut off the moment by turning to Shane. "And you. You don't do anything you're told, do you?"

Shane's boyish dimples deepened in a mischievous smile. "No, ma'am."

"Ma'am?" Reggie said with mock astonishment. "A sign of respect. Maybe there's hope for you yet." She returned to Lincoln with a stern expression. "No more. Next time it's someone else's turn."

"Don't worry," Ellis said. "Nobody's going to have to risk their life again. If we make it through tonight, we're going to go somewhere they can't get us. We can leave."

"Vale?" Ballard asked.

Ellis shook his head. "Lumen."

The sounds of boots crunching the gravel up the street reached their ears. The colonists who had gone for food, water, and supplies were returning.

"James!" Elena ran to embrace her son. "Oh my boy!" She pummeled his face with kisses.

"Hey, Lincoln." Ducard had two large, stuffed duffel bags hoisted over each shoulder. "You're alive. That's great."

The sentry noticed the colonists who had stayed to fortify the jail were silent and reserved. It was apparent to him he'd missed something. He set the bags down. "All right. What now?"

Lincoln bent a thumb toward Ellis. "He was just telling us how we're going to survive."

"Well, nerd, let's hear it."

Everyone looked to Ellis. The scientist shifted his eyes nervously. "So, uh, the ship that brought the First Families," he said. "We're going to use it."

Several people gasped. Ducard grunted in confusion. Clay cackled and slapped his thigh.

"I found James in the ship," Lincoln said, "and it didn't have power, did it, James?"

"No. Nothing worked."

"Oh, it still has power," Ellis said. "I assure you. The reactor is the same as the pillar's. Harnesses enormous amounts of energy and has a life expectancy of thousands of years. It's extremely stable too. The pillar and the ship are essentially the same structurally, but one was built to carry human beings through space, and one was built to create a world. The only real difference is our only real problem."

"Which is?" Lincoln said.

"The Dawnbreaker has an ascent rocket, which is what will get us to orbit. The engines that are powered by the reactor are only good outside of atmosphere. She's going to need fuel to reach escape velocity on her thrusters."

The survivors of Vale stood in silence as they processed what Ellis told them.

Lucy crossed her arms. "What good does an ancient spaceship with no fuel do us?"

"We have plenty of fuel. We'll use water."

"What? You can burn water?"

"No."

"That's what you just said."

"No it isn't."

Lincoln sighed. "Ellis, just explain."

"Water isn't combustible, but its constituent parts, hydrogen and oxygen, are. As I understand it, the Dawnbreaker's rockets are said to have run on water."

"Why water?" Ballard asked.

"In case the First Families got here and it wasn't what they thought," Lincoln said.

Ellis nodded. "Turns out it wasn't."

"So let me get this straight," Clay said. "You want us to leave our only shelter, cross the wild, and fly an ancient spaceship on the guess that it might still fly if we just add water?"

"Yes," Ellis said. "It was your idea."

Clay shook his head. "I didn't know it sounded so crazy. Where would we even get water? The lake?"

"There's a reason they landed in that field," Ellis said. "It was right on top of an underground river, and from what I hear about what you all saw in those tunnels, the water still flows. The ship will have a drill for extraction."

"You're sure?" Lucy asked.

Ellis waved his hand in the air as if to cast a fantastic image across the sky. "Imagine you're crossing the cosmos. You're light years from home, and something happens to your water supply. You can't exactly wait for it to rain. So you find a planet, moon, or asteroid that has water or ice, you land on it, and you take what you need. That's why it has the rockets too. The galaxy is filled with potential resource stations in case of emergencies. Not to mention the First Families would have needed water when they arrived."

The survivors were quiet, processing Ellis' proposition.

"You really think this will work?" Lucy asked.

Ellis thought about it for a moment. "Let's say it's fifty-fifty."

Ducard laughed. "It will, or it won't."

Ellis winked.

Lincoln was squeezing his children. "It has to work."

The colonists stood in the street, looking at each other, waiting for someone to say or do something. Nobody moved or spoke.

"Should we put it to a vote?" Ellis said.

"I think we just did," Ballard said.

Ducard nodded and hoisted the heavy duffel bags onto his massive shoulders. "Yeah."

"We'll leave at sunrise," Lincoln said.

"If we make it 'til then," Clay said.

Lincoln glared at him. "We'll make it."

"Let's finish inside and give ourselves the best shot we can," Lucy said.

The colonists each grabbed a mattress and marched into the jailhouse where they fortified as much as they could, their armor not against force but sight and sound.

Eight

Night fell. Through the barred window in the jailhouse, Lincoln and Lucy gazed out upon their home, which now belonged to the exos. The creatures patrolled the night, marching through the street like soldiers. They trod over Vale's ashen ruins, danced over the rooftops of vacant homes, and they unceremoniously stomped past Arokson Hall's toppled bell tower. They crept through the farmlands, rending any livestock they could find, and even crawled over the perimeter wall at the edge of the wild. The exos, no doubt, held dominion over all of that too.

Above them, the aurora swirled like the hands of a majestic symphony conductor, stirring a baton in the heavens.

Standing on the mountain in the distance, the pillar gleamed in the aurora's light. Dormant, the spire's lifelessness meant no more atmospheric clouds rose into the sky, and the aurora snaked around the tower like a python preparing to squeeze. Once, it was a herald of life. Defiled by the presence of the exos, the pillar was now a bastion of death. The exos clutched the heart of this world, and they refused to let go.

In nothing, though, was the exos' torment stronger than Lincoln's and Lucy's glassy eyes.

"The aurora is stronger than ever tonight." Lincoln was looking up, trying to forget, if only for a moment, that the exos were right outside. Although, even when he blinked, they were there on the backs of his eyelids.

"Lumen's dying." Lucy slid to the floor and hugged her knees. She bounced on the mattress beneath her, looking forward to the time when she could lay down and rest her weary body.

"It's happening so quickly."

Lucy looked at her brother-in-law, and Lincoln was still staring at the aurora.

"Good thing we won't be here," he said.

The exos thundered through the street and over the piles of crumbled buildings, but so far, the colonists' silent sanctuary held.

"For so long," Lucy said, "Aeron led our people. He was supposed to be the last warden. In our time, the pillars would finish their job, and then the people would be free to really make this world theirs. That's over. This can't be our home anymore. The others look to me for guidance now, and I just don't know what to do. We get through the night, you're going to have to lead us."

"For a while," Lincoln said, "I thought I resented Aeron because Dad chose him. But that wasn't it. I thought I resented him because I wanted to be warden. That wasn't it either. It was because he kept me out of it. He wouldn't let me help when I could have."

"He never wanted to hold you down. He felt it was his burden, and he didn't want you stuck with it like he was. He wanted you to have a normal life."

"It was my colony too. He put me outside those walls. He made me an outsider, and then the rest of the colony treated me as an outcast. But I had nowhere to go. I could have made a life in the wild, but I didn't want to do that to my children."

"Why not?"

"Because I wanted them to have a normal life." Lincoln was quiet for a moment, then said, "I wish I'd told him I was sorry."

"He knew."

"I loved him."

"He knew that too."

In the hall, a floorboard cracked. Lincoln scrambled to look outside through the window. An exo was perched across the street on the ruins of Gill's. The aurora danced over its shiny black exoskeleton. Its attention hadn't been drawn. It remained, thinking and doing whatever it was they thought and did.

Reggie stood in the cell doorway. "Time's up. You two should get some sleep." She entered the cell and handed them each some beef jerky. "Should eat too."

"Where's Ducard?" Lincoln asked.

"Relax," Ducard said. "I'm here."

The last sentry entered the cell looking alert and refreshed. Ballard appeared exhausted, as if the sleep had done her more harm than good.

Lincoln passed the silenced rifle to Ducard. "Reggie, is it weird for you to be in here?"

"No." Ballard yawned and rubbed her aching neck. "It isn't the first time. We used to use these cots to sleep on days when nothing was going on. The cot next door is actually the most comfortable."

"No sleeping this time," Lucy said.

"We'll be fine," Ducard said.

Lucy took Lincoln's hand and pulled his arm over her shoulders. "Let's go, old man."

They left the watch to Ducard and Ballard and went into the hall where piles of mattresses with sleeping bodies lay. Lucy lay next to her son and daughter. Lincoln found Bernie, and without opening her eyes, she nestled into his chest. Shane and Sera were nearby, embracing in their slumber.

Even though they didn't feel safe, sleep took them down into the darkness of unconsciousness. Lumen mercifully granted them rest until she turned and faced them toward a new dawn.

CHAPTER 12
THE COLONY

One

The tip of the pillar burned like a torch. Daylight slid with maddening indifference down the spire. From the jailhouse, the colonists heard the exos creeping through the marketplace and then diving into the earth. Their chittering and clicking faded, the sun washing them from the land.

When the sunlight covered the pillar, Ducard and Ballard decided it was safe.

They went into the hallway. Reggie roused Ellis with a gentle shake of his arm. Startled, the old man blinked and looked at her. He took note of the sunlight pouring into the jailhouse, shadows cut by the metal bars.

"What time is it?" he asked.

"Morning."

Reggie then went to Lincoln's side. She grasped his shoulder, and he snatched her wrist.

They stared at each other.

"Bad dreams?" she said.

"Yeah."

Clay swatted Ducard's hand away. He stood and marched out the front door.

"The hell is his problem?" Ballard said.

Lincoln popped his neck and sighed from the release. "He knows he needs us, and he hates it." He brushed Bernie's golden hair behind her ear and kissed her cheek. "Sweetheart, it's time to wake up."

Bernie whined and rolled over.

"Is it tomorrow?" Gabe asked. "Are we alive?"

"Of course we are, dingus," Shane said to his cousin.

One by one, the remaining colonists rose, rubbing their eyes and yawning. Because of the physical and emotional exhaustion, they moved slowly yet deliberately. They gathered the food and water, and they assembled in the street.

Lincoln and Lucy were the last out of the jailhouse, ensuring they had everything. They stood on the steps, presiding over the last of their people.

"If every night was like last night, we could make it a long time," Lucy said.

"But we wouldn't make it," Lincoln said.

Lucy released a deep breath and nodded.

The others watched them with blank faces, and Lincoln and Lucy took the first steps away from the jailhouse, the colony, their home, toward an uncertain future.

If they stayed, they could depend on a slow, inevitable death. If they left, they could count on escape or a quick, merciful end.

The last of Vale's colonists made their way through the marketplace and the commons to the perimeter, where they opened the gate and didn't bother closing it behind them.

Two

They entered an alien world of green the likes of which most of them had never seen. Trees towered and shaded them with a thick canopy. Bracken and tall grass covered the forest floor. Thick brush and bushy foliage blocked passage and corralled them in weaving paths, and when they needed to, Lincoln and Clay led the way with their swinging blades.

"Stay close," Lincoln said.

Dani was shaking in James' arms. "I think I came through here the night I thought I lost you."

"Why do you think that?" he asked her.

"I feel like I've been here before."

Bernie and Mel were cowering, their eyes wide with equal parts wonder and terror.

"It's all right," Sera told them. "It's weird how quickly you'll get used to all of this. It almost feels natural. Almost."

"No, it doesn't," Gabe said. "There's nothing natural about being out here."

"That's enough," Lincoln said.

The ground began to tremble. At first, it was only perceptible in sound, but it wasn't long before it threatened to knock them off their feet.

Clay was still hacking, and Lincoln snatched his forearm.

"Wait!" he said.

They listened.

"It's them!" Dani cried. "Run!"

Lincoln's hand shot up. "No! Wait!"

They heard the approach of snapping branches and cracking trees, like a hurricane whipping through the wild.

Lincoln's eyes shot open in alarm. "Everyone get close!"

The colonists huddled as a stampede of herebors charged through the wild right in front of them. Their massive antlers reached into the treetops and tore limbs from high above. Their muscles pumped and bulged under their hides, and their hooves pounded the earth, leaving deep divots in the soft soil. A buck crashed into a tree nearby, splitting the trunk. It snorted and kept going.

"Are they running from the exos!?" Lucy asked.

"I don't think so," Lincoln said.

A red mass darted through thick vegetation. Another followed. Then an herebor went down, and the herd scattered. The buck leading the stampede bore down on the colonists.

"Run!" Lincoln said.

They fled. Lincoln scooped up Bernie and stayed close to Shane and Sera. Reggie wasn't far. Lucy had Gabe and Mel.

The forest thundered as the snorting herebor herd engulfed the colonists. No matter how fast their legs pumped, the animals were faster.

Something growled and then squealed. Something else screeched, and a blood spray slapped Lincoln in the face as an herebor collapsed among the speeding giants.

"We have to get out of this!" Lincoln said, lost in a sea of rippling hides. He had Bernie in his arms, but there was no sign of the others.

He cut in front of an herebor. Then he cut in front of another. It screamed at him as it barely missed him. Lincoln worked his way laterally across the herd.

He crossed in front of herebor after herebor, and he could see no sign of an end to the herd. So he made a desperate move and put his back to a tree.

The giants flowed around him like water as he held Bernie's trembling form to his chest.

Three

Ellis lay face down in ivy and wildflowers, clenching his eyelids and burying his nose in the damp soil. Clay's knee dug into his lower spine, and his forearm pressed the back of Ellis' neck. It felt like Clay was killing him. But no, Clay was saving him.

When the herebors had redirected and split them from the others, Clay had thrown Ellis to the ground and lay on top of him, protecting the engineer's body with his own. It might have been selfless if not for the understanding that Clay needed Ellis to survive.

As the thundering footfalls quieted and faded, a horrible shrieking persisted, and in a moment, it occurred to Ellis that it was his own voice.

Clay slapped the back of Ellis' head. "Knock it off."

Ellis quieted and opened his eyes. He took stock of his body, expecting the pierce of pain but feeling none.

The knee in Ellis' back lifted, and Clay stood. He scanned their surroundings. The herebors had torn a path through the wild, and it unfolded into the distance. The incredible power of the animals had parted trees and ravaged earth.

Ellis joined him and gaped at the destruction. "Goddess."

"And they're the bottom of the food chain."

"Really? You ever kill one?"

Clay tilted his head. "Okay, maybe not the bottom."

Ellis took a timid step onto the path.

"Where you going?" Clay said.

"To find the others. They can't be far."

"They could still be running for all we know. We don't have time to waste searching the wild for them. It can get real maze-like out here real quick."

"What if they're hurt? What if they need our help?"

"That doesn't concern us anymore. What concerns us is getting to that ship and you getting us off this planet." Clay clutched Ellis' arm and motioned with his head. "This way."

Ellis watched Clay for a moment and saw something in his eyes that frightened him. Clay was desperate to get to the Dawnbreaker.

Ellis stood his ground. "I'm not leaving without—"

The fist came hard and fast and connected with his cheekbone. The impact shook his entire world, and after the shiver of the shock dispersed, cracks of pain bloomed in his eye.

"You're leaving with me now. We're getting to the ship. Then you're flying us off this planet. Do you understand?"

Ellis nodded. Clay pushed him, and he started walking.

"Keep going," Clay said. "They'll meet us there."

"What if they don't?"

The intensity of Clay's dead stare measured equally with his selfish will to survive.

Part of being Ellis meant looking beyond today or tomorrow. His weather forecasts kept his mind always in the next week. His study of the climate kept him focused on the next year. As Clay pushed him through the vines and ferns of the forest, one thought nagged him.

Assuming they made it to the ship, and assuming he could get it off of the ground and into orbit, what would Clay do to him if it came to rationing their supplies?

Four

The last of the herebors thundered past the tree Lincoln and Bernie had hid behind, and the trembling settled. The tree stopped its violent shaking; the shuddering calmed.

The herebors galloped into the distance. A pack of red riptens were chasing them, leaping onto their flanks and clawing with everything they had to bring the behemoths down. He'd never known them to be predators, only scavengers. Apparently the humans weren't the only ones who were desperate.

He looked down at his daughter and breathed. "We're okay."

"What about everyone else?"

He set her down. "Stay close." He cupped his mouth with his hands. "Shane! Lucy! Reggie! Anyone!"

Only the stillness of the wild answered.

Bernie's eyes were big and glassy. "You said not to go farther than we could hear each other."

"I know."

"How are we going to find everyone else if we can't hear them?"

"Bernie, I don't know."

She stepped away from her father, squeezing back the tears. It seemed every hour she was more afraid than she'd ever been, and now, even with her father, she felt alone. She knew they weren't lost. She trusted in her father to bring them back from the wild. However, that lonely, empty feeling evoked a whimper and sob.

"Hey," Lincoln said with all of the compassion he could muster. He kneeled in front of her. "Breathe, Bern. Just breathe. It's going to be okay.

We're going to find everyone, and we're going to be safe by tonight. You'll see, sweetheart. Don't you doubt it for a second, okay?"

She looked at him with those big, vulnerable eyes and sniffled. She nodded, and he pulled her to his chest. Then she wanted to cry for another reason. Her chest swelled with love, and the sudden snap between emotions left her feeling defeated. She breathed. She just had to breathe.

"Dad?" Shane's voice echoed through the wild.

Bernie's eyes shot open. "Shane!"

Lincoln held her at arm's length. "Okay, okay. Stay close to me." He rose and cupped his mouth again. "Here!"

The forest crunched and cracked and swished as multiple pairs of feet ran over the untrodden deadfall. A moment later, Shane emerged from a thicket with Sera in tow. Shane had a scratch on his cheek and a hole torn in his shirt. A cut on Sera's arm had released trickling blood, but it didn't look too deep. Aside from that and the dirt and filth from laying for cover and the dead leaves that clung to their clothing, they appeared all right.

Shane grinned as he approached his father.

Lincoln took a deep breath. "I'm glad you're okay."

"Me too."

A shrill scream pierced the wilderness, shattering their happy reunion.

Lincoln was already running. "Stay close."

They followed him as he chased the echoing sobs. They ran through the bracken until they encountered the fallen trees from the herebor stampede. They climbed over them and broke into the path of destruction the colossal animals had left in their wake.

The voice continued to sob ahead, and they crossed the herebors' path, breaking through the other side. They leaped over more fallen trees, and then they discovered Dani Hines on her knees. James was leaning over someone who lay in the grass and weeds.

Lincoln stopped and held the kids back, but he could do nothing to keep Sera away, and he wouldn't have felt right doing so.

"Mom?" she said. "Oh no. Mom! No, no, no!" She ran to her brother's side.

Blood ran down Elena's head from a split that crossed her brow, over her crown, and beyond her hairline. Her forehead was terribly bruised. Her leg was twisted at an unnatural angle, and she had cuts all over every exposed piece of skin from running through the thick mess of the wild.

"Mom." Sera squeezed her hand. "I'm here."

"Good." Elena's voice was a whisper. "Take care of each other. You need to take care of each other now."

Sera and James nodded.

"Your father," Elena said. "Your father would have been proud. I am proud. I am happy. I'm happy that you both found someone to make you happy. That is all we ever wanted for you. But you have to go now. You have to live. You have to make it." Her dimming eyes pulsed with sudden panic. "Where is Lincoln?"

He moved to her side. "I'm here."

"Good. Get them away from here. Give them a place to live."

"I will."

Hearing Lincoln's words, her body released a kind of tension. Her head settled, and her grip on her daughter's hand relaxed. The muscles in her neck receded under her skin, and she swallowed.

James kissed his mother's cheek. "I love you."

Lincoln touched Sera's shoulder.

"No." She shrugged him off.

"You have to," Lincoln said.

"No."

He whispered into her ear. "You don't want to see this."

He pulled her away, and she allowed him.

Lucy, Gabe, Mel, Reggie, and Ducard broke through the thicket. Lincoln returned to Elena and held her hand. She closed her eyes, her breathing unsteady. The blood from her head wound stained the earth.

The delirium revealed itself with a sudden wrinkle of her brow. She stirred, her body contorting with adrenaline as it fought to live long enough to convey a final message. It was something he'd seen before with his own mother, as he'd sat alone by her deathbed and endured the ugly end of someone he loved.

Elena clutched his arm, her wild eyes locked onto his. Her lips trembled as she tried to speak. A breath hitched in her chest, and she was gone.

Lincoln placed her lifeless hand on her stomach and closed her eyes.

Everyone was watching him when he turned.

Lucy grasped James' and Sera's shoulders. She brought them in for an embrace and looked at Lincoln across the expanse.

Five

For the better part of an hour, the colonists trudged up and down the herebor trail. The increasingly desperate calls for Clay and Ellis rippled through the wild.

The effort grew futile, and the colonists agreed to rest. Beside a moss-blanketed boulder away from the others, Lucy, Lincoln, and Ballard convened.

Ballard sipped from her canteen. "It's like they just disappeared."

"People don't do that." Lucy sighed in lament. "Not during the day, anyway."

Lincoln's pensive expression dug deep lines in his face.

"What's on your mind, Lincoln?" Lucy asked.

"There's another aspect to this I'm worried about."

"What is it?"

"Clay left us to die in that cave. I don't think he'd have a problem doing it again."

Lucy rubbed her eyes and brushed her sweaty red hair out of her face. "Is there something that makes you think that's what he's doing?"

"I can't find any tracks."

"Those animals tore through here like a storm," Ballard said. "Maybe Clay took Ellis and followed their trail."

Lincoln tilted his head, doubtful. "Maybe. There's one more thing though."

"What's that?"

"I don't know where we are."

Lucy and Ballard gaped at Lincoln. They were frozen. They didn't even breathe. The one constant in all of this was that Lincoln would know where they were going, and if he didn't, Clay would. It had been a desperate move. They'd had no illusions about that. The prospect of being lost in the wild meant they'd marched the last of Vale's colonists into a place where there was no refuge.

In pure amazement, Lucy uttered a single laugh. "What do you mean you don't know where we are?"

"The stampede moved us and changed things. I've lost my point of reference. I don't know which direction is which."

A haunted look crossed Lucy's face. She was shaking her head and clamping her teeth in an underbite that made her look mean and fierce. She wasn't ready to give up.

"We keep moving," she said. "No matter what."

Lincoln craned his head back. "Tree canopy's too thick to see the sun's position, but if we can get out in the open, I might be able to reorient myself."

Ballard rubbed her arms. "Let's just hope we find it before nightfall."

They returned to the others, who were sitting on a downed tree and sharing a water canteen. The remaining colonists eyed Lincoln, Lucy, and Ballard expectantly.

"We're going to head for the ship," Lucy said.

Ducard stood, his hulking form towering over the acting warden. "What about Ellis? We can't just leave him out here."

Lucy raised her hands in placation. "He and Clay are okay. Lincoln found their tracks headed east. Clay is more than capable of getting Ellis to the Field of the First Families. Isn't that right, Lincoln?"

Ducard's gaze shifted to him, and Lincoln nodded.

"We'll meet them there," Lucy said. "So let's go. Break's over. We have a lot of ground to cover."

Everyone stood and waited for Lincoln to take the lead. He surveyed the surrounding greenery. It all looked the same to him now, but he had to choose a direction.

"This way," he said, and set off across a field of bracken under a thick canopy provided by hundreds of old trees.

The colonists moved in silence, and Lincoln led them into a wild that only grew denser. The terrain became harder to traverse, and he had the nagging fear that they were moving south toward the mountains. With the constantly changing slope, he couldn't tell if they were climbing.

In the thick wild, with no direct sunlight, time became indefinite. As the colonists pushed onward through the morning, they had to battle the rising dread that dark was approaching. In the blinding green, the depleting energy levels took precedence for gauging the passage of distance and time.

Exhausted, Lucy stopped. "Okay, let's break for a few minutes."

The colonists dispersed, taking seats on nearby rocks or simply collapsing on the ground.

Lincoln heaved his pack over his shoulder and set it on the forest floor. He dug into a side pocket where he had stored a bag of nuts, and his hand grasped a metal disk. He removed it and analyzed the smooth silver backing of his father's compass.

In time, we find our way, the inscription read.

He looked at its face. The needle was holding steady. Lincoln shot to his feet. "We need to keep going."

Ducard looked up from his reclined position on the ground. "But we just sat down."

"We need to keep going."

Lucy regarded the compass with confusion.

"It works," he said. "All this time, it was never a compass at all. It was a clock."

"I don't understand."

"The pillars. They must have finished their work. Lumen has poles. And I know which way to go."

She smiled at him with reverence. They were saved.

"You heard him," she said. "We have to get to that ship."

The colonists moaned.

With the compass leading, Lincoln started walking northeast.

"Wait a minute." Ducard threw up his hands. "We were just heading the other way."

Apparently indifferent, the colonists passed him.

"Unbelievable," he said.

They delved back into the thick, and in time, Lincoln heard someone hurrying to catch up to him. He figured it was Ballard, but when he turned, he was surprised to find James Bellman.

"I want to thank you," James said. "On behalf of my sister and me."

"For what?"

"Showing respect to and being there for my mother. She looked peaceful."

Lincoln thought about telling James there was nothing peaceful about the way his mother had died, but Lincoln just nodded. The thought that had kept him silent was the hypocrisy of it. When his kids had lost their mother, he'd pushed them off on Lucy and sought his own refuge in the wild under the guise of work. He should have been there for them. If they made it to the Dawnbreaker, he intended to never leave them again.

"I'm sorry we couldn't spare the time to give her a proper burial," Lincoln said. "You know I would have liked to."

"I do," James said. "Still. It feels wrong to leave her."

"Yeah. It does." Lincoln grasped the boy's shoulder.

"She saved us, you know? Dani and me. We were running and didn't know an herebor was bearing down on us. Mom pushed us out of the way."

James shook his head as if to shake the memory away. Lincoln had no illusion that he could spare the boy his grief, but it was precisely that grief that would turn him into a man. Lincoln could only hope to give James enough time to grow up.

As they pushed farther into the wild and the colony grew more distant, they felt more conflicted. Part of them grew more anxious with every step about leaving their home, but another part of them understood they no longer had a home to go to. Vale had been decimated to its foundations, to its very idea. The colony had been more than its walls and fields, more than its buildings. It had been more than its people. Vale was the idea that humanity could exist on Lumen, and when the exos had torn that idea down, they had erased any possibility that Vale could be. It existed only in memory now, but the reality of that memory was that the potential they'd all dreamed of was only ever just a dream.

Vale could never have been on Lumen. Only for a time did its idea stand.

The people of Vale weren't refugees. In a way, they'd never really had a home, and now they were looking for one. They hoped to find it in the stars.

The idea that they could dream again, so soon and so readily, both terrified and comforted them. They had no destination, but they knew they were going somewhere, and for them, that was enough.

More hurried footsteps behind Lincoln caused him to turn. It was Reggie.

"Ellis is in good hands, eh?" she said.

Lincoln looked ahead at the thicket before them. He raised his bush knife and carved their way onto the pathway, which would lead to the Field of the First Families. He held out his hand to help her onto the path. "We better hurry."

Reg refused Lincoln's hand and stepped onto the path, but she did so without spite. She looked from end to end, the path disappearing as it curved, and then she smiled.

"I know where we are."

Snapping fallen branches and crushing dried leaves, the rest of the colonists emerged from the thick behind them, and Lincoln led them on their first definite steps toward the sunlight.

Six

The Dawnbreaker stood at the far end of the field, a gleaming shard of metal like a pillar fallen onto its side.

Bernie gasped beside her father at the edge of the field. Her eyes were wide and filled with wonder. "What is that?"

Lincoln kneeled. "That is going to take us into the sky. We're going to use it to find a new home."

"You mean we're going to where the skylights are?"

"We're going to go above that, sweetheart. We're going to the stars."

Something about her face touched Lincoln, if only for a moment. He gazed into her gaping, awestruck expression, and it occurred to him that this was the first moment in days that her fear had vanished. Seeing the legacy of the First Families, she was no longer afraid. She beheld their magnificence, and compared to the only world she'd ever known, it transcended all of her expectations.

The Dawnbreaker's majesty was a monument to a long-forgotten age of people they wouldn't recognize. It was their salvation. It had to be.

Lincoln led the last survivors of the colony Vale across the Field of the First Families, back across the arrival place of their kind, back to the beginning of everything that was this dream of a new world. Wading through the tall grass that swayed in the comfortable breeze, it felt as if they were being welcomed. The spirit of their people had always been there for them if they'd needed it, and it turned out they did.

They passed a wooden pole that had long since shattered. It had probably held a warning sign of some kind, but by the time Lumen's harsh elements had broken it, no one had been around to heed it anyway.

The perimeter fencing was so rusted and frail that, even though some of the colonists walked through gaping holes, others tore it apart with their bare hands, ancient metal turning to iron oxide dust.

The nose of the ship peaked like the head of a bird, and they gazed up at a great pane of glass positioned on the ship's throat.

Ballard pointed at it. "You think Ellis is in there?"

They felt the rattling hum of electric current in their bones as the ship began to shake the earth. An ear-splitting boom filled the air. Blinding floodlights illuminated around the ship's bow, and that great pane of glass lit up with a cool blue glow.

Lincoln and Ballard shielded their eyes and squinted into the window. Ballard released a guttural laugh and clapped.

"What is it?" Lucy said.

"It's Ellis," Ballard said, pointing. "He's up there. The old man got this thing running."

Behind that glass, Ellis was jumping and waving his hands like a madman.

Ducard shook Lincoln's shoulder. "Why so glum, chum? We made it, and Ellis is okay."

Lincoln frowned. "Where's Clay?"

When they heard the high-pitched whine of a charging rifle amplifier, they understood that Ellis wasn't making a dramatic display at a greeting.

He was trying to warn them.

Seven

The grass rustled. A man and woman stood from their cover in the tall stalks and flanked the survivors. Leveling their old rifles made of rusting metal and cracked wood, their gun barrels jumped from target to target. The tension in their faces and movements was a warning in itself.

Lincoln eased his hands up and eyed Ducard. "Let's not do anything we'll regret."

The sentry's face flared at Lincoln. The command was an affront to Alain's instincts and training to protect and never surrender. He grit his teeth and growled, knowing Lincoln was right. Harnessing all of his willpower, he lowered his weapon and took his firing hand away from the grip.

The colonists did not recognize these people from Vale. Their hair was wild and unkempt, tangled and clumped. The man had a beard that reached his chest. Their clothing was tattered and torn with old stains that suggested the rough condition was not as a result of recent exo attacks but of living in the wild without the colony's support.

A rifle barrel nestled into Lincoln's spine.

"This is how it's going to go." Clay's smile was audible in his voice. "You're going to do as I say, and if you don't, we're going to shoot your friends and family until you do."

"Why are you doing this?" Lucy's voice was steady, but her eyes were pleading. "We're so close. We can all make it. No one else has to die."

Clay leered at her.

"It's because he doesn't need us," Ballard said. "He figures the fewer people with him on that ship using resources, the better his chances."

"More or less." Clay stepped back. "Or maybe I just don't like you."

With eyes ablaze, Lincoln faced his enemy. Seeing Clay now, a surge of emotions rushed through his chest and squeezed the air from his lungs. He felt the pull to close the distance and take the man's life for everything he'd done, but he stuffed it down. The time wasn't right.

"I recognize you," Ballard said to the man and woman with Clay. "We were in your home when we were searching for James." She squinted with recollection. "Where are your children?"

The woman flinched, and her lips quivered. The man's knuckles turned white around the frame of his rifle.

"When the exos attacked their home, they ran out into the wild," Clay said. "Sadly, their kids weren't fast enough. After we found their home abandoned, I went back. You see, Thomas, Carol, and I are friends. I have friends everywhere. I'm a real likeable guy. I get along with everyone."

Lincoln was staring Clay down. "So what now, Mr. Nice Guy?"

Clay's smile faded, his face again hardening. "Now you move."

Eyeing Lucy, Lincoln shuffled toward the ship. She gripped the girls.

Clay followed a few steps behind and shoved his rifle barrel into Lincoln's back again. "Move it. Everyone else, Thomas and Carol will take real good care of you."

Lincoln and Ballard met eyes. Ballard tilted her head toward Ducard, who tightened his grip on his suppressed rifle. Lincoln shook his head. The message was clear: not unless he had to.

"Don't worry," Clay said. "They won't hurt your family. It's not my intention to kill anyone today."

"What is your intention then?" Lincoln said.

"You're going to help me get the drill working, and then we're going to leave you here."

"That's the same thing."

"Good point. Then if it would suit you better, I can put you all out of your misery before we leave. That I can do. Of course, the girls will probably be coming with us too. I'm not heartless."

"You know what your problem is?"

"What's that, Lincoln?"

"You're not very creative. You can't think beyond your next move."

"Tell me more about how I outsmarted you."

"I made a mistake in trusting that you'd accepted we were in this together, but what's going to happen when you need someone? No one's going to come. Certainly not me."

"Let's not kid ourselves. I burned that bridge in the cave."

"Yeah," Lincoln said. "Yeah, you did."

The men walked into the Dawnbreaker's great shadow and the plummeting temperatures of winter without the grace of sunlight. Seeing it again up close, Lincoln marveled at the alien exterior. Through the vines and moss, the pieces of the hull that the wild hadn't claimed over the centuries, the metal still gleamed. It sang even in shadow, a light source emanating from within.

They approached the far side of the Dawnbreaker's outer hull. A mechanical arm extended from a port like an arsenal of spears. Mounted on the device, a drill reached to the ground and kissed the dirt, ready to dive and find water.

A speaker crackled to life. "It's ready," Ellis said from the control room. "It works exactly like the drill on the pillar. Do you understand? Exactly like the drill on the pillar."

Lincoln traced the drill arm to the side of the ship, and above a nearby airlock, he found a small glass dome with a black eye. He could have sworn it winked.

"Yep," Ellis said. "I can see you."

Lincoln held up a hand in amazed greeting.

"Just like the pillar, Lincoln."

"I got it."

Lincoln kneeled next to the drill and inspected it. Then he huffed and stood back up.

"What's wrong?" Clay said.

"We're in the shade here. I can't see what I'm doing."

The speaker hissed. "There should be exterior lights. I could probably turn them on here, but I'm not too familiar with the subsystems. Check the control panel by the airlock near you."

Lincoln walked to the nearby airlock. Beside it, a small glass plate illuminated as he approached. He touched it and was amazed when it reacted. He found a box labeled "Exterior Lights" and pressed it. Floodlights on the hull snapped on.

"Can we get to work now, please?" Clay said.

Lincoln returned to the drill and guided the bit into place. He tightened the chuck and adjusted the pressure-release valve. He didn't want it to blow right away.

The red handle screeched as Lincoln threw it down, unlocking the bit. After that, the drill descended into the earth, guiding itself.

"That's it?" Clay said.

"That's it."

"I could have done that."

Lincoln shrugged. "There's a few tricks to it. Someone who isn't trained could have set the drill out of alignment, and that could have broken the bit."

"Okay then." Clay motioned with his rifle barrel. "Let's go."

"Backing the drill out is also tricky," Lincoln said. "You better let me do it."

"Why do you care?"

"You have a friend of mine on this ship."

"Looking out for him, are you?"

The earth trembled, a god slamming its fist. Lincoln and Clay stumbled in surprise and caught each other's gazes.

"The drill hit something?" Clay asked.

It still turned smoothly, its low, mechanical whir indicating it was in no hurry. Lincoln and Clay watched it spin, and then the ground shook again.

"It's them," Lincoln said.

"But it isn't even dark and—"

The pressure-release valve sputtered and exploded compressed air at Clay. His hands shot to his face in defense, and he stumbled. Lincoln leaped and grabbed the rifle stock as Clay regained his composure. Clay jerked the weapon, but Lincoln's grip held firm. They fell to the ground, and the rifle clattered away. As they wrestled, another bone-rattling tremor boomed across the Field of the First Families.

"*Everyone!*" Ellis yelled over the ship's exterior speakers. "*Get inside now!*"

Holding their weapons in place, Thomas and Carol eyed each other with uncertainty.

"Please," Lucy said. "Please."

Thomas blinked and lowered his head, something within him loosening. "Come on."

While Lincoln and Clay rolled over each other near the drill, the colonists raced across the field. They entered the Dawnbreaker's shadow and scurried around the ship's hull until they reached the open air lock.

"Lincoln!" Lucy yelled.

The men stayed locked in battle, striking each other and rolling to establish dominance. Seeing her father fighting this other man, Bernie froze as the others poured into the ship. Horrified, she watched.

"Daddy!"

Pressed beneath Clay's weight, Lincoln heard his daughter's cry and found the strength to turn the man over and shove his forearm under Clay's chin. Clay scuttled, but Lincoln stayed on top. He bucked, but still Lincoln held him down.

The ground stirred beneath them. It loosened and rippled, like waves on a body of water. Lincoln released his hold and rolled as the earth opened and swallowed Clay, his arms outstretched, screaming for help. In an instant, he was gone.

Shocked and awestruck, Lincoln got to his feet.

"Daddy!"

He raced for his daughter.

"Bernie!" Lucy screamed from the airlock. Ducard was holding her back.

Whether it was the exos, Lincoln's hurried strides, or his thundering heart, his world shook. For all of his ferocious need to protect his daughter, a primal rage to be strong and fast, it only took an instant for the earth beneath her feet to loosen.

"Daddy?"

The exos pulled the little girl down into a vortex of swirling dirt.

"No!" Lincoln dove to the ground and dug at the depression where his daughter had been. "No, no, no, no! Take me!"

"Dad!" Shane lunged for the doorway

Ducard grabbed him too, and locked him with his embrace.

Lincoln's hands dug with fury. They dug with love. They dug with hatred and malice. They dug with every ounce of strength he had left, no matter its source.

"Take me!"

Reason and logic fled. His mind burned with a relentless rage to do the impossible. For Bernie. To bring her back. She was not gone. He could save her.

The earth settled. The rumbling receded. Still, Lincoln would not relent. He would dig until sunset if he had to. He would dig until the exos were strong enough to take him. With the detonations in his heart, he was powerful. He was formidable. He was a machine of vengeance.

"Lincoln," Lucy said. "Lincoln."

Her voice struck him like a blow to his head, and Lincoln stopped and stared at Lucy with electrified eyes and trembling lips. His friends and family watched him, utter heartbreak in their open mouths and sorrowful faces, too grief-stricken to speak or do anything to help him.

In that moment, joined across the expanse of their despair, it was almost a mercy that the ground liquefied, the earth collapsed, and they pulled Lincoln down into the suffocating darkness.

Eight

Outside, the drill went on spinning. It hummed and churned the dirt into fine dust, digging deeper and deeper, rattling the earth like a beacon for the exos. Enraged, their slamming returned and persisted even as the last colonists of Vale gaped through the bay door at the depressions in the ground where Lincoln and Bernie had been drawn down.

BOOM

BOOM

BOOM

Though the earth shook outside, inside the Dawnbreaker, the air was still. Nobody spoke or breathed. Their collective consciousness was stuck, refusing to move on and process what had happened.

Shane broke the stillness when he cried out and fell to his knees. He reached toward the opening but couldn't risk setting foot on the ground. He knew there was nothing he could do, the precise source of his agony.

Lucy embraced him and pressed his head to her chest. She stroked his hair as he sobbed. She sobbed too. She gazed into the field with eyes of such sadness that any fire that had once been there was now extinguished.

They'd made it into the Dawnbreaker but at immense cost.

BOOM

The children whimpered, and Lucy remembered herself. She motioned for them to come to her, and they ran to her side, clutching her wherever there was an opening, a family in grief. They came together because, even though the exos could not get them now, if they did not cling to each other, they otherwise might have been torn apart.

At the doorway, Ducard grimaced at the depression in the field. He contemplated it as if it were a great mystery. Ballard shuffled to his side and rested her head on his shoulder. She was clutching herself and weeping. Ducard hung a great arm around her and squeezed. She felt as if he might break her bones, but she didn't care. She was already broken.

"Why did he do that?" Her voice trembled. "Why did he let them take him?"

Ducard's chest swelled. "For whatever reason, they don't always kill right away."

She turned her face up to his. "How do you know?"

"When we fought them at the pillar, they could have killed me, but they were trying to take me away. And they don't leave any bodies. For some reason, they want us alive."

"How do you know?" Ballard said.

He looked at her with eyes of great weight, and it was all he would say on the matter.

A door at the back of the room split open, and Ellis limped through. His glare was as sharp as a knife, and he searched the group with intention. The people he was looking for were sitting against the wall.

BOOM

He charged. "You filth! Hasn't there been enough suffering!?"

Ducard and Ballard intervened before Ellis could reach Thomas and Carol.

Thomas recoiled. "We're sorry, okay!?"

"Sorry!?" Ellis thrashed against Ducard. "You're sorry! What were you trying to do!?"

Carol bowed her head. "What we thought we had to."

"Well you didn't have to. We would have helped you."

Ellis stood back from Ducard and composed himself. Then he went to a control panel on the wall and closed the outer door.

"What are you doing?" Shane said. "He could be coming back."

It broke Ellis' heart to say, "When the tanks are full, it won't take long before the ship is ready. And I think we can expect it to get bad tonight. Very bad."

Lucy stood. None of the colonists were looking at her, but she knew what she had to say.

"We leave when we're ready. He would want us to."

Even with the doors closed, they heard the drill's whine cease and the water pump's hum.

BOOM

Nine

Lincoln started, the electric current of adrenaline shooting through his chest and limbs. His body pulsed with emergency. Every part of him shivered from the fire in his nerves.

Coming to, he gasped and gagged on the foul air. His lungs heaved to expel the rancidity from his body, but he clamped it down, swallowing a burning like acid in his throat and stomach.

Then he realized he could see nothing. He blinked to be sure his eyes were open, and he rubbed them to clear anything that might obstruct his vision, but by the smell and the moist feeling on his skin, he knew why he couldn't see. His eyes were fine. He was simply in a place where they were useless.

He was in their home, their colony.

He felt drugged. The creature that took him must have done something to put him to sleep. A sharp pain flared in his abdomen, and he touched a wet spot. The stingers on the ends of their tails, the creature must have stuck him with it to sedate him.

He didn't know exactly how he got here, but awakened in the exos' underworld without a hint of light to run to, here he was.

Bernie had to be here too.

His fingers grasped something lumpy and cold. As he pushed himself to his feet, it gave under his weight with a sickening snap. His boots shuffling backward on the rocky floor, he reached for the flashlight in his pocket and shined it on the place where he had woken.

Dead faces gaped at him, their open eyes glazed in the beam of light.

He'd made it alive, but many others hadn't. What did that mean for a little girl?

A scream pierced the labyrinth. A man was calling for help. His pleas reverberated through the caverns and surrounded Lincoln like an apparition seeping through the rock walls. Lincoln couldn't tell if the man was near or far. He couldn't discern which direction the man was calling from. The only thing he could be sure of was that the panicked voice came through an opening in the wall.

"Please! Help! Oh, please! Somebody! Help! Please!"

Then his screams stopped.

Lincoln found hope in that man's fate. The creatures weren't killing everyone they were taking. At least, not immediately. Bernie could be alive. If she was, he had no idea how he would find her. He couldn't call out to her, and she couldn't call out for him. All he knew was he wasn't leaving without her.

Leaving was a novel idea. He had no idea how he was going to navigate himself out of these tunnels, but one thing at a time.

His flashlight hit the opening in the wall. Dust motes hovered in the beam. Blackness awaited behind the light's reach. Lincoln climbed up to his exit and pulled himself through. His light illuminated a long tunnel. He looked back at the mound of dead. He had no choice.

He pressed on down the tunnel, convinced that each scuff of his boot on the hard earth, each choked breath, would draw one of the creatures down the tunnel to pulverize him into the ground. With each step, he stopped to listen, but nothing came lumbering from the gloom.

When he reached a bend, the earth trembled. Temporarily blinded, he choked on the dust that fell from the cavern's ceiling.

Another scream rattled the cavern, and a blast of warm air followed it. Lincoln had to press on.

He came to a chamber off of the tunnel. An exo clicked within, and he turned off his flashlight, hugging the wall. The creature pounded the chamber floor. He winced at the thought that it had seen the light and would come to investigate. He prayed under his breath, willing the thing to pass him by.

Lincoln heard the smacking of flesh on flesh and knew it was depositing another body. Lurching with articulate legs that pressed against the floor, walls, and ceiling, it came out of the chamber and did not pause as it turned away from Lincoln, following the tunnel away from him in a diminishing knock of bone on bone.

He squeezed his eyes shut, waiting for it to come back and end him, but it didn't.

In an act that defied every ounce of his instinct, he turned the flashlight back on, and peered into the chamber. More dead faces gaped at him. He raised a fist to his mouth to stifle a scream. Then a hand moved.

The fingers grasped the mound of bodies. A man was pulling himself free.

Lincoln tightened at the sight of Clay emerging from the limbs and faces. Despite himself, he felt an exploding urge to finish their fight, but Lincoln's breath caught when Clay pulled another person from the wreckage of people. The golden hair on her sweet little head gleamed so brightly that it pushed back the darkness in Lincoln's heart.

"Come on," Clay said. "It's okay."

Lincoln rushed into the chamber.

Clay squinted and raised a hand at the flashlight. "What's that?"

Lincoln scurried up the pile of bodies and clutched his daughter, pulling her from the cold of death into his warm embrace.

"Daddy?"

"We have to be quiet, sweetheart."

"Daddy?" she whimpered.

"Breathe, Bernie. Just breathe."

Clay struggled to be free of the dead. "A little help here?"

Lincoln's sharp look said everything his voice didn't have to. It said he should leave Clay. It said they wouldn't be here if not for him. It said he should take the handle of his flashlight and bludgeon the man for everything he'd done.

"I saved her," Clay said.

"You what?"

"It's true. Ask her."

Lincoln gazed into his daughter's horrified eyes. She was only seeing the bodies around them.

"Look at me," Lincoln said. "Just look at me."

"They're coming for us," Clay said. "One at a time. When I woke up, I found her. Then we heard one of them coming, so I showed her how to hide."

His daughter's face was pale and blank. Instinctively, Lincoln bounced her in his arms as he'd done to soothe her when she was an infant.

Clay grunted as he freed himself. "You're welcome."

In that moment, Lincoln had no time to consider how Bernie would probably never be the same. He had no time to think of how good it would feel to take Clay's life or that he might actually need the man. He only knew they had to get out of there and that the rest had to wait.

With Bernie in his arms, Lincoln returned to the chamber opening and eased back into the tunnel. Clay followed. They inched down the corridor for what seemed like an eternity, and with every tremble in the earth and every sound, Lincoln clicked off his flashlight and stood still and silent in the impossible darkness.

In those times, when he couldn't tell if his eyes were open or closed, his own breaths became the breaths of a stalking exo, easing down the tunnel to take them. With such a blending of senses, their own existence becoming horrifying due to the uncertainty of their end, they waded in an oblivion of endless time. The darkness seeped through their pores, through their muscle fibers, and stained their bones so that, even as they wept, they attuned to their threatening reality. Above them, crushing weight. Around them, suffocating gases. And always, the exos stalked.

Such was the assimilation to the dark that, when they discovered a blue light at the end of the tunnel, Lincoln questioned what it was.

"Must still be clear skies." Clay slapped Lincoln's shoulder. "We made it."

He took off running and laughing down the tunnel.

"Wait," Lincoln said.

Behind Lincoln, the earth thrummed. He spun and shined his light on a squealing exo. It recoiled and burrowed into the earth, diving through stone as if it were water.

The time for creeping through the labyrinth was over. Lincoln ran.

The light ahead blazed. He could already feel its warmth, a breeze flowing down the tunnel and striking his face. Behind him, exo feet drummed on rock. Clay's silhouette showed the way. Lincoln's legs pumped. His chest burned. His weakened body felt like it would give out, but he knew he only had to make it to that light. Then, Bernie would be safe.

Clay turned and disappeared at the end of the tunnel. Lincoln heard the exos behind him gaining ground, but he was almost there. It was only a little farther before he and Bernie would be in that warm light, and then the exos wouldn't be able to reach them.

Before he could make it outside, though, the blue glow softened, Clay screamed, and daylight extinguished.

Lincoln spun with his flashlight's beam burning down an empty corridor. The exos that were chasing him had vanished.

As he gazed down the tunnel in disbelief, the blue light grew behind him again. Bernie whined, and he hushed her.

He had no choice. He entered the chamber. Clay was backed against the wall, arms splayed as if holding on for dear life. Ahead, a pit was pulsing, the source of that blue light.

"It's coming back," Clay said.

Lincoln looked on in horror. An exo emerged from the pit, and it was unlike any of the others. It was three times the size, and its body was more bulbous, its exoskeleton more bulky and armored. Its jagged, spiny legs arched with several points of articulation, and that blue light was a kind of bioluminescence, emanating from its thorax, pulsing in flares like a calm, steady heartbeat.

They had come upon the center of the exo colony, and they were standing before its queen.

The creature rose from the pit, its limbs thundering with each step. The magnificence of its being froze them. It regarded them, evaluated them. Its black, beady eyes peered like spotlights of darkness.

Lincoln set Bernie down. He'd told her to look only at him, but the queen had drawn her terrified eyes, and she could not look away.

Confident and prideful, Lincoln clicked on his flashlight. He raised it like a saber, jabbing it at the queen's vision.

She didn't react. His light glared in her eyes, and she didn't even flinch.

Instead, she roared, and the glow of her body beamed like a brilliant explosion so bright the men had to shield their own eyes. The earth rumbled with her rage. She lurched forward. Lincoln only had seconds before she would be on them. He lunged for his daughter, intending to take her out a different tunnel than the one they'd come in, but he found it blocked by an exo. He scanned other entrances. Soldiers standing guard blocked all of them.

Behind him, the queen squealed with a frustrated cry, and then she raised her head to the chamber's ceiling and screeched, a call for aid. When she quieted, the glow of her thorax dimmed and darkened. Her tail followed, and Lincoln saw that the tip of her tail was connected to some kind of intestinal membrane that channeled the light down into the pit. Even as the queen's light diminished, the light in the pit persisted.

The exos at the tunnel entrances advanced. Lincoln held them off as best as he could, but with only one light source, he could push one back while others continued forward. Their only retreat was into the queen's embrace.

Clay grasped Lincoln's shirt. "What are we going to do!?"

Lincoln looked into Clay's pale, haunted face. Then he looked down to his daughter. She looked up at him with wavering reverence. She knew her father could not protect her. She knew this was their end. Finally, she understood death.

And Lincoln wasn't having that.

He threw off Clay's hands and grabbed the man by the throat. Spinning, he placed Clay between himself and the queen. Then he kicked Clay square in the chest, sending the man tumbling backward into the queen's waiting arms.

Clay screamed. The queen flared with blue luminescence. Her exos fled from the searing light.

Lincoln picked up his daughter and sprinted toward one of the tunnels he chose at random. Clay's cries resonated in Lincoln's ears. Long after Clay had been consumed and his screams ceased, their echoes remained in his ears and, for much longer, in his mind.

With Bernie in his arms, Lincoln raced on. His flashlight led the way, and he fended off exos in front of him. In the confined tunnels, they weren't able to move fast enough to catch him from behind.

The tunnel turned upward. Another tunnel branched off, and it continued the rise, so he took that. He took any tunnel that went up until his light struck roots hanging from the tunnel ceiling, and he knew he had ascended enough to touch trees.

The sound of rushing water grew like static, and it reinvigorated him. He pressed on and on until he entered the chamber with the underground river.

With the exos screeching behind him, he jumped into the cold water. The current dragged them, but Lincoln pumped his arms and legs, his daughter clutching his chest. The exos leaped in after them, but their digging limbs were useless in the water, and they were carried away.

On the other side, Lincoln wasted no time turning down the passage that led to the Dawnbreaker, to daylight, and to safety.

Ten

On the surface, Lumen was coming to life. The whole world quaked. Every piece of earthen surface, from the ground beneath Lincoln's feet to the boulders he palmed to steady himself, quivered with violent tremors. The din of such forces rose in his and Bernie's ears like waves of thunder. Though the sky had darkened, there were no clouds. The tension in the earth and the rumbling sounded like the approach of gods, and their footsteps were ejecting dust into the air to block out the failing daylight with a brown haze.

The hills were crumbling. Boulders rolled down the mountain facades, smashing trees and scarring the land.

Lumen wasn't coming alive. It was falling apart.

Behind them in the tunnel, the exos screeched and pounded, enraged animals demanding release from their prison. Their bony limbs glinted in the ambient light, and Lincoln shielded his daughter from seeing any more of their kind. She'd already endured enough nightmares for one lifetime.

He was going to take her away from all of this. He was going to get her someplace safe. What they were about to do seemed easier to him when he thought of it in those terms.

A whirlwind blasted from nowhere, stirring the dust into thick funnel clouds. Rocky debris struck Lincoln in the chest and face like glass shards, and he held his daughter tightly.

Frozen at the entrance to the exo layer, Lincoln strained to see through the rising dust storm, unable to see anything but an ocean of dark brown. The Dawnbreaker had been just ahead. He was sure of it.

The air crackled like the snapping electrical arc bolts at the pillar. The ship's engines hummed and roared.

"Daddy!"

Lincoln held Bernie to his shoulder. "Hold on tight, sweetheart."

He ran. Dust filled his vision and lungs. The ship's dark shape emerged. He had to keep moving. It wouldn't be long before the creatures came for them.

"Daddy!" Bernie squeezed Lincoln's neck. "Look!"

Exos streamed from the hole, dashing across the surface with the power and grace of a water torrent. The planet's skin had opened and sent forth a river flow of creatures. They leaped onto the Dawnbreaker's facade and spread across the hull like a growing shadow, turning the brown haze black.

"Just shut your eyes, sweetheart."

The wind whipped. The earth shattered. Lincoln kept running. Then he heard the familiar sound of the exos breaching the surface. The earth exploded to his left, sending rock shrapnel into his face and raining onto the Dawnbreaker's metal hull. Exos leaped from the opening like reaching limbs, arcing over Lincoln and Bernie, and punching the side of the ship.

Another breach opened behind them. They were breaking all over the Field of the First Families.

From the gloom, the drill emerged. It was still buried in the earth. If the Dawnbreaker took off, the drill would be broken, and their ability to harvest water would be destroyed.

"I have to put you down." Lincoln set Bernie's feet on the ground and pointed toward the camera on the ship. "They'll see we're here."

Lincoln went to work reversing the drill. He turned a latch, and the metal in the shaft thunked and clanged. The drill retracted with maddening indifference.

"Come on, come on!"

Bernie screamed.

A shadowy mass appeared in the haze.

Lincoln picked up his daughter and held her tightly. She clung to him as he ran to the door, her grip tight around his neck. The exos drew nearer.

He pounded on the airlock's door. "We're here! We're here!" He turned to face them. They marched with a measured patience, their front limbs shielding their eyes.

"Just hold me, sweetheart. Hold me tight."

The exos closed in, surrounding them in darkness. More breaches opened, and those exos crashed into the ship with incredible growing numbers. Above them, shadow soaked the hull like spreading ink stains. They were everywhere, more than anyone could count.

He looked into his daughter's frightened eyes. "I love you, Bern. You know that. And I'm sorry."

Bernie sobbed. She knew exactly what he was telling her.

Lincoln put his back to the bay door and held his daughter to his chest. He told himself that, as long as he could feel her in his arms, they were okay. He told himself that, as long as he held onto her, he wouldn't fail as a father.

The shadows in the haze took form. They moved like creeping hands, fingertips dancing gracefully, gently, over the face of the planet, with an undeniable power and ferocity to squeeze. They closed in like a falling veil, and with the expiring light, Lincoln understood that the darkness was coming for them. It was coming to envelop them, absorb them, make them a part of it.

He tensed for its strike. Every muscle fiber in his body clenched in reflex, embracing his daughter, folding in to protect something deeper, some sense of warmth of his being within, perhaps her soul.

He could hear the saliva matter drip from their teeth and splat in the dirt. Their rancorous odor made his insides feel hollow and putrid, yet Lincoln did not despair, because he remembered he could still wield light.

He spun and slapped the control panel beside the bay door. The floodlights on the ship's exterior snapped on, and the exos recoiled and screeched. In the growing darkness, there was a brief unwinding, like the threads of a rope loosening and unraveling.

With a sense of satisfaction, Lincoln watched them writhe in pain. He may have staved off the inevitable, but he'd bought some time, and no matter how horrible, he wanted every last moment, as long as it was with Bernie.

The airlock door split open, and Ducard marched forward, firing his silenced sentry rifle, launching a bullet storm that sounded like fully automatic whips. Its amplifier hummed and sizzled with electric current.

Another rifle roared. Ballard fired one of the independents' weapons, flanking the creatures from the other side.

Her stone face was immovable even as her weapon's recoil rocked her shoulder. "Get inside! Now!"

Lincoln scrambled into the opening with Bernie. In spite of the gunfire, the exos still advanced. When the creatures were almost within range to pluck them from the doorway, Ducard slammed the panel on the wall, and the door shut on the outside world. For a moment, it was silent; no rumbling of the earth; no roaring of the ship engines; only the cool whisper of air vents and the whir of computer systems.

Then the creatures started pounding. Under the enraged barrage of their strikes, even the armored door designed to hold the vacuum of deep space threatened to buckle.

Ducard stood back in awe. "We have to get to the control room."

Lincoln stood with Bernie still clinging to his torso, and he and Reggie locked eyes. Her rifle clattered on the floor, and she crossed the room and kissed Lincoln like a punch.

Bewildered, Lincoln reeled. "It's good to see you too, Sheriff."

"I'm not the law anymore. And you're done doing stuff like that. Understand?"

"That a new law?"

"Don't start."

"Yes, ma'am."

"This is sweet, and I'm real happy for you two," Ducard said, "but we have a planet to get our asses off of."

Running once again, Ducard and Ballard led Lincoln and Bernie through the ship. Their eyes landed on strings of cool blue lights and gleaming metal surfaces. Their boots pounded wrought iron grating. Bunches of piping ran below and no doubt went on for miles. The corridor branched and went off toward parts of the ship unknown.

The environment and technologies were utterly alien to them, but they didn't have time to investigate. With any luck, they'd be able to get intimate with every gadget and control in their new home.

The hallway opened above into a shaft obscured in a blue haze. Ducard stood in front of a blank, flat wall.

"What are you doing?" Lincoln asked.

The sentry smirked. "Watch this." He pushed a square on the surface, and it illuminated with a yellow glow. A bell chimed, and the wall split open, revealing a small room with windows.

Lincoln gawked at Reggie.

She smiled. "There's more."

They entered the lift, and the doors closed behind them. It shot up, and soon, the glass revealed a great, expansive chamber of red and green lights.

Lincoln pressed his hand against the window. "What is this?"

Reggie's fingertips went to her lips to contain a swell of happiness. "Ellis called it the 'stasis chamber.' It's where the First Families slept on their journey here. It still works, and Lincoln," she fixed her hopeful gaze on his eyes, "some of them are still sleeping."

Lincoln gasped. "We're not the last?"

Reggie laughed and shook her head. "We're not the last!"

The lift finished its ascent and chimed. A pleasant female voice announced they'd reached the command deck. The doors split.

"Look, Bern," Lincoln said.

The girl eased her face out of her father's chest and saw Lucy, Shane, Sera, Gabe, Mel, Ellis, James, and Dani all gaping at them. The sight of their loved ones standing in the sleek and unspoiled control room gave them pause. It was now that it hit Lincoln: they'd made it.

Lucy stepped forward with a smile a mile wide and embraced them. Shane, Sera, Gabe, and Mel did the same.

"This is great," Ellis said. "I'm glad everyone is okay, and I hate to be insensitive, but we have another problem."

Lincoln released his family. "What is it?"

Ellis pointed out the window in front of the controls. Over the field and beyond the forest sat the colony, the pillar still gleaming on the mountain.

"Look," Ellis said, motioning downward.

Below, the dusty haze was rising. The exos were churning the earth beneath and around the Dawnbreaker.

"They're trying to sink us," Lincoln said. "How much time until we can take off?"

Ellis gazed pensively at the controls. "Thirty seconds."

Powerless, they waited in agonizing silence. They could do nothing as the dust enveloped the command deck window and blocked their view. They could do nothing as the slight quiver turned into a powerful tremor, rattling metal components and toppling anything that wasn't fastened in place. They could do nothing as the Dawnbreaker keeled and began to sink.

They had endured so much and come so far, yet Lumen wasn't going to allow them to leave.

Ellis began a countdown. "Ten, nine, eight..."

With every syllable, the Dawnbreaker listed more. Its hull groaned and ticked.

"...seven, six, five..."

The rumbling from the exos and the ship's engines grew until it became hard for the colonists to stay on their feet. They held each other for safety and comfort.

"...four, three, two..."

Something beneath them cracked and boomed, and the colonists were tumbling. The ship's interior lights darkened, and all fell silent and still.

Lincoln got to his feet. Everyone else struggled to stand, and he helped them. Outside the window, the world was brown in the dusty haze.

"Was that it?" Lincoln asked.

Ellis' fingers danced on the controls. The tension in the room electrified them.

"Was that it?" he repeated. "Are we sunk?"

Ellis stepped back from the controls with amazed eyes. "We're up."

"What?"

"We have liftoff! We're off the ground!"

After living for days in the silence, for fear that speaking or making any noise would lead to their doom, the cheer that erupted crashed upon their ears with a force that set them on their heels and made the room spin. They embraced each other. Lovers kissed. Some of them cried in pure joy because they knew it was over. They were free from the colony's walls. They were free from the threat that, at any moment, a subterranean creature could drag them down into the earth and rend them in utter darkness.

They were free to find a home, the spirit of which they'd been promised when the pillars had finished their jobs. Now the pillars were, in fact, finished. The colonists could escape the bounds that had imprisoned them for generations.

Lincoln turned from Reggie's embrace long enough to tell Ellis, "Then get us out of here!"

The engineer pressed a slider forward, and the ship lurched. In seconds, they broke free from the dust and entered the red light and bruised horizon of dusk. The ship's thrusters pushed the ship west, passing over the colony and flying low near the dormant Pillar of Dawn. They climbed into the atmosphere, burning into night as they passed out of the sun's graces, carrying with them a torch of friction, a fireball ascending into the sky.

Ahead, the aurora formed, a veil to the unknown.

Bernie clutched her father and pointed. "The skylights."

Lincoln squeezed her shoulder. "We won't have to live by them anymore."

"There is no light in the stars?"

"We bring it wherever we go now."

The ship burst through the aurora, unveiling a blanket of stars, countless systems with unimaginable possibilities, and even so, all that mattered was that they were leaving this one.

As they entered the vacuum of space, a beeping alarm sounded, and Ellis interacted with the controls.

"What is it?" Lincoln asked.

"She's old. I knew there were some breaches in the hull, but those compartments are sealed. Nothing critical."

Lincoln nodded. "We're okay then?"

A look of genuine concern on the old man's face relaxed into cathartic relief. He sighed with tears in his eyes, and then he nodded. "We're okay."

Lincoln squeezed the man's shoulder, and he took Bernie and Reggie back away from the controls. He and his family left the command deck to familiarize themselves with the place that would be their home for a long time.

The Dawnbreaker entered Lumen's orbit and exited the dark side of the planet. The sun emerged into view, already a new day.

Below, the green and blue planet of Lumen graced them with beauty they had never actually known. Beyond Vale's borders lay an untamed wild that was as alien as it was inhospitable. Gazing over Lumen's face, the world on the other side of the colony's walls no longer meant endless potential. Even in sunlight, the exo hand spread wide and gripped the land. They saw that now.

TIMOTHY JOHNSON

They saw that the colony was always there, right under their feet, and with or without the humans, the colony would always be there, staking its claim to its domain, its right to thrive and live in its own way on this alien world.

The Dawnbreaker streaked into the cosmos and lit up the darkness.

ACKNOWLEDGEMENTS

Special thanks to Nick DeWolf and Slade Grayson for their invaluable feedback, support, and friendship. These guys are great authors, and they shared some of their greatness with me for this one. You can thank them by checking out their work.

To my beta and proofreaders, Laurie Bickett, Brice Bradford, Michael Cullen, James McReynolds, and David Ring, who read drafts, gave me good ideas, found mistakes, and reassured me I wasn't wasting my precious time on planet Earth, thank you.

To Dr. Sean Reilly, who always has my back while murdering aliens in simulated worlds and who humored my ignorance when bouncing ideas about science around, even stuff that isn't in his particular field but which he was gracious enough to comment on because he's, like, a really smart guy, thanks.

To Eloise J. Knapp, a fellow author who also has some amazing graphics skills because she's one of those talented people you hear about, thanks for squeezing me in and making this one look so good.

Thanks to my editor, Felicia A. Sullivan, who not only helps make my work better but also is a good friend and something of a speculative fiction community den mom, an indie writer's support pillar. Everyone should have a Felicia.

Finally, to my wife, Heather, who sacrifices more of our life together than I'm comfortable with so I can sit alone in a dark room and play pretend, thanks for your unwavering support.

ABOUT THE AUTHOR

Timothy Johnson is a speculative fiction author and editor living outside Washington, D.C., with his wife and his dog. His previous work includes the sci-fi/horror novel Carrier. He has an English degree from Virginia Tech, where he won the fiction award for his graduating class. He is a member of the Horror Writers Association. Nothing frightens him more than the future, so he writes about it in hopes he is wrong.

Learn more at www.TimothyJohnsonFiction.com.

www.ingramcontent.com/pod-product-compliance
Lightning Source LLC
Chambersburg PA
CBHW030920120726
47906CB00002B/418